D1177718

Gaston
de Blondeville

Gaston de Blondeville

OR

THE COURT
OF HENRY THE THIRD
KEEPING FESTIVAL IN ARDEN

BY

Ann Radcliffe

INTRODUCTION BY

Devendra P. Varma

WOOD-ENGRAVING BY

Sarah van Niekerk

LONDON
THE FOLIO SOCIETY
1987

Gaston de Blondeville was written in 1802 and was first
published posthumously in 1826. This text is taken from the
first edition. Readers should note that the author's
idiosyncratic spelling and punctuation have
been retained in this edition.

SET IN CALEDONIA
BY TRADESPOOLS LTD, FROME
PRINTED AND BOUND IN GREAT BRITAIN
BY THE BATH PRESS, AVON
USING WEST ONE ANTIQUE WOVE PAPER
DESIGN BY DAVID ECCLES

CONTENTS

INTRODUCTION   vii

GASTON DE BLONDEVILLE   1
  OR THE COURT OF HENRY THE THIRD
  KEEPING FESTIVAL IN ARDEN

THE FIRST DAY   28

THE SECOND DAY   36

THE THIRD DAY   72

THE FOURTH DAY: INTRODUCTION   106

THE FOURTH DAY   112

THE FIFTH DAY AND NIGHT   120

THE SIXTH DAY   154

THE SEVENTH DAY   179

THE SEVENTH NIGHT   208

THE EIGHTH DAY   222

CONCLUSION   225

NOTES   229

INTRODUCTION

Curio boxes and old caskets always reveal some long-forgotten and priceless trinkets. Such articles often arouse nostalgic memories. After the death of Ann Radcliffe, in one of her old trunks, along with some antique jewellery, wrapped in crumpled sheets of cambric and silk was found an unpublished manuscript containing sheaves of her last romance, *Gaston de Blondeville*. This work, along with *St Alban's Abbey and Poetical Pieces*, was published posthumously in 1826 by Sergeant Talfourd who also supplied the *Memoir* of her life, a very sympathetic treatment of the novelist's art.

Written in the winter of 1802, it was inspired by her visit to the ruins of Kenilworth Castle, and had certainly never been intended for publication. She found her subject fascinating; it struck her imagination and quick sensibility, and she became interested in exploring the history of that old castle.

The story purports to have been taken from an old manuscript dated 1256, dug up in the churchyard of what once had been a Priory of Black Canons. The book recreates an age of chivalry, tells a love-story, and includes a description of a splendid tournament which recalls the lists of Ashby-de-la-Zouch in *Ivanhoe*. It certainly has far more medieval colour than Leland's *Longsword* (1762), Miss Reeve's *The Old English Baron* (1777), or Miss Sophia Lee's *Recess* (1785). The scene is set in Kenilworth Castle, while the 'Court of Henry III keeps festival in Ardenne'; and it was only in this last novel that Mrs Radcliffe made use of old chronicles or attempted a reconstruction of history. By introducing an entirely fictitious narrative into a historical setting, connected with actual events only by the slightest of threads, she foreshadowed the emancipation of the historical novel from all educational trammels and its treatment as a purely aesthetic form.

Another merit of this work is that here Mrs Radcliffe makes her first use of supernatural machinery. Only in *Gaston de Blondeville* does she introduce a spectre which is not explained away, but stalks unabashed though Kenilworth Castle; and the accomplished manner in which she does it can only deepen our regret that she did not employ such machinery in her longer novels.

The spectre in this case is not a mere adjunct to the Gothic back-drop nor a scenic accessory, but stands as the protector of the innocent and the minister of divine vengeance. The apparition of a murdered knight glides up the stairs to stand before Gaston, his murderer; and when justice is not immediately done, three drops of blood fall on his robe, spreading until the whole of one side of his garment is crimson.

Shades of Walpole and *Ossian* have gone into the conception of this imposing ghost. Its awfulness is modelled on the good Alfonso of *Otranto*, though the progression here is not from scattered limbs to a complete figure, but from fleshly man (the minstrel) to apparent spirit. When it speaks, its words echo the heroic tunes of *Ossian*. Indeed, in her unbridled fancy, Mrs Radcliffe seems to have discovered a new power: in the trial by combat, the Unknown Knight makes a silent entry into the barriers and rides round the lists, while a tremor of cold fear runs through the hushed spectators. In the final encounter with the culprit, no words or blows are exchanged; only the power of evil, symbolised by the Baron, slowly withers and dies under the stony gaze of justice.

In her treatment of the supernatural, however, Mrs Radcliffe never lifted the horrid veil of the Occult. Her fancy never strayed beyond the native churchyard ghost or the angelic visitant, and her religion would have forbidden her to conceive a malignant spectre. Her best achievements in the field of the supernatural pale before the morbidity of Poe, or of Tieck in his youth.

But her techniques cast a spell over Sir Walter Scott, who

enriched his own art from the way in which she handled all things mysterious. He inserted, in *The Monastery*, the figure of the White Lady of Avenel. There is the Glenallan episode in *The Antiquary*; the mysterious warning given to Frank Osbaldistone in the crypt of Glasgow Cathedral, and his meeting with the stranger on the bridge at midnight, in *Rob Roy*; and there is the dungeon scene in *The Legend of Montrose*, complete, with darkness, a chained and desperate prisoner, and the uncanny sudden appearance of Argyle from a secret passage. There are birth-mysteries in *The Antiquary* and *The Legend of Montrose*; and in Scott's *Bride of Lammermoor* – in the dark scenes of impending fate, in the storm which brings Lucy under the Master of Ravenswood's roof, in the haunted well by which they plight their troth – Mrs Radcliffe's influence is abundantly apparent.

There is a close resemblance between the novels of Scott and Gothic fiction in general, since both drew inspiration from the same fount. *Waverley* and its successors drank deep from the waters of Gothic romance, though the outmoded Gothic motifs were replaced by Scott with plots that afforded similar excitement, but added to them the colour and conviction of reality. The wicked Montonis, the scheming Schedonis, the savage banditti and spectres of Radcliffe's pages, became in the works of Scott genuine outlaws, monks, highland chiefs, and phantoms of Scottish tradition. For the Salvator Rosa landscapes were substituted real mountains, forest-vistas, valleys and caves, and the impregnable castles of Scotland. The appeal of Mrs Radcliffe's romances cast a glow on the reader's mind, and when Scott breathed new life into the old forms, the general audience responded with the same enthusiasm.

Where Mrs Radcliffe visualised her characters, Scott vitalised them. Her aim was to portray a group of figures, through whose gestures she could impart the impressions of Gothic architecture and sublime landscapes. Her purpose was to obtain a harmony of conception; while Scott's motive was to achieve comprehensiveness. Consequently he was not interested in exciting a fear of the supernatural in his readers, but aimed to show the effect of such fear upon the characters in his stories. The incidents and scenery were Radcliffean, but the point of view his own.

The charm of the historical novel lies in the interplay of the strange and the familiar in human nature and human conditions. It has numerous variants. It may tread so closely on the heels of history that the flavour of romance may evaporate; it may drop so far behind that history may turn into a mere shadow. Mrs Radcliffe's knowledge of medieval literature and life, for example, was almost negligible; but moats and drawbridges, aisles and broken chancels, stained-glass windows and dilapidated tombs called forth such flights of fancie, such entrancing spectres of villainy, valour and romantic love, that it hardly mattered. In *Gaston de Blondeville* her fancy hovered round a few historical figures and incidents, and she did attempt a reconstruction of medieval manners. She had certainly studied old chronicles (see her notes on the text), and she may also have depended on oral legends clustering round Kenilworth. Ghostly legends fascinated her, and she probably amassed a hoard of traditions when she visited the castle.

But the historical novel proper had yet to be born. Mrs Radcliffe's world was still that of the Gothic novel with its romantic unrealities, its strange and sensational beauties, its flights of extravagance – it was the Novel of Adventure, the Novel of Escape. As Walpole once wrote: 'Old castles, old pictures, old histories, and the babble of old people, make one live back into centuries that cannot disappoint one.' As a reward, the reader – if not too restless, too impatient, and too modern – will find himself transported back many a long year from this atomic age to a realm of magic and marvels of knight-errantry and adventure, of combat and romance.

In such a world anything may happen so long as it is terrible; flashes of lightning are more frequent than sunlight, and, if we are not poisoned with a magic potion in the second volume, we are probably stabbed with a jewelled dagger in the third. It is a world of ungoverned emotion and hisses and swoons, a realm where laws and morals are consumed by passion, but one which remains, in the end, curiously reassuring. For Mrs Radcliffe's novels are in the nature of adult fairy-tales, and the reader responds like a traveller on enchanted ground.

The Radcliffean novel fell in with the literary mood of Europe of that period, and it processed and transmitted its themes to a successive generation of writers. All successful followers had to call to aid other means to make their works interesting. 'Monk' Lewis added sickly voluptuousness to his terrors, while Maturin, full of 'rich conceits', approached the borders of forbidden speculation and paradoxical morals. But greater names owed allegiance to Mrs Radcliffe. According to Montague Summers:

'Honoré de Balzac thought her romances admirable, and many of his first efforts were directly inspired by her pages. In some of his maturer work their influence still prevails, as it often does in Dumas, Victor Hugo, Eugène Sue, Joseph Petrus Borel, Baudelaire – and when I have said Balzac and Baudelaire what more can I add?'

There is a profound reason for her popularity. Those half-veiled splendours set against a background of dizzy crags and gloomy forests; those bizarre mysteries, in which love and death are wedded, provided sanctuary in the form of an imaginative domain. Fantastic recreations of the past, a remoteness of time and place, and a range of exotic settings – Oriental or Mediterranean, for instance – all conspired to produce a voluptuous dream world in which physical possibility and impossibility, the natural and the supernatural, real and fantastic, fused together. Mrs Radcliffe's romantic dissatisfaction with reality produced the finest flower of Gothic romance.

In the concept of terror lies, perhaps, the most extreme form of romantic escapism. Darkness and obscurity have a negative significance, but they also provide a gateway to the higher and spiritual life. The deep but dazzling darkness is itself some kind of mystical experience. We are all aware that the spiritual potentialities of life lie beyond the practical realities which circumscribe our existence on earth. The appeal of Mrs Ann Radcliffe lies in her recognition of our need for mysteries, and her enormous talent in conjuring them out of her imagination.

DEVENDRA P. VARMA
Dalhousie University

EDITOR'S NOTE

The numbers in the text refer to Mrs Radcliffe's notes on some of her source material which can be found at the end of this book.

ELL! now are we in Arden,' said an English traveller to his companion, as they passed between Coventry and Warwick, over ground, which his dear Shakspeare had made classic. As he uttered this exclamation of Rosalind, he looked forward with somewhat of the surprise and curiosity, which she may be supposed to have felt, and with an enthusiasm all his own, on beholding the very scene, into which the imagination of the poet had so often transported him with a faint degree of its own rapture. He was not, it appears, one of those critics, who think that the Arden of Shakspeare lay in France. But he looked in vain for the thick and gloomy woods, which, in a former age, were the home of the doubtful fugitive, and so much the terror of the traveller, that it had been found necessary, on this very road, to clear the ground, for a breadth of six acres on each side, in order to protect the wayfaring part of his Majesty's liege subjects.

Now, albeit the landscape was still wild and woody, he could not any where espy a forest scene of dignity sufficient to call up before his fancy the exiled duke and his court, at their hunter-feast, beneath the twilight of the boughs; nor a single beech, under the grandeur of whose shade the melancholy Jaques, might 'lose and neglect the creeping hours of time,' while he sadly sympathized with the poor stag, that, escaped from the

1

pursuit of man, came to drop his tears into the running brook, and to die in quiet. Not even a grove appeared, through whose deep vista the traveller might fancy that he caught, in the gayer light, a glimpse of the wandering Rosalind and her companions, the wearied princess and the motley fool, or of the figure of Orlando, leaning against an oak, and listening to her song: he could not even catch the last faint echo of that song, in a scene so different from the one his fancy had represented to him for the forest of Arden.

'Alas!' said he, 'that enchanting vision is no more found, except in the very heart of a populous city, and then neither by the glimmering of the dawn, nor by the glow of evening, but by the paltry light of stage-lamps. Yet there, surrounded by a noisy multitude, whose cat-calls often piped instead of the black-bird, I have found myself transported into the wildest region of poetry and solitude; while here, on the very spot which Shakspeare drew, I am suddenly let down from the full glow of my holiday-feelings into the plain reality of this work-a-day world.'

Here ensued a conversation on illusions of the imagination and on the various powers of exciting them, shown by English poets, especially by Shakspeare and Milton, which it is unnecessary to repeat in this place. Such was its length, that Mr Simpson's part in it had gradually become less and less active, while Willoughton's increased earnestness had rendered him less and less sensible of the deficiency of replies. At last, on his asking, rather peremptorily, whether his friend did not recollect some fine effects of the towers of Windsor Castle upon the imagination, Mr Simpson, fortunately concealing how nearly he had approached to a nap, answered, 'No, no; I do not recollect any thing of what you tell me; but you were talking a little while ago of Hamlet and towers; now, if you want towers that would do honour to Hamlet, go to Warwick Castle, and if we reach it, as we hope, this night, you can walk from the inn while supper is preparing, and you will find, on the terrace or platform before the gates, towers frowning and majestic enough. If the moon is up, you will see them to perfection, and, as you are so fond of ghosts, you can hardly fail to make an assignation with one there.' 'I shall delight in the advantage,' replied Willoughton, laughing: 'Though I am not so fond of ghosts in general, as you seem to think. It is only for a few of particular excellence, that I feel a friendship; for them, indeed, I am willing to own even an affection.'

2

Willoughton, not receiving a rejoinder, observed, that his friend had fallen again into his nap; and he returned to the busy thoughts, to which his first view of this land of Arden, the ground of Shakspeare, had led. Sunk in reverie, he was no longer in the living scene, but ranging over worlds of his own, till a jolt of the carriage awoke his companion; who, shaking his head, and looking out of the window, with the sudden alertness of one who thinks he has been losing time, now supposed himself bound to brush up his thoughts and to talk to his friend.

Willoughton could well have spared the interruption, till a remark, delivered with an air of self-satisfaction, touched the string that recalled him willingly to the present scene.

'There now is an oak,' said Simpson, 'that may have been of Elizabeth's time, by the hollowness of its vast trunk and the state of its branches.'

'Ay, long before her time,' said his companion, 'and perhaps Shakspeare's eyes have dwelt on it; perhaps he has rested under its shade:– O! we are coming now to something like the Forest of Arden: see how finely the woods rise in the distance, and what a rich gleam the western sun throws along the ground, beyond those low-hung boughs on our left.'

As the travellers advanced upon Kenilworth-chace, the country assumed a more forest-like appearance, and a new train of ideas engaged Willoughton, on approaching the venerable ruins of the once magnificent castle, at one period its prison, and at another, the *plaisance* of royalty, where Edward the Second groaned under the traiterous power of Mortimer, and his abandoned Queen; and where the crafty Leicester entertained Elizabeth, with princely splendour. The domain of this castle, with its parks and chaces, included a circuit of nearly twenty miles; and when a survey of it was taken in the reign of James the First, on its forfeiture by the voluntary exile and contempt of Sir Robert Dudley, the son of Leicester and of his first wife, the Lady Sheffield, – the woods alone were valued at twenty thousand pounds, according to Dugdale, who observes of the castle and its territory, that 'the like, both for strength, state, and pleasure, was not within the realm of England.'

Recollections of the long and varied history of this castle, crowded upon the mind of Willoughton, and he looked out, with impatience, for a glimpse of its stately towers in the distance, and then of its mouldering gateways, in the sun gleam, beneath the woods that now rose round him with majestic shade. Here,

3

at least, was a mass and pomp of foliage worthy of the noble ruin he was approaching and of the memory of Arden; and, when he first caught a view of the grey walls and turrets overtopping the woods, lighted up by the evening sun, whose long beams, slanting now under the boughs, touched with a golden flush the bending trunk of many an old beech standing deep within the shade, he uttered a note of admiration and curiosity that discomposed Mr Simpson, who immediately directed the postilion to make his way to the nearest gate.

Soon afterwards they found themselves in a valley, whose woody slopes excluded all distant prospect, and confined their attention to the venerable relique, which seemed to characterise, with its own quiet gloom, the surrounding landscape. They observed the several fine and detached masses of the castle rising on a lone rock in the centre of this secluded little valley; and, as they drove towards the only entrance of the area of these deserted courts, near the square-turreted gateway, which Leicester built for the grand approach to the castle, the impatience of Willoughton became tempered with a gentle and luxurious melancholy, and he forgot even Shakspeare, while he was influenced by somewhat of the poet's feelings.

But a sense of real life broke in upon him even in this scene of solemn grandeur, and it required somewhat of the patience of a philosopher to endure, in the full glow of his present enthusiasm, the clamorous impetuosity of idle children, who, on the first sound of wheels, were seen running to assail the strangers from every cottage on the neighbouring banks. The visions of quiet solitude and of venerable antiquity were, in an instant, dispersed; the chaise was surrounded, and the travellers, having alighted, made their way with difficulty to the little gate, that led through a garden beside Leicester's ruined tower into the area that was once the lower court of the castle, followed by a noisy troop, whom neither money, nor command, could for some time disperse.

The tower – the gateway being now closed up, – was no longer accessible to curiosity, nor could gratify it by any traits of the customs of former times. No warder's bench lurked within the gloom, nor portcullis hung in the arch. The warden's chamber for those, who, by military tenure, kept guard on certain nights of the year, was transformed into a light parlour, and the whole building changed into a modern habitation. From the green and broken square, anciently the lower courtyard, the travellers

4

looked up to the noble mass of ruins that yet stand proudly on their rocky knoll, and form three irregular sides of what was once the inner and grand court.

Of the fourth side, which separated the upper from the lower court, are now no vestiges, save in the inequality of the ground where their foundations stood, and where the walls, fallen from above, may lie buried under the turf and briers, that now cover the spot.

On the left, the shattered walls of that lofty pile, built by Leicester and still called by his name, advance proudly to the edge of the eminence that overlooked the lower court, hung with the richest drapery of ivy; on the right, stands the strong square tower, called Caesar's, which, though the most ancient part of the castle, appears fresher and less injured by time, than parts that were raised some ages later. This was the keep, or citadel, of the castle; and the prodigious thickness of the walls appears through the three arches in front, proportioned and shaped like some which may yet be seen in aqueducts near Rome; the walls here show a depth of fifteen or sixteen feet. The stone, of which this noble tower is built, is of closer texture and of a greyer hue, than that in any other part of the building; and this hue harmonizes beautifully with the ivy towers, which overshadow its arches and door-cases, and with the ashlings and elder crowning its summit, which highly overtops every relique of this once magnificent abode of princes.

'It should seem,' said Willoughton, 'that no human force could lay low walls of such strength as these; yet, as one side of the tower is destroyed, while the other three remain nearly entire, it must have been assailed by some power more sudden and partial than that of time.'

'Yes, sir, yes,' said a man, who had been standing by, observing the strangers with attentive curiosity, 'that part was pulled down by Cromwell's soldiers, and, if they had had more time on their side, they would have pulled it all down; as it was, they did a mort of mischief.'

Willoughton turned to look at his informer, and saw a tall, thin man, who appeared to be a villager, and who, without waiting for encouragement, proceeded: 'I have heard say, they destroyed all that stood between Caesar's and John O'Gaunt's tower there, at the end of the great hall, and a deal on the other side of the court, between the Whitehall and Lord Leicester's buildings.'

'Are those walls before us the remains of the great hall?'
inquired Mr Simpson, pointing to a picturesque mass of ruins,
standing on the third side of the upper court and seen in
perspective between the other two.

'Yes, sir,' said the man, 'that there was the great banqueting-
hall where' –

'Leicester entertained Queen Elizabeth,' observed Willoughton. 'How beautifully the ivy falls over those light Gothic
window-mullions and that arched doorway, so appropriately and
elegantly sculptured with vine-leaves! The sun now slopes its
rays through the arch, as if purposely to show the beauty of its
proportion and the grace of the vine that entwines it.'

'Ay,' said Mr Simpson, 'many a pitcher of wine and many a
baron of beef have been carried under that arch by the king's
yeomen, when Henry the Third kept his court here.'

'I doubt whether by yeomen,' replied Willoughton, 'for,
though yeomen of the household are mentioned, about this
time, yeomen of the guard, a part of whose office it afterwards
became to carry certain dishes to the king's table, do not occur
till the reign of Henry the Seventh. However, it is probable,
that, before the appointment of the latter, yeomen of the
household might perform this business on state occasions, and in
that very hall may have stood before the long tables, in double
row, with wine ewers in their hands.'

'Those were times worth living in,' observed Mr Simpson.

'Ay, those were jolly times! sir,' said the stranger man; 'it's
lonely and sad enough in that old hall now; nothing but briers
and ivy. Why, there is an ivy tree now against that old wall
there, partly as old as the wall itself. Look, sir, it is as grey, and
almost as sapless as the stone it crawls upon, though the trunk is
such a size, and hardly shows a green leaf, spring or summer.'

The travellers made their way among the briers to take a
nearer view of it; and, if verdant festoons of younger plants had
charmed them, Willoughton, at least, was no less affected by the
withered sinews and grey locks of this most forlorn and aged
tree, which had itself become a ruin, while adorning another.
He climbed over hillocks of briers and weeds, which now
covered the ruins of walls, fallen into this courtyard, and he
looked down into the area of the great hall, through a doorway
which had once led from it by a vestibule towards the white hall,
of which latter hardly a vestige remains, and to King Henry's
lodgings. Here he distinguished the upper end of that magni-

6

ficent banqueting-room, the very spot where the *deis*, or high table, had stood, which had feasted kings and princes, its lords, or visitors; where Henry the Third had sitten, where John O'Gaunt had caroused, and where Elizabeth had received the homage of Leicester.

At one end of this platform were still the remains of the large bay-window, opening upon the grand court, where the cupboard had stood, and the golden plate was piled; at the other end, a windowed recess bowed out towards the spot, where there had been a lake, and to woods, that still flourished. This also, on state occasions, had probably held a plate-board, or cupboard, and, on others, had been occupied as a pleasant seat, commanding the finest views of the park.

The four walls only of this noble hall marked its former grandeur, not a fragment of either roof, or floor, remaining; the ground, upon which Willoughton immediately looked, having been the foundation of a chamber, or hall, for domestic and inferior guests, under the great one, which was eighty-six feet in length, and forty-five in width.

Those walls, where gorgeous tapestry had hung, showed only the remains of doorways and of beautiful gothic windows, that had admitted the light of the same sun, which at this moment sent the last gleam of another day upon Willoughton, and warned him, that another portion of his life too was departing.

The melancholy scene around him spoke, with the simplicity of truth, the brevity and nothingness of this life. Those walls seemed to say – 'Generations have beheld us and passed away, as you now behold us, and shall pass away. They have thought of the generations before their time, as you now think of *them*, and as future ones shall think of you. The voices, that revelled beneath us, the pomp of power, the magnificence of wealth, the grace of beauty, the joy of hope, the interests of high passion and of low pursuits have passed from this scene for ever; yet we remain, the spectres of departed years and shall remain, feeble as we are, when you, who now gaze upon us, shall have ceased to be in this world!'

'Why, here is a stone bench yet in this old window,' said Mr Simpson; 'and a pleasant window it is still. This homely bench has outlived all the trappings of the castle, though, I dare say, it was little valued in their time!'

'You see, sir,' said the old man, 'it belongs to the wall itself; else it would have been carried off long ago.'

7

Willoughton turned at the now repeated voice of this stranger, whose intrusion he did not entirely like, though his knowledge of the castle might be useful, and his conduct did not appear to be ill-meant. To an inquiry, whether he lived in the neighbourhood, he answered, 'Hard by, sir, in Kenilworth. I saw you was a stranger, sir, and thought you might like to know a little about the castle here; and, unless you hap to light on such a one as me, you may go away as wise as you came – for, you will know nothing. No offence, I hope, sir.'

'No, no; no offence at all;' replied Willoughton; 'and since you are so well acquainted with this spot, let me hear a little of what you know of it.'

'Ay, let us hear what you have to say,' said Mr Simpson.

Willoughton, turning as he heard this, perceived his friend seated in the recess he had before noticed. Much remained of the beautiful stone-work of this bay-window, and it now showed itself upon the glowing west, where the sun had just descended, behind the dark woods of the valley. He advanced into it, and looking out upon the scenery, was interested by the stillness and solemnity that began to prevail over it. At some distance down the steep bank on which the castle stands, he could distinguish fragments of the walls that once surrounded it, with here and there some remains of a tower, or a banqueting-house. The ground below seemed marshy, but pasture of a better green stretched up the opposite slopes, and mingled with the woods, that, on every side, shut out the world! This valley seemed the home of a composed melancholy.

'But where,' said Willoughton, 'is the noble lake that, in Leicester's time, surrounded this castle, on which, as you may have heard, Queen Elizabeth was welcomed with pageants and so much flattery?'

'Ay, where is it?' echoed Mr Simpson, looking at the old man with an air that seemed to say, 'Now we have some use for you, and will put you to the test.'

But Willoughton, without giving him time to reply, proceeded:–

'I am doomed to disappointment in Arden. For many miles, I could not discover any thing like a forest-shade, that might have sheltered a banished court, or favourite; and here not a wave of the lake, that delighted a festive one, and which might have supplied me with a floating island, moving to the sound of invisible music, or to the shells of surrounding tritons and sea-nymphs. Nay, I cannot even catch a gleam of the torches, which, on such an occasion, might have thrown their light on the woods and towers of the castle, and have quivered on the waters over which they passed.'

'No, sir,' said the old man, 'it would be a hard matter to find any thing of all that now. Cromwell's people would have knocked all that o' the head, when they drained off the water, if such things had been there then.'

'Cromwell's people again! However it is as well to remember them. What had the venerable scenes of Kenilworth to do with politics, or freedom? But thus it is; if even the leaders in political agitations have a better taste themselves than to destroy, for the mere sake of destruction, they let the envy and malice of their followers rage away against whatsoever is beautiful, or grand.'

So said Willoughton to his friend, who smiled, as he perceived that the indignant admirer of antiquity had allowed himself to speak of a military operation, as though it had been a popular commotion.

'Where went the line of the lake, my man of Kenilworth?' asked Simpson.

'Why, sir, it flowed round two sides of the castle, as I have heard say; it went from the tilt-yard, all along the valley here, for half a mile, and spread out at the foot of these banks, – as wide as to the woods yonder, on the hill-side.'

'What a noble sheet of water,' exclaimed Willoughton, 'with lawns and woods sloping to its margin and reflected on its surface!'

'Yes, sir, all that on the opposite side was a deer-park then, as I've heard from the account of some book, except that low ground further on, and that was pasture for cattle.'

'For cattle!' exclaimed Mr Simpson, –'how they would poach such ground as that!'

'But what a beautiful picture they helped to make from the castle windows here,' said Willoughton; 'when, on a summer's noon, they lay under those shades, or stood in the cool waters of the lake.'

'Ay,' said Mr Simpson, 'to such as did not value the land.'

'It was just opposite the Pleasant, yonder,' said the aged historian.

'The *Pleasant!*'

'Yes, sir; if you look this way, I will tell you where it stood: – it was a banqueting-house on the lake.'

9

'O! the *Plaisance!*'

'It stood on the walls there, down in the valley, to the right of John O'Gaunt's tower here, and not far from the Swan Tower; but it is so dusk now you can hardly see where I mean.'

Willoughton inquired where the Swan Tower stood.

'Further off, a good way, sir; but there is nothing of it to be seen now. It stood at the corner of the garden-wall, just where the lake came up; but there is nothing to be seen of that garden either now, sir, though we know the place where it was. Queen Elizabeth used to take great delight in the banqueting-house, as I've heard.'

'It was pleasantly seated;' observed Willoughton.

'Yes, sir; but there was rare feasting and music too, I reckon. She used to be fond of sitting in this very window, too!'

'How do you know all this, my friend?'

'Why, sir, the place is called Queen Elizabeth's turret, to this day, because she took such a fancy to it; and it was pleasant enough to be sure, for it overlooked the widest part of the lake; – this bench had velvet trappings enough then, I warrant.'

'I have no pleasure in remembering Elizabeth;' said Willoughton, as he turned to look for his friend.

'No! – not in remembering the wisest princess that ever reigned?' said Mr Simpson.

'No: her wisdom partook too much of craft, and her policy of treachery; and her cruelty to poor Mary is a bloody hand in her escutcheon, that will for ever haunt the memory of her.'

'You are too ardent,' observed Mr Simpson; 'much may be said on her conduct on that head.'

'She inspires me only with aversion and horror,' replied Willoughton.

'She gives other people the horrors, too,' said the villager.

'How do you mean, friend?'

'There are strange stories told, sir, if one could but believe them; – there are old men now in the parish, who say they have seen her about the castle here, dressed in a great ruff about her neck, just as she is in her picture; they knew her by that.'

Here Mr Simpson, giving Willoughton a look of sly congratulation, on his having met with a person of taste seemingly so congenial with his own, burst forth into a laugh, or rather a shout, that made every echo of the ruin vocal, his friend smile, and the old man stare; who, somewhat gravely, proceeded –

'They say, too, she has been seen sitting there, in that very window, when there was but just light enough to see her by.'

10

'A ghost in a ruff and farthingale!' exclaimed Mr Simpson. in exultation; – 'that is, surely, the very perfection of propriety in the ghost-costume;' and again the roar of laughter rolled round every turret of the castle.

'Why does that strike you as so absurd?' asked Willoughton; 'this is only a ghost representing the familiar image of the person when alive. Can it be more ridiculous than the Scotch plaid for the supernatural being, whom we call a witch? And yet, when you and I used to discuss the taste of ghost-dresses, you did not object to that appearance; but justified it, as one with which popular superstition was familiar.'

'Yes,' replied Simpson; 'but though the ruff and farthingale accompany our idea of Queen Elizabeth, it is of her, as a living character, not in that of her apparition.'

'And yet,' rejoined Willoughton; 'if you remain in this ruin, half an hour longer, till you can scarcely distinguish the walls, you will feel less inclined to laugh at Queen Elizabeth's ghost in a ruff and farthingale.'

'Perhaps I might,' said Mr Simpson, 'if you had not let me so much into the secret of effect in these cases. Yet I question whether it would have been possible for Elizabeth's picture, arrayed in that ridiculous court-dress, supposing it actually to appear, to extort from me any thing but laughter.'

'They say, sir,' said the aged man, 'that she looked solemn and stern enough as she sat in that window, just where you do now, leaning her head upon her hand, or something that looked like one. She sat quite still, for some time, and old Taylor sat quite still looking at her, for he could not move; – but when she rose up and turned round, and made a motion with her hand – thus – as much as to say, "Go about your business!" he thought he should have dropped, and would have gone fast enough if he could.'

'Ay,' said Mr Simpson; 'there was the characteristical in manner, as well as in dress. This must be a true history!'

'Well, friend,' said Willoughton, 'and what followed?'

'Why, sir, then she went down this steep place you now stand upon, into the hall there, where *he* could not have gone, in broad daylight, without risk of his neck; she sank down, as it were, and he lost her awhile, it was so dark; but presently he saw her, all on a sudden, standing in that doorway there, – and I can almost guess I see her there now.'

'You are a silly old man,' said Mr Simpson; and he looked immediately to the door.

11

'You would not like,' said Willoughton, smiling, 'to inquire minutely into the difference between purposely avoiding to look, and purposely looking in the midst of this story; but' – turning to the old man – 'what next?'

'Why, sir, she stood in the arch some time with a very stern look; but I never rightly understood what became of her. Old Taylor said she passed away like a cloud; but then afterwards he was not sure but he saw her again, in a minute or two, in this very window.'

'And have you never been fortunate enough,' said Mr Simpson, 'to see any of those sights?'

'No, sir, no; I hope I have no need of them; though, if I was that way given, I might have thought I saw things too sometimes. Once by Mortimer's tower, down in the tilt-yard, I as good as thought I saw a man standing with a mask on his face, in a moonlight night, with a drawn sword in his hand.'

'That tower,' remarked Willoughton, 'was doubtless named after Mortimer, the paramour of the infamous Isabel?'

'They say, sir, some king was once shut up there.'

'Ay, Edward the Second, for a short time.'

'And they will tell you a power of stories of what was to be seen about that tower, before it was pulled down, and after too; but I don't believe a word of them. People are always conjuring up strange tales when they have nothing better to do. I have got an old book at home full of them, enough to make one's hair stand on end, if one could but make it all thoroughly out. I showed it to Mr Timothy, the school-master, and he could hardly make it out neither; but he said it was no matter, for it was full of nothing but nonsense. He read me some of it, and I could not get it out of my head again for a week.'

'Ay, it met with a thriving soil,' said Mr Simpson, 'it's well you got the nonsense out of your head at all. But how happened you to buy a book in a language you could not read?'

'I did not buy it, sir; and, as to the language, I could understand that well enough, but I could not read the letters; and Timothy himself bungled at the spelling.'

Willoughton inquired where this book was met with; and whether he could have a sight of it?'

'Why, sir, it was dug out of the ground, where an old chapel once stood, belonging to the Priory hard by.'

'O! I remember,' said Willoughton; 'there was formerly a monastery of Black Canons at Kenilworth, founded by Geoffry

12

de Clinton, lord chamberlain to the first King Henry, and the founder of this same castle too: but go on.'

'The place is used for a burial-ground still,' resumed the old villager; 'and it happened, that as Guy, our sexton, was one day going to dig a grave there, he lighted upon a coffin, or the chest, or whatever it was, that held a many things besides this strange book.'

'Indeed!' said Willoughton, eagerly 'let us hear a little about this.'

'We shall not get to Warwick tonight,' said Mr Simpson, gravely.

'Why, sir, it was one day last autumn, – no, I believe it was as late as November; I remember it had rained hard all morning; but whether it was October or November, I cannot be sure.'

'That, I should suppose, does not much signify,' said Mr Simpson.

'Come, now,' said Willoughton, 'do let him be as circumstantial as he pleases.'

'Willingly, willingly, only remember, we are not to sleep at Kenilworth.'

'Well, sir, I cannot be sure exactly of the time, only it had been a dismal day; but the rain was over, when old Guy came running to me in as great a fright as ever I saw a man, and said he had found something in the ground, he could to tell what, but he never felt any thing so heavy in his life; he could not move it, and desired I would go and help him to raise it; and he stared, as if he was out of his wits. When I heard it was so heavy, I thought we might as well have my son to help us, for he was a stout lad. Guy did not much like this, I saw, for he was thinking he should find a treasure, and Guy was always a close one, and for getting as much as he could; it was only two years before he got his money raised for tolling; and there is not one in the parish has liked him since. However, I got my son to go with me, and we set to work, without saying a word to any one; and it was so near dark that nobody was likely to see us in that lonely place.'

'Well! but if it had been treasure, it would have belonged to the Lord of the Manor,' said Mr Simpson.

'Yes, sir, I know that well enough; but you shall hear. We raised it out of the ground at last, and what should it be but an old oak chest. It was so large, a man might have lain down in it at full length; but what helped to make it so heavy was the iron bands that held it together, and three great iron locks, that

13

fastened it. Now, as the place where it was dug up was the east end of the church, Guy took it into his head it contained church plate, that had been put there, in troublesome times, by the monks of the priory. If you had but seen him! he thought his fortune was made; he threw away his spade, and cut a caper as high as a wall. I thought myself there must be something worth looking at o' the inside, but by this time it was so dark we could hardly see what we were about; so I sent my son home for the lantern, and then we tried with old Guy's crow to get the lid open. We got it off at last; and what do you think, sir, we found? Why, nothing but old parchments; some with seals dangling to them, and some old books, dropping to pieces with the worms, though the leaves were thick enough, too: at the bottom of the chest was a great heap of dust.'

'Did you find nothing else?' asked Mr Simpson, fixing his eyes on him.

'No, sir, nothing else,' said the old man, with a little hesitation; 'nothing else, except an old staff, with a large head; and there was a little silver on that and on a book I have at home.'

Mr Simpson inquired what had made the chest so weighty.

'Why, sir, it was made of solid oak, six inches thick, I warrant, and had a great deal of iron about it. I took a fancy to that book, though I could not read it, for I could not make out the letters; but there is some pretty pictures on the leaves, and the colours are as fresh as if they were just painted; and some of the great letters are done all over with gold as bright as the sun.'

'A manuscript, illuminated probably by some monk of the priory,' said Willoughton; 'can I see it?'

'Yes, sir,' replied the old man, 'I have it at home; but what made me wonder most was to see it look so fresh, after it had lain all that time in the ground; to be sure it was well wrapped up in parchment, and the trunk was thick enough, for that matter; but some of the other books dropped to pieces as soon as the air came to them.'

Willoughton asked what had been done with the parchments; adding, to his companion, that they were probably the leiger-book and some other muniments of the priory, hidden when the terrors of Henry the Eighth first prevailed in the monasteries, and afterwards pretended to be lost, first from some hope of their future utility, and then from a fear of avowing their concealment.

14

'When Guy,' resumed the old man, 'found what sort of treasure he had gotten, he was ready to throw himself into the old chest, to be put under ground with it again; but I said there was no need of that; so we took out some of the best of the books, but none of the others had pictures; and Guy took the old staff, and then we did lay the trunk in the earth again.'

Willoughton made many inquiries concerning the parchments with the seals, and the seals themselves, and whether his informant could find again the spot where they were deposited.

'Come, come,' said Mr Simpson; 'let us leave this place; it is almost dark.'

The old man said he thought he could find the spot; but that would be of no use; for it had lain so deep in the ground, that there had been depth over it for graves, and it was now beneath them.

Willoughton, shocked at this circumstance, said no more on the subject; but the old man proceeded.

'Among other things in the book, sir, is a view of this old hall. I should never have found it out myself; for it was no more like what it is now than nothing: but Timothy Crabb, our school-master, knew it at once by this very window – and he read something about this window, too, – and by a doorway in the wall, yonder.'

'How does it appear in the drawing?' asked Willoughton.

'Why, sir, – but you shall see the book, if you like. The hall had a high roof, like a church there, and a gallery ran all along the bottom of it, and such a chimney!——'

'Aye! like the remains of what we see here now, I suppose,' said Mr Simpson.

'No, sir, as different as can be.'

'O! perhaps,' turning to Willoughton, 'it was such an one as we saw at Penshurst; a raised hearth, with irons to hold wood, in the middle of the hall.'

'No; that style,' observed Willoughton, 'was of later date than chimneys in English halls. It came in, I apprehend, with the castellated mansion, of which style is Penshurst, the more ancient part of the building at least. In the hall of the older castle, a chimney sloped back from the line of the wall into the thickness of it, and let out the smoke through a loop above. Thus, the raised hearth, on which the wood-fire blazed, projected into the chamber, and was sometimes overhung by a canopy of stone-work supported by pillars, that gave it a

15

resemblance to a gothic porch, such as adorn some of our finest cathedrals.'

'Yes, sir, this in the book looks like something like a church porch without the sides, the top comes so far over the hearth. Then all down the hall are rows of tables, and gentle-folk and ladies sitting at them, and——'

'I must see this manuscript,' interrupted Willoughton; 'it appears to be a curious one.'

'Come,' said Mr Simpson, 'it is already so dark, we can hardly see our way hence. There is scarce a gleam of light left on the horizon.'

'No, sir, but the moon is rising yonder, and some gentry have a fancy to see this place by moonlight.'

'O! we have seen enough of it.'

'I recommend you,' said Willoughton, 'to avoid looking, just at this moment, towards the door at the bottom of the hall, lest you should see the stately form of Elizabeth in the archway; I had a glimpse of something like her just now; nay, I am not quite sure that I did not see the grave physiognomy of Leicester, under his small black velvet cap and feather.'

'We shall not get to Warwick tonight, said Mr Simpson, fretfully. 'They talk of the patience of a painful antiquary; think what the patience of his friend must be.'

'I have not the honour to deserve the former title,' said Willoughton.

'Between us, we approach to it; the painful part of it, you will allow, belongs to me.'

'In the old sense of the word,' said Willoughton, 'you do not claim it; and, as to the new one, your jests recompense you for your pain: I have all possible inclination to deserve the title, in its best sense; at least by cherishing those inquiries, which make us intimate with the characters and habits of our fellow creatures in past ages, which show them to us in their halls, their ceremonies, their tournaments, their banquets, their domestic usages and even in their monastic retirement. These pictur-esque visions, in which the imagination so much delights, and every discovery, however remote, awaken a peculiar kind of interest and of sentiment no less delightful, which render antiquity, of all studies, the least liable to the epithet of dry, though dull and dry people so liberally bestow it. Antiquity is one of the favourite regions of poetry.'

'Nay,' said Mr Simpson, 'your woods and your meadows are

16

the region for that. Who ever thought of looking for a muse in an old castle? But come, let us remember, that we are on the road for Warwick.'

'Before we go, my friend here must show me his old manuscript; and I must see this fine ruin by moonlight.'

'By moonlight!' exclaimed Simpson; 'would you really stay for so romantic a purpose? We have seen it already by sun-light, and almost by no light at all.'

'The moon is rising, now, sir,' said the old man, 'and by the time the gentleman has seen the book it will be risen high enough to give you light on your journey.'

'Meanwhile, the horses will have no objection to a little corn,' remarked Willoughton; 'nor the postilion to a little ale, if this good man will direct him where to get it.'

Mr Simpson having added, that he too should like a little Warwickshire ale, the old man replied, 'The ale they sell is not much to brag on; but, if you please, gentlemen, I will direct the lad where he and the horses may rest themselves, and, if you will step with me, you can taste some of my home-brewed, and see the book at the same time.'

The travellers assented, and their conductor, after having directed the postilion to a house, accompanied them to his cottage, where he produced the desired manuscript. It was written on vellum, and richly illuminated, and purported to be an account of what passed at Kenilworth, when Henry the Third there kept the feast of Saint Michael, and of some wonderful accident that there befel.

'There is a title-page written almost in the form of a triangle,' said Willoughton, 'and that about as closely as if it were printed. The date, which forms the apex of the reversed triangle, I cannot wholly make out, but it is twelve hundred and some-thing.'

At the heads of chapters and sometimes on the broad margins, there were made drawings of parts of Kenilworth Castle, as it had appeared in the time of Henry probably, with some of the scenes which had there passed, and sometimes with single portraits of the chief persons engaged in them. These gave vivid ideas of the customs and manners of that period, and were traced, with more knowledge of perspective and more attention to proportion, than Willoughton expected. Among them was a procession of knights and ladies, led by numerous harpers, returning from the tilt-yard to the great hall, which showed a high sloping roof, while the windows below, at a considerable elevation from the ground, had round-headed arches, instead of pointed ones. The doorway, leading into it, accorded with the place where one still appears; but the arch was differently constructed, and the receding mouldings seemed to have been ornamented with chevron work, or zigzag, instead of the elegant vine now sculptured there, which latter he had no hesitation in assigning to the time of Leicester.

Another drawing gave an inside view of the hall, as mentioned by the old man. The roof was of great height, open to the rafters, and with pendent beams below, formed into arches, ornamented with inverted pinnacles, nicely carved. Another drawing gave the inside of a chapel, of which there are no longer any remains at Kenilworth.

The original style of the building appeared very ancient, but this was mixed with one more light and elegant, like that of the pointed arches of the windows; and Willoughton conjectured this improvement to have been made by Henry the Third, who is known to have repaired the chapel of the castle for his own use, during his occasional residence there.

There was a representation of a marriage ceremony in celebration at the altar, where a numerous assemblage of dignified persons were arranged in state. A king was giving the hand of the bride to a young man, who was decorated with many military insignia, but who was so far from receiving the gift with joy, that he appeared to be struck with consternation, while the lady, by her attitude, seemed to be fainting.

In the margin was a portrait of a king robed and wearing a crown of gold, which seemed intended for Henry the Third, to whose statue in brass, in his monument in Westminster Abbey, it bore a considerable resemblance.

At the head of another chapter was an inside view of a tower, where a man was sitting alone near a lamp. In the background a face appeared at the grate. The same chamber was represented afterwards, with a man stretched upon a low pallet, but whether asleep, or dead, was not expressed by the drawing. The lamp had gone out, and, instead of a face at the grate, the moon appeared through a window beyond, and threw a pale light on the couch.

Another drawing gave a view of a chapel, or hall; Willoughton was not certain which: there was, however, something like an altar at the farthest end, near which stood a figure alone, the face concealed in a vizor, the left arm, uplifted, held a shield, the right a lance, but the feet were in a position of rest, though another figure near a door was departing, as if with the fear of being pursued, his hands outstretched, and his face turned back over his shoulder. There, too, the moon appeared through a window, and the light fell upon the lifted shield.

While Willoughton was musing what this could mean, the old man, looking upon the leaf, said, 'Timothy Crabb, sir, maintains this is a picture of the priory-chapel, he is sure, as it stood formerly. I should never have found it out myself, there is so little left of the chapel; but Tim makes it all out fine enough.'

'Does he tell you what that figure means?'

'Not as I remember, sir; but the book tells that, I reckon.'

Willoughton turned over the leaves near the drawing; the language, the orthography and the characters were all so ancient, that he hesitated much. What he did make out, however, fixed his attention so deeply, that his friend lost the small remains of his patience, and declared he would set off without him. Willoughton then told his humble host, that, if he was willing to part with the manuscript, he was disposed to give him his own price for it.

'Why, sir, I like to look at the pictures sometimes, and the gold is so bright it is a pleasure to see it; but the book for other matters is not of much value to me, though it may be to other people, seeing as I can't make it out; and, for that matter, if I could, I do not know any good it would do; for, what Tim did read made me as foolish almost as old John, and afraid to go near the castle, for some time, after dark, though I was always counted a little more sensible than some. But I see no good in such things, not I.'

'You are a sensible fellow,' said Mr Simpson, 'and I wish my friend here had a little less curiosity, and a little more such wit as yours. And now, Harry, do leave the book and come away.'

'No, I shall first console myself for the mortification of your compliments. What shall I give you for the book, my friend?'

'Why, sir, I don't know, I am sure; I don't know the value of such things. Tim Crabb said it might be worth its weight in gold for aught he knew; but I leave it, sir, to your generosity.'

'It is well you do not leave it to mine,' said Mr Simpson, 'for I should make a low reckoning of it.'

The sum Willoughton offered accorded with his own estimation of so curious a relick, rather than with the expectation of his

19

host, who heard it with exclamations of thankfulness; while Mr Simpson expressed not merely surprise but reprehension, and the vulgar proverb of 'Fools and their money –' was nearly audible on his lips.

'What other books did you find in the same place?' asked Willoughton.

'Ah! bless you, sir,' replied the ancient villager, 'I wish I had a score of them.'

'Well you may, my friend, if they would fetch you such a price as this!' was the ready remark of Mr Simpson.

'It is his honour's own generosity, sir, and I suppose he thinks the book worth the money, or he would not give it.'

'Come, Harry,' continued Simpson, 'here has been folly enough for once; let us be gone.'

'You are sure you have no other book like this? inquired Willoughton.

'There is another or two, that do still hold together, I think,' said the old man; 'They have got no pictures; but then they have the same kind of letters, that cannot be understood.' – He went for them.

'You will tempt the man to steal the parish-register, and offer it to you as a curious relick,' said Mr Simpson; 'and indeed it will deserve your money better than this.'

The old man returned with a small quarto, printed in black letter and bound in real boards, which had been guarded at the corners with brass; the marks of clasps remained on it and those of a lozenge in the centre of each board.

'Though this is of later date, much later date, than the manuscript,' said Willoughton, 'I see it is one of the earliest books that came from the press in England. It appears also by its contents, to have been intended to assist the purposes of the monks of that dark age.'

'A *Boke of Sprites*!' exclaimed Simpson, with a shout of exultation: 'a boke of sprites, with the signs they may be known by, and divers rules to keep you from harm: the like was never known before!'

'Excellent! excellent!' said Willoughton; 'and here is another black-letter volume. Well, friend, without looking further, what shall I give you for them?'

'This is past endurance!' said Mr Simpson; 'my patience is out!'

'O sir! I will give you these into the bargain,' said the old man, smiling; an offer which Willoughton would not accept, who paid the old man what he thought they were worth. Mr Simpson, then taking his friend by the arm, desired his host to direct them to the chaise.

'I must see the ruin by moonlight,' said Willoughton; 'but I will not detain you many minutes.'

'No, no; you will see the towers of Warwick by moonlight; which will be much finer.'

'My good friend here,' said Willoughton, 'will order the chaise round to the gate where it set us down; and, by the time it arrives, I shall have seen what I wish to see.'

'Be it so,' said Mr Simpson with an air of resignation; 'one is sure of you when a journey is to be begun; but never when one would end, or hasten it. I have not forgotten our midnight rambles about Stonehenge! Doubtless we were the first human beings, who had appeared there, at such an hour, for many centuries; and what astonished me afterwards, more than any thing I saw, was, that I myself should have been conjured there at such an unseasonable hour; I, whose brain never hatched any of those "high and unimaginable fantasies," as your poet Gray calls them, which distract the heads of some of his readers."

'Ay! those shadows of the moon at full,' said Willoughton laughing, as they walked towards the ruin, his friend remonstrating with him on the imprudence of this passion for antiquities and on his credulity. 'And can you really hold,' said he, 'that these books were found in the manner related; and that any of them, especially the *Boke of Sprites*, ever belonged to the library of the priory?'

'It does not seem probable,' replied Willoughton, 'that the old man should have invented the story he has related of the discovery of them; but, be that as it may, the books themselves announce their own genuine antiquity. The manuscript is laboriously illuminated, and it is well known, that such works were chiefly performed by the inhabitants of monasteries. The *Boke of Sprites* even was likely to have served the purposes of the monks. We know that the libraries of monasteries contained a most heterogeneous assemblage: Ovid, the *Romance of Charlemagne, Guy of Warwick,* and the *Rimes of Robin Hood,* have been found on the shelf with Homilies, and other books; which, although they might be tinged with the corruptions of the Papal school, ought not to have had such companions. You may recollect, that Warton, in the interesting sketches of

21

ancient manners which he gives in his *History of English Poetry*, mentions this very fully; and that, among others, the library of Peterborough contained *Amys and Amdion, Sir Tristram Merlin's Prophecies*, and the *Destruction of Troy*: and books of this sort were not only copied, but often invented by the monks, sometimes for their amusement, sometimes for worse purposes.'

'One of the old books you have relates to their castle, I think,' said Mr Simpson, looking up at the shadowy masses; which, shown thus faintly by the rising moon, seemed more majestic than before.

'Yes, and I perceive,' continued Willoughton, 'that even you feel a curiosity to know what may have passed so many ages back, on the spot we now stand upon.'

'Why,' acknowledged Simpson, 'when one looks up at the very walls now crumbling into ruin, that were once so magnificent, and that inclosed beings with passions as warm as our own – beings, who have so long since vanished from the earth, one cannot help wishing to know a little of their history and of the scenes they witnessed; but, for your legend, I fear to trust it.'

'It speaks of the times of Henry the Third,' said Willoughton, 'those were lawless enough to permit many adventures; and, if the citizens of London were then robbed in the streets even at noon-day, what could travellers in the forest of Arden expect? But this manuscript seems to tell of princely feasts given in the castle, and of adventures passing in the presence of the court.'

'Ay, if one could but believe them.'

'A great part of the castle,' pursued Willoughton, 'which then existed, is now gone; and much that we look at, stands in its place; but that noble hall, and Caesar's tower and several other towers, such as those where the moonlight falls, beheld the very court of Henry the Third, ay, and Montfort, on whom he had bestowed Kenilworth, and who added ingratitude to treason, by holding the fortress against his benefactor and liege lord.'

They stood for some minutes in silence, looking up at the ruin and listening, as the breeze rushed by, to the shivering of the ivy, that overhung it, – all the shining leaves trembling in the moonlight. The pauses of solemn stillness, that followed these sighings of the air among the old branches, were very solemn, and the sound itself – so still, uncertain, and sudden, Willoughton could have fancied to have been the warning murmurs of

22

one, who, in his mortal state, had lived within these walls, and now haunted the scene where it had once revelled, or, perhaps, suffered. It seemed like a voice imperfectly uttering forth some dark prophecy, and telling of the illusion of life and the certainty of death. To Willoughton's recollection this spectacle of the remains of ages past, now glimmering under the soft shadows of moonlight, brought those touching lines of Beattie——

> 'Hail, awful scenes, that calm the troubled breast,
>   And woo the weary to profound repose,
> Can passion's wildest uproar lull to rest,
>   And whisper comfort to the man of woes.'

Willoughton stood so wrapt, that he heard not his friend's inquiry, whether he meant to pass a night at Kenilworth, as a sequel to a former one at Stonehenge; nor was he immediately aware of the nearer approach of his aged conductor, who said, in a tone somewhat tremulous, 'You are now on the very spot, sir, where Mortimer's tower stood; it was the main entrance to the castle, when there was a lake, and it opened from the tilt-yard, that ran along the end of the water into the lower court: you see, sir, it was quite on the opposite side of the castle from Lord Leicester's great gate.'

Willoughton surveyed the place, but not a vestige of the building remained. 'Here then,' said he, 'the unhappy Edward the Second was, for a while, imprisoned, before he was removed to Corfe and Berkeley Castles, his last abodes.'

'If you please, sir,' said the man, 'the chaise is at the gate; and, if you will take my advice, you will not stay here long, for I cannot say I like it myself; I shall begin to think I see that strange figure again, and I had rather not.'

'Well, let us go,' and Mr Simpson, 'or I shall begin to fancy something of the same sort, too. What did you say, it had a mask on its face?'

'Yes, sir, and a drawn sword in its hand; but I don't like the place, sir, let us go.'

'Ay, ay,' said Mr Simpson, 'let us go; we – we – we shall not get to Warwick tonight.'

A laugh from his friend, which he too well understood, both vexed and ashamed him. 'I did not think it possible,' said he, 'that I could have yielded to the contagion of this folly thus; remember, however, it is not Elizabeth in her ruff and farthingale, that I fear, nor any thing else distinctly.'

Willoughton laughed again triumphantly. 'Better and better; your feelings are true to my arguments, in spite of your own. I desire no farther proof of the effects of time and circumstances – of solitude and obscurity on the imagination.'

As they passed by Caesar's tower, and inquired where the line of the castle-ditch had been traced, he observed, that probably the chief entrance had at first been over a drawbridge to that tower, though now no sign of it could be distinguished.

When the travellers were once more seated in the chaise, Mr Simpson betook himself to sleep; while, on their journey of four miles through the checkered moonlight of woody lanes to Warwick, Willoughton did not lament the silence of his friend, which left him to the quiet musings of his own mind, and to the peace of nature, reposing under this soft and beautiful shade. The air was so still that scarcely a leaf trembled of the lofty boughs that overshadowed the road; and when the postilion stopped to make some alteration of the harness, the breathing of the horses alone was heard through all this scene of night.

There is a peace of the spirits, which has surely somewhat holy in it. Such is the calmness which the view of a midsummer-dawn communicates, or that of moonlight on woods and green plains; and such Willoughton experienced during this short ride, till he drew near Warwick, when the beautiful towers of Saint Mary's appeared on the right, and the more lofty and distant ones of the castle on the left of the perspective; and these awakened the stronger interest of expectation.

Having reached the inn, and Mr Simpson, late as it was, having ordered a good supper, they walked out to take a view of the castle. Finding that, at this hour, they could not gain admittance by the porter's gate, they went to the bridge over the Avon, on the outside of the town, and thence had a fine retrospect of the castle, with all its towers crowning the high, woody bank of that peaceful and classic stream. One vast, round tower of most warlike air, looking down upon the precipice, delighted Willoughton more than any other. A part of the edifice, repaired and adorned in the time of James the First, containing the state rooms, which run in a long line upon the steep, was not in harmony with this tower, and gave very different ideas of the character and manners of the respective ages to which they belonged. The moonlight touched this tower with a fine solemnity, and fell on the tops of the dark cedars and other trees, that clothe the precipice, as it glanced to Shaks-

24

peare's stream below, where it rested in all its silver radiance, as if pleased to claim it for its home.

Willoughton leaned over the bridge, and looked upon the scene in silence. The brightness of the river, the dark, clear shade of the woods, reflected on its margin and rising with majesty up the steep, with the grey towers, in softened light, crowning all, formed a harmony of tints and of objects such as he had not often seen, and which recalled to him that state of holy peace he had so lately experienced.

Amidst the stillness of this scene, there arose a strain, as if commanded by Shakspeare's wand, and to which his words might have been applied. 'O! it came o'er mine ear, like the sweet south, that breathes upon a bank of violets.' It was the music of French-horns, sweetened by distance and by the water, over which it passed, accompanied by a few voices addressing the river celebrating the bard in the well-known song of Garrick and Arne, – 'Thou soft-flowing Avon!'

Nothing could exceed the beauty of some of the cadences, prolonged by the deep, mellow tones of the horns, or of the chorus, and of the close, that gave these words:–

'The fairies by moonlight dance round the green bed,
For, hallow'd the turf is, that pillows his head.'

They brought tears into the eyes of Willoughton, and drew from him a deep sigh long after silence had returned.

Mr Simpson looked about to discover whence this charming tribute to the memory of the loved poet came, and perceived two little boats stealing along the margin of the stream, under shadow of the bank that rose to the castle. The white awning of the first betrayed it to his eye, before it emerged on the moonlight; and now the measured trampling of the oars told its departing course upon the waters, till once again that chorus died along the air, and then the steps of the oars were heard no more.

The travellers remained for some moments, as if spell-bound, in thoughtful silence; and they left this enchanting scene, and returned to their inn, without having uttered a word. This was an unusual mood with Mr Simpson; he had caught it from his companion, rather than from the scene; and now, on the entrance of supper, he rejoiced to get rid of it, and to return to the more substantial pleasures of this world.

Willoughton, when he had retired to his chamber, and had, as

25

was his custom, looked out upon the night, now overcast with gloomy clouds, sat down to examine his manuscripts, instead of seeking repose. Bound up with that of the *Trew Chronique*, was another, entitled A *Trew Historie of two Mynstrells, that came by night to the Priory of Saint Margaret, and what they disclosed, and what one in the convent by his art, proved them to bee*. This *Trew Historie* was more difficult to be deciphered than the *Trew Chronique*, and Willoughton left it for the present, and took the *Boke of Sprites*.

As he turned over the leaves, curious to see the thraldom of superstition to which the people of a remote age were liable, he often smiled at the artless absurdities he discovered, the clumsy inventions practised upon the fears of the ignorant by the venality of the monks. Yet he sometimes found his attention seized, in spite of himself, by the marvellous narratives before him; till, at length, he began to feel that he was alone, to recollect that it was past midnight, to observe that all around him was still as death; and gradually to think he might as well lay aside the *Boke of Sprites* till daylight should return and the world again sound busily around him.

He did so, and again took the *Trew Chronique*, desirous of ending his long day, with some new traits of an age so distant from his own and of the style, in which they might be shadowed forth. The mere spelling did not render this so difficult, as the character in which it was written, with its abundance of abbreviations and contractions.

The following is a modernized copy, which he afterwards wrote out for the amusement of a friend, who was fond of the subjects it touched upon, but had not industry enough to work his way through the obstructions of the original. In this copy, while Willoughton endeavoured to preserve somewhat of the air of the old style, without its dryness, he was often compelled to regret, that much of the effect of the story was lost, with the simplicity, brevity and quaintness of the ancient manner. However, he often retained the old words, where they did not seem to form too glaring a contrast with the modern style, and, now and then, somewhat of the quaintness of the original, the title of which ran thus:–

26

A Boke

Contenynge a trew chronique of what passed at
Killingworth, in Ardenn, when Our Soveren
Lord, the Kynge, kept ther his fest of
Senzt Michel; with ye marveylous
accident, that ther befel, at the so-
lempnissazion of the marriage
of Gaston de Blondeville.
With divers things, cu-
rious to be known,
thereunto purtayn-
ing. With an
account of the
grete Turney,
ther held
in the
yere
MCCLVI
Changed out of the Norman tongue
By Grymbald, Monk of Senzt Marie
Priori in Killingworth.

THE FIRST DAY

At the head of this chapter was a drawing, of the King and Queen, with their train, passing under the towers of Kenilworth. Near the King rode a young knight of a very spirited air; in one hand he held his cap, bending towards the King, who seemed to be speaking to him, and with the other he reined in his fiery courser. At some distance, was a man pressing through the crowd, with eager gesticulation and a wild countenance, towards the King. The royal banner, on the tower above, was tinged by the setting sun, and the arms and caps of the soldiers on the battlement there glistened with the rays. The cap of one of these, who, as if to obtain a longer view of the King, appeared to have stretched too far forward, was falling on the multitude below; some of whom were laughing.

 T WAS at the feast of Saint Michel, that King Henry, the third of his name, with his Queen and sundrie of the nobles of the realm and a marvellous train of estates and gentils, came to keep court in Ardenn, at his castle of Kenilworth. The day was drawing to an end ere they arrived: and it was a goodly sight to see this noble company coming over the forest, till then so lonesome; and the last light of this day's sun glittering upon the helmets and lances of the King's guard; likewise on the gorgeous apparelling of their horses and trumpets, with their banners unrolled, that went before his grace; also on the litters of the Queen, covered with cloth of gold and with tapestry of rich colours, brought from her own land beyond the sea.

This noble train, with all the spear-men attendant on the King, was like unto a little army covering the paths and tracks, for many miles, as they wound amongst the woods of Ardenn; or like unto some mighty river, that flowing along, appears, where the shades open, in shining bends upon the plain, and is lost again as they enter beneath the gloom; but yet may you judge of their course throughout all the prospect. Like as you may the broken lines of the great aqueduct, stretching over the plains of our dear father of Rome; which, as we perceive its distant points athwart those solitudes, we connect in our minds into one great

28

whole, grander in its sweep than it might have shown when it stood complete.

There went before the King a hundred archers in pairs, sumptuously apparelled, and having the feathers of their arrows stained with green; the horns sounded before them through the woods: then fifty demi-lancemen, two abreast; then fifty pikemen; then trumpets, with their banners also displayed; then officers at arms, in their sur-coats, the serjeants with their maces. In the midst was borne up the royal banner, by six of the standard-bearers: the pipes of it were of silver, and were slided along the banner-staff; which was held with horn in a girdle of white leather, embroidered, worn by the King's chief standard-bearer.

The King's Highness came riding on a noble grey, widely encompassed about with pikemen, and attended by divers nobles of the realm and by knights and gentils, without number. His Highness wore that day a cloak of purple velvet, lined with yellow satin, and furred with martin and ermine; on his head was a cap of black velvet, bearing a sable plume. His countenance was goodly and gracious, and he often turned and spoke to those about him.

On his right hand, rode the young Prince Edward, holding in his fiery charger, yet looking as though he would fain spur him to the top of his speed. Next to him rode the Archbishop of York. On the King's left, was his brother, the Earl of Cornwall. The Bishop of Coventry would have been there, but he was then lying sick on his bed; but the Prior and divers of the monks attended on the King.

First amongst the knights, that waited on his grace, was Gaston de Blondeville, a young Provençal; whom King Henry had raised, for some daring exploits in his dominions beyond the sea, to be a knight of his household. He was of comely person and gallant air; and managed his proud charger with such easy grace, as a lady might, with silken bandage, guide a fawn. He wore a cloak of pale olive, lined and guarded with rose colour; his cap was of velvet like to it, and he wore his feathers in the French fashion: for he was of the Queen's country, and had all the gaiety of her nation in his countenance and 'haviour.

Yet were there some in the court, men of English ground, who liked him not; it may be, because he was a stranger in our land, or that he bore a proud defiance in his eye, or that they envied him his favour with the King.

29

Some way before the Queen, went fifty of the foresters of Ardenn clothed in green, sounding their horns. She was in her litter, tapestried with cloth of gold, and she was compassed all about with her ladies and her nobles and esquires. Her litter was borne by two brave coursers, right richly trapped with velvet, and led by pages apparelled in sumptuous liveries; other pages, in 'broidered doublets, went beside her, or following. Then came her master of the horses, leading her palfrey, very richly appointed, the bridle and breast-chain studded with jewels, followed by another of her palfreys, led by a page. Her Highness was adorned in a close gown of velvet, 'broidered about with pearls, and bearing upon her head a great hood of black velvet, richly sewed with large pearls. Following her Highness, came her ladies and gentlewomen mounted on fair palfreys, richly appointed and apparelled; a goodly company.

Then came her Highness's chariot empty, drawn by six horses, led by pages in jackets of scarlet damask, with the English crown 'broidered on their backs. They bore in their caps a white feather; dropping aside, in the manner of France, where-at the people murmured, and well they might; for such a sight of strangers, from her own land, the like was never seen! But the Queen bore herself so graciously towards the people, smiling upon them with her comely countenance, that she won away their discontent. Other gentlewomen of her court followed her car, mounted on palfreys.

Next came Eleanor, the widowed Countess of Pembroke, the King's sister, now Countess of Leicester, in her litter, with a sumptuous train: and then Cincia, the Countess of Cornwall, the sister of the Queen, right freshly apparelled, and sumptuously attended by noble dames and gentils; and a sight of people followed, in the different liveries of their masters.

Before the Queen, went her *mynstrells of music;* who, when they came nigh to Kenilworth, began to blow upon their pipes, and to strum their stringed instruments with most sweet noise – so that the bells of a village there, which were rung for mirth, could not be heard so far.

Amongst the damsels attending the Queen, none were so fair as the Lady Isabel, daughter of the Earl of Arundel, and the Lady Barbara, daughter of the Earl of Huntingdon; who followed her Highness, on white palfreys. Ychon of them was beautiful beyond thought: the Lady Isabel was the more stately and carried a higher brow; but Lady Barbara's smiles were blyther than the morn.

Soon as the towers of Kenilworth showed themselves upon the West, which, if it had not been for the glowing spears of those on the battlements, would hardly have been known from the dark wood-tops, – soon as they appeared, some half-score of the foresters rode forward with their bugles, to give sign of the King's approach; but were straight sounded back by the trumpets, which blew up a blast, that filled the forest, and echoed to the very castle walls, ere the proud trumpeters would stop.

Then his Highness courteously commanded, that those who had come forth so many miles, to welcome him on his way, should be appointed to proclaim him at the gates. They waited not for second bidding; but, tuning up so clear and sweet, set spurs to their hobbies, and flew swiftly as the arrows from their own bows.

All the way hence to Kenilworth was lined with other troops of foresters in green; who, at certain distances, saluted the King, as he passed, with their bugles, in spite of the trumpets, that charged so loud and shrill their minet-flourishes: and they followed in the Queen's train. The King's pike-men and lance-men going after of all.

At the first sound of the bugles before the gate, you might see the great banner of England raised upon the keep of Kenilworth. Then, the chief wardour of the castle appeared upon the turret; though he stayed not long there, but went down to join his lord, in their service at the gate. The archers behind the battlements stood in order; other bow-men and the lance-men ranged themselves behind the tower-walls, and the trumpets there answered the summons, with a blast, that shook the forests, and made the fair waters of the valley tremble; roughening the portraiture of towers and woods, which had seemed to sleep upon their surface, as in a glass of chrystal.

Then the Lord Constable, coming down from the keep, followed by a posse of his officers, took to horse and went out to meet the King. As he turned out of the gate, he met the Prior of Saint Mary's, with the twelve canons, and a long train processioning, all in full ceremony, bearing precious reliques, to welcome his Highness; after them came the priest and sundry of the parish-church, singing.

The press of people, from all the country about, was so thick,

31

that hardly could the monks make way among them. The castellan, a man proud and jealous of his high place, was not well pleased, that they should try to present themselves to the King, before himself; but they were soon right glad to follow in his train, for strait as he appeared, the crowd was forced back, and they passed, without difficulty, in that wise, full three furlongs.

The castellan, coming in presence of his Highness, leaped from his horse, and, on his knee, presented him the keys of the castle, on a rich plate; the which his Highness readily delivered to him again, with a gracious speech, bearing, that they were well in his custody. Then, the Prior and canons of Saint Mary's showed themselves in procession, with banners, and chaunting sweet anthems, and his Highness looked kindly on them; after which they went on to the Queen, and, paying duty, attended her to the castle. But my Lord Constable, remounting his horse, rode bareheaded before his Highness, to the very gates.

Immediately before the King, was borne his sword of justice, by the Lord Hubert de Lacey; where, on the sheath, you might behold, in letters of rubies, these words, 'Truth and Right'. As he passed all the people cried out, 'King Henry, King Henry, long live King Henry! and blessings on your sweet-favoured visage!'

Then, they threw forth on the air, for joy, among other tokens, corn and flour[1]; so that many of the nobles of the realm, nay, some of the King's guard, liked it not, for the flour-dust, falling on their garments, disguised them like unto grinders of corn: but they held their peace, as needs must, passing on in solemn stateliness.

Before the castle-gates,[2] a great show of the King's bow-men were drawn out to receive him, and the courts within were lined, and every tower and battlement was thronged with his soldiers. There, too, were the foresters ready at the gates, who, on the King's approach tuned up their merry bugles, with might and main; as though one breath sounded through the whole of them. But, when the heralds passed under the towers, their trumpets took their revenge, for they gave many blasts, that made every court within shake for joy; and showed more like a triumph of war than a flourish of festival. They on the ramparts now seemed to take the hint, and joined them with such warrior-sounds of fierce disdain, that the clear bugle seemed but as a shepherd-pipe beneath them, and, for a season, was not heard at all.

Certes, the noise of the trumpets and cornets, the clanging of bells, the trampling of horses over the bridge, the striking of swords upon shields, with, ever and anon, the shouts of the multitude, astounded cattle and fowl in the woods, far and wide. Old wives and they that might not leave their homes for sickness could hear the mingled uproar; and could know as surely, when the King reached Kenilworth, as those, who had journeyed thither to behold him. And many an outlaw in the forest, who feared to show his face among the crowd, lay hearkening in his den, or stalked under the old oaks, while he watched the minutes of the coming twilight, and reckoned on the booty he should seize from careless travellers, returning, at night, to distant towns.

Some too there were, who, in the pathless holds of this forest, heard the far-off voice of joyance and society, with bitter grief; finding out, too late, they were not made for that lonesomeness of heart their thoughtless vices had condemned them to. Alas! for such, let them shrive and betake themselves, as penitents, to holy cloister.

When the Queen's litter came near the gates of the castle, her minstrels of music sang with most sweet glee, and the bugles saluted her as she passed into the barbican, or first tower of defence; but, soon as she appeared on the drawbridge, the trumpets from the ramparts blew up a flourish, and then the minstrels stopped, though they had not finished their fit. And they did well; for hardly could there be heard the trampling of the horses' hoofs upon the bridge, nor the distant music in the courts before the King. The walls and turrets, thronged with faces, seemed to be alive, and to shout, as with one voice, 'Queen Eleanor! Queen Eleanor! Long live Queen Eleanor!' – but some few were heard to shout, 'Away with the foreigners! – away with all foreigners!' which the good Queen seemed not to hear, though she guessed in her heart what they said; and many a noble knight and lady near her knew well. She, with unchanged countenance, showed only sweet smiles to those numberless eyes, darting from the walls and battlements, all turned upon her litter, as it passed over the bridge, glittering in the last beams of this day's sun, and then entered beneath that deep and dark archway of the great tower, leading into the base court.

Beyond, in the sunshine, could be seen the King's Highness, preceded by the Lord Constable, and having the Archbishop on his right and Prince Edward on his left, passing forward to the

33

upper court; where, on the steps, stood the marshals of the hall, the stewards, the esquires of the household, with many officers of the castle, waiting to receive him, some with chains of gold on their necks: the royal banner waving over all. They stood so thick, looking over one another's shoulders, face above face, on the steps there, that they seemed like a rampart of heads; while, below them, in the same court, the lance-men and yeomen of the household stood waiting to receive the Queen.

And truly it was a pleasureful sight, to behold that vision of light appearing beyond the deep portal, under which stood, on either hand, the wardours in their niches, to the number of eight; so dim, they showed like shadows more than substance, albeit, they did not lack of that. And a more delightful sight it was to behold the Queen and all her train, winding through that dark arch into the beams beyond; the rich trappings of steeds and men, their breast-plates and spears and steel caps, all glancing in the setting sun. There, too, you might see, through the higher bars of the portcullis, the windows of the great chamber hung out with tapestry of silk and cloth of gold.

But that, which caused some surprise to those who watched without, was a sudden turmoil, that appeared around the King in the court, just as the Queen's litter was advancing forth of the archway. A man was seen forcing himself among the guards, towards his Highness, who turned his face backwards in the sun, as if to see what was going on; and seemed to rein in his steed, while he held forth his right arm to Sir Gaston de Blondeville, who, with cap in hand, leaned forward on his courser, as if receiving some command. The while, the heads and spears of soldiers gathered round, moving in tumultuous hurry, rising and falling incessantly, like unto those stormy white tops coming on over a darkened sea.

On a sudden, the King disappeared: some thought he had fallen from his steed, struck by the hand of the stranger; and then, such was the throng of people beyond the portal to get forward for more certainty, that hardly could the Queen's guard keep them back, till his Highness was seen ascending the steps of the high court.

At last, out of the midst of the confusion a shield was seen raised upon the traversed spears of six soldiers, and borne towards the outer gate, having upon it a man stretched, as if dead. But at the great portal the soldiers stopped, and drew aside to make way for the Queen; his Highness, meanwhile,

34

with his nobles and young knight, had withdrawn into the state apartments.

When her Highness was gone by, they brought the man upon the shield into the free air without the walls, and lowered their burden on the grass; but the tumult of the people was so great, (they suspecting that he had attempted the King's life) that the soldiers with their spears had much ado to save him from their fury, or to keep a little space open around him.

He was a man of goodly appearance, that lay there, seeming without life. Anon, he began to stir himself, and in a little while opened his eyes; the which, when the people saw it, redoubled their fury; and they demanded, that he should be had to prison, for 'he has assailed the life of our good King!' With that they made such a roaring, that the shouts of the soldiers, who wanted to set them right, could not be heard, the women brawling louder than all of them together.

Thus it went for some time: and then, the noise being hushed, they found out the man was innocent of what they had suspected.

When the stranger had recovered himself a little, he stared wildly; and, raising himself up, he looked round him, as if examining the countenance of every one, whom curiosity or anger had made to bend over him. And so he looked again and again, till they asked him, if he thought he saw the countenance of any one there, whom he knew. Then he fetched a deep sigh, and said, 'I as surely saw him as I now breathe, but he is not here.'

Divers present then asked him, of whom he spoke, but he only muttered to himself, 'I could not be deceived; it is impossible for me ever to forget him.' Then he shook from limb to limb, and was nigh going off into a swoon again. The people, meanwhile, pressed upon the soldiers to know what all this meant; and curiosity and pity began to take the place of rage.

The tale went, that, as King Henry had approached the entrance of the second court, this man, who had passed the portal amongst the King's horses, at the risk of his life, came beside him, and, having fixed his eyes with the greatest attention upon a knight of the King's household, cried out, 'Justice! most noble Henry.' Then, as if unable to utter something he would have spoken, he fell down in strong convulsions, and was nigh being trampled to death. His Highness, seeing the condition of the man, had commanded he should be taken forth of the court, and aid administered to him; and this was all the soldiers could tell.

There were some amongst the crowd who thought they had seen him before, and questioned him of his name, and wherefore he had presumed to approach the King in such manner; to all which he would nothing answer; but seemed heavy at heart, and as if his very sadness would not let him speak; only these words he uttered, once or more, – 'It was he himself! I should have known him at Cairo!'

Some still said they had seen the poor man before; naithless he proved to be a stranger in Kenilworth. When he could walk, he was led back to the little hostel, where he had taken up his lodging, and there he remained closely hid from the eyes of every one, all that night.

THE SECOND DAY

At the head of this chapter was a view of the tilt-yard, at the end of the great lake, with the towers of Kenilworth above. – In the lists were two armed knights, on foot, each poising his spear at the other. They were cased in complete steel; their visors closed, each bearing on his helmet his plume and crest. There was somewhat very impressive in the station and in the whole appearance of these armoured figures. Each stood with his right foot advanced; the right arm, holding the spear, was raised high, displaying at once the strength and grace of an accomplished warrior. At the end and along one side of the tilt-yard, were galleries hung with tapestry, where sat the Queen and her ladies, and the King and his nobles, waiting to behold the encounter. The opposite sides were open to the lake, the woods, and the castle.

N THE morn, next after the King came to Kenilworth, there was tilting in the great yard of the castle, at which his Highness, with the Queen and her court, were present. This was the day of Turney; but, although this noble company made a goodly show, they were not apparelled with that splendour they showed on the chief day, as will be hereafter rehearsed.

Among the ladies of the court, none surpassed for beauty the Lady Barbara, daughter of the Earl of Huntingdon and a favourite damsel of the Queen; her the King intended to bestow in marriage, during his sojourn in Ardenn. She was innocent and graceful, as the fawns that bound in our forest, and excelled in all the accomplishments of the court. She had fixed her heart on Sir Gaston de Blondeville, a young knight of the King's household, who had entreated her of her father in vain; for, though he was of a good family, it was a foreign one, being of the Queen's country, and he had little besides the favour of his master to depend on. The youth was of a comely person and gallant bearing; well practised in all martial exercises of war, of which he had given some proof in exploits, and had latterly so much displayed himself in a fierce adventure against some of King Henry's rebellious subjects, beyond sea, that his Highness had incontinently advanced him to be one of his own knights. Moreover, the King, on hearing of his ill-faring suit, had taken that matter into his special cognizance; and the King knew so well how to command the earl, that he consented to give his daughter to the knight, and his Highness determined the marriage should be solemnized forthwith.

But, on this very first day, after his arrival, his spirit was ruffled by a strange accident. As his Highness was returning from the tilt-yard, accompanied by the Queen, and attended by the whole court, his harpers playing before him, a stranger came forth of the crowd, and falling at his feet, called out boldly for justice. Many there present knew him for the man who, the night before, had showed such striking signs of a disturbed mind; and now, noting his unseemly vehemence, they stopped and asked for what offence he demanded justice. The King, too, remembered him; and listening what he should say, the man, observing that, addressed his looks and his voice eagerly to him, and exclaimed, that he demanded justice upon robbers and murderers who infested the highways of his kingdom with more violence and frequency than was ever known before, so that none of his peaceable subjects were safe from them.

The King, seeing the wildness of his look and the strangeness of his gesture, guessed the man was not rightly himself; yet he commanded him forthwith into the castle, there to wait, till he should speak with him, or order some others to do so; and the procession passed on.

Meanwhile, the King determined not to leave this matter, till he should have seen something more about it, with his own discernment. He went speedily into the white hall, which was the court of justice, keeping only a few of his nobles and other attendants, where he summoned the stranger before him, and had question put to him, who he was and of what particular grievance he had to complain.

The man answered, that his name was Hugh Woodreeve, a merchant of Bristol: and then he told his story – that, three years before, travelling with a very large sum of money in his possession, and, being in company with three other travellers, two of them merchants of good repute, and the other a kinsman of his own, they were attacked in the forest of Ardenn, when about two miles from Kenilworth, and robbed of nearly all they carried. They did not part with it quietly, it was so much. His kinsman, however, was the only one of the party that had good arms; he had served in the wars, and he now manfully resisted the ruffians, who directed most of their vengeance to him; he was murdered on the spot; for the rest of his company, they escaped with some hurts. No one of the robbers was killed, but two or three were wounded.

Here the merchant stopped and seemed ready to sink. His Highness, having declared his indignation at this villany, assured the merchant, that justice should be done upon the guilty, if they could be found, and asked whether he could swear to them, if he should see them again. The stranger straight replied, that he could truly swear to the murderer, and that he had seen him in the very court, nay, that he saw him at that very instant, standing even beside the King's chair.

King Henry, struck with astonishment, fixed his eyes sternly on the stranger, for a moment, and then looked at those around him. On his right hand, was his son, Prince Edward, and, on his left, his young favourite, Gaston de Blondeville, upon whom all eyes were fastened; for to him the answer pertayned, and to him the accuser pointed, with a look of horror, which convinced every one present, except his Highness, he did indeed believe he saw before him the murderer of his friend, whether his fancy deceived him, or not. For the King himself, he inclined to think the accuser was either disordered in his mind, or that, from some unknown cause, he was the enemy of Sir Gaston; and his Highness knew well of the unreasonable and deadly abhorrence, in which many of his subjects of Britain held some of those strangers from France, who had risen into favour.

At the boldness of this accusation, Sir Gaston stood, at first, like one stricken with dismay; then, moving his hand towards his sword, he said, 'but for the presence of the King, my master, I should soon avenge me for so foul a slander.'

To which the merchant, now much more tranquil than he had been, said, 'The same reason must restrain all; but I do not need it: I would not set my life against that of an assassin! I ask for justice from his Highness.'

At these words, Sir Gaston was hardly withheld from his accuser. King Henry commanded silence: and, as soon as all noise had ceased, he turned with a severe countenance to the stranger, and said, 'Know you not, that he, whom you accuse is a knight of my household, advanced to honour for his valour?'

'Yea, noble King Henry,' replied the merchant, 'I have heard so; but, I repeat, he is the man who killed my kinsman! I never can forget that face: if I had met him in a distant land, I should have seized him for the murderer!'

The King, more fully convinced of the unsoundness of his mind, said, 'Your passion has deceived you; thus far I am willing to pardon you; if you go farther, you must be taught what it is to dishonour a gentleman and a knight.'

Upon this, the merchant fell at the King's feet; and, with uplifted hands, again cried out for justice! Henry, hardly less astonished at the resolution of the man, than that one of his household should be thus accused, (although he might have bethought him of the law he had himself found it expedient to make heretofore at Kenilworth, respecting robberies then committed in a very extraordinary manner on the highways)— King Henry, though astonished, began to doubt. He fixed a look, in which there was somewhat of inquiry, upon Sir Gaston, whose visage was pale, though his eye was fierce; but who may say, whether fear or anger maketh some men pale?

The King held it to be the last; a momentary doubt had entered his mind; but he promptly dismissed it. His Highness was commanding, that the stranger should be removed; and, for the present, confined in the castle; when Prince Edward, who, young as he was, had closely observed all that had passed, craved humbly of the King, his father, to suffer the merchant to be further questioned; and the King consented thereto.

Then the man was asked, whether he could tell the year and the month, when the robbery he spoke of had been committed. He was ready enough with his answers, and said it was on the eighteenth of October, in the year twelve hundred and fifty-three, and on the chase; that he was sure of the time, because it was within three days of that, when he should have paid to a goldsmith the most part of the money, whereof he was robbed. Upon this, the King seemed to consider awhile, for he knew, that, about that time, a camp lay in the neighbourhood of Warwick and on the edge of the forest, and that Sir Gaston was there, he being then serving as esquire to Sir Pierse Mallory.

At the last words of the merchant, Sir Gaston moved towards the King, as though he would privily say something; but his Highness reproved him with a frown; and asked the merchant at what hour the robbery was committed, and what were the array and appearance of the robbers?

The knight interrupting the reply, then said aloud, 'Sire! I entreat you, be mindful of the condition of disgrace, in which I must stand, if you seem to give countenance to his scandalous accusation. I know not, that I shall be able to breathe, if it be thought, that your Highness could for one minute, think it possible I could have committed so foul a deed.'

King Henry, looking kindly upon him said, 'It is right you should be cleared with those, who know you not so well as I do; and chiefly with those, who love not men of your country; and, therefore, would I examine this witless charge to the uttermost.' His Highness then made all his questions over again.

The merchant considered awhile, and somewhat of his boldness seemed to forsake him: he then answered, 'the number of the robbers was three; they were most of them tall in stature; they wore cloaks about them, and had masks on their faces.'

'Masks?' said the King.

'Masks!' murmured the courtiers, with one voice.

The King, daunting the accuser with the anger of his countenance, said, 'You could swear to this knight, as one of the robbers, and yet you say, he had a mask on his face! I suspect you now for an impostor more than for a moody man. If it prove so, tremble! for I swear by my sword you shall not escape. I give you one more warning, to stop before you totally plunge into your ruin.'

At these words, delivered with vehemence, the paleness left Sir Gaston's face, and he made a profound obeisance, showing his gratitude to the King. The accuser, dismayed, could not immediately find his voice, as it seemed. Haply, he could not so speedily send back his thoughts to the rest of his story.

Incontinently, the most of the assemblage began to look ychon in other's face.

By-and-bye, the merchant said, that in the struggle between his companions and the robbers, two of the vizors fell off, and so he saw plainly the faces of the robbers, and he perfectly remembered the face of the knight. His Highness, without telling his thoughts on this, which many there present scrupled not to hold an after-invention of the accuser, commanded him to begin his tale anew, and to tell, one by one, every particular he could bring to mind of the alleged adventure; but before he began, Sir Gaston, surveying him, asked whether, about four years back, he was not at Embrun, in the Dauphiné.

Denying, that he had been at that place, the accuser then renewed his story, which purported, that he and his companions were travelling, about the close of day, through the forest, or chase, of Kenilworth, when they were attacked by robbers. He was bidden to repeat the number of them and of his company, which he did, without varying his tale. The King asked how long after sun-set it was when the assault began? which he could not readily tell; but said it was so nearly dark, that hardly could he see the figures of the robbers under the shade of the woods, from which they burst: the merchant paused a moment –

'Go on,' said the King, impatiently: –

'But I could, afterwards, see them plainly enough by a torch I took from my companions, who had lighted it, at a smith's in a village by the wayside; an iron-smith's.'

The King asked him if he knew the name of this village, but he knew it not; and whether he should know the smith again? and he answered, he thought he should. Then he was ordered to proceed with his story:

'My kinsman,' said he, 'was the only one of us, who was well-armed; and a braver spirit never lived. He fought with his sword that man, who now stands beside your Highness; it was a trusty weapon, and had done him good service in Syria, where he had it for booty, after a skirmish, as I heard. When my kinsman first made up to that man, I followed him with the torch, and to aid him, as I might, with an oaken staff I had in my hand; but I received a blow upon the arm, that held the torch, which was knocked to the ground, and the vizor of the man fell also, that very man, who now presses behind your Highness's chair. The torch was not extinguished, and, by its light, I plainly saw that same countenance, that now glares upon me so vengefully. I saw

41

it while he aimed the blow, which penetrated the head of my unfortunate kinsman, Reginald de Folville.'

The merchant paused, seemingly overcome by the remembrance of this event, while Sir Gaston exclaimed, – 'Was it Reginald de Folville? He was esquire to a knight of Saint John, and was then at Lydda: so much for the truth of your story in that main point.'

At the first words of Sir Gaston, the King and the courtiers had turned their faces upon him; but though his words were so strong and sufficient, they beheld in his countenance paleness and consternation. But he soon recovered; and, asking pardon of his Highness for the emotion with which he had spoken, accounted for it by saying, that Reginald de Folville had been his earliest friend.

'Your father's friend, you must surely mean,' said the merchant; 'for he was at the wars at a time, that would have made that possible. You must have been a child, when he went there.'

'I *was* then a child,' said Sir Gaston, averting his eyes from the stranger; 'and I must ever remember the kindness he showed me after the death of my father; I owe him much. He went from Provence to Syria; I heard he fell in battle there. Sure I am he never returned: he died in battle there.'

'He died in the forest of Ardenn,' said the merchant with solemnity, 'and lies buried in the priory of Saint Mary here. He died by your hand: that is his very sword by your side; I remember it now.'

The audacity of this assertion struck all present and none more than the King himself. His Highness desired to examine the sword, and asked the merchant why he had not sooner challenged it; to which he answered nothing. Sir Gaston, as he delivered it on his knee to the King, said – 'If I know my accuser, which I think I do, he is no stranger to this weapon: he knows well that I usually wear it; but it never belonged to Reginald de Folville. My liege, it was my father's sword; he won it in the plains of Palestine.'

The King examined it with attention. It was of eastern shape and finely wrought. In the hilt were a few jewels. Prince Edward, as he leaned over it, pointed out to his father a motto in an unknown tongue; and then, at some distance below it, a date, with the Roman letters, H.A., remarking, that probably these letters alluded to some exploit achieved in the year noted. The

King addressed himself to Sir Gaston for the meaning of the motto and of these letters; but he knew not their meaning, and said they were as when his father won the sword from his enemy.

Then the King addressed the merchant with the same question, observing, that, as the sword seemed to be familiar to him, he probably had been told the signification of the letters on it. With that, the merchant was hastily advancing to receive it of one, to whom his Highness had delivered it: when he suddenly drew back, covered his eyes with his hand, and stood immovable. Those near almost expected to see him fall, as he had done before in the castle court on the night last past. Sir Gaston, at the same time, stepping forward, presumed to take it, and to deliver it again to the King, with these words: – 'Your Highness will not tempt the villany of this man by putting him in possession of the sword he falsely claims.'

But the merchant claimed it not; nor could he even endure to look upon it. Heavy sighs burst from him, while with eyes still covered with his hands, he said, – 'That was the sword, with which the villain murdered him; and can I endure to take it in my hand, and to look upon the blade, on which his life blood flowed?' and he groaned more piteously than before.

There were some in the hall, who instantly thought this sorrow of the merchant was a mimickry, and asked how it could happen, that his kinsman was killed by his own weapon; to which, soon as he could recollect his thoughts, he made answer, that the robber, on wrenching the sword from his friend, struck him his death-wound with it. The King, returning the sword to the young knight, bade him keep it forthcoming till he should demand it of him again, and then said to the stranger these or such-like words: –

'You, a man unknown to me and to mine, and without a name, except as far as you have declared one, have dared to come into my court, and to accuse to me one of my own servants, a gentleman and a knight, of a crime most foul and incredible. You have related your story, and I have waited patiently for some evidence, that the murderer of your kinsman, if, in truth, he were ever destroyed by violence, was Sir Gaston de Blondeville. I find none, except your story. And in this you have not scrupled to affirm, that you would have seized him for the murderer, even in a distant land, though you also say, that your knowledge of his countenance was obtained only from the sudden (and,

43

therefore, the uncertain) light of a torch lying on the ground, at a moment, when the danger you were yourself exposed to, might, it may be readily believed, have prevented you from closely observing any face whatsoever. You must be held unworthy of credit; and I commit you into safe custody, till it shall be discovered who you are, and who those are, who urged you to this base accusation.'

When his Highness had ended, they were going to convey away the merchant from his presence, but he craved leave to speak, and it was granted.

'My liege,' said he, 'at any other than that moment of horror, I might have seen the face of this stranger, without remembering it the next; but the impression made, at that moment, will remain with me, as long as the strong feelings, which then struck me, shall return with the recollection of my kinsman's fate. On seeing the same face, I was seized with the same horror; your Highness's people can be witnesses, that yester-eve, when I saw that knight, I fell into convulsions, and was carried senseless from your presence.'

His Highness, remembering what had happened, and, on inquiry, finding, that this was the very man, who had then fallen senseless, perceived, that the merchant had not spoken this untruly. He asked again whether he was known to any person in Kenilworth, also whether either of the merchants, travelling in his company, at the period of the alleged murder, was at hand. The accuser stood, for a while, bewildered, and then repeating, that he was a stranger, having only passed through the place, a few times, on his way to or from Coventry, said, that of his two companions one was dead, and the other following his merchandize, in a distant land.

'Then,' said the King, 'it appears you cannot bring any evidence of the truth of your story; even so far, as that a robbery was actually committed. Your accusation of this knight is, therefore, likely to be impelled either by malice, or by some other bad motive. If it shall prove so, dread the punishment that awaits you'

'My liege,' said Sir Gaston, 'I think I know the man, and also his motive. He wronged my father at Embrun; and now his malice, – but this story is connected with family circumstances, that should only be divulged to your Highness; and, if you will suffer me to unfold them in private, I shall prove, not mine innocence only – for of that your Highness does not doubt – but that man's former and present guilt.'

44

At these words, the stranger fell again on his knees, and besought aloud justice on 'a villain'.

The King looked upon him and upon Sir Gaston, and sat pondering awhile. He then turned to the merchant, and, bidding him rise, asked him, a second time, if he were not known to any one person in Kenilworth? and received for answer, 'Only as a traveller.'

'An adventure as remarkable as that you have related,' pursued his Highness, 'must have been known here at the time it happened, and must be remembered now. It is strange, if there be none who can recollect you also.'

'My lord,' observed Prince Edward, 'he said his friend was buried here in the priory. If so, the prior must know him and his strange history.'

'Said he so?' quoth the King; and, turning to the stranger, he inquired how it happened, that he was not known to the prior? and who it was that commanded the burial of his kinsman.

The merchant said, he had himself ordered it, and had conversed with a monk and even with the Prior himself.

'Then you are known to the Prior, at least,' said the King; 'he will surely recollect your story: let him be sent for. It is strange you should have said you were unknown: you are either guilty of falsehood, or your senses are unsettled.'

The stranger raised his hand to his head and sighed. 'I recollect the Prior,' said he, 'but he may not remember me.'

'We shall see!' said the King, calmly, as he rose from his chair: 'If you are innocent, fear not! if you are guilty, you will lose your life, in seeking that of an innocent man.'

As his Highness left the hall, he looked somewhat sternly upon the accuser, and commanded, that he should be held in close custody, while more inquiry should be made. He then ordered Sir Gaston to attend him in his privy-chamber, and so departed forth of the hall, leaving the accuser speechless and dismayed.

As the merchant was led through this court of the castle to the tower, where was his prison, the Lady Barbara, sitting in her bower-window above, saw the passing crowd, and inquired the occasion of it; but none would inform her. While she gazed with curiosity, she observed Sir Gaston going to the King's privy-chamber; he looked not at her window, but went his way with a hurried step, and with such a countenance as she had never witnessed in him, till this time. At length, word was brought to

45

my lady, her mother, of what had passed before his Highness. The Earl, her father, was promptly filled with disgust; and thought the occurrence would be sufficient to prevent the marriage, which neither his English heart, nor his pride of ancient blood, had suffered him to approve. His daughter, the lady Barbara, was differently minded; she would not believe him she loved capable of even a dishonourable action, much less of so foul a one; and, assured of his innocence, she would have thrown herself at the King's feet, had that seemed always, as it did at first, proper, to urge his Highness to clear Sir Gaston instantly from the suspicion.

But truly the King needed no advocate for Sir Gaston de Blondeville; and so she thought, at last. His Highness's own inclination was sufficient; and so angered was his generous spirit by what he held to be not only a false, but a malicious accusation, that he had determined after proof of this, to give a signal warning by the accuser's doom; and this not only to prevent other false accusations proceeding from private motives, but to reprove and caution those of his subjects, who had a public prejudice against strangers, and were too likely to delight in the ruin of such especially as had risen to honours.

The King, therefore, willingly gave audience privately to the young knight, that he might explain to him the circumstances, which should assure him of his innocence. What Sir Gaston told his Highness was never assuredly known; some reports went on one side of the matter, some on the other: there was not one witness of what passed. Who then might know, unless they could guess by the countenances, and by what passed, when the hearing was over? But, if they had gone by no other guide, they would have been all for the knight, since he had made the King quite convinced; and moreover, the Earl of Huntingdon was summoned to the closet, where the King promised him the honour of the young knight would always remain unsullied in his opinion; and so commanded, that the marriage with the lady Barbara should be solemnized, as had been before appointed, on the day next following.

The Earl besought, nay, as some say, dared to remonstrate, that the marriage should be postponed till the stranger should have been lawfully convicted of falsehood; but his Highness said, 'Nay; lest it should seem that the accusation was probable enough to require such delay. It is already well-known, as a matter agreed upon, that the nuptials are to be held on the morrow, the preparations are nearly all made, and they are public. It is necessary for the honour of Sir Gaston de Blondeville, that the appointment should be kept. If you are not convinced, still you will not be required to make disavowal of any thought you may have; for I myself will lead your daughter to the porch, and will so, by my presence and by this act of parental kindness, show my estimation both of the fair bride and of him who shall become your son. Farther proof of my regard shall not be wanting hereafter.'

His Highness was peremptory, and the Earl, swayed by his master's positive opinion, and, it may be, by that promise of regard hereafter, at last obeyed.

While these things were passing in the King's chamber, the unhappy merchant was taken to a turret of the castle, called Caesar's Tower; and there, with nothing but a pallet and the bare walls, was left to think of his jeopardy. What his thoughts were I know not; but he was heard sorely to sigh and groan, and with good reason; for, if he knew himself perjured, he knew also, that he should find no mercy from the King; and, if innocent, he could expect little justice against so great a favourite. But, whatever were his meditations, they held not till night, for he was called and led forth of the tower into the presence of the King; and, before evensong, the Prior of Saint Mary's was in attendance upon his Highness. He was not an aged man, yet was he a stern one. When he was asked whether ever before he had seen the merchant, he answered resolutely, that he had no knowledge of him. The same question being put to the merchant, touching his knowledge of the Prior, he returned a like answer.

At this seeming self-contradiction, the King could scarcely command his anger, till it was discovered, that a Prior of Saint Mary's had died, since the time when the murder was alleged to have been committed, and that it must needs be he, whom the merchant meant.

'But, where is the monk, with whom you consulted?' asked the King; 'can you tell his name?'

'His name was Ewdwyn,' replied the merchant.

'He died yesternight!' said the prior.

At this there was a pause, and a dead silence throughout the chamber. Sir Gaston looked darkly on his accuser; his accuser directed his eyes to the King and then on high; but, in a short minute, he fell down, as though he were a dying man. The King, touched at his sufferings, commanded him from his chamber, that aid might be administered unto him. And then, that he might know whether this accusation of Sir Gaston were through malice, or mistake – for now pity inclined him to think the last – and also, that Sir Gaston might have mistaken, when he took this for the man, of whose deeds at Embrun he had talked; that he might know the truth on all this, he ordered the Prior to make inquiry in his community, whether the body of any person known to have been murdered in the forest of Ardenn, three years before, had been deposited in the chapel, or in the cemetery of the convent. Likewise, he commanded the Prior to have inquiry made in Kenilworth, whether any person remembered such an accident, or any house had received the dead body. And this he ordered, that it might always be seen he had desired to have justice done towards the wretched merchant, as well as for Sir Gaston de Blondeville.

This being appointed, the King departed to his great chamber, there to keep his state; the Prior to his convent, to resume his spiritual musings; the accused lover to his mistress; and the merchant was conveyed to his prison tower.

The King kept state, that night, with the Earl of Cornwall, the Archbishop of York, the Bishop of Winchester, the Bishop of Lincoln, Henry de Wernham, his chaplain, who also had the custody of the Great Seal, the Earl of Norfolk, the Earl of Hereford and a number of other nobles of the realm; but the Queen kept her state apart.

The King's great chamber was marvellous to behold. There were twenty-five wax-lights held by esquires of the household, all in the King's livery, gentils as they were; also twenty-five wax torches were fixed high up over the tapestry. The walls were, that night, gorgeous with the story of Troy-town in ancient tapestries; there you might see the flames burning and the towers falling, and old King Priam, with beard as white as snow, his crown upon his head, and his Queen Hecuba tearing her dishevelled locks for grief. And there was that renowned son, who carried off his aged father, with his little child holding by his garment, and his wife following, all disconsolate. This was a piteous sight to see pourtrayed: but that it were nothing save a heathen story.

The floor of that chamber was not strewed either with rushes or with litter of any sort, but was laid in little checquers of divers colours; and, where his Highness sat, under his cloth of state, was spread a silken carpet of full crimson, fringed about with gold, as likewise his chair and canopy of estate. But the finest sight was the cupboards, piled up with plates and cups of gold and silver, in readiness for the King, when he should take his VOIDE.[3] These were in that great oriel[4], which his Highness had newly made in this chamber, before the bay; and which was closed about with painted glass from the highest cup-board to the arched roof, where hung a silver lamp, that made the whole glow with its light.

There were, that night, playing in the chamber, the King's twelve minstrels, all clothed, for his honour and dignity, in sumptuous livery, with their virger to order their pipyngs and blowings. There were, besides, the children of the chapel singing, at times, from the brown gallery; so that, the doors being open, you might have heard them through all that side of the castle; and those, who sat afar off in the great hall, needed none other music.

There also was Maister Henry[5], the versifier, whose 'Ballad of the Giant of Cornwall' was this night rehearsed to the harp by Richard, the King's harper, as was his famous 'Chronicle of Charlemagne,' which lasted, till his Highness was well nigh weary, when he jocularly called out, having tasted of his golden cup, that Henry should have a butt of wine with his wages, if he would shorten his ballads by one-half. Maister Henry, who was a Frenchman, took this in good part, and, having especial care ever after to make his ballads nigher to too short than too long, became, in time, a notable rhymer. But let those do so who can. Some are famous one way, some another; for mine own part, I must be circumstantial, or else nothing, as this *Trew Chronique* in due time must show.

That night, the King played at Checkere with the Earl of Norfolk, on a board laid with jasper and chrystal, the checkmen being of the same. Some said the kings and queens were of ebony, studded over with jewels, but of this I know not.

But, the finest sight of all was the going of the chamberlain to the cup-board, accompanied of three nobles of the highest estate in the realm, that were there present, (save the King's family) to receive the King's cup and spice-plates; and then the bringing up of the voide before his Highness. And, first, the usher, having assembled the King's sewers, their towels about their necks, with the four esquires of the body[6] and the knights and esquires of the household, to the number of seventeen; these,

49

with divers other officers, being met at the cup-board, the Chamberlain took the King's towel, and, having kissed it, as the custom is, delivered it to the Earl of Norfolk, he being of the highest estate, who reverently received the same, and laid it safely upon his shoulder. Then, the said chamberlain gave the gold spice-plates covered to the Earl of Hereford; and then the King's cup of massive gold, covered also, to the Earl of Warwick. At the same time were given to the knights of the household[7] the Archbishop's spice-plate and cup, covered also, to be carried up, by the space of one minute after the King's.

And, certes, it was a goodly sight to see all these nobles and gentils marching up the great chamber (the minstrels playing the while), compassed about with esquires, bearing great lights to the number of thirteen, especial care being taken, as the manner all times has been at the voide, that the lights were odd in number.

First, then, went the usher, with his torch and rod, making passage; the chamberlain, with his chain and wand of office; then the five esquires, of the body, bearing wax-lights before the Earl of Norfolk, with the towel; then, three esquires about the Lord of Hereford, bearing the spice-plates; then, other three before the Lord Warwick, bearing the King's cup covered; then followed one knight of the household, bearing a single torch; so making up altogether the just number of lights. Amongst them went four knights of the household, well renowned for bravery and noble bearing, with the Archbishop's spice-plate and cup.

When this array drew near to the King, he, standing up under his cloth of estate, which was rolled up high, with the young Prince Edward on one hand and the Archbishop on the other, the Chamberlain taking the covers from off the spice-plates, gave assaye unto the Earl of Gloucester. The King, before he took his spice, made a beck to the Archbishop, that he should take his first; and the knights having advanced, as they well knew would be seemly, the Archbishop forthwith obeyed.

But, when the Chamberlain uncovered the cup, all the minstrels in the chamber blew up louder than ever, and so held on till his Highness took the ypocras, so that every roof in the castle rung with joy.

The King and Archbishop being served, his Highness's cup and spice-plates were again covered, but not so the Archbishop's. Then were the spice and cup carried to Prince Edward and the Earl of Cornwall, by the knights; to the bishops by the

50

esquires of the household, and to the other estates by the esquires also. Which being done, his Highness forthwith departed for 'all night', the trumpets blowing before him. Then, were three healths drank, one to the King, one to the Queen, and one to the Prince Edward; after which it were not meet, that the assemblage should remain, and straight the great chamber was avoyded of all there present.

The Queen, that night, sat in her bower with all her ladies. There were mynstrelsy and dancing to the harp and viol. The Lady Barbara was the marveil of all, that beheld her moving to the sound of viols like unto some sprite, rather than to a poor mortal. Prince Edward danced with her a round, and the Queen often honoured her with her pleasing speech. Sir Gaston, though he beheld her, showed not his wonted joy. He stood apart looking on, and, when her Highness spoke to him, he seemed nigh to senseless of the honour.

The dancing being ended, Pierre, a Norman and the Queen's chief minstrel, apparelled in the guise of his country, sang some of his ballads on the harp, in his own tongue, which, albeit, they were not esteemed like unto Maister Henry's, yet did they not displease. The first tuning was in words which have been thus rendered into English by one, who had learned much of the new speech, not then familiar, except with some few.

THE BRIDAL

Lightly, lightly, bounded the roe,
The hind o'er the forest was fleeing;
The small birds tuned on every bough,
In sun and shade their gleeing.

And purple cups, and silver bells
From the green leaves were peeping;
The wild-rose smiled in the mossy dells:
Nought but the thorn was weeping.

And so bright in the sun its tears did shine,
They showed like tears of pleasure;
And the airs of May, through the budding spray,
Breathed joyance, without measure.

For this was Isabel's bridal morn
Who loved each bud and flower,

51

The wild-wood shade, the mountain head,
The deep vale's mead and bower.

And now was her festival gaily kept
By hagled brook and fountain,
From the low green bank, where the violet slept,
To the blue hill-top and mountain.

And lightly, lightly, bounded the roe,
His footstep wing'd with pleasure,
And small birds sang from every bough,
Welcomes beyond all measure.

At the end of this ballad, the minstrel rang out his harp in full joyance; and then, falling note by note, he dropped into a faltering murmur, as of deep sorrow, and so continued for some space, till those who heard him, perceived the witch of melancholy stealing upon them.

The Queen, deeming such strain unsuitable to the time, commanded him to change the measure, and sound forth one more gay, a lay of Provence, her native land, whither she knew he had been for his learning; but he, enthralled by the magic of his own mood, loving not to be commanded, still hung his head over the harp, listening to that pleasure-full melancholy and heeding nothing but its sweet sound.

At last, being made to know fully her Highness's will, he sang the song of a troubadour; for, though he loved best the ditties of Normandy, his own land, there was scarce one of Provence, which he had not gained; and the Queen did not let him forget them, so often did she command those, which she affected best. And now he sang forth to his harp a 'roundel' in the Provençal tongue, made by a knight of the 'Order of Fine Eyes'. They, who then heard him, would have thought he loved any thing less than melancholy, so light and debonnaire was the music he rang out; and many could hardly keep their steps from dancing to that gallant measure. But it lasted not long; for, making a pause and looking wistfully at the Lady Barbara, he struck forth, on a sudden, some of his deepest tones, with a wild yet solemn grace, such as brought tears into the eyes of many a fair lady, and darted dread into the heart of one there present. It seemed as if the shadows of prophecy were moving over the strings, and calling from them some strange and fearful story yet to be. And then again did the harper's voice steal trembling forth, as do the moon's beams, when pale clouds pass over, saddening, but not fully obscuring their brightness: yet might every one hear plainly all his words. Here it is done into English by the same hand; but the verses be not all divided into equal numbers:

I

O'er the high western wolds afar,
  Glimmer'd some lights of yesterday;
And there, one bright, but trembling star
  Among the streaky shadows lay,
  The traveller's lonely warning.
But soon the winds, that sing day's dirge,
Did o'er that star the shadows urge,
  And hung the night with mourning!

II

  'What steps on the waste are beating?'
  He listened not long on the ground,
  'Ere he fearfully heard a sound,
As of trampling hoofs retreating:
And a dismal cry and a foot draw nigh;
'Stand ho!' 'twas an armed man passed by:
  But he spoke no sound of greeting,
  And seemed like a death-shade fleeting.

III

O'er the lone mountains riding,
  He gallop'd by gloomsome ways,
Where night-mists were abiding,
  Round the witch of evil days:
Her name is written on the wind,
That speaks in cliffs and caves confin'd.
  List there when the waning moon goes down,
  And thou'lt hear the call her spirits own;
    But as they pass, hold a chrystal glass,
Or thou'lt sorely rue the wild witch-tone.

IV

O'er the lone mountains riding,
  From a distant land he came,
No step his dark step guiding;

But he thought he saw a flame,
That bright, or dim, would sport awhile;
Then vanish, as in very guile;
He heard, as he passed, the witch-name sound;
And his startled steed, at a single bound,
Bore him away from that evil ground.

V

But o'er the mountains pacing
    As fast as he can flee,
Strange steps his steps are tracing,
    And a shape he cannot see;
And, though he flee away, so prest,
Whether to north, or south or west,
    Toward the past, or coming day,
    (So dim the night he may not say)
Still oft by fits did ghastly gleam,
A corpse-light, all unknown to him.

VI

He followed the light o'er deserts wide,
    Down in deep glens, where wild becks wail;
He followed by darkened forest side;
    He followed with dread, though link'd in mail;
Till it stayed before an iron gate,
Where battled turrets kept their state,
    O'er towers so high and massy strong,
    They seemed to giant-king belong.

VII

Sir Adomar looked him all around:
    Turret on turret hung on high,
    Shaping black lines on the dim sky;
Sir Adomar looked him all around;
    Nought, save this castle, could he spy,
Though, heavily clanged a death-bell's sound;
    And in each pause of the shuddering blast,
    Moans were heard as of one from 'neath the ground!

54

VIII

He struck on the gate with his good sword:
    'Ho! wardour, ho!' but never a word
Return'd the wardour from within.
     'The storm is loud, the night is dark,
     I hear from the woods the dog-wolf bark.
Up, wardour, up! it were a sin
     To turn a traveller from your tower,
     At such a lone and dreary hour;
A Saracen would let me in!'

IX

The wardour was watching through the loop,
How many were of the stranger's troop.
     He had left his torch in the cullis' bar,
And it let down a light on the lonely night,
     That showed him harnessed, as for war.
His coat was mail, his helm was steel;
His visor did his look reveal;
Yet o'er his brow it cast a shade,
That made the wardour more afraid,
     Than did the crimsoned plume above,
     Or the mighty grasp of his iron glove.
He would not let the stranger in,
Till one, awakened by the din—
One whom the wardour need obey—
     Seeing a lonely knight stand there,
     Bade the wardour nought to fear:
He feared still, but he said not Nay:
Yet he would not ope the portal gate
To an unknown knight, without his state;
     For neither squire, nor page, he saw:
     He bade him then to the postern draw.

X

The knight dismounted at the call;
The porter let him through the wall;
He turned the weary steed to stall,
And led the knight to the lordly hall.
I' the lordly hall, so wide and dim,
One drowsy squire awaited him.

55

The ashy wood lay, white and cold,
On the raised hearth, where late was told,
With fiery eye and accent loud,
The deed of martial prowess proud;
Where late was told, in whispers low,
Some tale of terror and of woe,
The while each listener bent his head,
Nor lost a word the trouveur said:
Till fear crept o'er each nerve and vein,
That late had swell'd to martial strain;
And shadows crept along the wall,
Such as the sinful soul appal:
Till each, who heard, look'd round with dread,
And saw some phantom of the dead.

XI

Now silent was the hearth and lone,
    Save that a stag-hound slumber'd there.
    The tables in disorder were,
    With relics of the evening fare;
The household to their rest were gone,
And now no light was seen but one,
The light that led the stranger on;
That show'd above steel armour gleaming,
And many a dusky banner streaming,
    From the black rafters of the roof,
    In the night-wind, far aloof,
Like to some flitting phantom seeming;
    And, stalking o'er the rushy floor,
    It showed the knight where steps of gore
Had stain'd its green, with foot-prints red.
And the stag-hound, as the knight passed by,
Sent forth a mournful fearful cry.

XII

The drowsy squire the stranger led;
(The wardour to his post was sped.)
They traversed the hall in silent march:
At the end was a door in a mitred arch.
The knight stood before that mitred door,
    And gazed on a warrior shape above,

That seem'd to watch the passage o'er.
  In his altered look strange passions strove!
The armoured shape leaned on its sword,
  And downward bent its steely face,
  As jealous who below might pace,
Or about to speak the challenge-word;
And it seemed the very form of one,
The knight perforce must look upon.

XIII

Thus, while he stood in wonder-trance,
  The squire upheld the torch on high,
  Viewing the guest with watchful eye;
And marvelling what strange mischance
So check'd his step, and fix'd his glance: —
'Sir knight, why gaze you on that steel?
  It is a baron's good and bold;
  Had he been here, no welcome cold
Would he have shown a stranger-knight,
Who trusted to his towers at night.'

XIV

The spell of fant'sie loos'd awhile,
The knight return'd a grateful smile,
With thanks for this so courteous style;
And, then with thoughtful accent said,
  While yet he stood, that shape before,
'The armour some resemblance had
  To that of a dear friend no more!
A friend!' – he paus'd, – 'a friend long dead!'
This, while he said, his colour fled.
The squire seem'd not to note his pain,
But, with fair speech, began again
Excuse to make for slender fare,
That it was night, and, not aware
Of honour'd guest approaching there,
The menials to their rest had gone;
A chamber should be fitted soon.
His squire and page should welcom'd be;
Right well he longed that squire to see.

XV

The wearied knight a gesture made,
And looked his thanks, but nothing said;
Save that, for rest alone he prayed.
He sighed, as through that guarded arch,
And vaulted gloom, he held his march;
And there, before his doubting sight,
Glided again a pale sad light,
Full often he had seen with fear,
Yet more he felt to meet it here.
Then came they to an iron door,
And the knight beheld that flame no more.
It opened to a second hall,
Where warriors frowned upon the wall;
And ladies smiled in portraiture,
With downcast eye and look demure.
An umbered flash the red torch threw,
Athwart each warrior's steadfast brow;
And hardly might the gleam declare
A baron grim from lady fair.

XVI

There is no need that I should tell,
*   What hasty fare the stranger took;*
*   Nor how the squire, with silent look,*
Watched, wondering, what had him befell;
So strangely gleamed his hollow eyes,
*   From forth the lifted beaver's shade*
So wan his lips, like one that dies,
*   So few the words and thanks he paid!*

Though round the hall his looks would steal,
Not well did torch or lamp reveal
The portraiture of warriors grim,
Or noble dames hung there so dim;
Their frowns and smiles were lost to him.
But once, when that he turned his head
Where the fix'd torch a gleaming shed,
A sable form, ill seen at most,

Went gliding up a stair, on high,
Passed through an open gallery,
And through a doorway there was lost,
That seemed to lead to antient rooms,
Such as where silence dwells, and glooms.
The knight, he felt a sudden chill,
    Though nought he said of what had sped;
    But the spicy draught he deeply quaff'd,
Whenever the page his cup did fill.
And from his spirits chaced the ill.

XVIII

The night-cheer o'er, the page led on
    The stranger to his resting-place.
He led the way, that form had gone:
    On the high stair he stood a space,
    Waiting the knight's reluctant pace,
Then, with mute reverence, marshalled him
Through many a gallery, long and dim,
Where helmets watched, in order grim;
Through many a chamber, wide and lorn,
Where wint'ry damps had half withdrawn
The storied paintings on the wall.
Electra, o'er her brother's urn,
There bent the head, and seemed to mourn;
There, too, as meet in room and hall,
Troy's tale* and Hector's piteous fall:
Here Priam's Court, in purple and pall,
Its golden splendour now had lost;
    But Helen, on the rampart stood,
And pointed to the Grecian host,
    Out-stretching to the briny flood.
Here Hector's wife sat in her bower,
Waiting her lord's returning hour;
And 'broidering 'midst her maiden train,
While her infant played with silken skein.
There – but it boots not that I say,
What stories once, in long array,
Lived on those walls, now ghastly clay.

----

*The 'Tale of Troy' appears to have been a very favourite subject in
ancient tapestry. It occurs often in old castles, and is mentioned twice in
this *Trew Chronique*, as adorning the walls of stately chambers.

The knight would oft, as he strode by,
Cast on their shade a searching eye;
And pause, as list'ning some drear sound,
That rose within the glimmering bound:
And start, as though some fearful sight
Passed along this gloom of night;
But, at a lesser winding stair,
(The long drawn chambers ended there,)
When to that narrow stair he drew,
He thought a robe of mourning hue
Went fleeting up that winding way;
No glimpse had he of shape or ray;
No foot he heard the stair ascend.
Yet still that seeming garment passed,
As though some fiend, with evil haste,
   Did up that lonely tower wend.

XX

The knight, he stood on the step below—
'Whither, my young page, dost thou go?
   Who dwells within this lonely tower,
Passing with speed, in sable weed—
   Passing with speed, at this dead hour?'
'Nobody, save the raven-crow,
   Dwells within this lonely tower;
   And here, sir knight, is your resting-bower!'
'But in this tower I may not rest,
Till I know who that stair has pressed;
Did you not see that black weed wave?'
   'Yes, knight, I saw the raven's wing,
   Glint up that wall with sudden spring:
And hark! you now may hear him crave!'

XXI

'It is not courteous, that my bower
Should be within this ruin'd tower!'
'But see, knight, 'tis not in decay;
The storm hath blown a bar away,

60

And the raven through the loop doth stray;
His nest is wet on the battlement grey:
Your chamber is a stately room,
Hung round with work of choicest loom;
And erst it was the resting-place
Of our dear Lady Baroness,
Before she went to stranger-land.
My lord yet strays on foreign strand.
The chamber has another stair,
Leading to many chambers fair;
But no step goes by night so far,
Since my lord baron went to war.'

XXII

The page stept on with torch before,
Far as that stately chamber's door.
'Page! lift that light—fain would I know,
Whither that second flight doth go?'
'It goes to a battlement up on high,
And to a turret perching by.'
'Doth none keep watch on that turret high?'
'None, but the raven with his cry!
Your rest, sir knight, he will not break;
To traitors only doth he speak.
They say he scents the new spilt blood.'
Upon the stair the raven stood!
He turn'd his dark eye on the knight,
And, screaming, upward winged his flight.
The wondering page looked back with fright,
And met the stranger's fiery glance;
Then, hardly daring to advance,
Lingered he at that chamber-door;
'On,' said the knight, 'with torch before!'
Scarce was the page the threshold o'er,
When check he made, and pale he turn'd;
Dim and more dim the torch-flame burn'd.
The knight look'd on, but nothing saw,
That might explain this sudden awe.

XXIII

A spacious chamber there was spread,
And, for his rest, a stately bed;
Fresh rushes on the floor were strewn;
Faint on the arras'd walls were shown
The heroes of some antient story,
Now faded, like their mortal glory.
Another form, as dark as doom,
Stood within that chamber's gloom,
　　Unseen by those who entered there.
His cause of dread the page thus said:
　　'Methought I saw, within that chair,
The baron's self, my very lord;
I saw it, on a true man's word:
I saw my lord return'd from far,
Arrayed, as he went forth to war!
He fixed his very eyes on me,
　　But looked not, as he wont to look.
Yet now no living shape I see,
And know that here he could not be;
　　For, long since, he these walls forsook:
Yet is it strange such visions pale,
Should o'er my waking sight prevail.'

XXIV

'Whose are these antient walls, I pray?'
The sullen stranger 'gan to say:
'Sir, know you not these towers and halls
Watch where the foaming Conway falls?
Who should these walls and towers own?
And the wide woods and forest round,
Even to Snowdon's utmost bound,
Save the brave lord of Eglamore?'
The knight explained his ignorance,
He was a wanderer late from France.
The page surveyed him o'er again;
He thought the wily knight did feign:
A deadly hue was on his cheek;
His looks spoke more than words may speak.
Yet to the page, though much it told,
He read not all it might unfold.

XXV

The knight perceived his doubting thought,
And drew a badge forth from his breast;
Some noble Order's golden crest,
Upon a field of silver wrought.
'This badge,' he said, 'with blood was bought.'
He turn'd with haughty frown away.
The page did not more doubt betray;
But service offered to undo
His casque and linked harness true;
But the stranger gravely said him Nay,
And refused that night to disarray.

XXVI

Wondering, yet fearing to demand,
Why to these towers from distant land,
The knight had come, without his train,
Pondered the youth his doubts again;
Again, as though his thoughts he read,
The knight look'd sternly down and said,
'My squire and my foot-page I missed
At night-fall, when the woods betwixt.
But they perchance may shelter find,
From this bitter-blowing wind,
In the deep hollow of some hill,
Till the dawn break, and the storm be still.'

XXVII

'But the wolf bays in the blast afar;
Sir knight, how may they scape such war?
I hear him now – he nearer howls!
Mercy! mercy! save their souls!'
'Hark!' said the knight, and stood aghast;
It was no wolf-howl in the blast;
It was a blood-hound's dreadful bay,
The stranger heard, with such dismay –
The blood-hound at the tower below;
That over pathless hill and dale,
Had tracked a murderer in the gale,
And came to claim his master's foe.

While listening to the lengthen'd yell,
The stranger seemed to hear his knell.
'A blood-hound loose, and at this hour!
    Your rest, sir knight, had ill been kept;
    Nor one within these gates had slept,
Had I been in my distant tower.'
The page he lighted a lamp on high;
The stranger stifled scarce a sigh,
That heavily for utterance pressed.
He heard the page's steps descend,
And go where the long chambers bend,
    Down to the halls, and th' outer walls.
The page knew not the chance he ran;
He was marked with the blood of a murder'd man!

XXVIII

The knight, he listened in silent dread,
    Till now, the blood-hound's voice was stilled;
But soon a low voice near him sped,
    That every nerve with horror thrilled.
He looked the way that lone voice came,
And saw, by the lamp's tall spiring flame,
A portraiture on the wall beneath,
Of noble dame, that seemed to breathe.
Robed in sable weeds was she:
    The gleam fell on that lady's brow;
There, written dimly, you might see,
    The characters of hopeless woe.

XXIX

Soon as that lady's face he saw,
    All other dread his heart forsook;
He gazed with fixt and frenzied awe,
    And vainly tried away to look:
For to his fearful sight it seemed,
    As though her eyes on his were bent;
And, where the pale flame wavering gleamed,
    As if her varying cheek were blent
    With lights and shades of death;
While round her lips a grim smile drew,
And the rose paled that on them blew;

And, with faint lingering breath,
'Prepare,' she said, 'thy hour is nigh!
Unpitying, thou hast seen me die;
Unpitied be thy mortal sigh!'

XXX

He heard the words – the words alone;
He heard not that deep solemn groan;
He heard not the clang of the 'larum bell,
Nor from the gates that horn-blast swell;
Nor heard the many-trampling hoofs,
    Nor voices calling in the gale,
And ringing round the castle roofs,
    Till they made the 'battled raven quail;
Nor heard the funeral shriek, that broke
Through every hall and lofty tower;
He heard alone the words she spoke.

XXXI

Nor saw he in the court below,
By the torches' umbered glow,
Borne upon his bleeding bier,
    With wounds unclosed and open eyes,
A warrior stretched in death draw near;
    Nor heard the loud and louder cries,
This piteous sight of horror drew
From every friend and vassal true.
But he knew that voice at his chamber-door,
And straight the witch-veil of glamour
Falls, and his wonder-trance is o'er.
He hears his summons in that sound;
It is the bark of the true blood-hound.
True to his murdered lord is he;
He has traced the steps he could not see –
Traced them o'er darkened miles and miles,
O'er glen and mountain, wood and moor,
Through all their swift and winding wiles,
Till he stopped before his master's door,
And bayed the murderer in his bower.

65

XXXII

The castle gates were strait unbarred,
And he sprang before his bleeding lord;
He passed the page unheeded by,
And tracked the stranger's steps on high;
Till at the door, that closed him in,
Loud and dread became his din.
The doors are burst, and the spectre-light
Betrayeth the form of the blood-tracked knight:
He was armed all over in coat of mail,
But nothing did steel that night avail;
He fell a torn corpse, beside that chair,
Whereunto the page did late appear,
By the dark glamour-art revealed,
His murdered lord with lance and shield.
The murderer fell, and his death-wound found
In the terrible fangs of the true blood-hound.

Here the voice of the minstrel ceased; and, after striking a few notes of his harp, full and deep, he rested with a look of sorrow. His eyes dwelt on the Lady Barbara—but she heeded him not; but sat with head inclined, as if still listening to his dismal tale. There followed a dread silence in the room, as of expectation of that which was to follow. Some there were, who said the ditty was already ended; yet they would fain have heard something of the pitiful history of that unhappy lady, whose portraiture was in the tower-chamber, and would have known what was the guilty motive of the knight against the Lord of Eglamore; and how it chanced he came so unwittingly to his castle. Others there were then present, who, having noticed the young Gaston de Blondeville to be ill at ease, the while the minstrel sung, and being, perchance, already moved by the merchant's strange accusation, scrupled not to think the story touched him nearly; and that Pierre rested, not because his ditty was at an end, or from weariness; but that he doubted whether it would be well to proceed to the second part.

However this may be, he needed not have stayed his strain, for Sir Gaston was no longer in the chamber. Whether Pierre knew this or not, he began once more to strike upon the harp; when, on a sudden, the king's trumpets were heard blowing up near the stair; and anon, his Highness entered the bower, it being almost time that he should go to his rest for 'all night'.

66

There was no more harping: Pierre tuning not up his second fit; and belike, if his Highness had been there at first, he would have bidden him to shorten his ballad by one-half.

The King looked about for Sir Gaston; and, espying him not, asked wherefore he was not there; but, before any answer could be given, the knight had returned, and now approached his Highness. He was then commanded to dance a round with the Lady Barbara, and he obeyed; but many there noted the sadness on his brow, though his steps were light and gay.

A more pleasureful sight could not be than the Queen's bower, as it was at that time, where she sat in estate, under a cloth of gold, her ladies standing about her chair, and her maidens on either hand, below the steps of her throne; and two young damsels of surpassing beauty and richly bedight, sitting on the first step, at her feet; the same, that were used so to sit, when her Highness kept state in the great hall at festivals.

Behind them, half encircling the throne, stood twenty household esquires, holding great wax torches, right richly beseen in the king's livery, and proud to wear it, gentils as they were, as I said before, and of ancient families in the countries from whence they came.

The arched roof was curiously wrought in that fashion, which King Henry had newly brought into favour; and, besides these lights, a great crystal lamp, that hung from the roof, shone over the chamber and upon the goodly assemblage, as they looked upon the Lady Barbara, passing so winningly in the dance. That night, the Earl of Richmond bore the Queen's spice-plate, and Sir Philip de Kinton her cup.

When the Lady Barbara had ended her dance, the Queen called her to her chair; and, making her take of the sweet-meats from her own plate, spoke commendable words to her, as did his Highness King Henry. Then the Queen, turning to the Lady Gloucester, took from her hands a girdle, richly beset with jewels, and, clasping it on the Lady Barbara, kissed her, and bade her wear it ever, for her sake and for her honour. Her Highness then stretched out her hand to Sir Gaston, who, kneeling, put it to his lips. 'May you, sir knight,' said her Highness, 'as well deserve this lady, as she deserves this token of my regard!'

Then, the King said many gracious things, and seemed so merry of heart, that he made all around him gladsome; till, the Voide being ended, he went forth with the Queen, the trumpets

67

blowing before them; and the chamber was then speedily avoided for all night.

While these things were passing in the chambers of estate, there were divers wassailings and merriments making in other places of the castle. In the great hall were feasting and revelling, but not of estate. There were tumblers and jugglers and morrice-dancers and mimicks and mummers, with pipings and blowings, that made the roofs ring.

The monks at the priory heard them afar, while at the last evensong, and long after; and well I wote, that had it not been the King's castle, there had been some rebuke, as indeed due, for such noise made. The Prior in his chamber sat alone; listening, I guess, in gloomy mood to the revelry; and, all that night, only Edmund the monk and master Peter with him: he came not forth to midnight-song.

But now I must return, and so must ye that hear, or read, to the castle. In the hall there was a dancer on stilts, playing the while on a recorder; there were dancers on one leg, and dancers upon the head; but that which most rejoiced many of the beholders, were the disguisings and the quaint antics of the mummers. There came a whole troop, some wearing the heads of asses, some of bulls, some of calves, some of cats, who brayed and kicked, bellowed and tossed, scratched and mewed, to the very life. Others, like stags and hares, hounds and apes, kept not so pertinently to their pretended natures, but marched on with solemn state, as much as might be, hand in hand, as if they had been loving friends and neighbours; yet each with a dagger stuck in his girdle. And others again, with fools' girdles and bells hanging to them; tossing their heads, and cutting such strange capers, to the noise of pipes and drums, as made the sides of many to shake with laughter, and roused up every hawk on perch there to shake his bells in concert.

But all this was child's play, though it was often done before the worshipfullest estates, in comparison of the sayer's art[8]; which, when he could be heard between whiles, when the loud revelry paused and held breath, was marvellous to hear: and, as soon as those mad-heads caught the words of that tale-teller, sooth to say, they soon were still and hushed, as though no living soul but he breathed there; listening to his dismal tirade, with tears in their eyes, or quaking for fear of the strange things he told them. He, the while, with solemn visage, showing as though he himself believed all the marvels he related, and not

68

showing roguish smiles, as some do, kept on always to the far end of his long tale: though some learned clerks would oft-times comment to their neighbours upon his marvels, as if he had purported lofty matter worth their notice, and did not merely strive to while an idle tide away.

In other parts of the castle were those gentils and honest gentlewomen, that, misliking the loud revelry of the hall, drew together in chambers apart; and delighted themselves with histories of times past, the sad hopes of lovers, or the deeds of brave knights, or otherwise in singing and harping, after their own manner.

In the lower hall too was feasting, and the mirth did not stop short of the 'Kuchane', so that every man to the lowest degree was joyous; and each chamber and tower rung with song, or laughter, save the prison tower of the poor merchant. He, as he lay on his pallet-bed, heard those sounds of music and jollity, in confused uproar rising through the courts, while his heart was stricken with fear and sadness; for, whether he were right or not in believing Sir Gaston to be the murderer of his friend, it is certain, that he had seen his friend murdered, and that too, as he said, in the woods of Ardenn.

He was, at this time, far from his home and friends, and had been travelling, over these parts, a lonesome stranger, along the foss-way from Lincoln, southward; having been on his merchandize into the north seas, and having landed on the eastern coast. Coming again to that place, where, a few years back, he had buried his friend, the remembrance of him broke out in fresh grief; and, hearing that the king was coming to keep festival in Kenilworth, he resolved to break the matter to him; as well as to adventure to tell him, the times were such it was no longer safe to journey in any part of his kingdom.

The most audacious robberies, certes, were then committed at noon-day with impunity; nay, the very thieves themselves feared not to be seen walking about, little attempt being made to seize them, or, in any wise, to suppress these scandalous outrages. Not only then did the sad fall of his friend, but also the fearful condition of the living, urge the merchant to make the truth known to the king.

With this design he had rested at Kenilworth, but not at the house where he had formerly suffered such affliction; and, on the king's arrival, had gone forth in the crowd to behold him, though he had not intended to present his petition in that time

69

of turmoil. But, when he saw near his Highness, riding as it were in the top of favour, the very man, whom he thought to be the slayer of his kinsman; when he beheld that look, which he felt to dart into his heart, and to revive there all the horror he had felt at the aspect of the murderer, at the moment when his friend had been stricken down – then it was, that, overcome by the strength of his feelings, he dropped down senseless in the castle court, as hath been related.

And now, what had he gained by his courageous demand of justice? Suspicion, contempt, fear, grief, a prison, and, perhaps, death. Yet did he not repent the effort he had made, so honest was his grief for the fate of his kinsman; so much was his mind possessed with the notion, that he had accused his very murderer; so confident was he that he was performing a duty; and, what is more, so sure was he, that to perform his duty in this world is the wisest, the most truly cunning thing a man can contrive to do. Whether his suspicions concerning the knight were just or not; these, his conclusions touching his own conduct, none but fools, or villains, that is, none but fools – will deny.

Thus he lay on his pallet, alike deprived of sleep by the jollity of others and by his own grievous reflections. A lamp burned beside him, but it served only to show the forlornness of his condition, in this high and distant tower. Sometimes, he would rise and look through his grated window upon the inner court of the castle, listening there awhile to the distant minstrelsy and to the confusion of numberless voices, footsteps and closing doors, that rose from many a chamber below. Anon, a torch-bearer would pass the court, a page, perhaps, or a yeoman; and would show the gloomy towers above and the steps of the guest he led at their feet. But, this passed, nothing could the prisoner see, save here and there, a lamp burning through a casement of glass (and a goodly show there was of such windows now in this castle) like stars through a clouded sky; but mostly the glorious beams of the great hall, that struck through the windows and lighted the air above. Once he heard the trumpets blow, and thought the King was coming forth, and once he fancied he saw, in the person of one who followed a torch-bearer, Sir Gaston himself. Then turned he from the casement, looked no more, and fell upon his pallet.

At last, every distant sound grew fainter; the noise of the dancers ceased; then the minstrelsy sunk low; the voices of the hall revellers became few; he heard less frequently the doors opened and shut; and then he heard the fastening of bolts and bars: and, afar off, the castle gates closed for the night; and soon all grew still, as though no living creature inhabited there.

And thus it kept, until the wayte piped his second watch in all the courts[9]. Then the stranger arose, and, looking again through his grate, saw him well, by the light his groom carried, piping the hour. And, when the man had finished his saye, he went round the court, his boy-groom holding up the torch, while he tried every door, and found that all was safe. By this light too, he perceived the wardour's men on guard; but no living being else was seen. The windows of the great hall were dark; and, the torch being gone, nothing glimmered through the night, save one great star, which wizards say is evil. It stayed, at his hour, right over King Henry's lodgings; but for whom it watched, who was there that might tell? The prisoner knew the star, and all that was thought of it, and he betook him to his pallet groaning heavily.

He had not long been there when, as he thought, a voice near him spoke his name. Now, there was a small grate looked out from his chamber upon the stair; and thence the voice seemed to come. The prisoner, raising himself from his pallet, turned, and saw there the figure of a man passing away. He kept his eyes fixed, for some space, upon the grate, but the figure appeared no more, and he sunk again on his pallet.

The voice, faint and passing as it was, had thrilled him with dread. Whose it was, wherefore it had called him by a name known but to few, and had then passed away, without communing with him, he tried in vain to understand; yet seemed it not wholly new to him.

Here was a drawing of the inside of the great hall, with the King
and Queen holding festival. In the back-ground was a sketch, of
what seemed to be a pageant acted there; and yet the spectators
appeared to be looking on, with an interest too serious for so
trifling a peformance. In the margin, also, was drawn, the chapel
before mentioned, with a marriage ceremony at the porch.

 N THE morrow, the Prior of Saint Mary's was
with the King, before the esquire-barber had
clipped his dread Highness's beard, or the
rushes had been strewed on the chapel-floor
for the bridal company, or even the ox-chine,
the manchets and the pitchers of wine had
been delivered out from the kuchane and the buttery-hatch, for
the breakfasts of the King and Queen and their lords and ladies.
He told his Highness, that no person of the name of Reginald de
Folville was on the burial lists of the priory; nor was there any
inhabitant of that house, or of Kenilworth, yet discovered, who
remembered that name, connected with the extraordinary
circumstances that had been related. It was, however, notori-
ous, that robberies had frequently been committed in the woods
and chases of Kenilworth, where many close and dark thickets
were the home of outlaws; and that no single person, and few
small companies, could travel in safety through any part of the
forest of Ardenn. He remarked, that, if the merchant had
suffered there the outrage he had alleged, it was extraordinary
he should now venture to travel over the same ground without
guide, or companion, to lessen his danger; for, it had appeared
from himself, that he was travelling without either.

It was no less extraordinary, that, if the calamitous adventure,
related by the merchant, had occurred so near to Kenilworth,
and so few years back, it should not be generally known and still
remembered there. From all these circumstances, and particularly from that of the name of Reginald de Folville not being
found in the cemetery-book of the priory, and from the absence

of every other memorial of such a person, save in the charge itself, the Prior scrupled not to insist, that the stranger, now in confinement, was an impostor, falsely calling himself a merchant; who, for his own private ends, sought the ruin and life of Sir Gaston de Blondeville.

His Highness seemed well satisfied that it should be so; and, in his indignation against the accuser, declared, that his life should be forfeited, for the crime of having sought another's. He called for Sir Gaston; and, having acquainted him with the result of the Prior's inquiries, assured him, that his honour should be cleared from suspicion, and his accuser openly condemned: and his Highness told him, that, since he would soon be unable to serve him as a knight of his household, such being batchelors only, as well as that all the world might have proof of his spotless honour, he would place him amongst the nobles of his land.

So saying, his Highness bade him to his intended bride, and to hail her Baroness of Blondeville; also to warn her to be ready for the appointed ceremony of her marriage, by then two hours were past: and forthwith his Highness departed the chamber.

The Earl, her father, when he heard of what had passed, in the presence of the King, and of the new dignity conferred on Sir Gaston, was well contented to receive the young Baron for his son; but the lady, her mother, whose tenderness, being more than her ambition, made her fearful of contrary tidings, was not yet completely assured, that this would be a happy union for her child. The Lady Barbara herself, however, nothing doubting the worth of her suitor, loved him not the less for having been accused, nor the better for having been raised to new dignity; nevertheless, she took the distinction in good part, rejoicing, that it should thus appear he had not fallen in the esteem of his Highness, the King.

She was now in her bower, aleady attired for the bridal, attended by her six maidens, the daughters of some of the first nobles of the realm. And, although this be not a gay history, chronicling the vanities of women, yet will we here report all that we heard of this lady, in so far as her appearance may tell what might be seen in the King's court, at this time. She wore on her hair a string of pearls of great value and a necklace of the same, given her by the young Baron. Her robe, white as the lawn of the Archbishop, was confined by the precious girdle, given to her by the Queen; and over all she wore the veil of a sister, and pity it was, that so fair a vestal should be relinquished to this world, instead of being retained in the community, which had once looked to have her their own. But I say not now more of her appearance, at this time.

King Henry, during his visits to Kenilworth, had newly repaired and adorned the chapel of the castle, and there the marriage was to be solemnized. By his command, the walls had been painted with the story of King Edward, the Confessor, giving the ring off his finger to a poor stranger. The floor was strewed with rushes and oak leaves, and with such sweet flowers as the season afforded, from the woods and the gardens. The lights were all a-blaze, so that they overcame the perpetual tomb lights of Geoffrey de Clinton, the founder of the castle, interred in the chapel here.

When the trumpets had sounded, there went forth in procession, first, the Queen and her court, her ladies pacing before her, two and two, according to their rank, preceded by her minstrels and the officers of her household. Next before her Highness went the bride, her six maidens strewing flowers before her, and Maria, the famous French poetess, who was then at the Queen's court, playing on her harp. Amongst the ladies encompassing her Highness, were the Countesses of Cornwall and Pembroke, (the latter then become Countess of Montfort) and the lady mother of the bride.

When these nobles and gentils had been met at the gates of the precinct of the priory, by a part of the choir, and by two of the secular clergy, and had been led to the porch of the chapel, they were more fully received beneath it by others of the clergy, repeating what is appointed to be there said; and were led into the chapel by those, who had received them, and so were they placed, every one according to their rank, unless when the Queen made any especial choice. Then, the King's trumpets blew up, and his Highness approached, accompanied of Prince Edward and the Earl of Cornwall, and attended by the knights of his Highness's body, the knights of his household, and a countless train of nobles – the young Baron conspicuous among them all, for that graceful and gallant air, for which those of his nation were renowned. The cloud, that was over him yesterday, had passed, and his countenance was joyous as the day.

And next to this young lord in grace, and high above in dignity, was the Archbishop himself: of lofty stature and of venerable and commanding aspect, he passed with slow and stately steps, preceded by bishops and others of the church, his

74

purple train borne up by two pages, and his own virger making due place for him and his part of the procession. Meanwhile, those of the clergy and of the choir, who had received the Queen, had returned to the precinct-gate, whence, with due sentences, uttered before the whole company, but 'specially before the bridegroom, they led him to the porch, where the banns were fully proclaimed.

I hold it not meet to speak here, with greater pourtrayment, of the more solemn ceremonies in the chapel itself, only that, when the Archbishop came to the lowest step, he stayed there some time, with bended head in silence, the bishops having passed to their places; and then the minstrels and the children of the chapel began an anthem, which ended not till the Archbishop, the King, the bride and bridegroom, had advanced to their proper places, and, the bride's veil having been thrown back, the Archbishop, on the special command of the King, began to read what is appointed.

There was that day in the chapel, among the crowd, by some unknown hap, a stranger, who seemed to observe, with more attention than the greater part, all that passed, yet did he never ask a question, nor speak to any one there. He was seen in different parts, although the press of people was so great, it was difficult for any one to change his station. At last, having reached the sepulchre of Geoffrey de Clinton, he leaned among the tomb-lights there, and moved no more. There was in his countenance a touching solemnity, while he watched the progress of the ceremony, which was noticed by many present; for, in his whole demeanour there was something, though it was difficult to explain what, that drew away the attention of many from the sight they came to witness, and that was pity, for it was such a sight as is seldom seen.

King Henry, of goodly stature and of comely countenance, was in a robe of dark blue velvet; and with the dignity of his carriage there was mixed an air of good humour, that made all men feel at ease in his presence. His son, Prince Edward, it was remarked, had a sterner look than his father. Many, who knew, that the King's heart was good, in many respects, lamented his weaknesses, and that his passions too often carried him away. He now appeared in his state and well able to enjoy it; but the Archbishop, with his firm, composed, and solemn countenance and lofty figure, made all other dignity appear as nothing. He was like some oak of our forest, whose grey top has braved the storms of centuries, and whose mighty branches still afford shelter to the storm-beset traveller, and to the plants and flowers at his feet. The Lady Barbara was the lily there; the Baron de Blondeville, a young beech, growing at hand, with all its glossy branches and light foliage, spreading forth in graceful beauty. What pity, if the lightning should sere those green leaves, and destroy its promise!

When the Archbishop asked, who gave away the maiden, his Highness advancing, graciously delivered her to the Baron, who bending on one knee, received her of the King; but, as he rose up, his countenance showed not joy, or love – it showed consternation. His eyes had glanced on the tomb of Geoffrey de Clinton, and were now rivetted, where the stranger stood. The stranger, as he still leaned admist the torches there, seemed, however, unmoved by the dismayed looks of the bridegroom; his gloomy sternness was unshaken. But the emotion of the Baron increased; his looks became deadly pale, and he could no longer repeat the words, that were necessary in the ceremony. All eyes were soon directed upon him, and then upon the Lady Barbara, who fell into a swoon, and would have sunk on the ground, had not the King's arm sustained her. Her maidens, and some of the Queen's ladies hastened to her assistance; but, though almost every one in the chapel looked upon her with pity and care, the Baron regarded her not, nor seemed to know what had happened to her. His attention was still fixed upon the tomb, whither, too, directed by his looks, all other eyes now turned; but they perceived only the extended marble image of the dead one within, and the torches burning round it. The stranger was no longer there. The hasty surprise of the King, the calm displeasure of the Archbishop, the severe curiosity of the young Prince Edward, the distress of the lady mother, and the wonder of all, where this might end, may not be told.

His Highness, inquiring of those about him whence this confusion had arisen, was answered, there was a stranger in the chapel, who seemed to be known only to the Baron, and it was surely the sight of him, which had occasioned this disorder. Then, the King commanded, that the doors should be shut, and search made for this unknown person, whom he suspected to be some secret colleague of the young Baron's accuser, come hither purposely to interrupt the ceremony; and he commanded also, that the service should proceed, as soon as the parties affected should recover their presence of mind. Many there thought the

King too hasty in this, and the Archbishop himself testified no willingness to proceed.

The Baron did not long remain in his apparent torpor, but, on his recovery, he seemed like one awakened from a dream; he looked round with fear and surprise; and, fixing his eyes again on the tomb, he was well nigh relapsing, though nothing there was seen, save the marble image and the torch-lights around it. The King spoke graciously to him, and, when the baron heard his voice, he made most humble gesture before his Highness, and craved his pardon for the disturbance he had created.

'You must ask pardon of this lady,' said the King, showing to him the bride, who was now nearly reviving; 'for it is she only who has suffered.'

Then, the young Baron seemed, for the first time, to know fully what had happened, and he hung over her with sadness and anxiety; yet divers of the courtiers thought he felt more for himself than for her, and of this number were those, who envied him the new honour he had attained.

When the bride had recovered, her lady-mother would have withdrawn her from the chapel, and she herself wished to go away from the great observance that had been drawn towards her; but the Baron, addressing himself to the King, besought his Highness to interfere on his behalf, and not to suffer, that the vain impulse of a momentary and wandering feeling, which had, at times, come over him even from his childhood should be taken in so serious a part. The Baron having knelt to the King, as he said this (and once before he did the same, but I did not note it on these leaves) the Archbishop could ill conceal his just displeasure, that the Baron should do reverence in that place to any human being; and the King said the Archbishop was right; and, making the Baron instantly rise, asked what had caused his dismay, and whom he had seen, that should have caused it.

Then the Baron anwered, that he had seen one like unto his dead father; but he now knew it to have been only an apparition, suggested in his own mnd; and he repeated, that to such like delusions he had been subject from his young-hood.

This was not said so lowly, as that the Lady Huntingdon heard it not; and she thought, that such a state of mind was a sufficient reason for withholding her daughter from the marriage; and the Earl, her father, taking up the objection, had begun to repeat it, – but he was soon silenced; for his Highness said, peremptorily, that, because of consent duly given, he had resolved to be present at the marriage, with his court; and it were not to be allowed, that a momentary infirmity of one of the parties, who instantly afterwards desired to have the ceremony renewed, should be sufficient for rendering all the preparations, which had been so great and so public, bootless. And his Highness commanded progress forthwith.

Yet the Archbishop had some private discourse with the King; and it seemed as though he were recommending delay, at least till that stranger had been questioned, whose appearance, he privately believed, had thus disturbed the Baron de Blonde-ville, notwithstanding the tale he had told. The Lady Barbara herself was questioned, as to the cause of the distress she had betrayed; but she answered only, that it was the sudden alteration in the Baron, that caused her spirits to fail.

When those, who had been ordered to search the chapel, were called upon, they declared, that no where could they find the stranger who had been seen, neither within the doors, nor in court, nor in chamber. Then, the King, without further delay, commanded, that the service should proceed; and it did proceed accordingly, and was concluded, without farther let, or hinder-ance.

So the King and Queen returned from the chapel to the great chamber, in due state and order, and the court dispersed for that day, until the evening, when there was to be a grand banquet, to honour these nuptials.

All that day, the young Baroness seemed grave and thought-ful; the lady, her mother, was not a whit more joyed; although the Earl, recollecting the honour the King had newly conferred on the bridegroom, and beholding, in his mind, other benefits likely to follow, seemed now again to be well contented with this marriage. But the Baron carried himself thoughtfully, for one in his circumstances; and some, who observed him closely, thought there was still a tale to be told, which he liked not to have known; and others, who envied him less his new title, held that this humour was but the remains of that, which had seized upon him in the chapel, and that it was the recollection of this and of the confusion he had there occasioned, which preyed upon his spirits. However this might be, he seemed desirous of shaking off that mood, and to appear at the banquet with the gaiety, which the time invited.

Surely the preparations for this feast were magnificent, though they came not nigh what had been made on some former

78

marriages, such as that given at Westminster, when Richard, the King's brother, wedded Cincia, daughter of the Count de Provence, and sister to the Queen, when three thousand dishes were served up at the wedding dinner; nor is it to be thought this was like unto that one afterwards at York, when King Henry gave his daughter Margaret in marriage to Alexander, the young King of Scotland; and my Lord Archbishop gave, for his share of the feast, sixty pasture oxen, which were clean consumed at that entertainment; but, nevertheless, this at Kenilworth was a right noble and princely banquet; and thus it was.

The King, that night, with the Queen, kept state in the great hall, which was thereunto, by command of his Highness, hanged about with that suit of tapestry, which setteth forth the story of our famous King Richard, Coeur de Lion, his deeds in Palestine; and be it remembered, that King Henry loved nothing better than to see on his walls the noble achievements of his ancestors and others, as the Queen's chamber here at Kenilworth showeth, where he had caused to be pictured forth, Merlin, King of Britain, and his three sons; the sailing of William from Normandy; the submission of Griffin ap Conan to Henry the First, and several other things.

This tapestry in the great hall was placed on all sides under the windows, down to the floor, except at the bottom of the hall, where the great gallery ran; and there the carved screens beneath were sufficient to hide the buttery-hatch, on the other side of the passage, and the doors leading down to the kuchanes. It hung on all sides, save here, and where the great chimney stood, which was guarded by a projecting stone-work, of curious carving, and like unto a canopy, or open porch. The wood, that was consumed within, was laid this night on andirons of solid silver, bossed.

On the top of this seeming porch, stood figures of armed knights, as large as life, such as were in the gallery before-mentioned. That gallery was covered with weapons and with complete suits of armour; some, with helmet and feet fastened against the wall, and others standing upright, like to living warriors, armed at all points; but doubtless, these last were well held up by some artful contrivance. Five figures, thus appointed, stood in the front of the gallery, as if watching who should enter from the screens beneath. Amongst these was one shape of black steel, larger than the rest and higher by the head; said to have been the very harness worn by the King's great uncle, Richard the Lion, in some battle in Palestine: and the very sight of it was enough to daunt with fear those unused to a field of war.

Certes, it was like to that worn by this king in the very tapestry, wherewith the hall was this night, in good part, adorned; and where he was shown fighting in all his glory. It has been said, the young prince was much moved at the sight of the daring deeds there pictured forth, and of that armour – but not with terror, rather with noble pride, to emulate such greatness; and that he was by this and such like things, often before his eyes, prompted to what he afterwards achieved; but of this I cannot say. The keys of this gallery of arms were kept in the care of the lord constable of the castle, so that no person might enter it, without his special leave.

In the back wall was a window, opening from the King's chamber, that looked over the gallery into the hall below; and where his Highness used sometimes to divert himself, with observing what was passing at the different tables there and with the games and sports, passing amongst his household and followers. He needed only to draw aside a curtain in that chamber, to see all that was doing in the hall below; and there, at even-tide, he might remain unseen, if it so pleased him; for the gallery received light only from the lamps in the arches high above.

Not the minstrel's gallery was this; never was it so at Kenilworth; nor in any great hall of prince or peer where state was duly kept. Their gallery was on the left, opposite to the great chimney, and nearer to the dais, where they sat all joyfully clothed in the King's livery.

At the upper end of the hall, raised by several steps above the rest of the flooring, was that dais, where stood the high tables. The King was under a canopy of crimson velvet, fringed about with gold; the Queen's was on the same platform, and with a canopy of the like form and stuff; but the canopy was lower by the valance.

A carpet of crimson silk was spread under the tables, and down the steps of the dais; below this, the floor of the hall was strewed with fresh rushes, on which were laid wood-flowers in plenty. In the bay-windows, at the end of the platform, or dais, a princely cupboard was set forth, stage above stage, of nine or ten heights, till they reached the bottom of the glass casements there; piled up with gold and silver cups and dishes and with basins of solid gold, some set with precious stones, and others highly wrought.

From the arched roof of these two bays hung lamps, that showed all their brightness, and illuminated the roial window above, and also the slender columns, that reached to the roof; and the curious fret-work of leaves and flowers spreading there; which had been newly done by command of King Henry, who loved such vanities, and had brought this new fashion out of Normandy. He had put such roial windows, perchance better painted, in his new church at Salisbury.

Those, who now beheld the pomp he displayed and his vast retinue, wherever he kept court, might say, with the venerable monk of St Albans, on occasion of the marriage of the Scottish King Alexander with this King Henry's daughter; 'If I were to describe the grandeur of this festival, the number of the noble guests, the splendor and various changes of their dresses, the abundance of the tables and the variety of the sports provided; those, who were absent, would think I was inventing.' There, Matthew, the good monk, tells us yet more of the Archbishop of York on that occasion, who expended four thousand marks in entertaining the courts of both kings and in every kind of munificence to the poor and sick. The two kings, Matthew further tells us, entertained by turns their whole courts, 'so that,' as he adds, 'the theatrical vanity of this world might show to all, as much as it could of its short and transitory gladness.' And vanity it was, as those of Saint Albans knew to their cost and sorely complained of, when the King went so often to the Abbey there.

But what would such have said, had they lived now, in our King Richard's days; who, the second of his name, is first in every kind of new extravagance, the like of which was never seen afore, and what it may end in, there is no one that dare yet say.

But now, to go back to the past King Henry; he proved himself, according to the account in the Norman tongue, which I have seen, not only an excellent 'meatgiver' here at Kenilworth, but a sumptuous bestower of many pleasures and a patron of every kind of mimickry, such as painting, carving, music and versifying, as this hall at Kenilworth fully displayed, on this very night. Before the feast began, it was a goodly sight to behold the serjeants at arms and the ushers, bearing the piles of gold and silver cups and the spice-plates to the boards; and the ceremony of laying forth the sur-nap on the King's table, in readiness for him to wash, which was thus:–

The King's sewer having laid the end of the sur-nap and a towel on the board, and the usher having fastened his wand to them, drew them to the other end of the table; and then kneeling down, the sewer at the other end kneeling likewise, they stretched the sur-nap smooth. Then the usher, laying up the end of the towel on the board, rose and did reverence before the King's chair, with his wand, as though his Highness had already been there. And, when he had kneeled down and amended the towel, he did reverence again in like manner.

On either side of the hall, reaching from the steps of the dais (for in this hall was only one dais) to the screens at the end, were ranges of tables, appointed for different ranks and degrees of the court: and it were goodly to see these nobles and gentils ranged in their places by the marshal of the hall. At one table, on the right, next below the dais, were those of the King's blood, who sat not at his board. Opposite, on the other line, sat the noble dames, all together.

Next below the King's board, sat the bishops and the abbots, each at their own table; then, the King's high officers of estate, such as attended not on his person; there were, besides, the four Barons of the Exchequer, assessors, and several other great servants of his courts of justice, which always followed him, wherever he might choose to keep the high fesitvals of the year, and to administer the laws of the realm.

Other tables were set apart for other ranks of nobles, not of blood; their wives and daughters sitting apart from them. Thus every table was filled, each with its respective rank, magnificently attired; the nobles in velvet and cloth of gold, the dames sparkling with jewels and bearing plumes on their hair; the bishops in their 'broidered copes and golden mitres, and the great officers of state in their own peculiar habits, with their golden chains.

But the table of the knights-banneret was that which made all, save the ladies' boards, look pale and dull. They wore their 'broidered mantles over a kind of light cuirass, each with a sash of crimson beneath, thrown over the shoulder and falling down to the sword. On their heads they had each a small cap of velvet, with a gallant plume of feathers depending on each side, which it was the King's pleasure they should wear, even in his presence. On the wall above, were the shield and helmet of each

82

knight, their banners waving over them. At the bottom of the hall was the esquires' table, where sat nineteen of them, arrayed in the King's livery. Every table had its own officers of service, as marshal-sewer, conveyers, almoner and butler, appointed according to the rank of the guests.

Now, the trumpets without having given warning, the King and Queen entered by a door leading from the state-chambers; attended by the young Prince Edward, the Archbishop, the Earl and Countess of Cornwall, the Lady Pembroke and Montfort, the Earl and Countess of Huntingdon, the bride and bridegroom, all the knights of the household then at the court, arrayed in their velvet gowns, the esquires of the body; the kings at arms, heralds and pursuivants, going before in their coats, – two serjeants at arms appearing to make way. Next before the King, went the lord marshal of the hall and his eight knights.

Thus, their Highnesses came in, with a brave noise of trumpets, and took their seats at the high tables. And immediately entered from the door, forty yeomen, each bearing a torch, who took their stations down the middle of the hall, between the tables, in two lines. Ten esquires of the household, most richly bedight in the King's livery, who had marched before his Highness, with the four esquires of the body, stood in a half-circle; each bearing a large wax-light, at the back of the dais, near the high tables: – while other ten, with lights, took their stations, in two divisions, at the foot of the steps of the dais; but leaving an open space, that all the guests might have sight of the princely board.

There, clusters of lights in golden candlesticks, showed the massive plate and the marvellous devices of the banquet, with the magnificent attire of those who graced it; and these lights, together with the numerous torches below, and the lamps depending from the points of every inverted pinnacle of the roof on high, cast such a blaze of splendour, not only on the banquet beneath; but on every painted window above, as made the hall as grand a spectacle, well nigh, for those without, as for those within; only that the guests could not be seen, by reason that the windows were so high above them.

Some travellers that night, coming from afar, through the woods, espying the blaze, wondered what it might mean. And some poor pilgrims, travelling from the shrine of Saint Hugh, at Lincoln, seeing through the darkness such painted light afar off in the valley, took it for some delusion, raised by evil wizards for their destruction; and they ventured not forward, till they had, after due observation, some assurance of the mortal reality. Presently, as they advanced, they distinguished better the gorgeous colouring of the windows, which they knew to be of the new manner, called roial, and then the towers above, though these were pale in the moonlight, and then they heard the revel sound of minstrelsy within; and so, coming to the priory-gate, they asked shelter and had it: for, though they were told, that the King kept his court, and, at that time, banqueted in the castle, they chose to take refuge in the quiet of our cloister, rather than to ask for any part, or sight, of such doings. But, to come back to the King's feast, of which much and marvellous is yet to be told.

At the King's table sat, on his right hand, the Archbishop of York; beyond him sat the young Prince Edward; and, on the left, the Earl of Cornwall. But, just before his Highness came to his place and sat, the Archbishop, as highest of estate, delivered unto him the napkin; and the young Baron, for his honour, was allowed, on that night, to bear the golden basin and ewer for the King to wash; although there were so many of higher estate in the hall. At the same time, was brought another golden basin to the Archbishop, who seemed to wait till the King should have washed: but his Highness made a beck, that he should wash; and he did so. When the King washed, straight five esquires gathered round him, and stood with their lights, till he made an end.

This ceremony done, they withdrew to their places, and the Baron took his behind the King's chair, who spoke merrily to him, while he served; and the Baron had recovered his good looks, and wore his gown of azure, 'broidered with silver, with as good a grace as any one in court. He was, most certain, of a brave figure, and of countenance, that, for high spirit, seemed to challenge comparison with every man he looked upon, which made him many secret enemies.

At the Queen's board, sat the Countesses of Cornwall and Montfort, and the young Baroness de Blondeville, and none other. A golden ewer, set thick with rubies, stood beside her Highness; and a basin of the same, with damask-water, strewed with fresh pulled lavender, was held to her to wash by one of her maidens, who duly sat at her feet under the board, the young Baroness bearing the napkin. Which done, two of her Highness's maidens, who waited behind her chair, delivered them to the Queen's pages.

And now entered the hall, Norroy, King of arms, heralds and poursuivants attending, all in their coats; the lord marshal, with his eight knights, and the steward, treasurer, and comptroller, walking before the first dish for the King's board; which was carried by the King's chief sewer, wearing his neck towel; his carver, Harpingham, wearing the same, surrounded by esquires, of the household bearing wax-lights, and followed by serjeants at arms and esquires and pages. But, when these had reached the middle of the hall, they all stood still, and made reverence to the King; the lord steward, with his wand; the carver with his great knife, and the sewer with his dish in his hand: and again, at the foot of the dais, they all stopped short, and bowed before him, the trumpets sounding the while.

Would you know what this first dish was? It was a warner of shields of boar, in armour, with mustard, served with malmsey. When the warner was ended, the first course, and so was every other, was brought up by seven sewers, with like state and with due taking of assaye of the King's meat, and with divers other ceremonies too tedious to relate.

Only amongst the dishes were frumentie, with venison; frumentie roial, with a dragon for a suttletie; browst of Almayne, potage of gourdis, and felettes in galentine.

At the Queen's table, amongst many other dishes and suttleties of curious invention, were these – tench in jelly; great custard planted for a suttletie; petynel, peronsew with his segue; goos in hochepot and browet tuskay.

There was, also, for an honour to the young Baroness, a special suttletie[10], presenting the Queen's bower, with her ladies ranged round, and the lady Barbara, receiving on her knee the jewels, which her Highness had given to her the night before; there too, was presented Pierre, the minstrel, playing on his very harp. The Baron de Blondeville had leave from the King to quit his chair, for a time, to visit the bride; and, when he showed this suttletie to her, she smiled; but it was the first time she had smiled this night.

There was another suttletie of archers in the forest hunting the hart, with foresters in green blowing their horns and the whole court following. In this, too, was the Lady Barbara, mounted on a milk-white palfry, her hair bound up in beauteous net; but not of gold and pearls, as it was this night, nor wore she

85

a mantle of white cloth like that she now had on. At a distance, within the shadow of the trees, stood an aged man alone, wringing his hands; but what this might mean none knew.

In the hall below, every table was abundantly served with dainties, according to the rank of those who sat there; and all were contented, as well they might be.

The King talked graciously and often to the Baron de Blondeville, and sometimes would send him with a dish of dainties from his own board to the Baroness; nothing doubting, that he would like the errand. And, when the Earl of Norfolk brought his Highness his cup, he drank to her; but the trumpets blew up too soon, so what what he said was heard not; but he bowed, and thrice waved to her his hand, the which, soon as the young Baroness saw, she rose up and curtsied low three times, to the great pleasure of all, who beheld her sweet grace and modesty. Many there were in the hall, who cried out, 'May she be happy!'

The King had given back the cup into the hands of the Lord Norfolk, and was resting him in his chair; when he saw the curtain drawn back of that window, which opened from his own chamber upon the gallery of arms, and a person standing there. While his Highness marvelled by what means any one could have admittance into that chamber, the keys being in the custody of the Lord Constable, the window was unfolded, and the person, advancing into the gallery, came forward to the front; and there stood still, and with great seeming confidence, beside the armour of Richard the Lion.

Although the light, that fell there from the roof, was not so strong that his Highness, at such distance, could distinguish the countenance of this person, yet, by the grey gleam reflected there, he seemed to be clothed in steel, with helmet on his head: and so like was he to the form of King Richard, that, had not his Highness seen him advance, and the real shape of motionless armour standing by, he would have thought this but a figure for show, like the others there. The King, no less surprized by the strangeness of this appearance, than displeased by the boldness which had thus openly defied his command, respecting that chamber, ordered an esquire to repair to the Lord Constable, who was himself in the hall; and learn whom he had admitted there. The Baron, who stood by, looking whither the King looked, on a sudden changed countenance; and his Highness again observed that stupor and dismay, which he had noticed in the morning, beginning to fix his eyes and to spread over every feature. The King spoke sharply to him, to rouse him, as was supposed, from his trance; but without effect, for he stood fixed and stiffened, like to a marble statue, yet with looks bent on the gallery, where the stranger stood.

Then, the King gave a beck that none should notice his condition; hoping he might recover himself, before the Queen and the young Baroness should observe him. When the Archbishop perceived that person standing in the gallery, he was observed to make the holy sign; and, when he looked at the Baron and saw his amazement, he repeated it: – it was said his Highness asked him why he did so; but that he answered not, save by a look of solemn reverence and by bowing of the head. That stranger, though the King fixed his eyes on him with displeasure, moved not; but his Highness, though unable to distinguish his features in that obscure situation, thought the intruder likely to be one not obscure, if known, but one who expected to remain unknown in a place so far from what was now passing; and his Highness, resolved, that he should not escape detection.

With the esquire messenger, came up the hall the constable of the castle, to attend the King's pleasure. His Highness turned to chide him for not having better observed his command, respecting his own chamber; and enquired who the stranger was, that had intruded there. With astonishment, the constable declared the keys of that chamber and gallery had not been out of his keeping, and that he had not admitted any one thither.

'Nay,' said the King, 'thine eyes may contradict thy tongue; look there, and thou wilt see one less willing to keep council against thee than thyself.' The constable looked to the gallery, but, perceiving only the known figures of armour there, he stood silent and amazed. Then his Highness, seeing the stranger was gone, said, 'I let this pass. Thy friend has seen thee, and profited by the warning. Be more heedful in future. Go now to thy place.'

The constable did reverence, and departed, marvelling much at the King's words and well resolved to enquire further into this matter. And now the Baron, not having been spoken to for some space, began to recover himself, like one awakening from sleep, and happily before those at the Queen's table knew what happened. The King made a sign, that none should speak, and

87

then, accosting him with his wonted graciousness, bade him go to the table appointed for his rank, and refresh himself there. The young Prince Edward looked on him with curiosity, but without pity; and spoke not to him. Meanwhile, the Baron gazed around with strange visage, as if he knew not well where he was, but in a short space bowed to the King, and withdrew. While this passed, the Archbishop was noted to look often towards the Queen's table; but he said nought.

The constable, the while, was making busy enquiry, who had been in the gallery of arms, but no one knew any thing of the matter; so he went himself to examine the doors, the key in his hand. The outer door, that led to the King's chamber, was fast. He unlocked it, and, leaving a guard there, went forward with lights through the whole range to the gallery chamber and there examined the window door, that opened towards the hall; which also was fastened, as he had left it.

Much marvelling, he went out into the gallery, and tried a door, at the end, that opened upon a stair, and found it not only locked, but bolted within, so that if any one had entered this way, he could not have gone out by the same. The constable had ordered the outer-door to be guarded, as I said, while search was made through the gallery and the whole range of rooms; but this was to no purpose, not any thing living being found there. And now he began to think that his Highness had tasted too often of the golden cup, and mistaken one of the armour-shapes in front of the gallery for a living knight, or other warlike person. However, he took care to make the doors secure, and forthwith he departed.

And now, when the second course was on its way to the King's table, the steward entered the hall, and called out loudly three times, 'Wassel! wassel! wassel!' and, incontinently, the cup-bearers went round to the different boards; and all of the court, standing up and leaning towards the high table, drank the King's health. Then, the verger of the minstrels giving them the beck, they all at once set up their pipyngs and blowings, with such a brave noise, that the castle might have been taken by storm, before those in the hall could have heard the thump of a single war-wolf.

There were trumpets and clarions and cittolles and tabarets and makerers and fithols; besides the King's five harpers, all beating, or blowing, or thrumming together. They were heard afar off in the woods; and many an outlaw lay on watch that night,

88

for those, who might be travelling from the castle homewards. The brethren of the priory liked not the noise, and the Prior, I guess, would have liked it as little, but that he was amongst those in the hall, sitting at the table of the abbots. The poor prisoner in the tower heard the revelry, and to him it was sad indeed.

It were making a cook's book to tell what dainties there were at the second course: these must suffice, for this little history: – There were joly amber potage; jiggots of venison, stopped with cloves; lamprey, with galentine; marchpagne; fritter-dolphin; leche-florentine: with divers suttleties of castles and dragons and voyages at sea; and cities in the King's dominions, beyond the seas; and a full tournament, showing knights on horseback, riding their rounds, and ladies freshly apparelled, in the galleries, looking at them. At the King's board, was a suttletie presenting his court of justice such as it was already prepared in this castle, against the feast of Saint Michael. There was his Highness, sitting in judgment, and all his great officers, sitting round on the benches.

At the Queen's table, was a suttletie with ballads, the which, as yet, I have not. It was of three stages: the first presented Sir Gaston, at some former time, mounted on a courser in a field of war, and this alluded to some valorous exploit performed in France; the second stage showed him kneeling before the King, who laid his sword on him, and rewarded him with knighthood; the third stage showed him in his Baron's robes, receiving from the King the hand of the Lady Barbara. There might you see every particular of the ceremony, as it had appeared that morning to the very life. There, too, was the tomb of Geoffry de Clinton; but the stranger, which had appeared there, was not mimicked. – While the Baroness looked upon this, with most serious countenance, suddenly she fetched a deep sigh, and fell from her seat like one dead. The Queen's maids and the bride's maids thronged about her, but none could tell the cause of this her sudden discomfiture. Though some readily guessed it was a recollection of what had happened to the Baron, that morn; others in the hall affirmed, that they had just heard a voice speak these words: 'Three tokens of death!'

But the Lady Barbara herself, when she recovered, feigned her swooning was from the heat of the hall and the noise of the music; and, in trowth, this last was enough to make a stronger one than her to faint; and how the Prior sat it, who used always to cry out upon loud doings at feasts, was the wonder of many:

but, that night, he seemed as joyously given as any there; yet held he himself with all proper ceremony, and remained always at the abbot's board, saying little, unless to those near to him. The lady Baroness, at the Queen's command, was led forth awhile for fresher air.

There entered the hall, about this time, a jongleur, or glee-man, with harp in hand, clad in a cloak of grey, and took his seat at the lower end. His sandals were stained with marks of many a mile's travel; and he sat awhile wearied and breathless. Those, who saw him, supposed that he had been to Warwick castle, there to exercise his art, as so many others of his craft did; that, having heard the lord of that domain was here, keeping festival at Kenilworth, and knowing a jongleur to be always welcome at such seasons, he had posted hither, with all speed, not waiting even to amend his guise. Yet, marvelled they how he had gained admittance, in plight so ill becoming a King's presence; but there was that in his look and stature, that agreed as little with his apparelling, as that did with the King's high presence; and which checked the questions they would have put to him. A page, seeing his weary look, offered him wine and meat; but he, with gesture that spoke as much as words, refused the gift, but accepted the good will.

And now, the second course and a third being ended, came the heralds into the hall; and, with loud proclaimings, called out, three times, 'Largesse for the King, the Queen, the Earl of Cornwall, and the Baron de Blondeville!' shaking, the while, their great cup on high. And first they cried it before the King, at the foot of the dais, next in the middle of the hall, and last at the lower end. And, in their officious zeal to exalt those, who yielded most to them, they made the Earl of Cornwall King of the Romans; but this was yet to be, which well they wot, also how wishful their lord, King Henry, was to gain this dignity for his brother, and how much he had employed his power and treasure therefore.

The King, as he heard that title given, fixed an eye of correction on him, that spoke it; yet was he not displeased with him in his heart, and he sent one to command, that he should again cry 'Largesse' for the Earl, and so remedy the mistake, which was straight done accordingly.

And now the minstrels came down from their gallery, and sat altogether, at the board's end, at the bottom of the hall, eating of the feast and partaking of the largesse-cup; there to remain, till the disguisings should enter. And it was a brave sight to see them all apparelled in the King's livery, guarded and laced with gold; their virger, more glorious than the rest, still directing all their doings. They eyed the stranger glee-man askance, and asked him not to their board, wondering why he came thither, where was no need of him, as they thought, and viewing his apparel with contempt and himself with disdain, as treading upon the skirts of their greatness, he being no better than a wandering minstrel. He seemed to read their thoughts, and his proud looks did somewhat daunt them; yet did his ruffled spirit take refuge with his harp and gain strength from it; for, he soon struck forth sounds so strong and clear, as rung up to the arched roof, and filled all the hall with sudden wonder. Maister Pierre himself could not exceed him in force and spirit, and amongst the whole five of the King's harpers was not one, who might not have bowed before him. Soon, the hum of busy tongues, that had often filled the hall with noise as of the murmuring tides, so that the whole band of minstrels might hardly at times be heard, (yet seemed not one tongue louder than another) – soon that hum was husht and still, – and the sound of that harp alone rose up out of the silence, and spread its sweetness over all the air. Every face was turned, with deep attention, one way, in search of the minstrel, and every head was hung aside.

Observing this, he quickly changed his measure to one more wild and abrupt, and his eyes seemed to send forth sparks of fire, while he sang, with full and clear voice, parts of the famous lay of Richard Coeur de Lion, as

'Him followed many an English knight,'

and other lines. Prince Edward, the while, seemed to lose not a word he sung. When he came to the words,

'By the blood upon the grass
Men might see where Richard was,'

the glee-man could not end them before the Prince, forgetting where he was, and, with fiery eyes, as if inspirited by them, stood like a conqueror on his field. The glee-man proceeded.

'As snow ligges on the mountains,
Behelied* were hills and plains
With hauberk bright and helm clear
Of trompers and of tabourer;

* Covered

91

To hear the noise it was wonder:
As though the earth above and under
Should fallen; so fared the sound!'

When the harper had ended, the King asked who played; and, being told a wandering glee-man, drawn hither by the fame of the festival, his Highness ordered he should be taken care of and well supplied with banqueting.

And now, supper being ended, damask-water was brought for the King and Queen and the Archbishop to wash with. After, the esquires of the household taking the royal boards, with all their suttleties, and the yeomen making off with those below in the hall, the place was cleared for dancing and disguisings. Then the Bishops, though not my Lord of York, nor yet the Bishop confessor attendant on the King, held it time to depart; the abbots also; and, with due homage to his Highness, forthwith avoided; but not the Prior; he remained in the hall.

It was then, that the King's Highness sent his presents to the bride's-groom; being a rich cup-board of plate, the chief wonder whereof was a great cup of solid gold, standing on a eagle's foot. On the cover rose the head of a bird, whose eyes were of emeralds, and with his stooping beak he held the ring, which was set with rubies, as though by pulling the ring he would lift up the lid; his wings, half-folded, formed the two handles. Great store was set by the King upon the workmanship of this cup, he having himself ordered the device of the eagle, and, as some said, to show thereby how he would encourage the aspirings of the young Baron. Besides this, were six spice-plates and six great bowls of silver chased and two basins and ewers of the same. There were also six great silver pots for wine, with vine leaves set with emeralds twining round them, the grapes being of purple amethyst so cunningly enwrought, you would have thought you could pluck them. Many other things there were of this cup-board, too tedious to relate.

To the young Baroness, who was recovered, and had now returned to the hall, the Queen sent a set of golden baskets for sweetmeats and perfumes, wrought, as was said, by a Frenchman, and of so seemly a fashion, the like had never been seen before, but which made some to murmur, that her Highness liked only the workmanship of her own country. For this, the Baroness, led by her lord, advanced nearer to the Queen, and thanked her, with most sweet thanks; and then he his-self paid homage to the King for his princely gift, as doubtless he should have done before, but, perchance, his bride detained him to uphold her in thanking the Queen, before so great a company. Having done this, he took his station by the chair, his Highness often turning to him, with merry speech, to drive away the gloom, that yet, at whiles, hung upon his brow.

Presently, the tuning of many instruments without the hall was heard, and the sound of the bugle drawing nigh and nigher, till suddenly the skreens were drawn away, and there entered, at the bottom of the hall, a mountain moving on unseen wheels, piled up with green trees of every shade, which rose to a height of forty feet, or more, and spread itself on every side. On the steeps of this mountain, stags – for so they seemed – were bounding from rock to rock, and foresters in green, with their dogs, were hunting them to the sound of bugles, concealed amongst the woods.

These were all lords and men of honour, in goodly disguisings, so that you would have taken them for foresters and bucks, as they climbed up and down certain steps of this mountain, at the risk of their necks, and all for sport, and to please the King's Highness by their agility. And a pleasureful sight, ywis, it was to see them all running together, lords and knights and hounds and men of honour, as who should be first in his Highness's favour. All acquitted themselves to the very top of excellence; for, they had been well taught in the knowledge of hunting, which is now called "the mysterie of the forests."

Amongst them was Sir William de Mowbray, who, being somewhat of the fattest, was often fain to stop, and blowed so hard, that, had but a hunter's horn been clapped to his mouth, it would have tuned up as high as the best of them. There was also the young Lord de Lomene, a foreign-man, as light as the flame of a waxen morter, and he, stepping falsely, rolled down the side of the mountain from stair to stair, till he settled on the floor of the hall, never the worse for his forced performance, where he was received with a chorus of laughter and plaudits from the whole court[11].

But anon the sound of the other instruments was heard, and another pageant entered. This was a goodly disguising of ladies, to the number of twelve, all freshly apparelled in silks of Italy, and shut up in a lantern. Around this lantern were windows covered with lawn; and within, amongst these ladies and women of honour, were forty wax lights, so that they might be seen and

93

known, through all their disguisings, by every one in the court. Thus, these ladies of the lantern came on sweetly singing, like unto a cage full of birds, and playing on lutes and dulcymers, claricords, claricimballs and such-like instruments, with so pleasing noise, the like to it was never before heard, till they reached the upper end of the hall. There, ere they grounded, they were turned round, before the King and Queen, that all the goodly machine might be beholden.

Then, the rehersed, disguised lords and men of honour, descending from their mountain (the lantern standing aside), danced awhile together by themselves deliberately and seemly-ly, playing, all the time, upon the recorders and regalls and tabors, in harmony with the music in the lantern, which might be called 'light of love'; and, at certain times, tuning up, with most brave noise, and singing 'Hayle, comely King, the cause of all our mirth!' And, presently, these ladies and women of honour, making a beck, that they wished to be let out of their lantern, the lords and men of honour hastened to open the door and to let them out, and help them down, and then they all fell deliberately to dancing, and gravely disporting together, in a most seemly sort, full curiously, and with most wonderful countenance. The while, the mountain and the lantern vanished together out of the hall.

When this pleasant company of estates and gentils had ended their sports, and had dispersed to their seats round the hall, there was a ceasing of the minstrels; and, forthwith the voide entered, with the heralds blowing up before it. Then came two score and more of lords and knights and men of honour, some bearing golden spice-plates, other bowls of silver gilt, others golden cups; followed by esquires and pages, bearing great silver pots of wine, to fill up the rehersed cups, as often as they were empty.

And now the King stood up, and spoke right cheerly to divers about him, who had not approached him before, and, amongst others, to the Prior of St Mary's, he being still in the hall, although it was past midnight, and those of his house were rising to keep the first watch of matin. His Highness was yet speaking to him, when my lord Archbishop, who stood deliberately on the King's right hand, was seen to make the holy sign. Those, who observed this, marvelled, and the King, gravely accosting him, asked why, twice this night, he had made this sign. But the Archbishop, as before, answered not, save by a look of awe and reverence.

The King, turning his eyes, saw, standing firmly at the foot of the dais, one, whom he took to be the same person he had already seen, this night, in the gallery of arms; and this he judged, not by his face, for his Highness had not then distinguished it, nor could he now fully see it, shaded, as it was, by his visor; but by his singular figure, arrayed in complete armour. It seemed, however, as if his melancholy eyes were fixed upon the King. He stood motionless, and spoke not to any near him, nor did those near seem to regard him. For a moment, his Highness's attention was rivetted on the object before him. He then sent an esquire to learn who it was, that had come thus unusually accoutred for a festive hall; but ere the messenger had left the King, the stranger had disappeared in the crowd.

And now, while the King and the Archbishop seemed severally to be pondering their thoughts, a solemn air of music was heard, without the hall, and the approach of another pageant withdrew his Highness's attention, who enquired why this had not appeared before the voide, but finished by supposing, that it was some mysterie the men of Coventry intended to surprise him. He, therefore, graciously took to his chair again, listening to the sad and sweet harmony that advanced, while he ruminated on the late extraordinary occurrences; for, indeed, the quiet mournfulness of these sounds promoted the musing of melancholy thoughts.

At last, the pageant entered, and there appeared in the hall the presentation of a sea-shore, with high white cliffs, so cunningly mimicked, that it was the marvel of all, who beheld. There seemed the very waves, flushed with the setting sun and bickering in the light, as also breaking with gentle noise upon the strand; and a ship riding at anchor near, with a little boat lying on the beach, as if waiting to carry some one away. Now, the absence of certain evil sprites from this pageant, would have been enough to convince his Highness, that this was no mysterie of the men of Coventry, without the beautiful deception of the scene here played forth, – and he marvelled.

Then there came in, the music playing sadly, a knight and a lady, with two little children following. The knight took them up tenderly, and pointed to the ship, and kissed them. The while, the lady wept sorely, and hung upon the knight, who tried to comfort her, and, pointing to the ensign on his shield, which showed that he was prepared for the Holy Land, he knelt down,

95

and raised his hands on high. She knelt beside him, and then the babes, lifting up their little hands, knelt too; the music, the while, playing solemnly and sweet. Then they rose up, and the knight again kissed the children, and held the lady to his heart. After which, mariners came in, and, launching the boat, the knight departed for the ship. But the lady stood weeping on that sea-shore, and motioning with her hand, till he reached the vessel, and it sailed away.

But still she stood, while it vanished in that gloomsome mist, which now seemed to rise from the ocean, and to stain all that glorious west, where late the day had been. Then, seeing the bark no more, she turned away, and wept piteously, leading her little babes, and so she departed.

Then the sea-shore was gone all at once out of the hall, and the music changing to warlike strains of trump and clarion, straight there appeared, as if by very magic itself, a field of battle, with knights and banners, on one side bearing the holy sign. Nor was there wanting St George for England, the English lion, with many other true-hearted ensigns. On the other hand, were shown Saracens, with their crescents, glittering, as if the sun shone on them. At a distance, on the slopes of the hills, lay tents, with palms and cedars overtopping them. Nearer, on the low sea-bank, was a city of Palestine, with walls and mighty gates and domes and pinnacles. Within that sea-bay, too, ships rode at anchor. The tide was bright as amber, save where a sultry mist seemed to sit on the horizon, as if brooding a coming storm. Nay, such was the cunning of the scene, that you might sometimes think you heard the muttering thunder, which growls by fits so sullenly from far, before a tempest.

The King could not but marvel; and seeing this pageant was so different from those mysteries he had beheld played heretofore by the men of Coventry, and from any pageant he had yet seen enacted by English joculator, he asked what jongleur from the east now played forth his art; for the like of deception and device he had never seen before. His Highness then bethought him it might be that stranger glee-man, who had, this night, come into his hall, and he meditated a due reward for his invention and for his loyalty, which he doubted not would lead him to display here some noble exploit in Palestine of Richard the Lion, whose deeds he had in part already sung.

'Who is there,' said King Henry, 'would not think that show were living truth? The light is on the hill, as if the sun shone there.'

While he spoke, there rose from behind the hill a line of spears and crescents as of a vast army of Saracens coming down upon the Franks. As they came on, you might perceive their helms and brazen visors, till they spread down all the hill unto the tents of the Franks. Then might you faintly hear the clash of cymbals, the dread bray of Saracen-horns and, ever and anon, the thump of tabours. And now the fight began between the armies; and King Henry joyed to see Prince Edward watching all that was here enacting; he seemed to have King Richard's heart in very trowth.

When the fight began, which was fought as if for very life and soul, the Franks fought with bows, swords, spears, iron-maces and battle-axes; the Saracens with spears and scymiters chiefly. Presently was seen the knight, who had set sail in the ship, fighting hard with two Saracens. There were few in the hall, that night, who, when they saw him so hard driven, did not think of the poor lady and her little children, whom he had left behind, and wish him victory for their sakes, as well as for his holy cause. These Saracens wore frightful masks of brass, and laid about them with so great strength, that it seemed the knight must fall. He broke his spear, and then he fought with his battle-axe, and was nigh being overthrown, when another knight attacked the Saracens; and the first, having now but one enemy left, went off the field fighting with him manfully.

And so the battle held on, near to a besieged city; the Saracens, who were in it, sending forth wild fyre, called fyre-grekys, most like in shape to dragons and other dreadful beasts. Those, who beheld this, wondered at the surpassing cunning of the jongleur, and began to think he was one of those from the East, who practised arts of delusion; for, some such they were. There were even wooden towers set up, without the walls, by the Franks, that played their darts into the ramparts like unto hail. There were also mangenelles, which cast stones, and the famous mategriffon, invented by Richard the Lion; yet still no where was he seen in this pageant, so it was guessed this showed not a battle of his time, though it was fought where he had conquered. Presently, there came a pell-mell of Knights and Saracens, hand to hand, and, amongst them, that same knight, who had first appeared departing from his own land. He was again hard beset, but he brought down his nearest enemy to the ground, and the others then betook them elsewhere. He disarmed him, and held his wrested sword over his head. The foe begged his life, which the knight granted, but kept the sword, and with its aid, rescued a brother-knight from an enemy, and then departed.

Soon, flames involved the city; then thick clouds of smoke involved the whole in darkness; the shouts and trumpets sunk faint and fainter, and then were heard no more, and that glorious sight was gone for ever, no one saw how! Attention still pursued the sounds, and there was yet in the hall deep silence, when other notes than those of war began to breathe, notes of such sweet and lively joy, as thrilled the hearts of all, who heard them.

As they drew nigher, there came into the hall that rehersed sea-shore, with that rehersed ship upon the waves, and you might discern the pilot at the helm, and the sea-boys in their places; and straight that knight was landed. He kneeled, then with both hands held his shield on high, and looked up to the heavens; then he kissed the strand, the music playing all the while so solemn and soft, that not only many fair eyes, but many manly ones too, shed tears. Then the knight rose up, and departed, and the scene disappeared.

And now other sounds were heard, but of what instruments none knew. They were grave and sad, with sometimes dreary pauses, that made many to shake. Then a forest appeared, with gloomy woods, and no sunshine seen, save one gleam, which showed travellers coming on, as if to some towers, the tops of which were seen over the woods; and many in the hall said these looked like the towers of Kenilworth; others said they were different. It was now, when the light was failing on these towers, that a torch carried by one of the travellers began to cast its gleam beneath the boughs, and showed them to be three horsemen well appointed, one of whom appeared to be the very knight from Palestine; who the others were none knew; but the King viewed them with close attention, and with seeming displeasure; and now not one word was spoken in the hall, and every eye was watching what would befall next.

Anon there came out from the wood three men armed, and with masks upon their faces, who soon came up with the travellers and attacked them. These defended themselves as well as they could; but the knight being armed, it was he who fought well nigh for all. Now many stood up in the hall, and a murmur and confused noise ran through it, for they guessed in their hearts what this meant.

The knight had his helmet on, but the visor was open, and thus was his face exposed; on his helmet stood a raven for his crest, with open beak and wings half-spread. He fought manfully with the stoutest of the robbers, whose mask falling down to the ground, it was too plain, that his countenance was the likeness of one then living in the hall and standing by the King's chair. On this, every one in the hall, not excepting the ladies, stood up, some looking eagerly to the high board, and others to the pageant, while his Highness spake not, but sat as if sternly determined to watch this extraordinary delusion to the end; nor did he once look towards any one, who stood near him.

The end soon came; for the robber, wresting in a great struggle a sword from the knight, plunged it through his open visor, and he fell from his horse, a dead man. Then was there a universal groan throughout the hall. The robber departed, with the sword in his hand, and darkness fell over the whole scene, which appeared no more.

Now, the King rose impatiently from his chair, with looks of anger, and was about to inquire who had invented this deception, when he perceived before him again, standing on the steps of the dais, that very figure, clad in arms, which had before appeared there; and he knew it for the likeness of that murdered knight, whose fate he had just witnessed. There stood the raven on his helm, and there too, within its shade, appeared a countenance of deadly paleness, shrunk and fixed somewhat angrily upon the King. His Highness, for a while, stood petrified and with eyes amazed, as if he saw something that might not, with any endeavour, be understood; he seemed to strive for speech, and at last faintly uttered, 'Who art thou, and what is thy errand?'

Then, the knight, pointing with his sword to the Baron de Blondeville, who stood, trance-bound, beside the King's chair, his eyes glared, and a terrible frown came over his face. The Archbishop made the holy sign, as he had already done, this night before, when the King had seen nothing strange near him; and then stood with arms extended on high.

The figure still pointed with his sword to the Baron. Again, the King vainly demanded of the stranger, who he was? and, receiving no answer, gave order that he should be seized.

Then it was, that the Prior of St Mary's, having approached the King, suddenly stepped forward to arrest the stranger; though such service pertained not much to him; but he might have spared his pains; for, where he would have seized upon the stranger, he eluded his grasp, and stood afar off in the hall; and the Prior, struck with dismay, attempted not to pursue him. Then, his Highness, in great disorder, commanded, that all the doors should be shut, that he, who practised this delusion on the sight, might be discovered.

And forthwith, his Highness was obeyed; but the stranger glee-man, who was the person suspected, was no longer to be found. A murmur went in the hall, that he was an Arabian jongleur[12] – for, wondrous arts and deceptions those from the East were known to practise; and he was sought for without the hall, in many parts of the castle; but no where could he be seen, or heard of; nor could Maister Henry, the versifier, be found in the hall, whom the King called for, thinking he might know something of this jongleur, or how that strange mysterie, which had been shown forth, was brought about. Hearing this, the King was much moved; and commanding that the search should be continued, he left the hall by a private passage, leading to his own chambers, followed by the Queen and her ladies; the young Baroness being among them, who went off to her Highness's bower.

The King, attended, by his especial order, only of the Archbishop, the Bishop confessor, the Prior of St Mary's and the Baron de Blondeville, withdrew to his privy-chamber. When there, and the door closed, the Baron fell on his knee, and besought his Highness not to deliver him over unto the malice and envy of his enemies, who had invented this device to work his ruin. His Highness answered, the devices of his enemies should cause their own ruin, and that soon.

Now came to the chamber, Maister Henry amazed and trembling; for he was one, who rejoiced so much in good fortune, that he could bear other as ill as any man: and the King's frown was now upon him. His Highness asked, whether he knew aught of the jongleur, who had been that night in the hall, or of the mysterie, that had been there enacted; for, in his heart, the King suspected, that Henry knew something of the matter.

Maister Henry, confounded by the King's angry looks, knew not well what he answered; which confirming the suspicions against him, his Highness hastily said, that if it should be found he had assisted in devising that delusion, which being an insult to the Baron, whom he favoured, was one also to himself, he

100

should sorely repent his misconduct; nor should he go entirely free, if he had obtained an entrance into the hall for that jongleur; and forthwith his Highness commanded him to depart to his chamber, there to remain, till called forth by his order.

Now it was that Maister Henry better found his speech, and it was to protest his innocence of that device; and his ignorance, touching the jongleur, who had that night appeared in the hall, there to practise the glamour-art; but this availed him little in the present mood of his Highness, till he entreated, that the master of the revels and the marshal of the hall should be called into his presence, and questioned, as to what they knew of the conducting of that pageant. The King consented, and they were called accordingly; the marshal being still busy in the hall, helping there to the finding out of the stranger, but in vain. This he now made known to the King, and scrupled not to say, he believed the whole to be the work of magic, worked by that jongleur and by the prisoner then in a tower of this castle.

The master of the revels said the same, for that he had no hand in that mysterie; nor had he seen any preparations made for it; nor did any one in the hall know in what way it had entered. Then he took his Highness to witness, how it was possible, so marvellous a pageant, showing so many changes, and such a multitude of people, could have been completed, without long pains and trouble; and therefore, how it could have been effected, unless by the glamour-art; but no prepration for this had been seen by any; nor knew he or any one how the different changes had entered the hall. The jongleur had sitten there the while, playing on his harp, but he had drawn from it sounds of many different instruments, that sometimes had seemed close where he sat; and at others far off in the hall; the music, that had been heard there, was not of the King's minstrels!

On this, the Prior of St Mary's came forward, and, having craved leave to speak, which was granted, told the King he doubted not, that the whole deception had been wrought by the King's enemies with certain spells of magic, such as were sometimes resorted to, in desperate cases, and in this it was not the Baron's downfall alone that they meditated, but the deliverance of their partner in guilt: the merchant now in jeopardy. Of such unlawful arts of magic, the Prior added, that his Highness himself had once proof[13], when the precious ring, that was to render him invincible in battle, was conjured away

101

from under the bolts and locks of his casket, (those remaining unbroken,) and was conveyed away by the Earl of Kent, as his Highness had declared, and given to his dire enemy, Llewellyn of Wales, then in arms against him.

The King seemed struck with this, but not well pleased with the choice of this time for remembering an occurrence, which, it is true, he had himself in council asserted to be supernatural; and had even urged, amongst other matters, in accusation of the loyalty of that lord. His Highness seemed not well to know how he should take this speech of the Prior, and he cast upon him an eye of doubt, but he said nought.

'My liege,' added the Prior, 'when I saw the astoundment, that came over the Baron de Blondeville, this morn in the chapel, I guessed it was a spell that fixed him. When I saw him in the hall, this night, twice in the same state, I held more surely it was so; but, when I beheld that marvellous delusion of the pageant, for who could suppose such surpassing scenes were wrought by hands – when I beheld that, I was convinced, in very truth, that magic was at work! and so I doubt not was my lord Archbishop, by his gestures.'

The King, assenting in his mind to this latter assertion, having observed, as before rehersed, the gesture of the Archbishop, turned towards him, and asked why he made that sacred sign? To which the Archbishop answered, he had used it to protect his Highness and all around from the evil, that he perceived was near him. At these words the countenances of the Baron and of the Prior brightened. Further the King inquired, why twice in the hall, when he had asked the same question, the Archbishop had returned no answer? To this, the Archbishop again made no reply; but bent his head with that look, both solemn and submissive, which he had before put on: till, being further urged, he replied, he 'had not dared to answer!' on which the King showed surprise and displeasure; but then seemed, on a sudden, to restrain the expression of either.

The Prior said, the Archbishop had done well; but the Archbishop showed no pleasure at this, and deigned not to turn an eye on the Prior.

'Did you,' said the King, 'think your answer would endanger you?'

'My liege, I knew I should be endangered by it.'

'How! when I commanded?' said the King; 'but you feared the force of magic?'

102

'No! my liege.'

The King looked again astonished, and the Prior curious. 'Whence then was your danger?' said his Highness.

'From the malice of an evil sprite, my liege!' answered the Archbishop.

At this, the Prior, with a sarcastic countenance, said, 'Perhaps, my lord Archbishop has not told the whole: I have heard it said, – speak it with submission, for I mean not to throw slander, – have heard it said he doubts of witch-craft, if so he may doubt of magic!'

On this, the Archbishop, turning loftily to him that spoke, said, 'The Archbishop of York comes not to the King's court to make confession to the Prior of St Mary's!'

Then the King, seeing the weighty displeasure of my Lord of York and the rising anger of the Prior, interposed, and put an end to further question between them; but the Archbishop's eyes were sternly fixed upon the Prior's, which fell beneath them. He then craved a private hearing of the King, for to-morrow, and departed; leaving the Prior angry and confused, but not dismayed; for, soon as he was gone, he said in a low voice, which yet might be heard by the King, 'so depart from me all prejudice and callousness of heart.'

To which the Baron said, 'Such is my wish too.'

The King, convinced, by this time, of the innocence of Maister Henry, the versifier, ordered with kind words that he should be dismissed, and then, commanding all present to avoid the chamber, save the Baron de Blondeville, and the Prior of Saint Mary's, remained in close council with them, though it were past midnight.

Meanwhile, the whole company below in the hall remained close shut up, while the search was yet going on in the chambers and gallery above, for those, who might have been concerned in this marvellous deception. There were the marshal, the steward, the constable of the castle, and other great · officers attending, to look after the little ones; but none of them could find either the supposed knight, or the glee-man. There were divers sayings and reports went forth on this matter, as, indeed, you must expect, without my telling; but most present held this strange accident was brought about with magic, and that by the inveterate malice of the Baron de Blondeville's accuser and his secret friends. Some few there were who remarked, that by this same power of magic, did he possess it, the prisoner had done better to release himself from prison bond, but these were soon put to silence by others; and, whatever was thought, nothing more was said.

And so ended the festival in hall, this night, every one departing to his lodging in the castle, or to his home in his own or his friend's castle, or mansion, with his own thoughts on the strange accident, that had befallen.

And, whatever might pass that night in this hall, raised up by beings of another region, nothing was known of it by those of this; for none would venture thither; and none, save the poor prisoner in his tower, would even look down from the chamber upon the windows of that hall. And so that place was in darkness and in silence, which so lately had been illuminated, had echoed with song and laugh, and was animated with the pomp of beauty and of a court—emblem of life and death!

The darkness of the hall was observed of the merchant from his turret lattice, for, he had watched much there this night, led thither by the sound of minstrelsy, and by a longing of his spirit to hover over the haunt of beings like unto himself. In the misery of his solitude, his heart would often change, and, like unto one tossing on a fever bed, who continually shifts his limbs in the hope of a little ease, so he went from his pallet to his window to escape from his own thoughts, and from his window to his pallet to avoid those sounds of joy and revelry, at which his heart sometimes sickened, when he remembered his wife and children, yet ignorant of his condition and his dead friend, whose cruel assassin was now his own dangerous enemy. Thus, he passed the hours, which to most in the castle had gone by with joy and abundance; he alone being ignorant of those marvellous appearances, which the Prior had not scrupled to say were raised by his art.

And so strongly did the Prior urge to the King, this night, the danger to be dreaded not by the Baron only, but by his Highness, from the powerful malice of the agents of the prisoner, acting by his art, if he were suffered to live, that the King resolved to have the matter fully inquired into to-morrow, in open court, his-self, sitting on the bench. But the Prior and the Baron, who had overheard the Archbishop's entreaty for a hearing, and feared he might unsettle the King's resolution, urged the matter still further, and representing the danger of waiting a jury-trial, dared to hint at sentence by other modes. The Baron even finished by saying, that not a moment of his life was safe, while his malicious accuser lived.

Whether the King fully understood, or no, what they meant by the words 'other modes', he did not fall into their plan, but repeated, that on the morrow, a jury should be summoned.

They then spoke plainly of trial by ordeal, but his Highness instantly rejected it. It was indeed over bold of them to propose such trial, knowing, as the Prior must know, that King Henry had shown his abhorrence of it, even in the first year of his reign, when he had abolished that cruel instrument of fraudulent oppression. And his Highness seemed not now well pleased; for, he straight dismissed them both, for this night.

Forth they went of the King's chamber together, and withdrew to consult further on this affair. It is plain the Baron had by some means gained the Prior, who was no true son of the church, to his interest. It was agreed between them, that he should lose no time in gaining admittance to the prisoner, for his own purposes, which might be done, under pretence of confessing him; and that before he left the castle, this night. Having fully settled their plot, they quitted the chamber, and were returning to the great stair-case through the brown gallery, now left of every one, who had rejoiced there, that day, when the Baron made a sudden stop, and, taking a torch from the hands of one of the silver images, which lighted that gallery, shook it on high.

The Prior, turning to inquire wherefore this was done, saw standing beside him, that same armed knight, who had appeared in the hall! While the Baron stood with eyes fixed upon this stranger, a wound in the forehead opened, and distilled three drops of blood, which fell unnoticed on the Baron's robe.

The Prior had well nigh sunk to the ground, but recovered himself enough to utter faintly, after some solemn words, – 'Who art thou?' The knight frowned upon him, but spake not; and presently disappeared, leaving the dismayed companions almost senseless.

They, however, left the gallery together; but, when they had reached the head of the stairs, the sound of cheerful voices was heard in an antechamber, and the Baron, encouraged by them, turned thither. But those, who talked, were only pages in waiting on some lord of the court, and they were still speaking of the marvellous occurrence in the great hall, that night, when the Baron appeared. Standing aside to let him pass, they wondered at his wild looks, as he went on to an inner chamber, where their masters sat.

The Prior, having also taken a light from one of the silver warriors[14], that held torches over the great staircase, descended alone, and was passing through the upper court of the castle, when, finding himself approaching one of the King's guard, on watch, he immediately extinguished the torch, and passed the man without it; but, whether he took his way to the prison-tower, or to the castle-gate, his further course was unknown; for, he was no more seen, that night.

THE FOURTH DAY: INTRODUCTION

Here was a drawing of a castle seated loftily on a rock, hung with thick wood, and having many towers on the precipice. In the margin was a portrait of an Archbishop, in his pontifical robes, probably designed for the Archbishop of York.

N THE morn next following the day of festival, my Lord of York had long speech of the King, and it was supposed, amongst other things, that he had been arguing against the truth of magic; for he was suspected of divers notions of that sort; it was also thought, that he had given no very favourable opinion of that same Prior of Saint Mary's. However this might be, his Highness, when he came forth of his chamber, was noticed to be thoughtful, and somewhat sad, and, though the summons for a jury was that day issued, his Highness seemed willing to let that matter rest awhile.

Instead of sitting in court of justice and on the judgment-seat, as he had sitten at Winchester[15], his Highness went hunting the stag in the forest, to his own contentment and to the great joy of his courtiers. And, ywis, this was a better chace, through these deep glades, and woods, than that upon the wooden mountain in the great hall; and more sweet and cheerily did the bugles sound along the valleys and upon the open hills than through the roofs and galleries of Kenilworth. There went with the King all of estate in the court (save the bishops) with the foresters of Ardenn, and also a train of gentils and gallants, to the number of many hundreds, and a great throng of people on foot.

The forest was covered with them, for miles, and nothing but the sound of bugles and other joyous instruments was heard through these deep shades, where quietness had dwelt, day and night, for so long a time before. Others there were, I guess, besides the beasts, lay hid in those pathless shades, listening to the revel rout afar off, and trembling too for very life, as it drew near; for, the forest was so wild and wide, spreading out on all sides and touching divers countries, that it was one of the chief hiding places for out-laws and desperate men in the whole realm of England, as those dwelling in the bordering towns knew to their cost. Many went wandering there, whom the world little thought of; and, who, had they been seen, could hardly have been guessed to belong to it, they had become so rude and uncouth in their seeming.

In the chase the King 'spied the towers of the Lord of Warwick[16], high over the woods, and that pleasant river of Avon, flowing beneath. The Earl, who was of his company, besought his Highness to repair thither, and to refresh himself in his castle; to which the King gave consent, that he might judge of it; his Highness being a great esteemer of the builder's art, and proficient in it, as his Abbey of Saint Peter, then rearing at Westminster, and the cathedral at Salisbury fully show; so he rode towards that castle; but, when he had mounted up the rock, he stopped before the great gates, in admiration of those warlike towers and hanging battlements, that rose to proudly over him. Then, he passed under the gateway into a court, surrounded by those towers, which all know to be of such vast strength, the bugles echoing through every arch and battlement, till he reached that pleasant side, where the turrets hang upon the precipice, that overlooks the Avon river.

As far as eye could reach, even in furthest west, to the broad hills of Gloucester, all the country, stretching below, was wood, or forest-pasture, with here and there the tops of spires and towers, whose convents and villages were so hidden in boughs, that, but for those little signs, you could not have guessed there were any goodly people dwelling in all that space. The King was well pleased with all that he saw at this castle, as he had been

107

before; but with nothing so much as with that broad and majestic round tower, standing guard, as it were, at the south-east end of the castle, with pending battlements, where, all night long, townmen marched around, and where, but high above, in that little turret, the warder keeps his watch.

Here Willoughton laid down the manuscript, and went to a window of his chamber, looking towards Warwick castle, that he might behold under the moonlight the very towers here mentioned. He easily distinguished the one here pointed out, and, although that called the Record Tower, at the other extremity of the eastern front, was admirable for beauty of proportion, he had many reasons for preferring the other; of which reasons there were two, first, that it was more ancient and had existed, at the time the manuscript referred to; secondly, that it wore an aspect of severer grandeur, and that by its singular construction, it showed forth much of the watch-and-ward habits and warlike foresights of that age. Willoughton thought he could never be weary of looking at it, under this shadowy moonlight; and already he fancied he could perceive half-armed men, on guard, pacing the battlement, and the warder's fire blazing on the summit and contending with the moonlight. The watch-signal too he heard; for, what else could be that, which passed on the wind, and which seemed to him so solemn, yet wild and so different from any thing heard in these 'piping times of peace' and luxury. Curiosity, as to the tale he was reading, brought him back, at last, to the manuscript and to King Henry.

King Henry stood long at a window of that side of the castle, which overhangs the Avon, and there he beheld, with delight, the great cedars[17] growing on a steep rock over the river, on whose out-spreading tops he looked down, as on a carpet of dark velvet, varied with silver. Certain, that castle of Warwick has a more pleasant scite, than this of Kenilworth; for, there your eye was carried, far and wide, over woods to the hills of other countries; where at Kenilworth, you see only the woods of its own valley, with the lake shining below them. Yet there were, who better liked the quiet shade of those majestic woods, that seemed to shut out all the world, save when the King brought it

108

hither, than the more free and lightsome prospect from the walls of Warwick; but, for mine own part, it was not so with me.

When that his Highness had tasted a manchet and had taken a cup of the fragrant Burgundy wine, of which my Lord of Warwick had good store, he hunted back to Kenilworth, followed by some of Warwick, whom he knew not of.

That night, the King kept his estate in the great chamber, with the Queen and all her court. There were the King's minstrels and there again was Pierre, the Queen's harper, who, by command from his Highness, sang forth a lay, made by Maria, the French poetess[18], who was now at the court, as aforesaid. She had presented her book to the King, full of marvelous histories, right pleasureful to hear, although they were not all true, nathless she had said to the contrary in the preamble to her book. The lay, played forth this night, was that of 'Guildeluce and Gualadun', or, as some call it, 'The lay of Eledire'. This was a knight of Bretagne famous for his high qualities, loved and honoured by his Sovereign, but envied and hated by many in the court, who, gaining the ear of their Prince, at length persuaded him to banish him they conspired against from the court and his country, leaving behind him a beautiful and excellent wife, whom they contrived to prevent from accompanying him.

It was said by many, in King Henry's court, that he commanded this lay to be sung, as a lesson to the enemies of the young Baron, that he suspected them of malice. Others said the example of Guildeluce might be a warning also to the young Baroness; for, they thought that of the two Guildeluce was the greater hero, as you shall hear. This wise and valourous knight, Sir Eledire, after vowing everlasting truth to his unhappy wife, set sail for England, there to seek adventures; and soon he found them. After achieving wonders, with the help of the ten knights he carried with him, in aid of a Prince of this country, he finished his exploit by falling in love with that King's daughter, contrary to all his former reputation, and setting his passion to fight with his duty, which had hitherto been sworn friends. There was a long contest, but unfortunately his passion conquered. Then, being recalled by his own Sovereign, who could not go on without him, having lost by his absence a great part of his territory, he carries off the young Princess, and returns to his affectionate Wife, estranged yet woe begone. The young Princess, who was as good as she was beautiful, soon as she

109

heard the knight had a wife, swooned away, and, not satisfied with that, died out-right. The knight goes nearly mad, and his distressed wife, to whom no one had told the whole truth, goes to a hermitage in a wood, to find out the secret cause of his distraction. There she sees the corpse of the beautiful Princess, and all jealousy and anger are lost, in compassion for her piteous fate.

Presently, the Princess by a charm is brought to life again; and what does this excellent wife, but determine to found a nunnery, and resign her beloved husband to the beautiful Princess. But the knight, her husband, would not be out-done in generosity, and what does he do, but build that very nunnery to receive her, and, having thus rewarded that excellent wife, he marries the beautiful Princess, without further fighting between affection and conscience.

Whether the young Baroness might be inclined, if tried, to profit by the example of this excellent wife is not known; but most surely some ladies would not; for, they scrupled not to take pains to say, that this was one of those lays of Maria, which were not true. They would not give it credence for a moment.

This lay, although we have here cut it short, rivalled Maister Henry's ballad for wearisome length; but the sweet thrumming of Pierre made the King endure it better; when it was well ended, there was great dancing amongst the ladies, and his Highness commanded the Baron de Blondeville to dance with the Lady Beatrice, and they went a solemn round together, to the joy of all that beheld them. You would have thought by his looks the young Baron had utterly forgotten what he had seen in hall and gallery, the night before; for, none in the court seemed more proud, or high in spirit, than he, or danced with a better grace.

The Archbishop of York was at the King's right hand, the whole even; but the Prior of Saint Mary's came not near the castle, all that night. Nothing happened to disturb the festival there; but at the priory was a strange accident.

It was before the first watch of matins, that a lay-brother went into the priory church to trim the lights, when, behold! the place, instead of being well lighted, was in total darkness, save that a gleam from the moon came in through the windows. Eadwyn could hardly trust his sight; for, never in man's memory, had the tapers there ceased to burn. But, while yet he stood amazed, he noticed something shining near the East end, as if a person stood there; and, the moon, soon after, coming out more brightly, he perceived the gleaming of steel; it was an armoured man standing still near a window, or rather under it.

Eadwyn had heard of what had passed, the night before, in the castle-hall; and he instantly became convinced this was the same appearance, which had caused so much marvel there. While yet he looked the figure pointed downward to the ground, near its own feet; but Eadwyn dared not to look again, but fled, as fast as age would permit him, to alarm the whole brotherhood.

Straight, they all flocked together to the church, failing not to bless themselves by the way; but, when they came there, the lights were burning as usual, and nothing new was to be seen in the place! Yet Eadwyn persisted in his say, and, pointing out the spot, where the supposed knight had stood, it was found to be over a grave-stone, without a name – so antient did it seem. The monks pored upon the stone; but, if a name had ever been there, not a letter could now be traced; and, if any present did guess whose bones were laid beneath, not one did choose to say.

The disturbance, caused by this strange accident, soon reaching the ears of the Prior, he forthwith came to the church, and, seeing the brethren in such number over this grave, it was noticed he looked more stern than ever; but, when they told what brother Eadwyn had related, he made light of the matter, and said, that his health must be looked to, for that infirmity of mind foretold infirmity of body. Then, he ordered him straight to his cell, there to diet on bread and water, for seven days.

Thus he ended the matter for this night, and in less than seven days did brother Eadwyn, poor man, end his sentence, for, he died on the fourth day, being above three-score and ten years, and of spare habit, having never been much in the Prior's favour. As he was proceeding to his cell, the Prior failed not to foretell from what he called the distemper of the brain, that his end was approaching; but all, who heard him, took not this matter, as he willed. He ended by warning the brethren not to go by night into the church, save at usual times, when all assembled, lest the folly of Eadwyn might disturb their minds with strange dreamings. Some, who heard him, smiled in secret, notwithstanding their grave deportment, and others, with wonder and trembling, promised to obey.

111

Here was a drawing of a forest, with a long cavalcade and procession, in other modes of the Court, winding under the shades. In the distance, where the light fell, tents appeared in a pleasant glade, and thence seemed advancing a body of Archers.

ING HENRY having commanded, that his court of justice should open, on the morrow, in the White-hall, in the castle, to administer the laws of his realm, summoned, this day, a court of pleasure, to attend him in the forest. The Archbishop was not of this train. Early in the morning, he had departed on his way to Coventry, a short journey from this castle, to visit the Bishop, Roger de Wesham, who there lay sick, at Saint Mary's. And this he did not only in kindness towards him, but for certain more private reasons. Since his discourse with the King, his Highness had seemed willing to move more deliberately in this business of the Baron, and to sift it to the bottom, that the foul slander, as he held it to be, which had been thrown upon his favoured servant, might be exposed, as well as that his life might in future be shielded from the evil arts of sorcery, if such should appear to have been practised by his accuser, in the hall of banquet.

His Highness guessed not, that other than just means might be resorted to against the merchant's life, while he remained in prison, friendless and a stranger, as he was, in this place; much less suspected he, that, in his own court of justice a verdict might be given against an innocent man. A jury had been summoned in this matter, and had been ordered to be in readiness, however suddenly called upon to meet in court. And there the matter rested, his Highness, meaning to keep up this festival with princely diversions, having gone forth, with the Queen and all his court, to divert himself in the chase of Kenilworth and forest of Ardenn.

The Queen was in her litter, hung with purple velvet, broidered with gold, drawn by milk-white steeds richly harnessed; six esquires riding before her; with divers of her Court, and six pages running beside her, and compassed all about, with noble ladies and officers of her state. Chiefest among the ladies, for gracefulness, went the Baroness de Blondeville, on a white palfrey. A palfrey of the like, led by two pages, followed the Queen, for her Highness to ride, when she should so mind. The Countesses of Cornwall and Pembroke-Montfort were likewise in their litters, gorgeously apparelled, with a press of noble dames compassing them about and pages and footmen.

Before the King rode the Lord Warden of this forest, attended by the Verderer and other guardians of the vert and venison, with fifty archers, clothed in green, moving in pairs, and sounding by turns their bugles, with right merry glee. First began the four nearest his Highness, and, when they took breath, eight struck up, further on; then again six sounded, and so the music rose and fell throughout the line with most sweet changes. The sound roused up the stags in the forest, and many a one afar off was seen to bound athwart the avenues from shade to shade. But the King came not to hunt, this day, nor would he let an arrow be levelled at any he saw, though this might have been done, without fear of hitting; for they flitted from gloom to gloom, like a sunbeam among clouds, and hardly could you tell when they had passed.

But that, which most delighted the Queen's ladies in these wild woods was to see the nimble squirrels climbing among the boughs, and springing from branch to branch, so full of happy life it was a pleasure to behold. And some, when they had gained the topmost boughs, would quietly sit, cracking the chesnuts and securely looking, with their full, quick eyes, on the company below.

There, I fear, were some, overborne by their own evil passions and galled by the consciousness of them, who might look up to those poor animals, with momentary envy. And doubtless many, who had not these painful reasons for choice, thought it were better so to live amongst these woodlands, in blessed ease and sprightly health, than confined in the golden trammels of a court, where every feeling was checked, that it might move only to certain steps of order, and nature was so nearly forgotten, that, if perchance she did appear, she was pitied and reproved for a child of ignorance, and straight altered after their own fashion. And there were few, who, when they came abroad amongst the hills and forests and the free air and the open sunshine, and heard the joy of birds, and saw the playful grace and glee of animals, there were few, who felt not

113

their spirits dance, although they knew not it was in sympathy
with free and guileless nature, which, if they never more could
resume it, yet could they never, even in spite of themselves,
entirely cease to love.

This noble company had not gone many miles under these
forest shades, ere their horns were answered by others, afar off,
that made every hill and dell to ring; yet feared they not what
this might mean, nor made halt to inquire. Presently, coming
where the woods opened, they espied in a green lane a demi-
circle of tents, and on the hills beyond a body of archers –
outlaws they seemed to be – three hundred at the least, drawn
up in battle-array, as if ready to meet them. The noble company
nothing daunted, still advanced, and the King ordered his
bugles to sound a parley; the which was no sooner done, than all
the echoes of those hills answered with horns, and straight the
captain of the band came down upon that little plain, attended
by twelve of his archers and by two pages, one leading a brace of
milk-white greyhounds, in a chain of steel, the other bearing his
bow and arrow. These approached the King, cap in hand, and
then, dismounting from their hobbies, the captain, who was no
other than the King's bowman of this forest, taking his bow and
arrow from the page, fell on one knee, and presented them to
his Highness.

The King, having shot off the arrow, graciously returned the
bow, with a purse of gold, and bade him rise, which he refused
to do, until his Highness, and the Queen should grant his
petition, which was, that they would repair to the tents, and
there rest; while his archers sought to entertain them with
their bows. This granted, the bow-bearer rose, and, leading
those snowlike greyhounds, whose necks were bound with
collars of ebony inlaid with silver, presented them to the King,
as lord of this forest. But they were the Queen and her ladies,
who best welcomed those delicate animals, admiring their
slender forms and dainty coats, white as the ermine on their own
mantles.

Forthwith, their Highnesses, with this noble company,
repaired to the tents, where they found venison ready prepared
for them, with other game, such as these woods afforded, and
wines and fruits of Autumn, all set forth on boards dressed out
with oaken boughs, so that every table seemed a bower. The
rustic seats of the King and Queen were raised on turf, not
carpeted with tapestry, but strewed with flowers, and, for their

canopies of estate, they had arching branches of chesnut, wreathed with sweet woodbine. The wine was brought in beechen cups, carved from that noble tree, that stretched forth its mighty branches over the King's tent, and then sent out its spray, so lightly and so proudly, above the flag of England waving there. Also, instead of damask water in golden ewers, water, clear as crystal was brought in beechen cups, and in hunters' horns, bound with silver, from the wild brook, that ran among the rocks, and that made, in its lonely course, still music under the green shadows.

It was a goodly sight to behold the tents ranged beneath the trees on the short sward, filled with fresh ladies and other noble company; and the King's tent, where attended the Lord Warder and all the officers of the forest, in their peculiar habits of ceremony – encompassed by his archers in green, with lords and knights in hunting habits, and with esquires and pages in his Highness's livery, glittering with divers colours. The place of every one was so well ordered, that there seemed not any crowd; each rank being set forth to the eye in due degree of beauty and proportion, one beyond another. And first, between the tents, stood the King's demi-lances, and the archers, who had run before him; behind these were the King's horsemen, and others of his train. Somewhat apart stood the Queen's litter, having her cloth of estate over it, with her richly caparisoned palfrey, and pages in waiting; near it were the sumpter-litters of her sister, and of the Countess of Pembroke-Montfort, with coursers, squires and grooms, countless. But the chief sight was the tents circling this pleasant green, all filled with estates and gentils, freshly apparelled, and with banquet-boards so gaily decked, and the lofty trees of beech and oak that overtopped them all.

On the hills, opposite to the demi-circle of these tents, were drawn out the three hundred foresters, who feigned to be outlaws of the forest, presenting Robin Hood[19] and his company.

And, when the King and Queen had refreshed themselves, the Lord Warden of Ardenne, his-self, who had withdrawn from the banquet, came riding up to the tent, blowing the ivory horn, which was hung about his neck with a chain of silver, and which was the sign of the charter, by which he held his office, and having done homage, asked, if it so pleased his Highness, to see his archers shoot; to which a gracious answer being given, the Warden gave signal to the bow-bearer, who straight made sign to his men, and the whole troop shot off their arrows, which had whistles in the head, with so loud a noise as amazed and rejoiced the hearts of all present, and roused the stags from their coverts, and sent the birds from their leafy homes in flights, athwart the sky.

Then, were many noble bows drawn to shoot at the deer, as they scudded away under the shades; but the Queen benevolently said, 'Nay; shall our delight in these pleasant woods, be the cause of suffering to their innocent tenants! Let every beast and bird be free and happy now, as we are.' And his Highness said it should be so this day, and forbade them to shoot. A fence had been fixed, as was the worthless way, and the game was to have been driven into it, and there shot at by her Highness and the ladies of her court. For this purpose, also, there had been prepared arrows, plumed with peacock's feathers, and having heads of bright silver; and now, that a better sport might not be lost, hazel wands were set up, at due distance; from which were suspended garlands of roses, roses of Provence, the Queen's country, for such they seemed, whether the work of nature or of cunning skill; and at these garlands the ladies of her Highness practised for prizes, which the Queen distributed, who, naithless that this adventure had seemed to fall out by accident, was well aware of all that was to happen, and came prepared for it.

His Highness's sister, the Lady Pembroke-Montfort, won a golden arrow, and the young Baroness de Blondeville a silver bugle; which the Baron, her lord, tuned up in most sweet triumph of her victory.

After these feats, the archers of Robin Hood practised with their bows, the hazelwands having been removed to more than treble the distance; and they played off such cunning skill, as made marvel all those, who had before prided themselves in their own performances. Often were the rosy garlands scraped by their darts; or the hazel-wands that held them, shivered. A sheaf of silver arrows and a bow were the prize of the Lord Warden, the captain of the band, who was also well-known to be the best bow-man. After they had ended this sport, they went through divers courses and devices on horseback, feigning a battle, and sounding their bugles, and hiding in the woods; and then coming back, in pursuit of one another, to the great delight of the whole court; and to none more than to the Prior of Saint Mary's, who was in the King's train; for he joyed in sports of the forest more than well became one of his calling.

And no sooner was this ended, than there was heard from that woody brow, behind the tents, a sound of sweet minstrelsy, of tabours and flutes and viols and other joyous instruments, the which signal was well understood of many present. Straight, the King and Queen, with the chief nobles and gentils of their courts, departed thither-ward, whence the sound came, leaving the rest and the archers of the forest, to make merry in the tents.

Having gone up, beneath the woods, their Highnesses came at last to that lofty brow, where the minstrels were assembled, and which overlooked the country, far and near, except where the forest-oaks now and then interrupted the prospect. There might you see, as you looked down under their dark branches, the towers of Kenilworth far off in the sun; and, beyond them, all that wide forest-region, reaching to the Charnwood-hills in Leicestershire; so distant, they seemed blue as the air above them, and none here would have guessed what ancient woods were on their steep sides, dark even as these oaks, which stretched their boughs athwart that lightsome blue.

But neither the lofty spire of the abbey church of Leicester, Saint Mary de Pratis, nor the town could be spied; for they lay low at the feet of these hills. On another side, you had but to look down, where you could find an alley in the woods, to behold the Castle of Warwick proudly over-topping the vale, and seeming the very lord of those plains, that spread out on all sides, even to the hills of Gloucester, which his Highness had noted from that castle's walls. Some said you might perceive the stately tower of Gloucester Abbey; but of this I know not; for, my eyes could never make it out; yet it might be seen by others, which had not pored so many midnights by the blunt light of tapers; for, this makes things of day, if they be far off, invisible to eyes so used.

I do remember me, when Robert of Gloucester[20] vaunted of his abbey, Saint Mary de Pratis, at Leicester, he said from top-most spire you might see beyond a hill of Ardenn; but I believed him not, taking it for a triumph over our priory, which he said was so darkly closed in of forests, it seemed more like a cell of penance than a good prior's house. And when I asked him how often in the princely castle, that stood nigh his abbey, King Henry had kept his court, he was put to silence, though he might have remembered that our good King did, at his abbey, first receive the crown he wore.

117

From this hill, too, you might espy the town of Coventry, with Saint Mary's, and the convent spires of that village of Eaton, called of the nuns, Nuneaton. Certes, this was a pleasant brow; for, wherever the woods opened, these wide prospects spread; yet, turning from them, you seemed hid in boughs and lonesome wilds, where neither town nor castle could be seen, nor any pomp, save that blessed one of these shades; nor any living thing, but what they bred.

And here, where the oaks stretched round a green plat, leaving only a little opening towards those blue forest hills of Charnwood, here was a noble tent prepared for King Henry and his court; there was none other on this spot; but seats were cut in the turf around, under the boughs for such as were not of estate; and there, too, sat the minstrel, tuning up with merry glee, opposite to the King's tent, where the woods parted.

When this noble company had rested awhile, and had taken leche lardys and wine, and had spied out from this summit all, which those, who knew the country, pointed out to them, the Countess of Cornwall went forth of the King's tent; and, according to the pleasant fashion of her country, danced on the green-sward under the trees, with the Lord Simon de Montfort. She moved with a noble grace, as was reported by those present; first, in a bass-dance; and then, springing up with lighter grace, she ended with a measure that showed off all the gaiety of her own land, and so much rejoiced the heart of the Queen, her sister, that, but for her dignity, she would have danced also. I guess it brought back to her mind the festivals of her father's court, in that pleasant land of Southern France, called Provence, where they love to sport in the open air, nigh the shade of woods, and will pass a summer's day to the sound of flutes and viols; their banquets being of fruit, fresh gathered from the orange-trees and the vines, and being laid forth on the grass, beside some windling brook.

And it was to pleasure the Queen, with a banquet like to what she had been 'customed to in her own country, that King Henry had thus come forth into these forest-shades. This was a day, that suited well his purpose; it was a calm, sunshine day, when the air, so balmy soft, showed every near object as if nought but crystal interposed – and every thing distant – hills, water, sky, as it were dressed in azure; it was surely a blue day, such as is seldom seen in our Island prospect, save in the parting month of autumn, though often in that pleasant part of France, where these diversions seem devised to make the most of the climate.

When that the Countess of Cornwall had ended her dance, the Queen invited several foreign noble lords and ladies, visitors from her own land, to dance divers rounds of their own country. Amongst these the Baron de Blondeville figured; and truly, when he led off the dance most joyed in by the villagers on the banks of the Rhone, none did so lightly bound, nor throw up his cap in the air, with gayer grace than he. As for the young Baroness, who could trip more blythely, or more delicately express every joyful feeling than she showed here, this day?

> Lightly as the willow-spray,
> Dancing to the airs of May.

And thus this noble company disported themselves, until the day was far spent; and then set they forth in state and order for Kenilworth, the whole troop of forest-archers attending the King to the gates of the castle, whence they departed not till after due regale, nor till the sun had well nigh gone down. As they went, his Highness's command was conveyed to them, that they should attend him to hawk on the river of Avon in the forest, and should there partake his banquet.

119

THE FIFTH DAY & NIGHT

Over this Chapter was a drawing of the poor Merchant's prison-chamber; it was night; for, a lamp burned beside the pallet, on which he lay stretched. A face appeared dimly, behind the grating in the back wall.

HIS DAY, the King's Court of Justice was opened in the White Hall of Kenilworth, and divers matters adjudged there; but the cause of the merchant came not on. It hath been already related, that King Henry was inclined to move more deliberately in this matter than he had at first been; but there were some about him who were desirous to urge it to a conclusion, before the return of the Archbishop of York from Coventry: and for this they had weighty reasons of their own. It has been shown, that the Archbishop inclined somewhat to the cause of the poor merchant, and that he was no friend to the Prior of Saint Mary's. Now, neither the Prior, nor the Baron de Blondeville, augured well to themselves from the Archbishop, seeing the manner in which he had held himself towards them; and they sought, by all means, to have the prisoner disposed of, before the return of that powerful and intrepid prelate.

This day, the Prior came to the castle; and, after a private conference with the Baron, in which they settled their plot, the Prior craved hearing of the King, and set forth somewhat of the strange appearance at the Priory, on a late night; but he told only as much of the truth of that adventure as suited himself, and added to it as much falsehood as he dared. Having then declared the whole to be some new artifice, practised by the secret friends of the merchant, he besought the King to relieve the Baron from the unseen dangers, made to impend over him by the malice of his enemies, and which, he said, would not cease so long as his accuser remained unpunished; for that the accusation was a guilty one he had no doubt. To this entreaty the Baron joined his, that the King would end this matter, as might seem right to his Highness, pleading that his peace and honour were alike in jeopardy, during every hour of this season, in

120

which he had looked only for joy and gladness; since, however fully and highly he was honoured by his Highness's favour, and however he his-self might seem, in the face of the court, to bear the slander, neither he, nor any one of those most dearly connected with him, had known one moment of real comfort, since the accusation was first made.

The truth of this King Henry admitted; yet was he firm in refusing to hasten unduly the trial of the merchant; and they, suspecting that his motive for this was chiefly to have the Archbishop present when it should come on, urged their petitions, till his Highness's visible displeasure put an end to further hearing. And thus the business rested for this time: the Prior departing for his chamber, and the baron to prepare himself to attend the King, in the great chamber, where his Highness was to keep state. There was rehearsed before the King a Servantois, composed by Maister Denis Pyramus, setting forth divers brave deeds of chivalry. Nothing extraordinary happened this night; and the court broke up at the usual time, every one seemingly well contented and at peace. But, what human being may look into the secrets of the heart? many, that lay beneath this roof, from King down to serving-man, were pressed with heavy cares, each in his way, but none more heavily than the Baron de Blondeville.

Now every one was gone to his own chamber, for all night, and the wayte, with his groom bearing the torch, was going his second round, when a person passed athwart the upper court, who answered not the watch-word. Both the old man and his boy saw this person beside them; but he was gone, before the challenge was repeated; and he was so muffled up in his garment, they could distinguish neither shape, nor feature. But they had marked the way he went, and they followed his steps, which led them to that great tower, still called of Caesar, which was the keep; on it pended the prison-turret of the merchant. Marvelling who might go there at this hour so privily, they tried the door of entrance, but found it fast, and then the bars of the tower windows, and they too were safe. The great gate of the portcullis, where the wardours kept guard, opened not into this court, but over the ditch, on the other side of the tower; or the wayte would have speedily given the alarm, for he thought all was not right.

He guessed he had mistaken the way this person had gone; but, stepping back and looking up at the tower, his boy spied a light passing by a casement, on high, which he knew led up a staircase to the prison-chamber. So the old man suspected some plot was going forward for the liberty of him confined there, and he gave an alarm at the door beneath; presently on which, he heard the keeper's voice within; who, being asked whether any one had just entered the tower, answered 'No'; and, being then asked whether any one had passed up the staircase with a light, he said he knew not, others were dwelling in the place, besides himself. The wayte told him what he had seen in the court, and that he suspected some one had entered the tower with a false key; to which the keeper answered, that could not have been without his hearing; and bade him go on his watch-way, and, if his sight had not deceived him, he would find, perchance, the person he suspected lurking within the court, in the porch, perhaps, of the great hall, or under the archway of the white tower. Though the old man thought all was not right, he went his way, and searched the places noted and every other corner of the court; but he found no one. The more marvelling, he determined to look well to the prison-tower, and, if any one came forth of it, to seize him, if he might be strong enough.

And so, having sung out his second round, for this night, he concealed his torch, within a buttress-nook, where it lay smouldering; and then, with his boy, he took his station in the front of King Henry's lodging, which was opposite to Caesar's tower. Little did his groom-boy help him; for, he was soon asleep and snoring loudly enough to bid any one lurking in the court to beware of his master; the torch itself could not more surely have betrayed their station; but the aged man, who could better wake than slumber, sat still and watchful on the bench, within that porch, often silencing, though it were but for a minute, his drowsy companion. Still and watchful did he sit in that gloomy porch below; but there was one as still and wakeful in the tower above, lying on his pallet, full of grievous care and dread of what might happen.

This poor merchant, when he knew of what he was accused, saw, that his destruction was appointed, and that the Baron de Blondeville, to save himself, had contrived this pretence of delusions and evil arts practised by him. He had been told to prepare himself for trial 'on the morrow'; and he suspected not that he was deceived, or that there could be any motive for deceiving him, in that respect. The King, as before said, had steadily refused to have the merchant tried on the morrow; who, notwithstanding, had been bidden to hold himself in readiness for that day. And to that morrow he now looked with dread and despair; for, how could he defend himself from that terrible shadow, which he heard his enemies designed to raise up against him? how strike a phantom, which, though armed with the deadly weapons of malice, was invulnerable as the air – the phantom of sorcery? Thus, he foresaw that his sentence was passed: and, when he thought of his distant home, his wife and children, who, ignorant of his wretched state, were now expecting him with fond impatience, from a foreign land, and whom he must never more behold; – when he thought of this, he was little able to meditate what he should say, or do, when he should be confronted with his enemies. Thus he passed several hours.

At last, when he considered the virtuous motive, which had led him into this jeopardy, and the wickedness of his accusers, pious confidence began to possess his mind; indignation struggled with his grief, and his apprehensions vanished. In these moments, he believed himself capable of rousing conviction in the minds of the judges, by the strength and eloquence of indignation alone. He forgot, that it had hitherto failed him with King Henry; but such courageous hope rose and fell with his sorrow, giving place to deep despondency and weakness, whenever he thought much of his wife and children.

The suddenness of his first appeal to King Henry prevented him from perceiving the danger of accusing the favourite of a prince; nor considered he his own helplessness, though he was in this place a friendless stranger: he felt only a generous sorrow for his murdered kinsman; he balanced not the difficulties with the justice of his purpose. And, truly, his peril arose not from any indifference of the King to do what was right, but from the want of steadiness in his mind, and from that mis-directed kindness of heart, which made even a suspicion of guilt in one he had esteemed and trusted so painful, that a conviction of it seemed not to be endured. It is well-known, that a weak mind, rather than have such a suffering, will turn aside, and take shelter in willing credulity to its first opinion; a strong one, meeting the worst at once, will proceed straight forward, and, freeing itself from an uncertainty, will do both that, which is just towards others, and, in the end, best for its own ease. Which of these ways King Henry took will be more fully set forth hereafter.

Such thoughts as these had not occurred to the poor merchant, when most he needed them; but now, in the stillness of his prison, he considered of many things, which, amidst the interests of busy life, he would have passed unheeded. And much and often he pondered on what he should say, on the morrow – the day, as he supposed, of his trial – endeavouring to prepare himself for the questions, that might be asked him. Importuned with such thoughts, he was resting on his pallet, a lamp burning above him; when, without any previous sound even of a step, he heard the key turn in the door of his chamber, and with such cautious gentleness, as if some person tried by stealth to enter. He lay still, listening to what might follow; but the door opened not, there being a bolt within, that secured the prisoner from nightly intrusion. Of this, the person without knew not; for the key was still moved in the lock; and this showed to the prisoner it was not the keeper, who sought to enter. With a dread of some nigh evil, he looked round, and saw, through the grate opening on the passage, a light, that seemed to come from the stair; and, while he watched, behold a hand came through the grate, and tried to reach the bolt, which held the door within.

The poor merchant shuddered, when he saw those bony fingers stretched forth, with no weak impulse, to force back the bolt; and he started, when there came a face behind the grate, and he knew it to be the Prior's of Saint Mary's. His hand could not push back the bolt; and seeing, that the prisoner was now awake and watchful, he called to him by name, and desired him to unfasten the chamber. The prisoner demanded who came, at that unseasonable hour, and what he wanted; on which the Prior told his name, and that he came to confess him and prepare him for his trial, on the morrow. When the merchant observed, that the hour was extraordinary for such a duty, he was answered, 'it is never too late for a good work'; and was desired to open the door, without further speaking.

But the prisoner, misliking the visage of this Prior, whom he had noted, on a former occasion, and fearing some concealed mischief, still delayed to comply, saying, that for his trial he was as much prepared, as an innocent conscience could prepare him. On this, the Prior was angry, and said he came by the King's order, whose chamber he had just left, and, in his name, demanded entrance.

'If so,' answered the prisoner, 'I marvel the keeper is not with

124

you. Why come you alone, and at this dead hour? I beseech you let me go on with my night's sleep, which will best prepare me for the morrow's trial.'

'The King's order is sufficient for my appearance alone,' said the Prior. 'I require not the keeper's attendance at a confession; and, for his key, it is already in my hand; therefore, delay no longer, but draw that unlawful bolt.' The merchant said again he had no confession to make, and that, even if he had ought to tell, he could tell it through the grate, and there only would he answer, this night.

'You know not,' said the Prior, 'the good you are refusing; let me in, and you may hear that you expect not. Why should you suppose I come to you as an enemy?'

'Father,' said the prisoner, 'I have desired rest; and, in so saying, why should you suspect I take you for an enemy. I have never injured you, and am even a stranger to you; if, therefore, I ought to fear admitting you to this chamber, you best can tell why. But I crave rest; this is the reason for it, and well may I marvel you have chosen such a time wherein to visit me; and, yet more, why you come alone, without witness.'

'Come nearer to the grate,' said the Prior, 'and I will tell you.' The prisoner raised himself from his pallet and advanced. 'Come nearer,' said the Prior; to which the poor man, astonished at this eagerness, replied, that, where he stood, he could well hear even the lowest speech.

'Others, too, may hear. What I would say, is to yourself alone.'

'And what inducement can you have to confide any thing to me – a prisoner, without help, without council, without comfort, other than that of a good conscience? Since, then, I cannot administer to myself, what can I administer to you, that you should seek my confidence?'

'You may find, perhaps,' said the Prior, 'that you are neither without council nor help, if you will listen to me;' and again he bade the merchant draw nearer; on whose doing so, he asked him, if he wished for liberty? On this the prisoner smiled contemptuously.

'I hear the first matin-bell,' said he; 'it calls you – you had done better to be in your place than to have come hither, at such an hour, to tempt me by such a question.'

'I begin to think so too,' answered the Prior, 'since you are so obstinately bent against yourself; but open the door, and I will convince you I am your friend.'

125

'You must convince me of that, before I unfasten this door.'

What other arguments the Prior might use are unknown, but they answered his purpose so far, that the poor prisoner, at last, gave up his fears, and admitted him to the chamber. Having thus entered, the Prior fastened the door again, and, holding up the lamp to examine whether any one was concealed in the room, the full light fell upon his forehead, and showed a deep scar, that seemed to remain from a sword wound.

While the merchant stood observing his face, under this peculiar light, the scar suddenly engrossed his attention; and he thought he had seen the same countenance, at some former period of his life. He had little time for recollection; but he thought this was at an inn, between Tamworth and the Chase, as he was travelling with his kinsman from Worcester; the latter having landed at Milford, on his return from beyond the sea: but the recollection was indistinct; and he checked the fear, which was beginning to return upon him.

The Prior, after his survey of the chamber, met one glance of the scrutinizing eyes, that were directed upon him, and he immediately withdrew his own; and, sitting down on the low pallet, he thus addressed his prisoner: – 'Now shall you know me for your friend; for, here I tell you, that, if you wish to escape this night from the trial that threatens you, I have in my power the means of assisting you; and am ready to use them, on one condition!'

The prisoner, surprised and distrusting the motive of this offer, answered, 'You said but now, that you came hither by the King's order! Is it also by his order, that you bring me this offer of escape? He has only to will my freedom! and I shall go forth from these walls without any contrivance, or secret methods of my own.'

'Yes: and then you may, without further let, or hindrance, again sound forth your accusations against an innocent man! It is on one condition only, that his Highness consents to your escape. As to your going openly forth, with his known consent, free of punishment for your accusation against the Baron de Blondeville, that cannot be, and he preserve his honour: liberty, granted to you on such terms, would be the Baron's condemnation. This you must acknowledge. There is but one way, that can secure both his honour and your safety – only one!'

'Name it!' said the merchant.

'It is, that you set your name to this paper, containing a

recantation of all, of which you have accused the Baron before the King; and that you leave it behind you ere you take your secret flight, in sure testimony of his innocence.'

The prisoner, rising up with indignation, exclaimed, 'Never! I was witness to the crime, of which I have accused him, and never will I cease to demand justice for it! Nor will I believe King Henry would, in this way, shelter a man, whose honour he would fear to bring to trial!'

While he said this, the countenance of the Prior darkened; and, after a short silence, he replied slowly: 'I cannot doubt your knowledge of the crime; but I as little doubt the innocence of him you have accused. You err not as to the deed, but as to the criminal; and *your* crime lies in this, that you have rashly, and with unmeet confidence, charged a man with a dreadful offence, whom, even if he were guilty, you could have small means of knowing to be so. Your obstinacy, too, in persisting in this charge, when you have found who the accused is, takes away from you all claim to mercy; and, understand from me, that, on your trial to-morrow, you are not likely to find any. At this hour, to-morrow night, if you shall be then still amongst the living, you will remember, in despair, the opportunity, now offered you and now passing away.'

Scarcely had the Prior ended, when the bell of Saint Mary's sounded, and his visage altered, while he faintly uttered the latter words. He was mute awhile, and then he said, 'If you have resolved to proceed with this denunciation, I must leave you: if you doubt, mercy is still open to you; but no time is to be lost – I must be gone!'

'Could I doubt, for an instant, as to the person of the murderer,' said the agitated prisoner, 'I should indeed, be infamous, in accusing the Baron de Blondeville, and equally foolish in hesitating to accept your offer; but my memory is faithful; I never can forget the countenance of him, who murdered my kinsman, in my sight.'

'It is extraordinary your memory should have received so false an impression, if, indeed, you speak according to your conviction; it is extraordinary, that, considering the short opportunity you had of observing the robber's face, you should be so confident in that impression; you saw him only for a moment, and then by a torch lying on the ground. A light, so placed, might give a false appearance to any countenance.' He ceased, and the merchant remained thoughtful and silent.

'It is extraordinary, too,' said the Prior, 'that, recollecting so

127

clearly, the countenance of one of the robbers, you should have no remembrance of the others.'

'I saw not the faces of the others. You were present, when I related this matter to the King; can you have forgotten, that I said the other robbers were masked during the whole outrage?'

'I recollect you said so. And you say so now again? You are sure they were masked?' said the Prior.

'Yes, I am sure,' replied the merchant.

'Yet is it strange, that the man, who committed the murder, should be the only man of the four, who exposed his face.'

'The four! I saw but three,' said Woodreeve, eagerly. He looked at the Prior, who was, for a moment, silent. 'You must remember, I told the King, the assassin's *visor* fell off in the struggle with my brave kinsman.'

At this close recollection of the very manner of the deed, the prisoner was much moved; he groaned heavily, and threw himself again on the pallet, saying, 'Talk no more of this cruel transaction, I beseech you; it goes to my heart.' His visitor made no answer, and the merchant remained, for a short time, with his face hid in his hands, as if in an ecstasy of grief. When he raised himself and turned, he found the Prior standing close beside him, with an expression, which he did not, at the moment, understand.

'I must begone,' said the intruder; 'you will repent that you have neglected the opportunity; another will certainly not occur; and you deserve not that it should, since you can persist, on such slight grounds, in accusing a stranger of what would affect his life. I know the Baron de Blondeville to be innocent.'

Woodreeve was struck both with the emphasis and with the tone, in which this was uttered; it was not the usual voice of the Prior; yet did it seem the natural one, and not wholly unknown to him. Looking earnestly upon him, he said, 'Who is with me?'

His visitor, turning quickly at the question, answered not the scrutiny of the merchant's eye, but scornfully asked, 'Know you not the Prior of Saint Mary's?'

'I did know a Prior of St Mary's;' said the other sadly, 'you are not he. Moreover, your speech was but now changed, I knew it not for yours; not for the same I had heard a few minutes before, though it seemed not unknown to me.'

'That is strange; but your observance of my voice, seems to be about as certain as your recollection of the Baron de Blondeville's features; and I should not much marvel, if you were to

128

denounce it as a party in the same adventure. But I must leave you, and shall add nothing more, since you had rather remain a prisoner, with death before your eyes, than doubt the correctness of your memory, or recant from an error, when in so doing, you might save the life of yourself, or, perhaps, of an innocent man. Call not that a love of justice, which is blind vengeance in its blackest shape.'

There was something in these latter words, that now struck the harassed mind of the prisoner, with a force, which had not accompanied any similar exhortation from his adviser; a dreadful possibility was once more placed before him, and the moment was passing, in which by acknowledging that possibility, he might put an end to the fearful alternative, in which he stood, of losing his own life, or taking that of another.

'What if there be one possibility,' said he to himself, 'out of thousands, that I have accused an innocent person!' and he shuddered with horror.

The Prior instantly perceived the hesitation of his mind, and he waited awhile, that it might end in further doubts, which he knew would be stronger, if his now readier listener should forget them to have proceeded from his promptings, and should mistake them for his own. When he thought they had taken some hold, he threw out hints and argument to confirm his apprehensions; and this with so much success, that the merchant was no longer sufficiently confident in his own recollection, to adhere to a purpose so surrounded with danger, either to his life, or, what was truly more important, and what he always held to be more important–to his conscience. But, although this shade of distrust might influence him, to desist from a further prosecution of the Baron de Blondeville, he was not persuaded to sign the recantation proposed to him, nor any recantation whatsoever. On this point, every suggestion made to him, touching his own security, or advantage, was vain; at this moment, he held it just possible the Baron might be innocent, and, therefore, was he willing to desist from his accusation; but he also thought it far more probable, that he was guilty, and, therefore would he not affirm that he was innocent.

The Prior, feigning more satisfaction than he felt, as to the progress of his suggestions, said, 'You think the Baron guiltless; your recantation must therefore follow, when you have had a few minutes further consideration. Else where would be the love of justice, of which you have said so much?'

'I only doubt of his guilt,' said the respondent in this dispute, 'and that carries me no farther than a relinquishment of the prosecution.'

'But you certainly do not doubt, that this must be insufficient to satisfy his honour. He has been publicly accused, and it is necessary, that he should be as publickly cleared. It is also necessary, – here the speaker delivered himself with greater emphasis – 'it is also necessary, that his accuser, if he be obstinate, should be punished for his attempt. Think you that punishment is likely to be slight? If you remain here, certain destruction awaits you; if you go away, and leave behind this recantation of your error, you will save your own life, and testify so far to the Baron's innocence, as to render a pursuit of you unnecessary to his reputation.'

'I knew not,' said Woodreeve, 'that you were so warmly my friend, as you profess yourself to be; you seem as anxious for my welfare, after I may leave this place, as for the Baron's reputation.'

The Prior liked not this remark. 'I know not,' said he, 'why I should be thus anxious, since you are so distrustful of my good-will, although there be mixed with my wish to save your life, a desire, that you should restore the reputation of an innocent man. I marvel you should hesitate to accept my kindness.'

The merchant still refused to sign a recantation, which went so much beyond his own conviction. 'My flight, without this,' said he, 'would afford sufficient presumption of my doubt, and even that is rather a stronger word than ought to be applied to my mere admission of a possibility.'

The parties remained for a while in silence, one considering whether he should waive the recantation he had so strongly insisted upon, the other, whether he should trust himself with such a companion, even if he no longer required it. He feared some treachery in the proposal; the offer of an escape might be made, only with a design to draw him into a virtual acknowledgment of guilty motives for his charge, the more certainly to accomplish his destruction. 'Suppose I were on the outside of the castle walls,' said he, 'how may I proceed, when beyond them, since I have neither horse, nor friend, to expedite me?'

'You consent, then, to sign this?'

'No,' replied the merchant, lifting up his head, with a resolute and indignant countenance. 'If you insist on such a condition,

130

here, I entreat you, conclude your visit, and leave me to my rest.'

The Prior now yielded. 'There is a place, without the town,' said he, 'where you may lie hidden, till the dawn, or, if you fear not to traverse the woods by night, a horse and guide are in readiness for you. I am sufficiently your friend to help you, without insisting on further conditions.'

Still, the prisoner hesitated. He knew of no previous good-will of his adviser towards him, that could account for so much preparation for his safety; he liked not to trust him, with such an opportunity to ruin him. But, while he thus feared treachery, on one hand, he saw destruction threatening him, on the other; if he trusted to the present offer, he might perish; if he awaited a doubtful contest with enemies so powerful, and so greatly inflamed by revenge, he felt little hope for his life. To declare in court, his mere admission, that the Baron might be innocent, would not be sufficient for his own release; further his consci-ence would not let him go, and yet it was apparent, that he should be pressed to go further, and should be treated as a criminal, if he refused; nothing would be sufficient to his own safety, which was not so to the Baron's views; his admission would be attributed only to fear, and it was not fear in him, which his adversaries wished to prove. After he had weighed these thoughts in his mind, he told the Prior he was ready to depart.

While he yet spoke, he heard the bell of Saint Mary's strike, for the third time; the Prior heard it too; and he stood still and thoughtful. Then, starting from his mood, he said, 'Your determination is, perhaps, too late; let us begone.'

On being asked why he feared this, he answered, 'That bell was to serve as the third signal.' On being asked for what purpose it was to serve as a signal, he replied, without explaining, that it concerned the escape, adding, 'Not a moment is to be lost; while we are talking, your opportunity is fleeing;' and he arose and unlocked the chamber-door.

'Are you sure of the keeper?' said Woodreeve, 'and how are we to pass the castle gates?'

'There is no time for answers; follow in silence.' They left the chamber; a light was burning on the head of the stair, which the Prior, as he descended, took up in his hand. The merchant perceived no one on the stair, save his conductor; but he looked fearfully at every doorway he passed, expecting each

131

moment, to see some one on the watch, ready to start out upon him.

Having descended two flights only, the Prior turned into a chamber on the left, making sign for the merchant to follow; who, fearing he was not leading him forth of the tower, stood still on the stair, and pointed downward, as though he would go that way only. But, the Prior still beckoning, and retiring with the light, he could not but follow into what appeared to be a state-room of this tower, and which did in truth belong to the constable of the castle, though not then used by him. Wood-reeve marvelled, wherefore he was led to this chamber, which, for height and greatness, nearly equalled any at Kenilworth, and which, though scant of furniture, was yet hung with ancient arras, that fell from under the high windows down to the very floor.

The Prior again beckoning him, he passed on, without inquiring, fearing lest the sound of his voice might call forth some one, who should have been on watch. This chamber led into another, separated, as was a third, by a wall, which, though lofty, did not reach the roof, except by a row of round arches, that appeared above the arras, and rose to a vast height, making the whole extent of these three large chambers visible on high, like unto the aisle-roof of a church, though the partition walls concealed it below.

On the top of these walls, stood many figures of armour, beneath the arches and piles of arms, which none could reach, save those acquainted with the secret ways of the chambers. These shapes exhibited every device of harness known – of plain steel, of brass, or coat of mail; with helms and visors of divers sorts; some to lie flat before the face, leaving only an opening for the eyes above; others hiding the eyes, yet allowing sight and the passage of breath through the iron bars of the projecting visor, and some with beaver down, as if there were a visage behind too ghastly to be exposed. These were the state rooms of the great tower, or keep of Caesar; but although assigned as the habitation of the Constable, they were never used by him, except in time of siege, they were so cold and comfortless. Hung they were with like arras from the line of the windows and arches, down to the floor, but they showed little sign of the living beside.

The merchant, coming to the third chamber and seeing no sign of an outlet beyond, liked it not; and, halting at the door, made signal for the Prior to return; but he, waving the lamp over his head, noticed this only by a gesture to come on. As he did so, his companion could almost have believed some evil sprite was before him, so dark and strange he looked under that gloomy light. When the Prior had reached the end of this chamber, he stood still, till Woodreevre came up; and then, checking all further question, he put the lamp into his hand, and, lifting up the arras, unfastened a door behind it; beyond which appeared an arch made in the solid wall, of twelve or fourteen feet thickness.

Several steps led up to a stone landing-place and to a loop beyond; where, in time of siege, two archers could stand, and shoot forth their arrows, unseen of the enemy without. And there were many of the like in these chambers; but the arras hid them from those, who might be guests.

Woodreeve, marvelling why the Prior had led him thither, looked forward into the depth of this arch; and there saw, by the dim light, a figure stand: which, for aught that then appeared, might be a mere bowman, ready to shoot; till the Prior, snatching the lamp from the merchant, who had no power either to resist, or to flee, held it forward at arm's length, and it gleamed upon the armour of one, who seemed appointed like a knight.

Instantly, the lamp shook in the hand of the Prior, and Woodreeve wondered not less to see his visage change to deadly pale, than at the shape before him, till its harness of a knight seemed to remind him of his dead kinsman. The Prior, recovering from his ecstasy, said, ''Tis but the armour of the Lord Constable, which used to stand in this recess; 'tis strange I should have forgotten this: come on; you have nothing to fear!'

But the merchant thought not so; and liked not being brought hither, whence, as it seemed, they could go no further; but in this he was mistaken. A key having been applied by his conductor to a door in the side of the archway, it opened upon a passage, made in the thickness of the wall, which led to many secret places of this tower, and elsewhere, unknown to few, save the Lord Constable and the wardour: how the Prior came to be acquainted with it, may appear hereafter.

The wind, that poured through this door, had extinguished the lamp, had not Woodreeve let fall the arras; and, when he found himself inclosed in this arch, he lamented his attempt; and still more when he saw the Prior standing darkly, at the foot

133

of a narrow staircase, looking up it, and beckoning him to come on. His heart failed him, and he demanded whither he was to be led, saying he would go no further, till he should receive an answer to that question. The Prior spoke in a low voice, as if he feared to be heard, a precaution, which seemed to be unnecessary here, and said, 'Within the thickness of these walls, there are galleries, which lead to many points; you will presently find yourself at the foot of the tower.'

'How can that be,' said his companion, 'when the stairs do not descend, but rise?'

'Come on, and you shall see; but first let me secure this door.' The Prior stepped back; and, as he locked it, hung the key to his girdle. As he flung back his weeds to do this, Woodreeve thought he saw the glitter of steel within. Other keys might hang there; but he almost thought he saw a poniard, and he doubted whether it were safer to attempt going back to his prison, or to proceed, without betraying his suspicions. His conductor left him little time to meditate; for, taking again the lamp, he went up the stair, bidding him tread lightly, and speak not.

It was a short flight of steps, ending in a narrow passage, where once and again a loop supplied the place of windows. Now, there were within these walls of the grand story, galleries, that ran round the chambers, below the windows, which were made for secret communication to distant parts of the castle; and, for means of security and escape, in tirres of siege; some led up to the battlements; others down to the donjon and to subterraneous avenues; but whither these went finally there were few that could tell. The Prior was acquainted with them all, and, when the King's court was not at Kenilworth, he could, had he been rebelliously inclined, have surprized the ten knights, who kept garrison here, and have delivered the castle unto an enemy. But his treachery took not so wide a compass.

Woodreeve followed through this gallery, in watchful silence, and, at the end of it, saw the Prior make halt, where the wall fell into a recess, as if a turret were at the corner of this tower. On coming up, he perceived in the floor a large opening, or well, such as is found in the strong holds of many castles, and is used, when great balls of solid stone or balistas, catapultas, and other engines of war are to be drawn up, for defence, during the siege.

The Prior bent over it with the lamp, eyeing the depth; and, while Woodreeve did the same, he saw, far down within, a flash of light, which showed him a high and narrow arch at the bottom. A stronger flash made him look up to the lamp his conductor held, supposing it might have come from that; but his eyes settled not on the lamp, but on the looks of the Prior, which were fixed in dark watchfulness; and again the countenance struck him as having been seen by him, under other circumstances than any, which had lately occurred at Kenilworth.

He stepped hastily back from the opening; his conductor stepped back also; and he heard, at the same moment, a voice say, 'Wardour, mind the hour!'

The merchant's heart sunk at the sound, which seemed to him the same he had heard, this night before, in his prison, and he looked again at the Prior; but his lips were motionless; and, when he had made a sign for silence, and had beckoned the merchant forward, he turned quickly this angle of the tower into a gallery like that they had left. It ended in another turret, but here appeared a narrow stair, leading, on one hand, up to the battlement, and, on the other, descending; it was so narrow as to admit only one in front, and so steeply winding, that he, who followed, could hardly keep in view him, who went before.

It ended in a small chamber, where the Prior again made a stand, and, giving the lamp to his companion, he drew the bolts of a strong oaken door, so thickly barred and studded with iron, that the weight of it could hardly have been moved by the Prior alone. Here the spirits of Woodreeve revived; for, this seemed by its strength to be a door of outer defence, and he willingly assisted to force it back. His disappointment was great, when he perceived, that it opened only on a straight and steep flight of steps. Again, he questioned his conductor, who, once more, bade him be patient. The steps led to another door, which opened to a covered gallery, or passage, judged by the merchant to pass under the castle-foss, and, when they came to a third strong door, and ascended a short flight of steps, he doubted not the Prior was leading him forth of a salley-port, beyond the ditch.

At the top of these steps, a fourth door appeared; this was so stoutly fastened with bolts and bars, that together they could scarce undo them. And sorely was Woodreeve daunted, when, instead of finding it opening to liberty and fresh air, he saw beyond it only a narrow and dismal chamber, more like to a prison than even that he had left. His loud remonstrances alarmed the Prior, who again besought him, as he wished for freedom, to be circumspect and silent.

'We have passed,' said he, 'along the castle wall, through that covered gallery, which leads from the Constable's chambers to the gate of entrance into the bass-court, and may be within hearing of the wardours. Four knights below keep castle guard, to night, within the great portal, the King being here, at Kenilworth. You have, perchance, already betrayed yourself; but wait here, while I go on and examine, whether the way be clear; if you hear me speaking loud, retire into the covered passage, and bar the iron door; but be not heard the while; if all be still, stay here, till I return.'

Woodreeve eagerly desired to follow, his heart misgiving him of treachery, and because also, that he even shuddered at the thought of being left alone in this dreary place, without a light; for the only lamp they carried the Prior must take to light his own steps. But his conductor objected, that, their way now lying near the ground, it was unsafe for them to go further together, till he should have made sure, that the wardours were aloof. To this the merchant remarked with some surprize, that this did not agree with the assurance he had given him, that he had safe means of escape, for, it now appeared that, although their passage lay so near to where the wardours, or others watched, it seemed not that he had secured the good-will of any one to help them. A keen sarcastic smile was on the countenance of the Prior, which, certain, the poor merchant did not read aright.

'If you have deceived me already, how can I resolve to proceed further with you? you said you had prepared a horse and guide, without the walls.'

'Hush,' said the Prior, 'you are delivering us both to destruction; speak not; be confident and patient; you will soon have reason to find that your distrust has been folly. I will return immediately, unless I am seen. If you hear my voice, remember the retreat, that remains for you, and that you secure the door without noise; I shall find means of extricating you another way. You know you are not to expect me to call to you; it will be sufficient if you hear me speaking loudly.'

Having said this, he laid his finger on his lips, and then, shading the lamp by his garment, left the chamber by a narrow passage, and was speedily out of sight. Woodreeve, awed by the darkness of this lone spot, tried, notwithstanding the injunction he had received, to follow his steps; but no sound of them could he hear; a little ray from the lamp alone giving him a faint glimpse through that passage into a lofty chamber, where he just discovered the light vanishing through a distant doorway, with the Prior's shadow beside it. And here Woodreeve made halt, lest he should not be able, in this darkness, to find his way back to the covered passage, should the signal for retreat be sounded, and lest his following steps should be heard of the Prior, who his-self moved so stilly, as though he had meant to observe whether he was followed, or not.

The merchant listened attentively, but heard no sound: he watched a considerable while on this spot, without perceiving any sign of the Prior's return. His heart again failed him, and again he trusted, that he, who was guiltless of any crime, and whom pity for a murdered kinsman had exposed to this danger, would not be left to be destroyed by any artifice of man. Still the Prior did not return, nor was his voice heard in any direction. Now, taking his way towards the door, through which he had seen him depart, he determined to know the worst, and either to make one desperate effort to escape, or resign himself into the hands of any guard he could find. The chamber was so spacious, that hardly could he find his way through it, but that, as he advanced, he perceived a glimmering of light, which led him to the very door, where his conductor had disappeared. Here he saw the rays shoot athwart another room, through the arch of an opposite door. Listening and hearing no sound, he advanced cautiously, that he might observe, without entering that further chamber, what was passing within it.

It was a large and lofty chamber, having no window, save one, but many loops in the walls, which were dimly seen by the slanting light from a lamp near the high roof. On the opposite side, were large grooves and pullies of extraordinary strength, such as he had never seen before, and could not now comprehend the use of; but, in the present temper of his mind, he readily assigned for them some terrible purpose; in which conjecture he was not mistaken. Near them were a row of large iron spikes and many bars, that covered the wall to a great height; and he then understood this to be the portcullis room. But what surprized him was, to see light springing up through the floor, at regular distances, by small apertures; for, he knew not that there were used the machicollations, for pouring down melted lead and hot sand on the heads of enemies, who might have forced the first gates, or even the portcullis itself; and that this glimmering came from the watch-lights of the guard in the portal beneath. Still, he neither saw, nor heard, any living

137

person in this chamber; till, venturing a little within the door, he observed, at the farther end, a torch, gleaming through a passage, and the Prior himself standing in the archway, between two men, who lay along on stone benches in the wall.

He bent over one for awhile, and then over the other, as if communicating something to them; and Woodreeve, suspecting that he was betrayed to those, who would not scruple to dispatch him, stood rooted by terror to the spot, and saw the Prior advance alone towards the door, where he watched. He was presently observed of him, and the looks of his conductor, on discovering him, seemed to express dismay; but this soon passed from them, and, putting himself back, within the door, he said, 'All is right; follow me through that passage; but step lightly and speak not, for your life.'

'For my life,' answered the merchant, imprudently, 'will I not follow you thither, where two men are lying in wait; I have seen them.'

'Then you have seen the wardours of this cullis-chamber in their niches, keeping guard; and good guard will they keep; they will not wake of one while; their liquor has been such as I wished.'

This seemed so probable an explanation, that Woodreeve received it for truth; yet was he surprized, that so great preparation had been made for his escape, and he asked how it were possible to be certain this sleep was not feigned, and who had prepared their drink. The Prior answered, with sarcastic smile, 'Four knights do service in the portal below; there is one among them, who has spared not to make these inferior wardours merry.'

He then checked further question, saying, 'Come, let us pass; time speeds; this moment we may use, the next, perhaps, we may not.' Without more words, the merchant followed him through the portcullis-chamber, and, drawing nigh the place of guard, did, in trowth, perceive the two wardours fast asleep in the niches, where they usually kept watch. But, hardly had he entered the gateway, when one of them began to move himself on the bench, and cried out, 'Down with the portcullis, they are coming over the bridge;' and, stretching forth his arm, he had nigh knocked the lamp from the Prior's hand, and the merchant, as he passed, was touched.

They stayed not to see whether he had waked himself, but, turning into a little projection of the passage, went down a round

138

stair. And now approached the greatest danger of discovery; for, this led down into a room that opened under the great portal, where the wardours of that place usually sat. There were stone seats within the wall appointed for them, where they watched out the night in all seasons, save of the bleakest weather of winter, and then they sat by fire in the guard-chamber, which was in the opposite tower opening under the gateway. But those, who, this night, kept castle-guard under the great portal, being there on knight's service and unused, save for a certain season, to be from their beds, at this time, minded not to watch within the niches; and, the drawbridge being securely up, they sat in that guard-room, there beguiling the time with dice, or they contented themselves with now and then a turn under the great arch, to see that others did their duty; and then reposed themselves.

When the merchant saw whither that stair led, he asked how they were to pass, unseen, through the portal, where the wardours watched, and received for answer, they were not to go out to that portal, secured by gates, as well as by guards and by the raised drawbridge, but by a secret way in the tower-room below. Now, hardly had the Prior spoken, when, on coming near to the bottom stair, he checked his steps, and stood still and watchful; for, he saw the door of that room standing ajar, which he had reason to hope would have been shut and even fastened at this hour; and, presently after, a wardour was seen passing there, by a light hanging in the archway.

Darkening his lamp with his garment, he stood, fearing to venture forward, lest his steps should discover him, ere he could get through that room. He also feared, that the noise of raising the trap, by which he would depart, must be heard, even if he should get safely through the room. Before the passing of many minutes, the Knight, watching there, began to sing an old Norman song, the burden of which was taken up in chorus by his comrades dicing in the guard-room beyond, making a kind of hoarse music, which was soon joined by the sound of a single clarion, repeating a few notes in an under tone, both solemn and terrific to the poor merchant, who thought it was some signal of alarm.

But his conductor, who knew it to be only a sign for changing the guard at some post without the gates, took courage at the noise, and, boldly stepping forward, shut the door that led to the portal, and drew the gate within. Yet, ere he could find the trap, the knight, who had heard a bolt drawn, was calling and then striking heavily at the door. Finding no answer, he ordered a clarion to be sounded in the portal for a call to the wardours, of the portcullis chamber above, and to gather those below to inquire into this matter.

And now was Woodreeve most fearful, lest those sleeping wardours above should by these loud soundings be roused from their trance: and hardly could he hold the lamp to the ground, while the Prior searched for the trap, which lay hid in the corner; there, having found a grated opening on the floor, Woodreeve pointed that out for the trap, little guessing he stood over the castle dungeon, where condemned criminals were kept, and where he might yet be laid. It was of great depth, and what little and glimmering light it ever had was received through this opening, by which also food was let down to the wretched prisoner.

Undismayed by the noise without, now that he had secured the door, the Prior continued to search coolly for the trap, knowing, perchance, better than his companion, that the wardours would not soon wake, and that amongst the knights below, was one, who was enough the friend of the Baron de Blondeville and his cause to manage his unthinking comrades, till they should be willing to suppose the alarm had proceeded from some mistaken cause. Had the merchant been also aware of this, he might have thought himself safe; yet might he have erred, when thus secure, and have found that his worst enemy stood close beside him.

The Prior having, at length, found the trap, applied the key, and, with his companion's aid, lifted the door. Beneath, appeared a steep and narrow stair, and now again, when Woodreeve, after such long toil and so many changes of anxiety, looked down into this dark abyss, his distrust of his companion returned with new force; he pointed to the fearful descent, and urged, that, even if it could lead them without the walls, they must be unable to get over the foss, which was broad and full of deep water. A thundering sound upon the portal door and a loud blast of the clarion silenced this remonstrance, and prevented the Prior's reply. He thought the sleep of the wardours above must needs be the sleep of death, if it fled not at the noise: so thought some under the archway, and they redoubled their blows and their hallooings; but as yet to no purpose.

The Prior the while, having found it no very difficult matter to thrust, as it were, his harassed companion down the opening, lowered and secured the trap and followed down the steps. As Woodreeve now stood with the lamp, at the bottom of them, the light it cast upward to the Prior gave a ghastly hue to his visage, which again brought back his former faint recollection of having seen him, at some other period, and under circumstances of danger. It was by such an upward, darting light, that he had seen the murderer of his kinsman, at the moment when the visor fell off; and he now almost thought he saw before him that very murderer.

The suspicion was far from being strong, but the mixed expression of terror and firmness, with which he fixed his eyes upon him, did not escape the Prior. With less firmness than usual, he almost started and threw a keen and frowning glance upon his companion. Dark and thronging thoughts cast their shadows upon his countenance. But recovering, by degrees, his usual aspect, he stood awhile at the foot of the stair, listening for the sound above. It had ceased, and all within and without this gloomy vault, was still.

He knew not, whether to understand, that the noise had brought down the wardours from their sleep, and that the portal was opened, or that the Baron's friend, who watched there with the rest, had succeeded in quieting their suspicions. The thickness of the trap, and the depth of the vault, in which he stood, would prevent him from hearing their footsteps, even if they were trampling over his head; but should this be so, and should those knights, who were strangers to the secret ways of the castle, have discovered the trap-door, he trusted to the strength of its inward fastenings for a sufficient time of security. Woodreeve stood, the while, silent from terror and expectation, and hardly did he know whether it were better for him to be o'ertaken by those above, or to proceed with his murky conductor. 'What, if he has brought me into the depth of this vault only to destroy me?' thought he. Then he considered, that hardly would any one, after the alarm which had been given above, hazard himself by so atrocious a deed, and his spirits, in some deal, returned.

But he demanded again, and with more resolute tone, whither they were going, and was answered, 'To a sally-port.'

'But how are we to pass the ditch? Is there a boat then waiting for us?'

'Come on,' answered the Prior, sharply.

141

Woodreeve followed, without further question, yet misliked he the manner of his conductor more than ever. Nor had he failed to observe, that, unless at intervals, when reproof was to be conveyed, or hope raised, no eyes met his, so bent were those of the Prior towards the ground. They passed on through other vaults, and, whether it were the bad air there, or apprehension of what might follow, Woodreeve felt himself so faint, that hardly could he drag his steps along. Soon they came to a round chamber, whose roof, supported by a central pillar, rose in vaultings, that terminated in corbeils of lions' heads, upon a cornice of noble simplicity. The place seemed intended for a hall of some sort, but the merchant, who looked round it with surprise, could perceive no windows; there were two arched doors opposite to each other, and to one of these the Prior led. Having gone up a few steps, he undrew the strong fastenings, and unclosed it, Woodreeve hastily following him, for he once more felt the fresh air breathe upon his face. His conductor pressed forward, but suddenly checked himself, and drew back; he had nearly fallen into the foss below.

'I have mistaken the way,' said he, 'this is a sally-port long disused, and the steps from it are removed.'

He had in trowth mistaken this for a sally-port, that had led under the rampart, and the castle ditch; but, this entrance having been considered as an inlet dangerous in times of siege, the steps had been taken down, and the door strongly secured. For the hall, it had once been a principal entrance to a tower on the walls, although it lay under a lofty flight of covered steps, that led obliquely to a larger portal, guarded by strong doors, one of which was of iron.

Woodreeve, breathing awhile the fresh air from without, recovered strength and courage; he almost blamed himself for his want of patience, and for having failed to allow, that an escape from a castle so spacious as this of Kenilworth, and so fully occupied and inhabited, as it now was, could not be made, except by many devious and tedious ways. But he did not long enjoy this free air; the Prior suddenly closed the door, made the bars fast, and then, turning away, began to examine the wall, at a little distance, where he applied a key to a door, not seen till the lamp was held close to it; thence a steep stair descended, as if into another vault. They stepped upon it, and the Prior bade Woodreeve go first, while he locked the door; but here again distrust returned to the still baffled prisoner, for he

142

perceived that this door was greatly different from that of the sally-port; so much so that he marvelled how one could be mistaken for the other; and he stopped, fearful of what might follow.

Yet had no apparent purpose been answered if the error were wilful; and, if the Prior had an ill-meaning, so far as to intend him bodily harm, in their lonely track, he seemed to have missed an opportunity fitted for his purpose, since it would have been easy to push him into the dark moat below. This thought encouraged him now to proceed; but he would not have been so soon consoled, had he known as much as his conductor knew. He asked, however, whither this second flight would lead them, and was answered, 'Beyond the walls, where you shall soon find yourself at liberty; if you like not to proceed, return and deliver yourself up to justice.'

The merchant followed down a very long flight of steps, ending in a passage, which he supposed lay under the foss. Here the air was so changed by an unwholesome vapour, that it was painful to breathe it; and the lamp burned so dimly, at times, that he feared it would expire. The Prior often stopped to nurse the flame, and once, as he lifted the lamp high, and it revived, his garment flew back, and Woodreeve now saw, beyond all possibility of doubt, a dagger at his girdle.

His eyes were fixed upon it, till his conductor saw that he observed it; and then, laying his hand upon the hilt, he said, 'In times like these, every one should be somewhat armed.'

But now another object had seized the attention of the merchant, and he stood in horror. In drawing forth the dagger, his companion had turned aside his vesture, and, behold! a chain of gold hung about his neck, which from its ponderous but highly wrought ornaments, Woodreeve instantly thought was the very chain worn by his kinsman, at the time of his death, and he doubted not, that in the Prior he saw one of his assassins. A sort of amulet box was suspended to the chain, but of that he had no recollection.

At this conviction, he lost all presence of mind, so that he foresaw not how much he might hasten his peril, and lessen his chance, if there were any, of finally avoiding it, in betraying his thoughts to the Prior, whose revenge might be accomplished in such a place, without danger, as it appeared, from any human means of discovery.

He seized the lamp, and, holding it close to the chain, cried

143

out, 'It is the same – there are the very links, that shape – the initials of his name.'

'Of whose name?' said the Prior eagerly, and as he spoke, Woodreeve recollected the voice of the very robber, to whom he had delivered up his own treasure. The Prior, still without having changed his voice, repeated the question.

'Of my unfortunate kinsman,' answered Woodreeve; 'I now know you.'

Instantly, the discovered ruffian, without one word, drew the dagger from the imperfect grasp, which Woodreeve had of it; and upraised his hand with a fierce and deadly intention, but the blow descended not; the poignard fell from his hand, and his eyes seemed fixed upon some object beyond.

The poor merchant, who, for an instant, had been motionless and confounded with terror, seeing this, gathered courage, and turned to discover what held his enemy in this trance; but nothing could he perceive, save the dusky avenue. Then, losing not another moment, he fled, with the lamp, along that unknown way; but he had neglected to seize the dagger, which had fallen on the ground, and might easily have been made a weapon for himself.

He followed the avenue, till his breath failed, and he was compelled to stop; but, soon thinking he heard steps behind him, he again went on, and, flying for very life, hope and fear supplied him with strength. He had now gone a great length of way, without having discovered any thing like an outlet, and he rested again for breath, and to revive his failing lamp. He listened, and, though he heard no footsteps in pursuit, he remembered the soundless steps, with which his treacherous conductor had, this night, passed along several chambers, and he was not convinced, that he was distant, though unheard. The intenseness, with which he listened for any remote, or lone sound, seemed to sharpen his sense of hearing, like as the seaman's sight discovers things so small and distant, as are unseen of others.

Thus, now while Woodreeve listened, he thought he heard – not footsteps, but, a little strain of music so faint and fleeting it was more like the moonlight shadow of a fleecy cloud, that glides along the hills, and fades ere you can say it is, than any certain truth. It served, however, at first, to revive his hopes; he judged it came from without the castle walls; but then perhaps, from soldiers on their watch, and, if so, his deliverance could not be nigh. Still, as his only hope lay that way, he hastened forward, and presently he again thought he heard music. He stopped and no longer doubted this; the sound was nearer, and he gradually distinguished a faint, solemn swell of voices and instruments. As he advanced, they sunk and were lost awhile; and then a high and long continued strain of many mingling voices was heard. Soon after, it sunk away, at a distance, and he heard it no more.

But now he fancied steps were coming behind him, and, quickening his own, he came to a bend of the avenue, and espied a door, which seemed to close its dreary length. Three massive bars secured it, but there was also a lock. While he stood before it, and looked back on the long sloping avenue, almost as far as his lifted lamp could throw its blunted rays, he heard no sound of either step, or breath, from within, or from without that door; nor saw the Prior advancing through that dim way behind him.

The bolts gave way to Woodreeve's returned strength, and even the lock did not long resist. Already, he thought he felt the fresh air from without the castle walls; but, opening the door, he stepped not out upon a platform of grass, or under the boughs of the free forest; he stepped upon a little winding stair, that went up a turret, as he verily believed, of another tower, some out-post of the castle. At this, his heart sunk nigh to fainting; for how should he escape detection from those, who guarded it, and whose voices he now thought he heard singing, in dreary chorus, on their night-watch.

Having considered, a moment, to little purpose, for he had no choice but to go on, he went up the stair, and came to another door. He listened for awhile, but all within was still, and he undrew the bolt that held it, and would have stepped forward, but was baffled by what he thought a curtain, that hung before it. In this he deceived himself. It was the tapestry of a chamber. Perceiving this, he stopped again, before he lifted it, to consider how best he might disclose himself, if any one were within; but, all being silent, he ventured to lift the arras, and found himself in a great arched chamber. A lamp was burning near a reading-desk; but no person appeared, and he looked round, with a mixture of terror and curiosity, still holding up the arras, with one hand, and with the other his lamp, to survey the limits of the room; and he still kept one foot on the threshold-step, as ready to retreat, on the first alarm.

At length, perceiving that he was indeed alone in this chamber, he let the hangings drop, and ventured forward, in

145

search of an outlet, through which to escape; but he saw none. The walls were covered with tapestry, which concealed whatsoever doors might be within them, and presented in colours various good deeds. A large oriel-window of fretted stone-work rose in sharp arches, closed with glass, stained in a mosaic of divers rich colours, like unto those in the great church of the city of Cologne in Germany. This window showed also the emblazoned arms of Geoffrey de Clinton, with many a golden rule in scrowl-work and labels on the glass.

All this Woodreeve espied, while, with his lamp in hand, he searched around for some outlet, to depart by. It seemeth not expedient to set down here all the objects he saw in this chamber; suffice it to say it was an oratory, and the histories on the tapestry and all the garniture were such as are meet for such a place. On a table lay divers folios well bossed with silver; among them was *Matthew of Westminster* and the *Golden Legend*. An arm-chair, with purple cushions, stood by the reading-desk, on which lay open a copy of the venerable Bede, and a Missal beside it, freshly illuminated.

At all he saw his mind misgave him, that this was some chamber, not of the castle, but of the priory; and, if so, whither could he turn, to flee from destruction. His eye again glancing round the walls, he observed a part of the tapestry inclosed in a kind of frame-work, different from any other part of the arras; and, hoping there might be a door behind this, he was advancing towards it, when he heard a rustling sound in another part of the chamber; and, turning, beheld the arras lifted, and the Prior himself standing in the same arch, through which he had entered.

His countenance was livid and malicious, and he held in his hand the dagger he had dropped in the avenue.

Hardly did Woodreeve cast a look behind him; but, rushing towards that frame-work, he found it held a door, which opened upon a vaulted passage of the priory, ending in a cloister. As he fled, he turned to see whether his pursuer advanced, and observed him standing at the great door of the chamber, making sign for his return; as if, after having let that dagger and that murderer's look be seen, it were possible to lure him back again.

It was Woodreeve's aim, should he be unable to get out of the monastery, to take refuge at the altar; and, with this intent, he proceeded hastily along the cloister, which opened, as he expected, into the chapel; and thence he soon heard the sound

146

of voices and instruments; for the monks were now chanting the last matin, and he recollected the strain he had heard in the avenue. But, ere he could reach sanctuary, the Prior's steps were heard, along the cloister, and his voice calling loudly for help, and saying his life was in danger from a prisoner escaped of the castle; and, commanding, that they should stop him, ere he reached shelter. The monks, engaged as they were, at this hour, in service, heard not the alarm; till a lay brother, coming forth of the dormitory, raised a cry, which brought out from their cells a few sick brothers, who now joined in the cry, which those at matins presently heard.

Woodreeve, however, pursued his course; and, opening a folding-door at the end of the cloister, found himself in the chancel, and gained the sanctuary, ere his pursuers reached him, or the amazed brethren there could understand they were to stop his way.

By this time the service had ceased, and all was confusion; the Prior pressing forward to seize the poor merchant, even at the altar-steps; and the monks flocking round him, to prevent sacrilege, and to learn the motive for his attempting to commit it. Scarcely was he kept back by the monks from offering violence to Woodreeve, who was still breathless and fainting, from the thought of peril so hardly escaped, though he turned, and in some sort, faced his enemy.

But, before he was calm enough to speak, the Prior began his say: he asserted, that, while he was sitting in the great chamber, studying, a secret door of the room opened, and he saw this stranger enter. He knew him to be the man imprisoned in the castle, for having falsely accused the Baron de Blondeville, and whose trial for unlawful arts of magic, designed to delude the eyes and minds of the whole court, by a false presentment of the crime imputed to the Baron, and thereby to prejudice the King against him, to his utter ruin, was shortly to come on in the castle-hall. How he had escaped from prison he knew not, nor how he had reached the priory; where, perchance, he had come undesignedly. On perceiving him quietly sitting at his reading-desk, the prisoner, possessed either by despair, or by desire of vengeance, for the part he had taken against him in the King's presence, drew forth a dagger; and, having vainly made a blow at him, fled, as they had witnessed: 'And here behold the instrument of his intended crime,' said the Prior, 'turned aside from my breast by my own hand. I found it on the floor of my chamber." And he held up the poniard.

Astonished and confounded by these audacious falsehoods, Woodreeve stood aghast, and his very looks would have condemned him, with the greater part of the brotherhood, could they even have questioned the truth of their Prior; who, however, was little loved amongst them. With one voice they cried out against the stranger, so that he almost gave himself up for lost; but, when his enemy said, that no place ought to protect such a criminal, they all at once stood up against violation of sanctuary, as became them; and marvelled, that he showed so little reverence for so high a privilege. Then the Prior, forgetful of what became his office, said that his life was yet in danger, unless the prisoner could be dislodged from the monastery; for, although the law of sanctuary could protect him, it could not restrain him; and, as the doors of the church could not be locked, he might come forth, at some convenient hour; and not only escape from the monastery, but, on his way, accomplish the very crime he had meditated.

The monks made answer, that the doors of the church should be watched, but that they never could consent to afford a precedent for violation of sanctuary; and much they were astonished, that their superior his-self, who ought to be the first to maintain this right, should wish to renounce it. But they excused him, seeing his terror of the evil he had just escaped. Then, the Prior perceiving he was betraying his own cause, and turning those against it, of whose good-will he should hereafter have much need, gave up that point, but threatened sentence of exclusion against any one of the community, who should relieve the stranger's hunger. And thus was he nearly condemned to a lingering death more miserable than any, which the common law of the land could have pronounced against him, since it was improbable, that any of the villagers should venture to brave the anger of the Prior.

Adversity had now well nigh persuaded Woodreeve, that, however just his cause, it would avail him nothing, where the criminal had such powerful support; and he forbore, at this time, to increase his difficulties, by accusing the Prior as an accomplice of the Baron de Blondeville. He spoke only to make a solemn denial of the charge against himself, adding, that, if the brethren would send to the castle for a guard, he would instantly relinquish the privilege of sanctuary, and deliver himself up to the King's officers, but to no other. This pleased not his enemy, who dreaded the tale he might unfold; and, however strange that might appear and hard to be believed, he knew, that in those lawless times, there had been instances of rapine, committed by wicked intruders like himself into the fold, and, therefore might some parts of the history be not wholly discredited; the more especially as the lord Archbishop seemed to be not wholly his friend. So, he resolved to take his cause into his own hands, and to attempt that by poison, which he had failed to perpetrate by steel, when the merchant, as has been related, had imprudently made a charge against him in so lonely a place.

For, it is not to be guessed, that the Prior, in leading him forth from prison, had, at first, any other motive than to turn him loose and let him make his way to a distant part of the country, where he would be so well contented by having saved his life, as never again to hazard it, by endangering that of the Baron. However this might be, he now, in his folly and wickedness, as wickedness leads on to wickedness, and blinds its followers, judged it necessary for his own life, that the merchant should perish, and that, before he could have an opportunity of communicating with the King's officers. But to accomplish this it would be necessary to practise somewhat of the cunning dexterity, which with him supplied the place of wisdom, and which he was well content to mistake for it.

He, therefore, feigned to relax somewhat of his severity; and, saying the criminal should be allowed bread and water, while he remained in sanctuary, was so departing. But Woodreeve, now remembering the golden chain, worn by the Prior, and considering how helping it must be to his own cause to have that matter known, which might never be, if not now, wished to devise some means of making him show it to the brethren, before he had taken the precaution of laying it aside, if indeed he had not already done so. Yet, to mention this chain, without putting him on his guard to conceal it, were not possible. That was however done for him, which he had not the art to compass.

When the Prior was departing from the church, Woodreeve, again appealing to the brethren, bade them bear witness, that he utterly and solemnly denied all attempt or intention, to commit the crime now alleged against him, and that he could, at a proper time and place, unravel the mystery of his appearance there; 'Look at me, who am scarcely of middle age,' said he, 'and at the Prior, who, though large, is past his prime, and say,

149

whether, if I had attempted his life, his arm alone could have withstood me.'

'I say not, that I escaped by my own strength,' replied the Prior, 'I wear a charm, which protects me against evil sprites, whether instigating human beings, or acting as shadows.'

'If so,' said Woodreeve, 'why do you fear me, that you, but now, refused to grant me sanctuary, lest I should step forth from this place, and aim at your life. It cannot be credited; you have no such charm.'

'You are a deceiver,' said the Prior; 'here is your falsehood proved,' and he drew forth the amulet, suspended by the chain, but, in an instant, withdrew it, perceiving whither fear and anger were leading him. On seeing again this memorial of his dead kinsman, Woodreeve was so much disturbed, that he had almost slipped off the place of sanctuary, as he reached towards it.

But, checking his steps, he cried out, 'Wretch, whence had you that chain? Would it had been annexed to any real charm of defence, when my poor kinsman wore it in the forest of Ardenn! He would now, perchance, be alive to claim it.'

The brethren looked on Woodreeve, with surprize and displeasure, while no one, save the Prior, understood fully those words; and his countenance, nathless all his art and boldness, fell when he heard them. 'Venerable brethren,' continued the merchant, 'mark well that chain; for hereafter it may unfold a tale which ye guess not of.'

Upon this so pressing a call, they thronged round their superior, entreating, indeed, to see the amulet, but wishing chiefly to see the chain attached to it; and the Prior, who saw their motive beneath their pretence, was aware, that he could not resist them, without giving irremediable strength to their suspicions.

As they looked on it, Woodreeve said, 'You will observe, above what he calls a charm, three golden letters, being part of the chain itself, and also three jewels, the middle one of great value; the others are rubies.'

The monks then ventured to examine it further, and found it was as he said.

'In the clasp of that chain,' said the merchant, 'is a painting, the likeness of a noble lady, my unfortunate kinsman's wife; it was drawn by a Florentine, a famous illuminator.'

'We see nothing of that,' answered the brethren. 'There is no such thing.'

While the Prior now exclaimed eagerly, 'Mark his falsehood.'

But Woodreeve, addressing himself to the brethren, told them there was a secret spring; and, instructing them how to find it, said they would then behold a fair and unhappy lady. They did as he directed, when, a golden plate of that noble clasp flying up, they beheld, not the portrait of a lady, but that of a knight in armour, whose look was mild and full of thoughtful sadness. On seeing this, they cried, that he knew not the chain; for that it showed only the semblance of a knight. Hearing this, the merchant stretched forth his hand impatiently, and descended two steps of the sanctuary to examine the portrait, ere he well knew what he was doing. Then he entreated them, that they would allow him to see it; for, it was surely the likeness of his deceased friend; but they all assented to the Prior, that it must not be so entrusted.

At last, however, two of them yielded so far to his loud and earnest entreaties, that they held up to him the picture, beyond his reach, but where he could yet distinguish the features by the strong light of the tapers. On viewing that well-known countenance, tears stood in his eyes, and his looks alone might have convinced many, he had indeed spoken the truth, touching that chain, though he his-self was amazed by the portrait, having never seen it before. The Prior failed not to make his advantage of this unexpected circumstance; but, while he was yet triumphing, the merchant bade the brethren press once more that golden plate, as he directed, when a lid on the reverse side opened, and behold! a lady's countenance, meek and fair, with lifted eyes, and like unto some blessed saint.

They all at once exclaimed, 'it is here,' and passed the chain from one to another, some looking with wondrous dread, upon the prisoner, and some again on the Prior, who stood darkly watching, and they cried out, 'How may this be!'

Then the Prior, with looks of derision, said, 'Can ye ask that question, knowing as ye do, that the man before ye is about to be tried in the King's Court for practice of unlawful magic? It avails not, that he has been prevented from touching that chain with his hand; he has exercised a stranger power upon it, than if he had touched it. Those paintings were not there before; the chain has long been mine, as most of ye know. I bought it, before I was of this house.'

'And thus it may well be,' said one of the monks, 'for this is not so marvellous as those delusions conjured up in the castle-hall.'

151

And they blessed themselves and delivered up the chain to the Prior, who received it, with secret triumph.

'You now behold the charm which has preserved my life from the attempt of that ruffian,' said he, pointing to Woodreeve; 'and will no more doubt, why his strength failed, when he assailed me.'

Too late, the prisoner then perceived, that, in compelling his enemy to produce this chain, he had brought out an argument against himself. The monks had not refused their assent to their Prior's assertion; and, if there were any amongst them, who compared what he had asserted of the protecting virtues of this charm, against the malice of the poor merchant, with what he now said of the magical influence of the man upon this very chain, even while it was in his own hands, they did not dare to point forth the contradiction. The Prior, still dreading lest the prisoner should throw himself into the hands of the King's guard, as he had offered, now determined, in order to deter him from so doing, to make further use of his over-sight; and, holding up the chain, he called out, 'When you shall have surrendered yourself up to justice, here is an evidence, that shall convict you of unlawful arts, if others fail. This picture, which you have conveyed hither by secret magic, shall be more than a living witness against you.'

The latter words of the Prior were resounded, it might be by an echo of the aisles: 'more than a living witness against you.'

The brethren looked round, and Woodreeve listened. There were some among them, who fancied they heard a moaning from the ground underneath, between them and the north wall; others took it for the wind murmuring in the vaults near; but none of them spoke his thoughts. It might be the hollow blast, that sounds, at fits, before a tempest; for a storm came, soon after, which shook the walls. However this might be, Wood-reeve shuddered often as he heard it; and, looking round him, recollections rushed suddenly on his mind, that filled it with dismay. He examined eagerly the spot he stood on, and found, that he had indeed taken sanctuary near the grave of his unfortunate kinsman, though no name now appeared on it.

On this discovery, the blood rushed back to his heart, and he was nigh to falling into the like convulsions he had suffered under, when first he saw the Baron de Blondeville, beside the King. On recovering, he knelt down on the grave, raising his hands and eyes, and so continued, for some time. Then, rising and turning to the Prior, who seemed little affected by any thing

152

that had passed, he calmly said, that he was willing to deliver himself up to the King's officers, soon as they could be brought hither. To this the Prior answered he would send early on the morrow; but, as not even the King's officers might enter that place of sanctuary, to take him thence, he must come forth of himself, ere he could surrender to them. Woodreeve, fearing treachery on the way, liked not this; and so the Prior had foreseen, who for his own purposes, further said, that the officers should wait for him, at the outer gate of the priory, that so all the world might bear witness the church had not betrayed him to the secular power.

'And, when the world shall bear witness, that my surrender is voluntary,' said Woodreeve, in order to daunt the Prior from his purpose; 'then will it judge me innocent by that act alone.'

So resolute a reply convinced his enemy he had no time to lose in effecting whatever wrong he might intend to perpetrate, in pursuance of his wretched policy; and he now departed, meditating on the means of accomplishing it.

Leaving a guard of monks behind at the entrance of the chancel, he gave sign to Wischard, a brother, whom he had long favoured, to follow him to the great chamber. How to compass the death of the prisoner, in so short a space by any poison, that should not betray itself, and bring suspicion on its inventor, he knew not. Sometimes, he thought it were better to give him his liberty to flee away; and so he would have done, could he have been certain the liberty would be so used; but he was rather certain, from what had lately passed, that this would be otherwise; that the prisoner would urge his offer of an escape, as evidence against him, on a charge of having been an accomplice in the murder; and that other things might come to light, which would be more easily proved than the guilt of the Baron alone.

With these doubts and fears upon his mind, he remained in the arched chamber, in close consultation with Wischard, till all in the priory were at rest, save the poor merchant on his kinsman's grave, and those monks who watched him there.

At the head of this chapter was an illuminated drawing of the inside of the White hall, with the King's court assembled. The King was in a chair, but without a cloth of estate over it; and near him was his high Justicier, who sat on the same platform, in his robes of office. On the steps, near the King's chair, stood a youth, with an observing countenance, intended, no doubt, for Prince Edward; also at the footstool knelt a young man, with a spirited air, offering a chain to the King, who seemed to gaze on him, with amazement and terror. Throughout the hall appeared general consternation; many of the Bishops and Barons stood up, and leaned forward, as if to view what was passing near the King's chair.

ARLY on the morrow, the Prior of Saint Mary's was at the castle, in close conference with the Baron de Blondeville, and awaiting a hearing of the King. And, when they had obtained this, having already settled their plot, they set forth, in their own way, so much of the adventure of the night before at the priory, as they thought necessary to win the King's consent, that the trial of the merchant should be had, on this very day. His Highness had designed to defer it awhile, both because the argument of the Archbishop had taken some hold of him, and because he thought it not for the honour of the Baron de Blondeville, that this matter should seem to be held of such importance as that, just at this time, it must be further inquired into.

But now, being sore pressed upon by those about him – and it was ever his weakness to be ruled by those nearest at hand rather than by fixed principles either of his own, or of those wiser in council than himself – being sore pressed by the false representations of the wily Prior, he yielded his consent, that the jury already warned should be summoned to attend in court, this day, the trial of the poor stranger for divers practices of magical delusion and of the black art, in the great hall. Should they fail to substantiate this head of charge, the Prior had another in the tale he had already told the King of the merchant's pretended attempt upon his life, and his evil practices upon the golden chain.

As matter connected with this charge, he also told his Highness, that the merchant had escaped from the castle to the priory, where he then was and where he might be secured; for that he, trusting to his own arts, yet unable to elude the vigilance of the brethren placed there, had audaciously declared he would resign himself to the King's officers, and throw himself upon justice. The Prior failed not to point out, that there was a daring artfulness in this giving out, and to caution his Highness against the seeming consciousness of innocence, which it was meant to imply. And thus the King seeing, that each day brought forth some new danger, plotted, as it appeared, by the merchant, against the peace and even the lives of his quiet subjects, commanded without further hesitation, that his trial should commence, on this very day; and his Highness determined to be present his-self in court, the while.

The court had indeed already met in the White hall, and divers small causes had been tried there, the preceding day; many others remained to be settled, during this time of the King's keeping court, at Kenilworth; but it was resolved, that the charge against the merchant should be inquired into immediately on the meeting of the court, which was now beginning to assemble. Notice of this was speedily given there, and the jury and witnesses, being all nigh at hand, were easily brought together.

Meanwhile, a guard was despatched to the priory gate, there to await the surrender of the merchant. Nor was it without extreme anxiety and fear, that he, on receiving their summons, stepped from the sanctuary, and passed along the passages and chambers to the outer gate, where he gave himself up to justice, and was soon after again a prisoner in the turret. A night of watchfulness and terror had ill prepared him for the approaching trial; but he endeavoured to support, with the consciousness of innocence and with a recollection of his just motives, the burden of calumny and danger now laid upon him, and to meet, with calmness, the malice of his enemies.

Nathless, so haggard and wan were his looks, when he came before the court, and beheld his accuser, the Baron de Blondeville, that many there scrupled not to say he was guilty even before he was tried. And, as ignorance is always a child, so

155

were there many nobles then in the hall, who, profiting nothing by their years, did hold that magic could be wrought by such as fully applied themselves unto it, and that it had been practised in the banquet-hall by this poor stranger, or by those in league with him. And, as vanity never grows old, but changes its shape only with the stages of a man's life, so many an aged Baron, now sitting in the King's court, who, in his youth, had valued himself for a handsome person, gorgeously apparelled, and, in his maturer years, for the number of vassals and the abundance of his castle-banquets – many such a Baron, now in his age, as freshly priding himself on sagacity, such as no arts could baffle, came hither, fortified against the evidence, to abide by his first opinion.

There sat in the White hall that day, many bishops and barons of the realm, such as usually composed the King's court, when he wore his crown and held the high festivals of the year. These seldom had been kept at Kenilworth, but, when his Highness was not at his palace at Westminster, either Winchester, or Windsor, Salisbury, Gloucester, York, or other great cities of the realm were the scenes of them. At such times, not only was justice administered to his subjects, but the great councils of the realm were held, and laws were made. Then also were honours dispensed; the King making some knights, others barons, as it so pleased him, and the opportunity required. There too, sometimes, were contracted, or solemnized, such marriages of his own family, or of his nobles, as he countenanced; and too often was it said of King Henry, that he bestowed upon strangers, favourites in his court, the richest heiresses of his kingdom.

At these high festivals of the year, he was in trowth a sovereign, wearing his crown, sitting on his throne, and swaying all the princely power of his sceptre. Then he received homage of his tenants in chief, knights and other; levied fines, and with the help of his justicier, barons and prelates, managed his revenues. How far his Highness was governed by their council, when he was so hard upon the golden citizens of London, who, in his reign paid in fines for his favour, twenty thousand pounds, I know not. But, never did he practise such cruel means of extortion as did his father, King John.

At such times, too, were decided trials by combat; and among the gorgeous spectacles, then held forth, tilt and tournament surpassed.

156

But to come back again unto this festival of Kenilworth. The King sat not, this day, upon his throne in court, but upon a chair, beside his justicier, whom he wished to do his part there. He meant not his-self to speak sentence upon the prisoner, as at Westminster he had done upon Peter de Rivallis, his treasurer, whom he sent from open court to the tower of London, by his own word of command. Amongst other of the King's chief officers, who this day kept state in court, were the Earl of Hereford, Lord Constable of England; the Earl of Norfolk, Lord Mareschall of England; Simon de Montfort, Earl of Leicester, the King's Seneschall; the High Chamberlain; the Chancellor, and the Treasurer. The Archbishop of York was not there; being, as the Baron de Blondeville and the Prior of Saint Mary's well knew, yet at Coventry; and, therefore, had they so hurried forward this business.

It was suspected, that the Baron and his friend had taken special means, that the jury, chosen for this trial, might be such as were likely men to serve their views; and they feared not, that the King would now do as he had formerly done at Winchester. There, as is well known, some merchants of Brabant, having accused to his Highness some of his household of having robbed them, the thieves, on being brought to trial, were acquitted by the jury; who, though wealthy men, were proved to be in league with the offenders; on which, the King, without scruple, commanded them to prison; and caused another jury to be summoned, who found them guilty of that they had been charged with. But the Baron trusted enough in the King's kindness not to fear he would do the like now.

What passed in the merchant's mind, while now in court, waiting his trial, may not be told, within compass; save that he resolved, when opportunity should come, boldly to charge the Prior with possessing the golden chain, worn by his kinsman when he fell, and of having been an accomplice in that foul deed.

For, well he now remembered, where he had first seen his face and heard his voice. This was at a little hostel, where he and his companions had rested them awhile, a few hours before the robbery. There, in the settle, beside the blazing logs, sat that same Prior, drinking mead. He wore not then the garments of the church, which he should never have put on, but the livery of war; and the merchant had taken him for a common follower of some knight, so coarse and worn were the clothes beneath his

157

hauberk. When they were departing, he asked which road they went, feigning to be fearful, in those times, of passing alone through the forest; and, having learned their way, said his was different, and bade them well to Kenilworth, ere night should come on.

Afterwards, during the perpetration of the crime, the merchant, who discerned not his person, nor his features, through the disguise he had taken, soon as he spoke, recollected the voice; and, within a short time, he had recognized both voice and features in the same man; though the countenance was so changed and bloated, and the present voice so artificial, that this recollection had not come, but by accident. The present dress of the Prior, too, and his station had gone to retard this, But now, when tones and countenance had been partly recollected, and that golden chain was seen on the same individual, Woodreeve was not suffered to doubt, that the Prior of Saint Mary's was one of those, who had robbed him. Nor was that so wonderful in times, when lawless violence had almost overrun the whole land; and when the King, as has been seen, found it necessary to commit to prison twelve householders of Hampshire, for having leagued with thieves in his own household!

But to come back, once more, to what passed this day, in the court. It were tedious to tell of all this – of the names of such as assisted in the judgment, or of the forms and ceremonies, observed during the trial; though these were curious to behold, and in themselves most grave and princely. Nevertheless, some things shall be related, which more nearly concerned the prisoner, and which struck many persons with marvellous dread. We vouch not for the truth of all here told; we only repeat what others have said and their selves credited; but in these days what is there of strange and wonderful, which does not pass as current as the coin of the land; and what will they not tell in hall, or chamber, seated by night over blazing logs, as if their greatest pleasure were to fear?

Some, who tell the story, say they were witnesses in court of what passed there, and that the marvels brought about, were through the arts of that same joculator, who came into the banquet-hall, before the visions there shown, and who, they scrupled not to say, was one of those magicians, from the East, who were well known to have raised strange delusions in many a hall here in England. But this man was not seen in court, that day, nor had he been seen, any where, either in the castle, or town, since that memorable night of the festival, though strict search had been made for him.

The accusation against Woodreeve ran thus. It charged him with having raised up certain delusions, by means of unlawful arts of witchcraft, or of magic, to the end of persuading the King and his nobles, that the charge of a dreadful crime, imputed by the prisoner to the Baron de Blondeville, was true. And it farther alleged, that he had by witchcraft acted upon the person of the Baron, causing, at divers times, a suspicion of all his faculties, and, as it were, binding up his whole soul in a trance, so that he could neither speak, nor see, nor move. There were, it was affirmed, hundreds in the court, who had seen the marvellous pageant, which had appeared on the night of the great banquet, and not one could tell how it came thither, or by whom it was invented. They were many also, who had seen the Baron's condition, both in chapel and hall.

And it seemed plain enough, that all this was the work of evil sprite, in league with an artful man. Who this might be, whether the poor merchant, or that strange minstrel, that had entered the hall of festival, who was there, that might tell? Many and divers were the opinions and sayings upon this affair; but, though all thought the delusion supernatural, none held the merchant to be guilty of it. Nay, there were not wanting those, who willingly credited, that the Baron was guilty of all, which the vision seemed to accuse him of; yet none dared hint such thought, knowing the place he held in the King's favour. And, perchance, this very high favour, shown forth by the new title granted to him, did incline many, though the cause was unknown of themselves, to judge the worst of him.

Now, when all the proceedings were finished, the jury thought the same as the many, that, though there had been evil practices, there was nothing to show that the prisoner knew ought of them; and so they said by their verdict. But when all looked to him to remark his joy, they saw his countenance still anxious and fearful. The trowth is, he dreaded the Prior, more than any other enemy, and that he would pursue him far more artfully than the Baron had done.

The King was much disturbed at the verdict given, and the Baron would have been more so, had he not trusted to the further measures of his friend.

But now it was, that the poor merchant, finding himself detained and seeing the peril in wait for him, accused the Prior

159

of Saint Mary's, of having been one of the robbers, confederates of the Baron de Blondeville, affirming that he his-self had seen on his neck a chain, which had been taken from his murdered friend.

By the King and most present, this accusation was considered as the effort of a desperate man; and it took away from him all pity, and turned their hearts against him. Others there were, who judged less hardly of him, and these suspected, that his brain was disordered by the fits he was subject to have at times, and would have had him withdrawn from the judge, and taken in hand by the physician.

But the Prior had already delivered in an accusation against him, not only of having practised magical arts, but of having forcibly attempted his life; and the court must do their duty. So, a new jury having been called, this second trial of Woodreeve began, at the especial petition of the Prior and by command of the King. The Baron remained in court, and some observed he seemed as earnest in the Prior's cause as he had been in his own.

This latter charge having been fully stated, the first witness examined was the prison-keeper of Caesar's tower, and the jury scrupled not to hear his say, though he must condemn himself of want of vigilance, at least, if he did not accuse the prisoner of arts superior to human resistance. This man said, that he had secured the prison-chamber, at the usual hour, and that, during the night, all had remained so still, you might have heard a leaf stir, save, that, at the second watch-piping, the wayte had called out to him, that some one had entered the tower; when he, finding the strong door fastened, as he had left it, and not having before heard any noise, knew this could not have been, and so had told the wayte. On the morrow, going as usual to the prison-chamber, he found that door secure, as he had made it, but when he undid it – the merchant was no longer within! He could account for his disappearance by no mortal means; and so he ended his say.

Then the knights, on service at the great portal, were questioned, and their answers were partly to the same purpose. One of them, indeed, said he had heard a noise from the room over the dungeon, soon after the wayte had piped the third watch; but, on trying the door, he found it fast, and so thought no more of it. And now it cannot be doubted, that the knight, who was the secret friend of the Baron de Blondeville, had tampered with his companions, or, in some way, had deceived

160

them, since they could thus slightly treat that, which had caused a clarion to be sounded. But, they could truly say, as they did, that they had seen no one go forth of the gates, or move any where, save their own men. And, knowing that they had been too bountiful of wine to those of the portcullis chamber, they might dislike, and avoid to say anything, that would lead to a discovery of the condition of those drowsy guards.

These wardours of the portcullis room being questioned, touching the fastening of the tower-door, one of them took that matter upon himself; for, though none of them knew what had happened, yet did they, for their own credit, conceal their ignorance, save he, who said, that he thought one came in the night and gave him a blow; but he knew not how he got away, nor any thing more about his assailant! 'You were slumbering on your post, carle,' said his examiner; but this he stoutly denied, to the admiration of the poor prisoner, who knew the whole party had been in such deep sleep, that he had heard them snorting two chambers off. For this the Prior had his-self accounted, as before rehearsed; but he allowed not himself to smile.

Next were called the wayte and his groom; and the old man deposed he had seen some one pass through the upper court, as he was going the second round, so closely muffled up, he knew not who he was, and the person had passed by so quickly, that, though he pursued his steps, yet could he never see him after. He thought he had gone to Caesar's tower; but, on giving an alarm there, he found he had mistaken, the keeper having declared he had seen no one enter. Afterwards, he had searched the upper court, and questioned those on guard there, but they had neither seen nor heard any thing. Still, not being satisfied that all was right, he had taken his station in the porch opposite to the great tower, and there watched out the night, save when he had piped his rounds; but he had not seen any one come forth of the tower, nor any persons but the guard, the whole night long. This testimony of the wayte the guard confirmed.

During these narratives of the witnesses, the Prior kept an unconcerned countenance, and none present suspected him of being that unknown person; while many thought the prisoner his-self was the man, on his way out of the castle, and that the wayte had mistaken the course he took.

When the sentinels of the ramparts and posterns were questioned, all were found to agree, that no living thing had been seen, or heard, from wall or battlement, to pass forth of the

161

castle, during that night. Then were most of the persons present confirmed in their suspicion, that the merchant possessed some secret art, by which he had conveyed himself from the castle into the priory. It signified not to their apprehension, that such art, if he had possessed it, might have conveyed him clean away from his enemies; they troubled not themselves to think so far; or, perchance, they guessed there were certain limits and boundaries to the power of magic. But, whether the limit here drawn was consistent with the end designed, who was there, that could judge?

After these witnesses, the Prior his-self came forward and repeated his own tale, at length, such as he had already related it to the King. And he brought several of his monks and others of the convent, as evidence, that the prisoner had, in the midst of the night, fled from the great chamber of the priory to the church, and then sought refuge at the sanctuary, as if he dreaded punishment for some crime. They dwelt on the disorder and emotion he had betrayed, the seeming conscious-ness of guilt, and the boldness and desperation, with which he had accused the Prior of having unlawfully possessed himself of the golden chain, which he, this day in court, had made the subject of accusation against him. This chain, they said, pertained to an amulet, which had preserved their Prior's life from the dagger of the assassin; on which chain the prisoner had, though standing apart at the sanctuary, so wrought, it being then in the hands of certain brethren of the house, as to cause a painting to appear, that was not there before.

While this tale was telling, the Archbishop of York, who was just returned from his visit to the Bishop of Coventry, then lying in grievous sickness, had entered the court, and had taken his proper place. He it was, who inquired, whether this golden chain were at hand; on which the high justicier ordered it should be produced. Then, the Prior, who pretended a wish to show it, drew it forth from his neck, and, it was carried to the King, who examined it, looking long on the painting of that fair dame, the widow of the unfortunate knight. Close within the rim of that picture was drawn a little face, like unto a cherub looking up, in peace, to the lady, who seemed to smile upon him, in tender affection. The Archbishop, when he perused the picture, was wonderly struck both with the resemblance to the shadow he had seen in the hall, and with that of the fair dame, which had been there presented in the pageant.

162

The King, looking again upon the picture, acknowledged the likeness, and then summoning the Baron to his side, showed him the portrait, and put the chain into his hands; who, having received it on his knee, rose up, and withdrew to a window, the better to examine it. Thither followed him the eyes of the Archbishop and the Prior, but each with different interest and motive for watchfulness. My Lord of York observed the chain to tremble in its holder's hand, and believed, that Woodreeve had spoken the truth.

The Prior saw, that the countenance of his associate was altered, and hoped that he would be resolute, during the whole trial; each was contented, in his own way, and awaited calmly what might follow. But, when the Baron had gazed awhile, he became agitated. He seemed to shrink, and, averting his face from the object he contemplated, he held it nearly at arm's length. Then, he looked again, drawing the portrait nearer to his sight, and then, again withdrew it, while a livid paleness overspread his countenance, and he seemed hardly able to support himself.

Then, as if regaining all his courage, he left the window; but, instead of returning the portrait to the King, he was conveying it to the Prior, when my lord Archbishop cried out, 'My lord, his Highness, hath not yet done with that chain; give it into his hands, from which you received it.'

The Baron stopped; he seemed to be angered, and, half turning with a haughty mien and frowning look, he answered, 'I obey no command but the King's.'

On this the King, graciously smiling, said, 'I desire it of you.'

The Baron, immediately advancing to the state chair, dropped his knee, and presented the chain; on receiving which and looking again upon the picture, his Highness spoke with surprise to the Baron, who bowed, with a disclaiming gesture, and said a few words, which none nigh could hear; while Prince Edward, who stood on the steps, below the King's chair, viewed him with a suspicious eye; for, young as he was, he had observed that in him, which he liked not. And now he saw with wonder, the earnestness, with which his father looked upon the picture; for he knew not, that it showed the likeness of the knight, who had appeared in the banquet-hall.

Unknowingly, the Baron had touched the spring, which disclosed this portrait, and had shut up that of the unhappy widow. Prince Edward looked again on the Baron, thinking he

163

had wrought some change in the picture, leading to mischief and designed against the prisoner, to whose cause his heart secretly inclined him. From all that he had seen before, and on this day, he judged him to be innocent of evil intention; and he had not failed to tell the King, his father, privately all his thoughts.

But his Highness, whose understanding was often baffled by his humours and by the arts of cunning men, thought not with his son in this matter; and, he moreover, suspected this change in the painting to be wrought by the merchant, or his agents, as the Prior had before affirmed; or by some new art of magic. Still his sight dwelt on that portrait, whose look of quiet sadness so much remembered him of that, which the knight in the pageant had shown, when departing from his family and his native shore. After long perusing the portrait, the King lifted his eyes from it, and beheld! once more before him, the form of that very knight, such as had appeared on the steps of the dais.

It was in truth the very image of this shadowed forth here in miniature; the same armour, worn in the same way, with vizor up, and the eyes showing that same solemn and resigned look, save that they were now fixed, somewhat sternly on the King. It seemed as if his Highness only perceived this person, while he sat motionless, and, for some moments, silent.

Then he rose hastily, and commanded, that the stranger should be secured! Vain command. Those, who heard it, perceived not for whom it was designed; but looked upon each other with wonder and amazement: and many there were near him, who feared his Highness was stricken with sudden distemper. Whether the Archbishop saw aught, or only suspected the cause is not known; but he was observed to make that holy gesture, which formerly he had used in the greater hall. The King, with some anger, repeated his command! but he whom he would have seized, no more appeared.

For awhile, his Highness seemed struck with dismay; he sat and covered his eyes with his hand, reclining him in his chair. Then, imputing this appearance to the same art as the former, dread gave way to indignation against the prisoner; and he resolved to have immediate justice done; not only in punishment of past offences, but to put an end to those deceits and mischiefs, from which it seemed, that even his-self was not secured. Sometimes, too, he doubted whether this man might not be an agent of his bitter enemy, Lewellyn of Wales; by whose evil arts he had, as he deemed, been formerly robbed of that precious ring, which was to render him invincible in war. If this were so, the prisoner added to the guilt of being a spy and a traitor, that of feigned agitations and sorrow, touching a deed never committed.

Order being given that the trial should immediately proceed, the Baron de Blondeville, who, while this image had remained before the King, was busied in another part of the hall, and thus escaped its influence, advanced to the chair, and received again the chain, with intent to deliver it to the Prior. Now, that which follows, was reported of many present in the court, with what truth I know not; but it is here faithfully related.

No sooner had the Baron received into his hand that golden chain, than the eyes of all near were fixed upon his robe. It was the same he wore on the night of the banquet, and on which, when passing from the King's chamber, through the brown gallery with the Prior, and meeting there the marvellous stranger, three drops of blood had fallen. These had been partly erased; but they were now not unnoticed, though none knew whence they came.

No sooner had he received this chain of the deceased knight, than each little drop began to spread, till that side of his garment became covered, as it were, with crimson, seeming to maintain the notion, that is gone forth, that after some prolonged presence of the murderer, the blood of the deceased will become fresh again, wherever it may be found, as if newly shed.

The King, 'tis said, beheld this in silence, not knowing what it might mean, though guessing it to be some new device of sorcery. The Prior remained in his place, with downward look; while the prisoner in his, lifted up his hands to Heaven.

My lord Archbishop rose and turned himself to his Highness as though he would address him; but he did not. Prince Edward's looks were bent steadily upon the Baron, as were also most of those, that composed the King's court, but no one spoke, each awaiting for what another might first say. There was a general confusion and amazement in the hall.

The Baron his-self stood looking down upon his garment, with the chain trembling in his hand. How long he might have continued standing there none knew, had not the King's voice recalled him from his trance, and bade him deliver the chain to the secretary at the table, there to remain, till the trial should conclude. He obeyed with looks, that seemed to say this command foretold some diminution of favour; and, after his having delivered it, behold a new marvel; for that great crimson stain began to separate into three parts, and then to lessen and fade away, till it wholly disappeared, leaving his robe bright and rich as before.

Then there was a general tumult and outcry in the court of, 'justice, justice! the prisoner hath spoken the truth! The chain of the deceased hath borne witness against the Baron, the Baron de Blondeville.'

At these words, the Baron seemed to recover all his spirit; he threw a glance of indignation round the court, and then, walking firmly up to the King, did homage, and remained on his knee, ready to plead for protection, when the tumult should subside. Again my lord, the Archbishop, turned towards his Highness, calmly awaiting the return of silence. The Prior also stood up, and was haranguing, with vehement gesticulation, though no one could hear a single word he uttered. But the poor merchant, having seen this second marvellous sign in his favour, testified no presumptuous joy; he had sunk down, overcome with humble gratitude, unable either to speak, or to shed a tear.

In vain the King raised his arm on high, and his chief justicier stood up, with stern countenance, to restore order; each individual spectator followed the promptings of his own thoughts, and uttered them without scruple, though scarcely any one could be heard. And thus it went, for some time, till divers of the crowd, without the hall, hearing that something extraordinary was passing within, pressed forward to the court, so that those sitting there became afraid for their lives, and the King's guards were called upon to do their duty, which they at last performed, with no small difficulty.

At this so flagrant a breach of good 'haviour in the King's court and in his very presence, his Highness was much moved, and he willingly attributed it to the malignant passions of pride and jealousy directed against the Baron de Blondeville, who was doubly obnoxious, as being a stranger by birth and exalted by favour. So his Highness became more warmly attached to his cause than before, and more resolute to protect him against the united force of his enemies. Silence being at last restored, his Highness bade the Baron de Blondeville 'Rise and fear not; for justice shall overtake the guilty.' The Archbishop liked not the King's frown, as he spoke these words, and he sat down disdainfully, without uttering what was in his mind.

Not so the Prior of Saint Mary's, who had been impatiently

166

watching for the moment, when he might be heard, and who now boldly cried out, 'My lord Archbishop, will you now credit the truth that is before you? Will you now deny the power of sorcery? Here, in this very court, this false accuser has unwarily betrayed his guilt; here, in the face of justice, exercising his art, with a view to deprive the Baron de Blondeville both of honour and of life, he has made evident the truth of my accusation against himself. You yourself, have now witnessed, that a spell is in that chain, which his presence has put in movement, and you can no longer question what I have related of yesternight, or of his motive for exercising his infamous art. He has caused these paintings to appear in the chain, that he may claim it for his deceased kinsman's, who, he pretends, was murdered, that by this circumstance he may prove the extravagant and ridiculous charge he has fabricated against me. By the same arts of sorcery, exercised upon the Baron's robe, he would confirm the other slander he has uttered – that against the Baron de Blondeville; and, by connecting this second marvel with the first, he would fain make it appear, that the Baron and myself were confederated in the same crime. But, in so doing, he has proved nothing but the force of his spells and of his malice, and has turned them unwittingly against himself alone, since his Highness cannot be deceived. My lord Archbishop, will you now deny the power of sorcery?'

When he had ceased, the Archbishop rose with calm and dignified countenance, as of one, who holds the balance in his own hands; and, without deigning to notice the Prior, he called upon the justicier to put an end to this irregular proceeding, and to make the trial go on. It was only in submission to the King, that this disorderly interruption had been permitted by the High Justicier, his Highness having given him a sign, that the Prior should be heard; but now he willingly resumed his duty. However, the words of the Prior had not been in vain; for, they took effect upon the minds of many in the court, to the prejudice of the poor merchant, and to a confirmation of both charges against him, that of socery, and that of attempted assassination. And thus it seemed, that the very marvel, which at first made against the Baron, being now warped and twisted by the so crafty Prior, was likely to end in the prisoner's ruin.

Then, the merchant his-self was examined; but the truth which he told, of the Prior having come to him and offered him liberty, appeared less plausible than his accuser's falsehood.

167

That he should have hesitated to accept the freedom thus offered, few could credit; yet the testimony of the wayte, seemed to support Woodreeve's story, which, had he been suffered to proceed, would have been further proved by his account of the many secret ways, through which he was conducted, and which were so little known, that by hardly any other means than those of experience, could he have been made acquainted with them. But, when he began to tell of that door in the Constable's great chamber, which led into those passages of the walls and so, by covert windings, down into the portcullis room, and to those hidden vaults below, he was suddenly checked in his story. Those, who willed not, that these secrets, and, partly, safeguards of the castle, should be made public, denied that there were such; and, feigning to be weary of so long-winding a tale, they brought it to a speedy conclusion, by commanding the prisoner to be less tedious and to account for his appearance in the Prior's chamber, which surely was not in the castle, but in the priory. Now, how could he fully do so, but by tracing to all his steps thither? And this he was forbidden to do; and he could not but see, that he should be resolutely contradicted by those, who, if they had no concert with his enemies, fancied they were required by duty to tell a falsehood – as if any duty to man could require that! Being then, forbidden to take this course, he only related, that, having followed the Prior into a subterraneous way under the castle-ditch, hoping it would lead him to the forest, his life had been threatened by the Prior, on his discovering and claiming that very golden chain, which had been shown this day in court. He further told, that, having escaped from the uplifted dagger, he had fled along that avenue, which brought him to the Prior's chamber, whence he had again been compelled to fly from pursuit, which had scarcely permitted him even the rights of sanctuary.

While the prisoner was telling this part of his story, the most profound silence reigned throughout that hall, where lately not one voice could be heard from another; nay, hardly the trumpet of the King's guard, amidst the stormy multitude. Many, while they listened, found themselves inclining to the merchant's cause; and some would entirely believe, that he had spoken only the truth.

Amongst the latter, were the young Prince Edward and the venerable Archbishop – ingenuous youth and discerning age. Always, indeed, had the conscientious sagacity of the

Archbishop inclined him to Woodreeve's cause; and what he had heard formerly and lately at Coventry, respecting the Prior, confirmed his opinion. He knew also enough of the ways, employed by some in those times to procure riches, to be incredulous of the strange history of this Prior, whose unaccountable wealth had procured for him his present rank from the Pope's legate.

Others present there were, who, though but too well acquainted with the lawless and desperate manners of those days, yet refused to acknowledge, that a man of the Prior's office and rank could be guilty of the crime. Amongst those, who inclined to the prisoner, were some of the jury; when now there came into court, one Aaron, a Jew of Lincoln. He came in not by accident; but, as some shrewdly guessed, was sent by those, who, knowing the man, and his way of trade, designed to make him an instrument on this occasion.

The business, that first brought him to Kenilworth, was to pay the Queen that usual surplus of a King's fine, called 'Aurum Reginae'. This man had been heavily fined; and, as it is said, for having falsified a charter. However, this might be, he had now to pay, to the Queen alone, about six hundred marks; in present payment for which sum, her Highness took of him a transfer of a deed, by which this Jew held in pawn of John Vavasour, the manor of Hazlewood, which that ancient family had held of the de Percies, even in the Conqueror's reign. The deed, thus rescued by the Queen from the Jew, who had withheld it, that he might extort for it an exorbitant sum, was by her returned to the same John, on his paying to her the rehersed sum of six hundred marks. But this circumstance is here related only, that it may appear what sort of person this Jew was, on whose word might probably depend the life of an innocent man. Now, this Aaron, when he came into the hall, and was produced as a witness, desired to see that same golden chain, worn of the Prior and sworn to of the merchant, as having been about the neck of his deceased kinsman, at the time of the murder.

On this, the Prior, looking hardly at the Jew, feigned to remember him, saying, as he delivered up the chain 'You should know it well; for, if I err not, it was of you that I purchased it. I was then returning from a pilgrimage to the shrine of Saint Hugh, at Lincoln.'

'You are right,' quoth the Jew; 'this chain, I remember me, I sold to you for fifty marks of gold, some five or six years back.

169

Your were not then Prior of Saint Mary's, but a brother of Coventry.'

'Behold!' said the Prior, 'one who can bear testimony against the false story of the prisoner. Let an oath be administered unto him.'

'He is a Jew!' cried out a voice; 'his oath may not be taken.'

'The *law* is against it,' said another; 'but who may prevent his word being credited?'

The Prior then demanded of him whether he remembered any paintings concealed in the chain? and the Jew replied, that there were no paintings, when he sold it to him; but to the chain itself he could swear, if he were permitted to do so. He had bought it of a goldsmith of London, then living in Chepe; it was of fine gold, and of the best workmanship; for that citizen of London had in his workshop one Giocondi, a Florentine, who was famous for such things; and by him was it made. With those fine paintings, he should have valued the whole at not less than one hundred marks.

Here again was a contention, whether the oath of a Jew could be received; some saying the law was against it; others, that, when King John's reign ended, that law had ceased. And thus it went, for some time, till the King, rising from his chair, commanded that an oath should be administered, and this was done, after the Archbishop had obtained of the court, that the oath to be taken of the Jew should not be such as we swear. Then the Archbishop, turning towards the Prior, demanded of what house in Coventry he had been a brother, and at what time he had purchased the chain.

'At the time of my pilgrimage to Saint Hugh, of Lincoln,' answered the Prior; 'then I purchased that chain of Aaron.'

'Of what house were you a brother?' repeated the Archbishop sternly.

'Of Saint Nicholas.'

'Of what order.'

'– Of the Benedictine.'

'I know not of any house at Coventry, that is both of that name and order,' observed the Archbishop.

'I said not I was of Coventry,' replied the Prior.

'Your *friend* has said so,' urged the Archbishop, 'and till now, you have not contradicted him.'

'The Jew is mistaken,' said the Prior; 'I know not that he is my friend; if he were so, in trowth, he would have been better acquainted with my former abode.'

170

'Answer, without further evasion,' said the Archbishop, 'and tell to what town and brotherhood you belonged at the time of your pilgrimage.'

'I was then of the Priory of Saint Nicholas, in Exeter.'

'Your's was a long pilgrimage,' said the Archbishop, fixing his eyes attentively upon the Prior.

My lord Bishop said not more, but listened constantly to the further evidence of this Aaron, which went hard against the merchant, touching the matter of the chain, and when one, who pleaded for the Prior, drew up each particular of the prisoner's tale, such as he had his-self related it, many improbable circumstances appeared on the face of it. To those unacquainted with his enemies' true history and character, there seemed to be little motive for his attempt to lead away Woodreeve from his prison, to give him liberty, if that were in trowth the end he had in view, when he was said to have conducted him from the tower; and, if that were not his end, and he had designed to prevent any discovery of his own former guilt, by the assassination of the merchant, why, said they, did he pass over the opportunity, afforded by that avenue described by the prisoner himself, as so secret and remote. To these persons there appeared neither cause sufficient to have urged the Prior to draw forth a poniard with intent to kill, nor, having done so, any motive to restrain his hand, in a place so convenient to his purpose.

For Woodreeve, when he related that the Prior appeared horror-struck at the moment of aiming the dagger had not explained the cause of this, nor did he his-self know it, though by it his life had been saved. Neither, if he had known and related it, would they, in all likehood, have heeded him; but it was afterwards supposed, that the Prior, at that dangerous moment, had been awed by the appearance of the deceased knight.

These considerations, together with the evidence of the Jew, at last determined the jury against the poor merchant, who was adjudged guilty of having attempted the life of the Prior and of having practised arts of sorcery, which, it was supposed, had been made visible this day, in open court.

On this verdict, many made known their satisfaction, and approached the Baron de Blondeville, and the Prior, with joyful words. But there was not one to shed a tear with the prisoner, or who dared to show him any sign of sympathy.

171

My lord Archbishop seemed much disposed to do so; for, his countenance expressed grave displeasure, when all was joy around him. Even the smiles of the King could not move him to any show of accordance. It became plain he thought the condemned person innocent; and perhaps, he suspected, that the witnesses and even the jury had been unduly practised with; but of this he spoke nothing. Prince Edward, too, seemed not well pleased with this transaction; for, his eyes were sometimes sternly fixed on the Prior, and even on the Baron himself, whose heart was now at ease, who stood on the steps of the King's chair, cap in hand, discoursed to by his Highness.

But there was one present in the court, though unseen, whose joy did equal his. This was the lady Baroness, his fair bride, who, from a gallery on high, concealed from view by a lattice-work, had anxiously watched all, which passed in court, and now, that the honour of her lord was rescued from what she had been taught to think was but the malice of a secret enemy, she had nearly sunk under the tumult of the contrary feelings of joy for one, and pity for the unhappy instrument of the other.

Woodreeve, weighed down with grief and despair, was led back to his prison through a curious and busy crowd, too many of them willing to see him suffer death without delay, eager for some new spectacle. But his sentence was postponed, during the King's pleasure, who, well contented with the verdict, meant not that the dreadful infliction should take place, till after his own departure from Kenilworth; and thus the court broke up; Woodreeve to his prison-tower, there to await his fate; the Prior to his home, secretly to exult in the success of his wicked wiles, and to plot new ones; the Archbishop to his chamber, there to meditate alone; the Baron, to rejoice with the unsuspecting Lady Barbara; the King to refresh himself, and the whole court to talk over what had passed; and to prepare them for the diversions and merriment appointed for the approaching evening, unsuitable as they were, at this time.

The merchant, when he had once more taken possession of his solitary turret, desired means wherewith to send a letter to his wife – for he could write – that she, now at a distance, and in daily expectation of his return, might be somewhat prepared for his fate. But, even this poor request was denied him, under pretence, that it was feared he might work, with unlawful characters in the black art, further evil against those he had accused, or those, who had the custody of him.

While the trial had been proceeding in the White hall, the Queen, with many noble ladies attending, went into the Hall of Banquet, to view the shields of the knights, candidates for prizes in a tournament, which had been appointed for the morrow; and there a strange accident happened. The shields were hung in array, round this gorgeous hall, and the banner of each knight waved over his shield. An officer of arms attended, who called aloud to whom each shield belonged, with the name and full titles of the owner; that, it any lady had cause of complaint, against any knight-candidate, she might touch his shield; and, without aid of words, this action was sufficient to cause that shield to be taken from its place; that, if, on inquiry, there were reason to suppose him guilty of any 'haviour derogatory to the honour of chivalry, his name might be erased from amongst those of the candidates, and himself adjudged unworthy to break a lance on the field.

There was now in the hall a great display of shields; for, besides the many nobles and knights of the realm of England, who had entered their names for the lists, there were knights, drawn hither from all quarters; some from France, some from Scotland, and some from Germany. Amidst this show of shields, which had been here for some days, and which had not been disturbed by the late trial, three spaces on the walls betrayed, that three knights had been already accused. To many, who looked upon these vacancies, the blanks there seemed to plead for those whose shields had been condemned; when, perhaps, their enemies could not have proved aught against them, had they been accused in any other manner. The Baron de Blondeville's was not one of these proscribed shields.

Now, it happened, during this visit of very many ladies, that one amongst them went from shield to shield, examining the bearings in each, without awaiting the due progress of the herald, in his course of explanation, around the walls. Looking deliberately at every shield, she stood still before several, and seemed to meditate. Meanwhile, the singularity of her conduct and appearance drew the attention of many persons. She was not habited in the fashion of the court, or in any dress of ceremony, but wore a mourning robe and a veil, that flowed to her feet, but this had been lifted, while she was examining the shields, and even now partly betrayed her face. She was not of

173

the court, nor was she known of any of those, who gave attention to her; yet had she an air of distinction and of graceful ease, with, as some thought a foreign aspect; and each, who knew her not, supposed she was known of some other, and had good right to be there; perhaps, the sister of one of the foreign knights.

Her beauty was faded, yet seemed she young, and she had a look of sorrow and of wildness, too, that touched the hearts of many, that beheld her. By her own thoughts she was so much enwrapt, that she observed not how much she was noticed, though indeed little was said, her Highness the Queen being present.

When the herald came to the shield of the Baron de Blondeville, which was blazoned high, with all his new honours, he called forth loudly his name and titles. Then, on a sudden, this lady seemed to know where she was and what she came there for. With grave air, yet confident, walking up the hall, she stayed her steps before his shield, and examined it deliberately, the herald somewhat lingering the while. Having so stood, some little space, she bent her head, and, covering her eyes with her veil, she seemed to weep.

Then, lifting up her veil she stepped towards the shield, and touched it, looking at the herald, as she did so; but she spoke not one word. And this was sufficient, as the custom went. Immediately, the officer at arms advanced, to take down the shield from the wall, which he did not without some difficulty.

The Queen, seeing what was done, and that it was the Baron de Blondeville's shield, that was displaced, inquired who was the lady, that had caused its disgrace. But no one could tell, and she had already left the hall, well contented with what had been done. Then her Highness, blaming the herald for his speed, commanded, that the steps of this fair accuser should be followed, and her name and rank declared, that it might appear now whether her act were worthy to take so much effect, and, afterwards whether she had just cause of grief and complaint. And, until these things, or some of them, should be known, she bade the herald replace the shield on the wall.

So the Lord Marshall of England, who was attending upon her Highness, was then compelled to speak; and he said, with submission, that might not be done; the laws of chivalry forbidding, unless by especial command of the King. So her Highness let that pass, well knowing, that the King would order the shield to be replaced, except insurmountable cause should

174

appear against it. And then, having viewed the remaining shields, she, with all that company of noble ladies, withdrew.

But this accident caused much marvelling in the court, many thinking it was occasioned by some new offence of the Baron, and that a great deal yet remained to be told against him; others, that the unknown lady was the widow of the knight, who, it was said, had been slain by him; and that she had not gone away, so far, or so fast, but that her name might be easily learned by the heralds, if they were more fully ordered to discover it. Others, who held the Baron innocent, said this was only some new device of his enemies; and that, if any such female had really appeared in the hall, she had doubtless got out of the reach of discovery, into some sufficient, though near concealment.

The King, soon as he heard the report of this adventure, commanded, that strict search should be made for the lady-accuser; and that, meanwhile, the Baron's shield should be restored to its place, unstained by suspicion; there to remain until the morrow's tournament, or until surer cause should appear for removing it.

This night, his Highness kept state, not in the hall, but in the great chamber; my lord, the Archbishop, being ever at his right hand, whose gravity seemed not to yield, for one moment, to all the mirth around him. In trowth, he was not a man to be capable of festive enjoyment, when a fellow-creature had been recently condemned to wretchedness, had he even thought him guilty; but he thought not so. On all that passed, he looked with equal eye, and said little, answering only when his Highness spoke to him. Some thought he looked with displeasure on that extravagant pomp, which was here displayed in every thing, at a time, when the King had little in his coffers, and knew not well how to fill them.

With this King Henry it was ever so, on the score of money; good as he was, on many other points, he ever lived for the present hour, and suffered the next to shift for itself. His brother, my Lord of Cornwall, did otherwise; he took good care to gather up some of what he saw so bountifully scattered; and to keep it safe for his own purposes in time to come.

He had both cooler heart and head than King Henry; who spared neither trouble nor money, to advance him to the height, which he had obtained for him, and had caused him to be chosen King of the Romans, although he had once nearly raised a rebellion, with no better motive than that he wished to possess

175

the manor of Berkhamstead; and so no more of such matters. Only those, who attributed the Archbishop's more than wonted gravity, to the wasteful magificence, which was then displaying itself before him, did not reach the whole course of his so thoughtful mood.

It was, above all, the weakness of the King, which subjected him to the sway of designing men, and to be drawn aside from the administration of justice, that alarmed and grieved the bishop. And, this day, he thought he had beheld in him a striking instance of blindness to the cause of the oppressed. He knew, better than any one, the efforts he had made to warn the King against the Prior of St Mary's; and to persuade him, it was quite as possible the Baron de Blondeville should be guilty of one crime, as the prisoner of another; so that his Highness should listen, without prejudice, to what appeared on either side; but he could not so persuade.

Now, before the Archbishop had left Kenilworth for Coventry, the King had been so far influenced by his advice, that he had promised to postpone the intended trial of the merchant, till some further light should be thrown upon so extraordinary an accusation, and one made with astonishing hardihood; and it was chiefly to obtain this information from the Bishop of Coventry, that his good brother went so hastily thither; but it was of a bootless hope. The Bishop and the Prior there knew little of the character, or the former history of the Prior of Kenilworth; what they could communicate, confirmed the former suspicions of the Archbishop.

This day, when the trial was ended, he had despatched a messenger to the Prior of Saint Nicholas, in Exeter, to learn whether he knew aught of the Prior of Saint Mary's, and whether the Prior had spoken the truth, when he said, that he had been a brother of the Benedictine priory, of that name, in that city. Yet the great distance to be travelled through difficult roads, made it doubted whether his messenger would return, during any delay, which he might have sufficient influence to obtain of the King, in counteraction to that of the Baron de Blondeville and the Prior; who, for their own supposed security, might be urging, unceasingly, for speedy sentence upon their accuser.

If the Archbishop, on this night, looked sad in this courtly chamber, so did not the Baron de Blondeville. He had now regained all the gaiety of his nation and age; and danced a

176

measure to the joyance of all present; the Queen and her ladies declaring their admiration to the Baroness. Then, was there solemn dancing of many lords and noble dames; the King's five harpers playing the while.

Prince Edward, with the Baroness de Blondeville, performed a bass-dance, to the noise of the harps only. And then, finding himself oppressed with his mantle, which was of velvet, thickly embroidered, and besides heavily guarded with gold lace, he impatiently threw it off, and danced a round right merrily in his jacket, to the sound of the recorders, and to the great diversion of the King and Queen. Which dance being ended, the Prince brought his fair partner in his hand, up to the Queen, who said many gracious things to her; and, certes, for either high or solemn dancing, there was none that excelled her.

After the dancing, Richard, the King's minstrel, sang to the harp one of Maister Henry's best ballads, which were so bright and cheering, raising up the spirits and the laughter of all present; and this, if it flowed not from the famous Helicon, certes, it might be supposed to have come thence, and all held that it well deserved the butt of sack, which his Highness had lately bestowed upon him.

There was not any banqueting, or late wassailling, this night in the hall; for, on the morrow was to be the great tournament, and the most sumptuous feasting yet given; and every one was willing to prepare for it by taking an early rest. And thus, after Ypocras, and wafers had been served, with the usual state, the King and Queen avoided the Great Chamber, for that night, followed by a goodly train of estates and gentils. Each departed to his own bower; some to think on what had passed this day; others to forget that such a day had been; and others again, to watch for that, which was to come; since joy, or the hope of it, often makes the young as wakeful, as habitual care doth the aged; and many there were, whom delightsome expectation of the finery and pomp they should display, or behold, to-morrow, kept sleepless, till the wayte had piped the third watch and longer, knights and esquires, lovers and ladies, country folk, serving-men and waiting-women, many a one; and all impatiently looked for the coming hour; but specially the young knights thought how they should triumph, in all the pride of prowess, before their courted fair ones; and doubted not, that the happiness of their whole lives depended upon the coming day.

And thus the prompt feelings of youth gave shape and colour

177

and consequence to small circumstances, wrought into visions of their own imagination; all vivid and expansive now, but which would be dim and cold and contracted, as their sun should decline. But woe to him, who would have taught them to detect these bright illusions, which belong to youth, as do the golden lights and songs of joy to morning! Woe to him, who would have set before their eyes the severe form of experience, and have reduced the gaieties of their boundless hope to the many checquered scene of real existence! All in its season, comes the noon-tide ray, and melts the beauteous visions of the morning; all in its season, comes the evening ray, when lengthened shadows fall on the long landscape – when the purple cloud loses its golden edge, and the world below sinks into shade, which leads again to the bright tints of dawn – to the brighter, oh! how much brighter tints of a cloudless and limitless dawn! Are we, who would derange this order, and cast the hue of twilight before the morning or the noon-tide sun, better sighted than the Wisdom and the Beneficence which have ordained it otherwise? We may watch and regulate – to do this is our duty; and let us neither omit it by careless and total indulgence, nor spare our vigilance by total proscription; – gradually we may prepare the mind for the great truths, that time will cast over the thousand hues of hope and joyance; and gradually a sense of the vanity and nothingness of this fleeting part of an eternal existence, instead of being a melancholy, will be a complacent perception, more than reconciling us to the shortness of its imperfect joys and deeply consoling us for its sorrows.

Here was a drawing of a field of tournament, bordering on the lake, beyond which appeared the towers and lake of Kenilworth. A procession of knights, before a lady, drawn in a stately car, was moving round the field, trumpeters on horseback going before them, and dancing figures following. On the opposite side of the lawn, other knights appeared at a barrier, on whom seemed directed the chief attention of the company in the numerous tents and galleries around; who stood up, and leaned over one another, in their eagerness to view what was passing, or approaching.

Below, on the margin, stood a King crowned, in his robes, designed for King Henry; for it bore resemblance to his image in brass, placed on his monument in the Abbey of Saint Peter, called the West Minster.

UT, BEFORE rehersing the events of this day, let us not forget the night, which the poor merchant passed in his prison. There, when all noise in the castle had ceased, and sleep, as he thought, rested on every eye save his own, it was said he heard, at first, sounds of the most mournful warning, and, afterwards, others so sweet passed by his turret, as seemed to remember him, that not for any crime was he condemned, but for the grief and generous indignation, which had urged him to point out the murderer of his friend and kinsman. It seemed as if the image of that friend stood before him, not wounded, and with face of wretchedness, such as of late his memory had been haunted with, but with look of heavenly peace and kindness. Woodreeve knew this image was only in his fancy; yet, as the sounds went by, it seemed to stand more clearly there, and to smile on him with so benign a feeling, as imparted hope and comfort to his heart. He wept, but not in suffering sorrow; his tears were now such as hush the mind in deepest stillness, and strengthen and refresh it, like as the dew of heaven the withered herb.

The day of this great tournay, to which the King had invited lords and gentils, far and wide, was now come; and all was bustle and expectation in the castle and country round. It was a pleasant day to behold, and most fresh and sweet was the forest-air to those, who came prancing through it, and delightsome

179

were those shades of green and red and orange-tawney, that over canopied the way, and seemed in stately mournfulness to bid farewell to summer. The redbreast, piping his lonely song amongst the leaves, seemed to have stolen their livery, and hardly could he be distinguished from the beechen bough, on which he sat. Thus stood the beech, the elm and chesnuts, the slender ash, and lordly plane. Not so, with mark of past prime, stood the oak; warrior of winter – he yet stretched forth his mighty limbs, clad in strong verdure, to defy frost and storm, and, when he should doff it, to brave, in his crimson surcoat, even old Yule, when, with shrill whistle on the sharp north, he should come to scatter snows on his tawney crest.

It were most soothing now to melancholize under these shades, and think on many things in air and earth, real and unreal, that fly the lightsome noon; and thus might you ruminate till time should bring you to the verge of your part in it, without your perceiving, that he was carrying you on your way, all reckless of its better use, so stilly wouldst move beneath this quiet gloom. But those, who passed through the forest-tracks this day, went with the swift foot of hope and high spirits; they came not to melancholize: and a greater number of courses, palfries, hobbies, and other steeds never, ywis, tramped on the ground of Ardenn.

Ever since the first dawn, you might espy them passing among the woods from towns, and villages and hamlets and monasteries, whither they had gathered over-night; and now drawing on towards Kenilworth, and the castle, where, over the great gate, hung the helmet of invitation to all courteous knights, a summons not sighted by any, whether courteous and knightly, or humbly and civilly curious, or rude and forward.

It was in a fair meadow, which some call a plain, below the castle, on the opposite side of the moat, that this tournament was appointed; as a place were the Queen, and her ladies might behold it from the castle, if the autumn weather should forbid them to be present: but all that great space was prepared and set forth at the sides, with tents, and stages, and galleries, as if nought might keep them away; the whole hung with arras, or cloth of gold. These you might see from the towers and walls of the castle; nay, from the bay-window of the great hall, standing like a little town of palaces and castles; for so were many of the tents, fashioned in the midst of the woods, which rose up on all sides, around them, save where the lake spread its broad light to the foot of the Swan Tower and the rampart-walls: and, certes, it was a noble sight to see those pavilions ranged around the open meadow, all amongst the green shades, with vanes and banners glittering in the sun, spreading to the very edge of the water, which there lay, smooth and bright as polished silver, and giving back this glorious vision.

And then again, to those in the field the castle itself was a goodly sight, with all its towers and battlements thronged with faces; the great banner of England, waving on the keep, and over-topping even the forest-trees behind; the whole pictured forth on those sleeping waters, as if falling into the blue deep below. Every parapet, or tower, or rampart, where foot could stand, or arm could cling, was clothed with living forms, and every window and little grate was full of watching eyes, and showed shoulder beyond shoulder, and head crowding over head, looking towards the field, with an eagerness, that made all below, who had seen them, turn their eyes the same way, and feel yet a stronger eagerness for the spectacle they were expecting. Even behind the loop-holes there were faces; some of them, I ween, such as had never looked out there before; the darts of these warriors not being in their hands, but in their eyes.

Those in the castle could hear the trumpets blow up amain, and see the heralds on their great horses riding about the place of contest, before the knights appeared; and could clearly discern the different tents, and make out to whom each belonged. The King's pavilion of scarlet cloth of gold was raised on a platform, above every other, and stood in the centre of that half-circle, formed by the rest. The platform was covered with silken carpets; and there, in front of the pavilion, but just within the canopy, were placed two state-chairs for their Highnesses. The curtains were drawn up in large folds, held up with golden ropes; and within them were showed seat above seat, filled with ladies of the court, gorgeously apparelled, awaiting the royal train: and below, on either hand, were ranged esquires and pages in the King's livery. Over this tent played the royal banner; and the vanes showed the King's crest, glittering almost as high.

On the right of this was the pavilion of the young Prince Edward; but his was raised only by a few steps above the turf. It was of green and white silk, not in any feigned fashion, but in that, which belongeth to tents in war; and it had a golden lion on the top for a vane. On the left of the King's pavilion, raised only one step from the turf, was that appointed for the great officers of state, when they were dismissed from standing about his Highness's chair; and for other nobles of the realm, with whom were some bishops, but not in their state, though the King were present; and some abbots, also not in their state. Near this was the tent of the Baron de Blondeville, of white and azure, having for the crest an armed hand with a javelin poised in it, ready to strike at a shield.

It were tedious to tell of all the different pavilions and galleries, adorned with velvets and rich tapestries, that spread so gloriously round this fair meadow; or of the ladies, so sumptuously arrayed, that appeared within, delighting the hearts of all who beheld them.

But the tent of the challengers, whose chief was William de Fortibus, Earl of Aumerle, standing at the eastern barrier; and that of the defenders, whose leader was the Lord Simon de Montfort, nigh the western barrier, deserve notice. The Earl of Aumerle's was shaped like a castle, beset with gilded turrets and bastions, the entrance gate showing a lofty arch, hung round with goodly trappings of purple velvet, 'broidered and fringed with gold; and having within, hangings and seats of the same. But my Lord of Montfort's outdid this glittering pomp; his tent was in shape of a princely palace, yet with walls and towers, approaching in some sort to a castle. The entrance was into a bannered hall, with stately crimson and gold beneath the banners; and of crimson and gold were the seats and cushions. Figures in armour stood round that hall, as though he would assert himself a warrior and a prince; and truly King Henry needed such, if he might find them true to him.

The lists were forty feet wide, and they ran nearly the whole length of the field. On the outside of them was a raised space to keep off the crowd, which was guarded by knights and their esquires, in armour, but bearing no weapons; and so, too, were the barriers guarded. These knights, as well as all the attendants of the combatants, had taken an oath not to assist either by word, look, or gesture, any of the combatants, not even when wounded and unhorsed, except as the Marshal of the Field should allow; but this oath was not on pain of death, as at trial by combat, in law.

The eastern barrier was for the entrance of the challengers, with the lady-prize; the western was for the defenders. At these points of the field were the greatest press and throng of the people; amongst whom, to wile away their time of waiting, ran many stories of the deeds of some of the knights expected.

Anon, the heralds, who were riding about the place of war, drew aside to the barriers, and their trumpets blew up aloud for a long space, summoning the lords and knights, challengers and defenders, to the field, in manner of war, with such a stirring sound, that no man could abide in the castle, that thought he could get one foot into the field of tournay; but all ran speedily thither, not one allowing, in spite of eye-sight, that it was impossible to find the smallest space, not already filled. And then many, that had been on the walls, would fain have been back there again, for scarcely a glimpse could they get of the field; the fencing, the pikemen, and the horsemen being so deep around it, that the nearest to them had but a sorry peep. And, as for the stages and galleries, raised up for those, who came first, or who had some favour, they had been filled for hours, some having taken their seats there at sun-rise.

Presently, the heralds were answered by the King's trumpets afar, which drew near and nearer, until they came into the plain, and took their station before the King's pavilion, still blowing up, with their banners displayed. There, rode two King's at arms, Garter and Clarencieux: then was every eye turned thither in expectation of what might follow; and presently came into their tent the King and Queen, with a long train of nobles, and ladies, and took their seats on the chairs prepared for them, standing a little out on the platform.

His Highness, this day, wore armour, and was attended by the four esquires of the body. His helmet, with the vizor open, was circled with a crown, surmounted by a crescent, encompassing a blazing star.

The Queen was in purple and palle, and on her head she wore a crown of jewels. The Lady Cornwall, her sister, was ceremoniously apparelled with a coronet of pearls; as was the Lady Pembroke-Montfort, her sister, whose lord was, this day, to enter the lists. All the ladies present were ceremoniously attired, with fillets in their hair, or garlands, each according to her rank. And amongst those who stood by the Queen's chair, none looked more lovely than the young Baroness de Blondeville; her head was circled with costly pearls, and she wore a thin scarf of silver azure, drawn over her breast, the colour of her lord's banner.

183

Soon as the King and Queen were placed, the trumpets at the barriers sounded a charge, and a great many of nobles and knights entered the field. Amongst them was the young Prince Edward; for he liked not to ride alone, in the order that had been settled for him, but came in pesle-mesle with the rest, and so busy with his mettlesome steed, that he noticed not the observance which, nathless all the hurly-burly, was paid to him by those, who rode near him.

Cased in complete armour and mounted on a brave charger, he came, accompanied by his brother Edmund, a noble youngster, apparelled in mail, to witness the disport, though not to share it; sorely against his will was Prince Edward restrained from trying to break a lance this day. His heart beat high for martial deeds. The King and the Queen joyed to see him sit his horse as manfully, as did any knight in the field; and the Queen, although it was by her especial command that he forbore to try his skill with others of his age, looked on him, with even more delight than his father. In him she might have foreseen the corrector of such insults as were afterwards given to her by the citizens of London, when, by hurling of stones at her from the bridge, as she was flying by water from the tower, almost for her very life, they stayed her for a time, from her purpose of repairing to the palace at Sheen. And in him too she might have foreseen the queller of rebellion, the corrector of abuses, the restorer of general order, the enactor of wise laws, the administrator of justice, the mighty ruler, who, by his wisdom and vigorous perseverance, bound up the wounds of his country, strengthened its sinews, and pruned aways its exuberant vices, which the tyranny and weakness of King John had by turns provoked and encouraged; and which the incapacity of Henry had suffered to engraft themselves on and to encumber almost every useful institution.

This young Prince, in whose character yet lay hid the virtues which were hereafter to restore the kingdom, now came into the field with high spirits; and, having paid his duty before the King's pavilion, took his station. Perchance, it was with remembrance of his delight in this tournay, that, in after-times, when he his-self was King, he caused that magnificent feast of chivalry to be enacted here, which brought a hundred knights and as many ladies to give more fame to Kenilworth, for, they trooped to that festival from all parts, even from over sea, to witness its splendours and to increase them: yet did he not, I ween, delight so much in that, as in this present, now before his eyes, when all was new to them and wore the gloss of his own youth.

Soon after Prince Edward had so placed himself, the Baron de Blondeville appeared; and none came on with a more gallant air, (the white plume depending aside his cap to show the easy sway, with which he adapted himself to the curvetings of his managed horse,) or rose on his stirrups with more courageous grace than he; and the whispers and smiles of the ladies seemed to say this: the young Baroness, proud of his affection, and of his distinction, looked on, with beating heart and with tearful smile. Having paid reverence to the King and Queen, his banner was bowed also before his bride, and he saluted her with a homage, that seemed to say he was ambitious only to prove himself worthy of her love.

In this magnificent show, it was a question, which most excelled in gorgeous array, or seemed most proudly conscious, the knights, the ladies, or the coursers.

And now the trumpets, without the barriers, sounded a charge; for the challengers drew nigh the field, and were answered by others already there. Then it was, that neither Prince Edward nor his steed could longer endure restraint, so that both set off full tilt, coursing the plain, round and round, with most courageous bearing, the latter prancing, curveting, bounding, to the great joy of all, who beheld him, save the Queen. Her Highness, though herself of good courage and well skilled, for her sex, to manage her horse, feared he would be thrown head-long from his charger, while he rejoiced, with firm hand and steady eye, to urge, to watch and to command the strength and spirit of the noble animal.

A loud murmur of applause ran from tent to tent and from tower to tower, afar; and then might it be said the warlike people began to feel for their Prince the affection and respect, which hereafter assisted him to rule them. Where this curveting would have ended, none knew, for, the Prince was nothing weary, had not the appearance of the challengers at the barrier checked his career, when he turned slowly towards the King's tent, sitting his charger with a proud negligence, as he looked back on the approaching knights.

Now, the Lord Marshall of the field, the Earl of Norfolk, richly apparelled in arms, and with his truncheon in his hand, riding a brave horse, right bravely trapped, and attended by his king at arms, heralds and poursuivants, rode up to the eastern barrier, and, in the King's name, demanded of the champion, abiding there, completely armed, whence he came, who he was, and the cause of the grief that brought him hither thus clad in steel.

To which he made answer, his herald, with his banner, standing at his side. 'I am William de Fortibus, Earl of Aumerle;' and then he delivered his challenge, engrossed on embossed vellum, in which he defied to arms any one, who should deny the peerless beauty of his lady-love. Then the Lord Marshall made him undo his vizor, that it might appear he had rightly called himself; which being done, the knights, his aids, did the same. Then was administered to the champion and all his followers the oath, that they came not armed with any spell, or word, or other instrument of magic, but with lawful arms only. After which, the knights of the Lord Mareschal and those, who guarded the lists, took oath also, not to assist either champion, during single combat, by word, look, or gesture.

This ended, the Earl of Hereford, High Constable of England, who stood by with his staff of office, ordered the barrier to be thrown open; and forthwith the herald of the champion, attended by his poursuivants, to the number of four, entered the lists, the herald bearing his banner, and standing aside, where he proclaimed, with potent voice, the name and titles of his lord, and whereupon he came hither in array.

Having done this, he threw down the gauntlet, and advanced to the tree of honour, where he placed the written words of the challenge on a bough, and where also were suspended the shielded arms of all the knights, who, this day, meant to run their course of chivalry on the field. Then straight the Earl of Aumerle and his followers were admitted to the field, bearing up the King's flag, nearly in the state and order as here set down. First, came, in solemn march, eight trumpeters, four abreast, blowing up amain, in their yellow tabards and high caps, their banner rolls displayed; then cornets, drums and clarioners, in warlike fashion. Then came twelve knights armed, two and two, on foot. Next came the banner of the King's Highness, carried by a knight completely armed, and borne up by four other knights armed, but bareheaded, each having his two shield-knaves (now called by most, shield-bearers, or esquires) beside him, carrying his spear, shield and helmet. Then followed eight knights, appointed like the first, each with his two knaves, bearing his helmet and shield; then forty yeomen, in doublets of scarlet and gold, bearing their partizans upright, their coats broidered with a golden lion and the King's crown above, surmounted with a crescent and blazing star. Then followed two score of demi-lances, four and four.

Next came four trumpeters on horseback, blowing up; then four esquires; then a herald at arms; then the banner of the Lord Mareschal, borne high by a knight armed, four esquires walking beside it. Then appeared the Lord Mareschal his-self in complete harness, mounted on a barbed steed, right nobly and gorgeously trapped, with crimson velvet, embossed with gold and the shielded arms of his lord; esquires and pages going beside and following.

Then came, in separate order, the champion's five knights, his aids, armed cap-a-pé, mounted on goodly coursers, richly trapped, each having his banner borne before him, and four trumpeters blowing up; also with esquires and pages in his livery.

The Earl was cased in gorgeous armour, bossed with silver and laid in with gold. His helmet bore a scarlet plume and, for his crest, a winged griffin of solid gold, as were the bars of his vizor. The head-piece and breast-plate of his steed were bossed in like manner, as was the shaffroone and crivet for the neck; and the high pummels of his saddle were also edged with gold. Over this lord was borne by four esquires on horseback, wearing his livery, a silken canopy, the colours of his tent, fringed also with gold and surmounted by his crest, in silver.

And now were heard sounds of sweet minstrelsy, and, immediately following the champion, came the minstrels and the lady-prize, seated in a chair, covered with crimson cloth of gold of Florence, having a canopy of crimson silk, bearing a white plume, which played upon the air, and drawn by four milk-white harts, for so they seemed. Each was led by a page apparelled in rose-coloured silk, striped with gold, and holding in his hand his cap of velvet, wreathed with roses, and laced with gold. Their buskins were all of swan-down white as snow. These milk-white harts had their horns tipped with gold and hung with roses, with chainlets of the same round their necks. The reins were of crimson silk, studded with gold and precious stones, as were the traces. Within this so sumptuous car sat the Lady Aveline de Bohun, daughter of the Lord Constable, the Earl of Hereford. She was beautiful as morning, rising from the sea; her look was peace and joy. She wore a robe of palest silver,

187

and her hair was coronetted with eglantine, in bloom, and with pearls, that night might have scattered. In front of the crimson canopy above her, beamed a diamond star of purest splendour. Four knights walked beside her car. And thus she came on to the sound of dulcimers and harps, with her maidens playing on timbrels and lutes and sweet bells. Ever and anon they stepped dancing-wise, tossing the tabors on high and turning with so sweet a grace, as was the marvel and delight of the whole court; although many present liked them not the better, for that they were of the Queen's country. Still, as this lady passed, welcome, peace, and joy, spread around her: she was called the Lady of the Morning Star.

Then followed a goodly train of esquires, and gallant youngsters, in shining trim, wearing the livery of this Earl, to the number of twenty-five, riding on noble steeds; their trappings glittering in the sun, and tinkling with silver bells, that made merriment as they advanced. After them forty of the Lord Aumerle's yeomen, on foot, appeared in his livery, with his badge in silver, on their sleeves.

And thus, with proud paces, these processions passed on the field of tournament, till they reached the King's tent; and then they halted and did homage. So fair and pleasant a show was never seen before in woods of Ardenn. The crowds on the castle-walls beheld the whole order of it, and better than many that were nearer; yet were they not contented; and often, as the shouts of the people mingled with the clangour of the trumpets, they bemoaned themselves, that they were so far off. Yet those on the level of the field beheld not half of the show at once. Three times that gorgeous train moved round the field, to the sound of trumpets and other brave instruments; never failing, each time, their homage at the King's tent. From the very topmost turrets, those there perched, could see this processioning; the sun glittering on the armour of the knights, and glancing on their crests and helmets and on the heads of their spears, as they moved.

They could see, when the procession had the third time reached the King's pavilion, that it rested to deliver up the lady-prize unto the fair company there assembled, to remain in safe custody, till the end of the tournay. They could perceive her approach the Queen, who turned graciously towards her, and that then she retired amongst the crowd of ladies, behind her Highness's chair. This done, they saw the Lord Mareschal, with

188

four knights, advancing towards the centre of the field, in front of the grand pavilion, there to plant the King's great banner; but they could not see every one of the ceremonies, that attended this, nor hear the chaunt of the minstrels, which accompanied each part of them, though they caught the swelling strain of the louder minstrelsy; and on every charge of the trumpets and every shout of joy, did they set up fresh lamentation.

'If I was but in that tree,' said one, 'how much nearer I should be.' 'Why do not you see,' said another, 'the branches are so full already they can scarcely bear up the people? they will break presently, and tumble them into the lake.' 'But look,' said another, 'if there is not the roof of the Swan Tower, with neither man, woman, nor child upon it. Oh! if I was but there, I could see and hear every thing; I will try for it.' 'You may as well stay, where you are,' observed a fourth; 'you may be sure, if the roof could be reached, it would have been full of people long ago.'

Then would come a loud blast of the trumpets and a great huzza, but nobody could tell what it was about. 'Why this is worse than seeing nothing at all, to be tantalized in this way,' says one. Then another spies out some friend, at a distance in a valuable place, as he thinks, and hallooes out with might and main, 'Can you make any room for me in that tree? Do my good Hodge. If you cannot, speak to Ralph for me; he will, I know.' Straight, some score of faces are turned at his shout, but his friend maketh not out that he is spoken to; all hear him but his friend; till another shout comes amain on the wind: 'Hodge o' the Chase-side, I say, can you make any room for me?' and then a dismal 'No!' silences the non-content, and makes those laugh, whom he would have left behind; and thus they went on murmuring, and wasting what pleasure they might have had, because they could not have all, just like their betters; for thus it is in life, that we often employ our wits only to turn good to evil.

Those below, at the castle-windows, ladies and gentlewomen, who could not get places in the tents, or on the galleries in the field, murmured too; but not so much for that they could not see every thing there, though that seemed to be their grief, but that they could not their-selves be seen, dressed as they were in apparel, which they had gotten from Coventry, long before. They saw plainly enough knights, esquires and pages, prancing, or pacing, about the field, in all their splendour; and lady-aunts and lady-cousins in the galleries, in all their sheen and joyance, and fain would they have shared with them. Some too there

189

were, who spied out their knights looking towards the windows, yet were they unable, for the crowd there, to make themselves distinguished; and some few there were who, often as he, that each esteemed, advanced, in glorious seeming, shrunk back, with timid glance, fearing lest they should be noticed.

Above them all, perched in his prison-turret, was the poor merchant, looking upon this splendid field, with different eyes from every other that beheld it. Too little interest had he in what was passing there, to view it with curiosity. No vanity had he to make him feel the jealousy of rivalship, or the fretfulness of disappointment, where all around was pomp and pride, or mortification, or joy, from another's triumph; or aught but sense of his own misery and fond remembrance of his home. The weight of grievous evils left him no leisure to feel the pressure of small ones. How blessed would he have thought himself, were it possible for him to have considered, as disappointments and causes of murmur, any of those trifling circumstances, which now prevented the peace and joy of hundreds, possessing here health and liberty and prosperous estate, now looking on the same spot with himself!

He had been lying on his pallet, thinking on his hard fate and on that of his dead friend, when first he heard the trumpets blow up, and the hum of many voices from walls and battlements and tents below; and, judging this to be some pageant pertaining to the marriage festivities of his triumphant enemy, he had no heart to witness it. But anon, this noise of trumpets, with the heavy trampling of hoofs on the field and the loud ringing of the harness, and, at times, the shouts of the multitude roused him from his weighty sorrows; and, looking through his little grate, he, perched so high in air, like a poor bird shut up in prison-cage, looked down upon that field of warlike seeming and princely magnificence.

There he beheld the King's dreaded person, on whose single word life, or death, depended, sitting calmly in his estate, and right glad of heart, thoughtless of the suffering he now inflicted, or reckless of it, having persuaded his weak and willing mind it was just. There, too, he could distinguish the Baron de Blondeville, caressed and honoured by his Sovereign, admired by the court and loved by his fair bride. Then, as the memory of all that had passed in the woods beyond, returned to Wood-reeve, his very heart bled, while he beheld, as he too well believed, the guilty author of his woe, standing amongst

190

honourable men and gallant combatants, attended by a noble train, and ready to achieve the fame of noble deeds in arms.

Now, the challenger and his five knights, directed by the Lord Constable and Lord Mareschal, having planted the King's banner in the centre of the field, the Earl of Norfolk delivered unto each his lance, and they withdrew to the Tree of Honour, standing on a little hillock, raised near the King's pavilion and bearing on its boughs the shields of all the knights, who offered themselves, this day, for the lists. There they pointed to the words of the challenge, which having done, they retired in procession to the eastern barrier, where their tent and the empty car of the lady-prize stood, there to await the appearance of the defenders. And not long did they wait, ere they heard the trumpets sounding without the western barrier, which were well answered by those within, and straight appeared the chief defender, with his five knights, all clad in white harness. These, having passed through the same ceremonies, as had been already performed by the challengers, and a herald having proclaimed the name of their chief in the field, having hung his words of defiance on the tree of honour, and taken up the gauntlet of the champion, their procession entered.

And here it were tedious to set down all the particular splendours and doings of it; but some things may be told, both to be a record of certain remarkable appearances and also to show some traces of the characters of the chief persons, who played their part in this pageant.

The chief of the defenders, as has already been rehersed, was the Lord Simon de Montfort, the same whom the King's Highness had created Earl of Leicester, and on whom he had bestowed his widowed sister, the Countess of Pembroke, with this his stately castle and wide domain of Kenilworth; how worthily it needs not for this history to declare, since it is known to all, that he armed this very fortress against his King and benefactor. He, this day, wore on his scarf the Lady Pembroke's colour, and he was in truth her champion; his five knights were Sir Stephen de Segrave, Sir John de Plesset, Sir William de Cantalupe, Sir Robert de Grendon, and Sir Osbert d'Abrissecourt, a foreign man.

And, first of these, after heralds at arms, duely appointed, esquires and pages in pairs, and, after his raised banner, all in form and order much like to the procession of the challengers, came Sir Stephen de Segrave. He was on a stately charger,

191

trapped with flame-coloured velvet, bossed with his arms and hung round with little lions, in silver, such being his crest; his horse white and heavy, with broad chest, whose head-stalls and bridles were studded with precious stones. The lion on his helmet was rampant, and his plume and scarf of flame colour. Four esquires walked beside him, followed by four pages; leading spare coursers. Then came twenty-five gentlemen, clad in the colour of his scarf and having also flame-coloured plumes in their caps. Fifty of his yeomen, apparelled in the same hue, but of different fashion, followed; and a crowd of his servants closed his pageant. He was of lofty stature and surpassing strength, and moved upon the field with looks of sullen pride. Some present augured not well from this, and indeed his pride was so plain, that King Henry liked it not.

Next came Sir John de Plesset, Earl of Warwick, of most graceful person and demeanour, though he was a stranger, being Earl of Warwick only by right of his wife, who was sole heiress of that house and by the King's courtesy. He was mounted on a noble roan, whose breast-plate was chased with silver; and he was most gallantly caparisoned. His plume and scarf were of rose-colour, and the crest on his helmet was a leopard. He came attended by a brave show of esquires and gallants, with a train of fifty yeomen, besides forty servants, all in his livery of the colour of his scarf, and making a most stately show.

Then came Gaston, the young Baron de Blondeville, who had changed his cap for a helmet, and was duely caparisoned, as a knight; for, his shield, which the King had caused to be replaced in the hall, had not again been challenged, nor had any one made complaint to the Lord Mareschal against him. He rode so fiery a charger as hardly might be restrained, within the pace of dignity; yet, being curbed with his hand, he moved with proud and stately steps, well suited to his lord and master, who kept his seat, with gracious ease and looks of happy triumph, knowing he was admired of all, who saw him. His banner was well carried before him. Four esquires were at his side, and four pages, leading spare steeds, followed. Twenty-four gentlemen succeeded, and a goodly train of yeomen and servants, all in his livery of light blue and silver, brought up the rear. His plume and scarf were of azure, but not of the fullest hue, and his train of pages and servants, in the gallant fashion of their apparel, were outdone by none.

When he came opposite to the King's pavilion and paid his homage, his courser, whether he was frightened at aught he saw, or that he gloried in the loud noise of the King's trumpets, or that he was secretly goaded for the purpose, began to curvet and play off such high tricks, as terrified the lady Baroness sitting there. But, after he had gone through certain paces and high threatenings, the Baron the while commanding him with unmoved countenance, he fell into a gentle mood, and followed, with due order, in this pageant chivalry.

And now came a knight in most curious device, riding upon what seemed to be a red dragon, conducted by one personating a giant, as he might well do, who bore in his hand a spear of immense size, which incontinently he applied to the dragon's throat, which forthwith sent forth fire and smoke, to the great diversion and delight of all beholders. Following him, a page led his courser richly caparisoned, and he was compassed all about with brave gallants and followers. This was no other than Sir William de Mowbray, who at all times, was fond of mirth, and certes, he caused much; for, on his displaying himself, tents and walls and battlements and turrets, nay, the very trees, up to topmost bough, sent forth peals of joy and laughter. He was much beloved of the crowd, and well liked in the court, none envying him.

Next came Sir Hugh de Bois, mounted on an iron grey. His plume and scarf were of orange colour, and he was not wholly wanting in esquires and servants to fill up his estate; yet was he far from being on a par with the rest, his means being much smaller. So, I say not more of his appearance, seeing he made not much, when compared with others, on that day; only this I will add, he was of a most compassionate and honest nature; and might have vied with the rest, if he would have pressed harder upon his dependants, or would have mortgaged his lands, as so many did, to the Jews.

Next and last, came the chief of the defenders, the Lord Simon de Montfort, in his estate, under a fair pavilion of silk, with turrets and battlements shaped like unto a castle, his banner flying over all. This was carried along by six stout men; but it appeared to be borne by a multitude of his servants, in purple jerkins of silk, laced with gold. His charger, trapped in purpled velvet, bossed with his arms in gold, was led by pages; and its frontlet and breast-plate were so brightly burnished, that, as the sun shone on them, the splendour cast around him was enough to dazzle, if it could not daunt, any knight, his adversary. And this was made ground of complaint against him by his first adversary in the lists; so that, when he began to place himself for combat, he was commanded by the Lord Mareschal not to advance against the sun; but, in the changes and shiftings of the struggle, this command availed but little. Squires and gallants and pages followed almost without number.

Of kingly purple were the Lord Simon's plume and scarf; and his golden helmet seemed one blaze of light. He bore himself with a most lofty carriage; looking as though he thought none, but the King's Highness, might compare with him, and hardly that either. Not more audacious, I guess, could he have looked, when, in after-times, he traitorously gave his Sovereign lord the lie, in the field at Evesham! and there paid with his life for his ingratitude and rebellion.

Little weened King Henry now, when he saw before him this knight, arrayed in the pomp of chivalry, that he beheld one, who would hereafter turn his arms against him, excite his subjects into rebellion, and lead him prisoner through his own kingdom, until his life and liberty should be rescued by his brave son, Edward, here beside him. Little weened his Highness of this, or he would not have raised him to highest honour; bestowing upon him that sister, who had withdrawn herself to convent-life, and taken the veil, but not yet the ring, that would have wedded her to it; else not even the Pope his-self might have sent her dispensation. Happier had she been in her peaceful cloister than living in the world, with so proud, yet base a spirit, that could walk in arms against the Sovereign, who had lavished favours on him with so lavish hand. Yet were there some near his Highness's chair, who, from what they say this day, could guess something of what high favours might work in him; the venerable Archbishop was one of these.

The defenders having passed in solemn pomp, three times, round the field, paying, each time, due homage at the King's pavilion, their chief received from the Lord Mareschal his lance, which had been duly measured with that of the chief challenger, and his shield from the Tree of Honour; and then the defenders withdrew to the western barrier, and took station before their own tent, till the summons of war should sound.

They waited not much, ere the trumpets blew up a charge loud and long, which set the hoofs of every steed in motion to prance and curvet, with proud impatience for the onset, so that

194

hardly could the knights, whose turn was not yet come, rein in their arched necks. Then the Lord Constable of England, and the Lord Mareschal rode gravely round the lists, to see that all was right and in due order; and examined again the lances of the two chiefs, who, upon the second charge of the trumpets, advanced each from his station, near the barriers, and, each crying out aloud the word of combat given him by his lady, they ran together furiously.

The Lord Simon first brake his lance upon the Earl of Aumerle, shivering it into splinters, and with the blow making the Earl stagger on his courser. It was the marvel of all, that he fell not; but, adroitly recovering himself, he passed the sword-guard of the Lord Simon, and struck him on the chest, with a force, that made his armour flash fire, shivered his own lance into a thousand pieces, and had nigh brought his enemy, both man and horse, to the ground. Then the trumpets sounded, for victory, the cries of the people cheered him, and a murmuring sound of many voices rose from the King's pavilion.

A second round was run by these chiefs with lances duly delivered to them, while tumultuous shoutings from the more distant spectators on the castle walls and towers and on the trees encouraged them, those nearer being kept in order by the laws of the field, which forbade any to make sign by word, or deed, during the time of combat. But the knights, who, in armour, kept the lists, found it no easy task to preserve silence there; for, as the fate of the battle swayed, so was the clamour of hope, or joy, ever ready to break forth; and it was well these knights carried not arms, lest they might have been provoked to turn them against the unruly people around them. Those afar off, on the walls, being beyond the reach of the laws, seemed to shout forth in very bravado, as if to revenge themselves by liberty of voice, for that which was denied them of a better view. And how incessantly they did peal forth, sending out all the signs they could to either combatants, and calling loudly a 'Fortibus', or a 'Montfort', followed by hooting, or applause, just as their humours chanced!

The combat of these chiefs lasted, till each had broken on other several lances, but was at last decided, in favour of William de Fortibus, who unhorsed the Lord Simon and broke his shield.

Then was victory proclaimed by the heralds, to strains of minstrelsy, the name and titles of the victor being repeated, on every pause of the music, with these words, 'Renown to heroes and to the sons of heroes.' Immediately there rose from the lists cries of joyous triumph, and the woods resounded, far and wide, with the multitude of voices proclaiming the conqueror's name and 'Renown to heroes'. Convents, buried in the wilds of the forest, opened their gates, and let forth the startled monks, to listen to 'Renown to heroes'. Never had they heard such sounds, till then. Travellers from far, journeying through the forest and hearing such sounds of joy and triumph, where they expected only lonesome silence, or the joy of birds, looked round, on all sides, under the boughs; but, seeing nothing, save the sunlight, and the farther woods, that close them in, they feared this might be some witchery to deceive them. Coming, perchance, to a village, or hamlet, of the forest, they ask what mean these sounds, of aged men, or little children, the only inhabitants left there, and whose opposite extremes of life alike disabled them from following to Kenilworth. And then, having learned somewhat near the truth, the travellers urge their weary hobbies over deep roads, at the risk of their necks, that they may come in for a glimpse of the spectacle of chivalry. So they leave behind these lonesome cottagers to the quietness, which (ah! ungrateful man!) they now think dreary, and would fain exchange for the many pains of another entrance into crowded life; the distant shouts tantalize the curiosity of the young, and bring back the regrets of the aged; the old man reflecting on his long-past youth, and the child anticipating his, when he shall no longer be left at home, while his elder brothers go to fairs and to King's tournaments.

These shoutings of the multitude and the clamour of 'Renown to heroes', recalled to his prison-bars the poor merchant, who, on sight of the Baron de Blondeville, prancing in procession amongst the defenders, had, in the bitterness of his heart, withdrawn and thrown himself on his pallet, there to calm his throbbing spirit. Returned to the barred window, he there beheld that, which he could not well understand, not having witnessed the combat. This was William de Fortibus courteously returning his lance to the Lord de Montfort, together with the golden chain of his mistress, which he had worn on his shield in combat; at which rose up fresh shoutings of applause, but both were received by the vanquished with a very ill grace; and his countess might rejoice that she was not known to have bestowed this chain upon a conquered knight.

This ended, the chiefs withdrew, each to his own tent, and

then advanced four knights, two of each party, and ran their courses together. They combated with strong spears, of great breadth, and ran with most courageous skill, to the wonder of all beholders. It were hard to say, until the very last, which of the four most excelled; but then, at last, one knight of each party bore away the prize, worn on the helmet, or shield, of his adversary, to whom it had been given by the lady of his love.

Next advanced to single combat the Baron de Blondeville and Sir Robert de Grendon. On sight of the Baron, Woodreeve turned from his grate, and his heart sickened to behold the assassin appear before the whole court and the multitude of the people, arrayed for triumph, or, at least, for honour. Yet might it not be so; for, the triumph, and even the honour might attend his adversary. It was, however, long before such possibility occurred to Woodreeve; soon as it did, he resolved to abide the sight of the contest, yet were his fears much stronger than his hopes.

And now the trumpets blew up the field, and the onset began. They fought with spears, and such was the shock of the first encounter, that both knights were nearly unhorsed. At the second course, the Baron brake his spear on his opponent. At the third course, Sir Robert shivered his on the Baron's shield. Then, they ran with lances, or long spears, and the shock, with which they met, brought both combatants to the ground. The Baron quickly recovered himself, and, as some thought, made a blow at his adversary, ere he was fully risen. On this, there was a great outcry, and the Lord Mareschal rode up, and stood before the King's tent, but said nought. Then, the King commanded, that the combat should proceed. On this, there was a murmur of discontent; but, each knight being now remounted, it did accordingly proceed. Some said Sir Robert had received the Baron's blow on his head; others said it had missed him; Woodreeve now, as he watched, thought he sat not steadily on his courser.

However this might be, his horse tournayed, and passed with him along the lists, to meet the Baron, like unto a glance of lightning. The Baron, now well prepared to meet him, sustained the shock, and the combat was renewed with such force, as though it were but just begun. It lasted not long. Sir Robert seemed to support himself with difficulty, and sometimes almost to stagger on his steed; and, at the last course, he sank beneath the Baron's blow, and fell to the earth. Then he was borne away

197

to his tent, and his armour unbraced, and the tale went, that he had been hurt unfairly.

The Baron, having snatched from the shield of his enemy his mistress's pledge of favour, a tress of her hair, bore it triumphantly on the point of his lance unto the King's tent, where sat with the Queen the Lady Baroness, his wife, and presented it to her. Then their Highnesses said many gracious things to the victor, and many noble ladies there assembled testified their joy no less. Then was his name proclaimed, as victor, by the heralds, and his song of triumph chaunted round the King's banner.

The poor merchant, from his turret, seeing how matters went, and that nought but applause and honour seemed to follow the steps of him, who, in justice, deserved only shame and punishment, felt as if his last hope was gone. His pang of sorrow was at the uttermost. He turned from his grate, sickening even at the pleasant light of the sun, and once more he threw himself upon his pallet.

But why do the trumpets now blow up so loud a charge, so shrill and dread, that all, which went before, was sleep and silence in comparison of it? No shoutings mingled with this charge, nor was any other sound heard contending with it in the vault of the sky, where it rolled alone. So long it lasted, that it roused the prisoner again from his pallet, and recalled him to the window.

Thence beheld he, in the field below, not among the combatants, but among the spectators there, an extraordinary turmoil, and a sort of solemn, or fearful, curiosity, very different from that which they had before showed. Their faces were all turned one way, that was towards the place whence the sounds came, which was not from the heralds at arms. In all the tents the company were standing up, but none there, or in spots more exposed to his view, seemed satisfied, that they knew what was going forward. On the place of combat, the prisoner saw only the Lord Mareschal and the Constable of England riding about, and the heralds gathering at the barriers, to answer the summons (of which it seemed there would not, for a long time, be an end), and the knights, who kept the lists, watching for one to enter.

At last, Woodreeve saw, at the eastern barrier, a knight enter, armed cap-a-pé, mounted on a black charger. There, the Mareschal, who was ready, demanded in the most urgent terms, who he was, whom he came to challenge, and what was his cause of grief? What was answered, those only, who stood nigh the barrier, might know; but the stranger's herald was seen to raise a banner before the Mareschal's eyes, that he stood gazing on, like one amazed! while the knights of the barriers drew eagerly round him; when the Lord Mareschal again demanded, why he came? The knight his-self made a sign in the air with his lance, and held it raised; and, during the wonderment, which this spread around, a herald, not waiting for order, but moved by his own notions and fears, administered to him the oath, that he came not armed with any unlawful weapons, or means of harm; after which, the stranger-knight dropped the lance into its rest.

The Mareschal seemed still to marvel and to be at a loss, how he should proceed; but then, recollecting himself, he advanced close to the knight, as is the custom, to unclasp his visor, that it might appear he had spoken the truth, as to who he was: but he, drawing back, his-self unclosed it. What face the Mareschal discovered within, the prisoner, from his turret, could not know; but he saw both the Mareschal and the Lord Constable turn aside their steeds, and the knights of the barrier step back; while a tumultuous noise arose amongst the pikemen behind the barrier, as if they expected the stranger would attempt to retreat, and they intended to oppose him.

But he showed, that he meditated not any such thing; for, swift as an arrow from a bow, he cleared the barrier; and, having done so, moved upon the field of war gloomily and sullen, like unto a thunder-cloud, spreading terror as he passed. All the multitude of voices was hushed around him, and the air was so still, that nothing was heard but the sound of the charger's steps; and, sometimes, the unknown trumpets sending their clangour to roll away amongst the woods.

His banner was borne highly before him, in good state, and with ceremony of demeanour; but what it displayed the prisoner could not, at his height, discern; neither could he see the face, nor the crest, of the stranger. As he advanced, a murmuring ran through the crowd, mingled with faint shrieks; but, when he was present, an interval of hushed silence followed; as if suspense and wonder held the breath of every gazer. Slowly, but strait and with due steps, as showed an accomplished knight, the stranger rode up to the King's pavilion, and there stayed his horse, yet making no sign nor gesture, nor having even his banner lowered by his herald. Immediately Woodreeve perceived a rising up, and some confusion in the pavilion; the King motioned with his arm; the Archbishop made a sign in the air; some of the nobles, who stood round his Highness's chair, pressed forward – others drew back; and those behind, seemed to move to and fro in disorder.

The Queen and her attendants appeared no less agitated; her Highness turned away her face from the stranger-knight; all her ladies on the seats behind, rose up, and some so eagerly leaned forward, that they had nigh overbalanced themselves, and fallen down to the platform. The Baron de Blondeville, who, after his course and triumph, still rested, beside the pavilion, sat fixed on his courser, with his arm holding his spear on high.

Those on the field saw upon the knight's banner the image of a murder; they saw, too, upon his black helmet, a wing of fire, for a crest; but what his face was they knew not; for his visor was now closed; and his eyes only appeared above the flat bars of it; and they, it was said by many of the beholders, gleamed like flame. Some went so far as to say, though they saw too little to warrant such guess, he was the same who had appeared in the banquet hall; others thought not so, and eagerly denied it.

On the banner was a motto, which greatly disturbed the King; for, soon as he saw it, he called for the Lord Mareschal and the Lord Constable, and his own trumpets sounded a summons. My lords, the Mareschal and Constable, were still at the eastern barrier, the confusion there having detained them, and very great it was, though no one, at the distance of the King's tent, knew the cause of it, not a foot having stirred from that barrier of all, who witnessed the first turmoil, on the approach of this so strange an intruder.

Every one there was either too busy, or too curious, to run to spread the half-known news. Some, who had been thrust aside after their first glimpse, said the Mareschal had fallen off his charger; others, that he was dead; and others again, that he was held in thraldom of the Lord Constable, and the knights at the barrier; which last was but an unlikely tale. But let this pass; whatever the cause was, there he was at the time when the stranger-knight, advancing a few steps nearer to the King's pavilion, did make somewhat of an obeisance, and then held up, far as his arm could reach, before his Highness, a sword of strange shape, unknown in our tournays; which, as some nigh affirmed, bore on the scabbard, in characters of fire, the word 'Justice!'

Whether this were so or not, on sight of that sword, the King was sore disturbed; and straight commanded his Lord Chamberlain, who stood close behind his chair, to ask of the knight his name and style, and why he approached in so extraordinary a way.

The knight made none other answer than by pointing with the same sword to the Baron de Blondeville. Then, the King guessing him to be that secret enemy of the Baron, who had appeared in the festal hall, and that he was in league with the prisoner; nay, suspecting he might possibly be that man his-self, escaped by his supposed potent arts, disguised also by them, and instigated with designs against the life of the Baron de Blondeville, promptly despatched a messenger to the Lord Constable, with orders to secure the stranger; and he also privately sent one to know, whether the merchant was safe in his prison? and again bade his trumpets sound a summons for the Mareschal of the field!

For the merchant, King Henry might have spared his page the trouble, and his-self have seen, with little pains, if he had leaned that way, the poor man's face through the grate of the turret-window, looking upon what was passing, in this place of now-disturbed pomp, and knowing less about it, than did his Highness, little as that was; and, for the Mareschal, he was now leaving the barrier and slowly advancing over the place of war, like one faint, and hardly able to support himself on his steed. Two knights of the barrier followed his steps, hardly less in dismay.

Meantime, the stranger-knight, having remained awhile, pointing with that sword to the Baron de Blondeville, who, sitting on his courser, upheld his spear seemingly without power to launch it, if he had been so permitted, or to advance a single step; – the stranger-knight, this having passed, withdrew a few paces: yet he fled not, because of the approach of the Mareschal and the Lord Constable, who gave orders that he should be seized; but stood in the place, to which he had slowly receded, with his lance couched and his shield lifted, as if he defied all attack.

No one of those, who heard the command, had approached him; whether they were withheld by fear, or by reverence; and, when the Lord Constable his-self indignantly rode forward, demanding why he thus unlawfully intruded upon the sports, and disturbed them, with intent to turn that, which was designed for recreation, into revengeful and malicious war, he received no answer; but saw the stranger suddenly in a distant part of the field, in the same attitude of defiance.

Then was the King's anger changed into an ecstasy of amazement; and, turning to address himself to the Archbishop, who was at his right hand, he beheld, in the solemn tranquillity of his countenance an image rather of death, than of life. It seemed to bear the reflexion of some awful truth! while his eyes were directed to some object, which so engrossed his attention, that he appeared to be insensible, not only of the King's words, but of his presence! His Highness, on then looking for that which caused such deep interest, beheld again the stranger-knight, on his charger, before the pavilion, with the sword again raised: where, as many say, appeared that word, 'Justice!' in letters of blood, and now also the name of Gaston de Blonde-ville!

Then the knight's visor flew open, and his Highness beheld the very countenance he had seen in the banquet-hall; that countenance looked upon the King more sternly than before; the eyes were not, as then, dim and melancholy, but seemed to shoot forth fire; and the stranger pointed again with his sword to the Baron de Blondeville, who wore one, that resembled it in the hilt, though not in the shape, and who now, after having sitten so long motionless on his charger, dropped his spear; he seemed to totter in his saddle, his head leaned aside, and, in the next moment, he swayed, and fell to the ground, a dead weight. The clash had drawn all eyes towards him, when his terrified steed, running wildly along the lists, conveyed to the distant spectators, some knowledge of the truth. His two esquires, and others who were near, hastened to his assistance, and a general consternation ensued.

The King, who had not observed his fall, and understood not rightly the occasion of it, seeing his fiery courser fleeing over the place of war, guessed he had taken fright, and thrown his master; meanwhile the Lord Mareschal had ridden forward to secure the stranger.

With confusion and almost palsying terror, the Queen and her ladies had witnessed the truth. Some swooned; others who were the least overcome, endeavoured to convey away the Baroness de Blondeville, who had sunk down, and was senseless; others, on recovering from their first sensations, pressed forward to learn what might further happen; and others retreated, wishing to avoid all further view of so distressing a spectacle. Those

202

farther off, on the castle-walls and windows, who beheld this uttermost turmoil and consternation, wished only for wings, that they might fly forward into the midst of it; for, the vexation they had suffered from their ill-satisfied curiosity and their imperfect view of those pageants and courtly imitations of war, was nothing in comparison to that caused by this glimpse of truth.

The fall of the Baron had been seen by the prisoner from his turret; and immediately he heard shrieks and the busy hum of mingled voices loud and deep: he saw the charger flee, and somewhat of the confusion in the King's pavilion; he observed the Lords Mareschal and Constable riding at full speed towards it, and that the armed knight, who had stood alone before the King, was no longer there, yet he had not observed, which way he had departed, nor his herald.

Now saw he his Highness rise up, and turn to leave the tent; while his esquires and pages raised the Baron on a kind of bier, and carried him from the field.

Then, the Queen and her ladies, supported by divers of the lords, departed as speedily as might be. The Earl Mareschal continued to ride about the field; as did many of the knights, that those, who guarded it, might not think their duty at an end; a double guard was placed at the barriers, and all was hurry, examination, and suspicion. His Highness, when he had understood the Baron's condition, conceiving that he had swooned in consequence of having seen and of having been viewed by that extraordinary personage, whose presence had before dismayed him, sent his physician to assist him; and commanded, that strict search should be made for the person who had caused such repeated consternation.

But, when he learned the whole truth, and that the Baron's life was irrecoverably lost, his grief and horror were unspeakable. He broke up the present field, and with all his court, save such as were left to assist in guarding the barriers, while search for the stranger was going on within them, quitted the scene, and withdrew to his privy-chamber, with the Archbishop and a few of those whom chiefly he trusted.

That honest prelate failed not, on this occasion, to give sincere and wholesome council; which, though his Highness little liked it, he was observed not to speak against, at first, save that he said his thought, that this was no mortal business, but a deed of sorcery; to which the Archbishop answered, he thought not this was an act of sorcery; it might be otherwise accounted for, when an innocent man was in so great peril, and justice was to be brought on a guilty one, against whom other means might not prevail, before judges unfortunately prejudiced in his favour.

At this so bold avowal of his opinion of the deceased Baron, whom now the King most sorely grieved for, and charge implied of injustice in himself, his Highness became angry, and answered sharply. The words of the Archbishop had fallen upon his wounded mind, as boiling oil upon a wounded body, exasperating it almost to madness. When he had departed, one craved admission, who better knew how to turn the passions of this Prince to his own account.

This was the Prior of Saint Mary's, who, having learned the fate of the unhappy Baron, came hither to provoke immediate vengeance on the poor prisoner, and to ensure, as he hoped, his own safety; and, for that purpose, he had recourse to his old subject of sorcery. And he seemed so deeply to sympathize with the King in grief for this sudden death of the Baron, that his Highness listened to all he said, and was inclined to do whatsoever he entreated. The Prior urged, that, if speedily justice had been done upon the merchant, the Baron's life had probably been spared; and were justice long deferred, another innocent life, it were not unlikely, might fall under his mischievous arts; nay, that the life of the King himself might be assailed. He reminded his Highness, that he had both urged and dreaded the probability of what had happened, when he supplicated, that his false accuser might be punished, without delay; nay, that the unfortunate Baron had his-self urged this, and, if his entreaty had been attended to, he had, in all likelihood, been now living.

On this, the sorrow of the King redoubled; he seemed to accuse himself as a cause of his favourite's death; and, before the Prior left the chamber, he had promised to sign a warrant for the prisoner's death, bidding, that he should be told to prepare himself against the morrow. Then the Prior departed, grieving less for the Baron's fate, than rejoicing that his enemy would soon be destroyed.

On learning this fatal resolution of the King, the Archbishop again claimed hearing; for, he was of his Highness's council; and he tried by every argument to counteract the pernicious advice that had been given. He could now no longer conceal his suspicion of the Prior; and he entreated for a delay, at least, of the sentence, hoping that his messenger might, in the mean time, bring from Exeter some certain intelligence, on the subject of his suspicions. But the misled King, accusing himself bitterly for former delay, as the cause of the Baron's cruel end, and having been moreover prejudiced by the Baron, for his own purposes, with a notion of some pretended cause of the Archbishop's dislike of the Prior, refused now to listen either to remonstrance, or to entreaty.

Sorrow and remorse, arising from a misapprehension of the truth, alone seemed to occupy the King, who now, with the intention, as he persuaded himself, of preventing further evil, was about to execute an act of injustice and stern cruelty. And thus it is, if kingly power pertain to a weak head, not carefully warned by early instructions against the dangers, which must beset all power, whether public or private, whether in Prince or subject; for, the passions are the helm, whereon designing men seize to steer into action, as they wish. And thus was pity now about to be made the instrument of cruelty.

Prince Edward, though young, saw this matter more clearly than did his father; and he entreated for the poor merchant; nay, he even dared to express his opinion that he had used no unworthy arts. But the King was yet obdurate; and he bade the Prince remember that precious ring, which was to render him invincible in battle, how it had been conveyed away from his secured cabinet to his enemy Llwellyn of Wales, who had triumphed accordingly.

On this, the countenance of the Prince showed fiery red, and indignation sparkled in his eyes. 'Give me an army,' said the Prince, 'that I may fight your enemies, and prove that ring to be not invincible.' The King turned his eyes upon his noble son; and, for the ardour of his spirit, forgave him his importunity.

The Archbishop's brow relaxed, and his look dwelt long upon the Prince, with high benignity; while the young Prince cast down his eyes, which had met those of the prelate, and he felt, that to deserve such dignified approbation, he could encounter worse enemies, than he had spoken of.

The King now dismissed his suitors, even his son, and abandoned himself to grief and to ill-placed remorse. But what was grief, like his, compared with that of the distracted Baroness de Blondeville? who, innocent herself, had loved and honoured the Baron for such as her imagination painted him, not for what, in truth, he was. But what, had he lived, must she hereafter have known him for? She must have known him for the perpetrator of that lawless and wicked act, of which he was accused, and moreover for the cruel destroyer of domestic faith and happiness.

A tale was yet to tell, that would have abolished her peace for ever, and which that unknown and unhappy lady, who in the castle-hall challenged his shield and then departed, could have sadly related. The person of that lady was here a stranger, but somewhat of her story had gone forth, and was partly understood by divers at the court, amongst others by Pierre, the Queen's minstrel, who, in her bower, had darkly told it on his harp, enwrapping and disguising truth with fiction. There the Baron de Blondeville had heard it, and he alone knew how to separate one from the other; he had heard it, and with such consternation, that he stayed not in the bower to inquire how Pierre drew the line between them.

On that same night, there had been also in the Queen's presence one distantly related to the most unhappy character in the minstrel's lay, and whom the guilty Baron then suspected of having prompted it. He burned to tell him so; but he dared not, since that would have brought to light a truth, which would have ruined and disgraced him, for ever. Whether this suspicion were just, or not, is uncertain; but he bore deep rancour in his heart against that supposed suggester of the truth, and, on the first opportunity, determined to act, as if he had full proof that insult was intended.

And, this very day, he had done so, when, in the field of contest, he had encountered Sir Robert de Grendon, and had cunningly given him that dangerous wound, which had felled him to the ground. Those in the court, who knew the lady's mournful history and her relationship, though distant, to Sir Robert, questioned whether, even on his part, the encounter with the Baron was wholly accidental.

Nay, some suspected, that he had forborne to appear formally as her champion, only because he knew, that the King would then forbid the combat, and that he should be laid in jeopardy, like unto the poor merchant; wherefore, they said, he had concerted with his kinswoman her challenging of the Baron's shield. All this well might be, but nothing certain was known on the subject, nor has it come to light, to this day. Sir Robert, however, was so sorely stricken by the Baron, that the King's physicians long thought his life in danger.

The poor lady, his kinswoman, pined and died hereafter of

grief and remorse for her own former misconduct. With such a husband as the Baron de Blondeville, how then could his unfortunate wife have known happiness? But he died ere she knew him!

Woodreeve, who, from his prison-window, had seen the Baron fall from his charger, and had beheld him afterwards borne away from the field, knew not yet the whole truth; but this sudden reverse, appearing like a judgment on the crimes of his enemy, had filled the poor merchant with hope, yet with a kind of solemn astonishment, – a sort of tranquil awe, which fixed him in earnest gaze at his grate, till all the multitude of the people round the grand plain, in gallery, tent, or on tree, on coursers, on hobbies, or on battlements, had dispersed and vanished away, like cloudy freckles before the morning breeze. And thus was this tournay so soon broken up, to the sad discomfiture of those who had come from distant parts, many a weary mile, to behold it. Many, who had been up with the dawn, and had endured hunger and uneasiness for hours – neither the King's castle, nor the villages round, having wherewithal to supply the wants of the vast multitudes here assembled – were now compelled to return home, with curiosity as little satisfied as their appetites, unable to tell the real conclusion of the festival. They did, however, carry with them a vague knowledge of a spectacle more marvellous than that they came to behold; and widely did they spread it into distant towns and other shires; some to the heaths of Lincoln, some up the pleasant hills of Leicestershire, some to the forests of Nottingham, and some to the high regions of Derby.

207

Here was miniatured a stately chamber, in part richly illuminated. Under a canopy, was a long sleeping-couch, but no person appeared there. In another part of this spacious room, where the light prevailed less, sat one, who leaned thoughtfully on a table, his hand covering his eyes; another figure stood near, but so obscurely drawn, that for what designed could not be certainly known. Images, holding lamps, were pictured in the chamber.

HAT SAME night, King Henry signed the death-warrant of the merchant; and he gave notice, that, on the morrow, he would depart for his palace of Woodstock. And that same night, as was said, the prisoner thought he heard again his death-warning; the same song of peace passed by his turret, as at this hour of the evening before. Others there were, also, about the castle, who, that night, heard strange sounds, and witnessed more than they cound well understand.

Amongst these, were the wardours of a postern, near the north walls, who reported they heard grievings, and, more than once, saw some one pass, almost within reach of their spikes. When they spoke the watch-word, it answered not, and, when they raised their spears, it fled. The same appearance, though not the same moanings, was heard of those, who kept guard on the east ramparts; and the groom wayte, it was said, as he sat within the porch of King Henry's lodgings, on a sudden, saw some one standing still before it. He had not heard a step, but, on raising his head, perceived that figure. It was suspected he had been slumbering, and had dreamed of the strange accident, which had befallen the day before. But, whether this appearance were a reality, or only an impression of his fear, certain it is, that, being on watch alone, for his master had never piped the first hour, since the night of his alarm, he had not-courage now to speak, or even to step forward, till the object of his terror had passed away. Then, he came forth of the porch to little purpose; for all, without was still and lonesome, and nothing to be distinguished, save the huge shadowy towers around the court, and the stars twinkling bright above them.

But he also heard, at times, a strain of mournful music, and thought it was a requiem in the chapel. Remembering the late strange occurrence in this very court, as he had paced his round there, he began to think this was in very truth the Prior of Saint Mary, come again on some secret errand of mischief to the imprisoned merchant; and straight he wended to the keeper's door, in Caesar's tower, to give alarm.

But no one heard him there, the keeper being, at that very time, in the King's hall, waiting his command. Then he went to call the ancient wayte, his master, who was sleeping out his sleep in his own lodge; and, by the time he came back with his groom, this unknown person was no where to be found. If these men, in the midst of the castle, were confounded with fearful thoughts, the poor prisoner above, distant, forlorn and distressed was no less so; for, as he lay, in watchfulness and sorrow, ruminating on the extraordinary occurrence in the field of tournament, suddenly he thought a voice, without his door, called upon his name. He would not turn at the sound, fearful of beholding behind his grate the dim visage of the Prior of Saint Mary, as he had seen it on a former night. He knew that malignity alone could lead him hither; and, dreading even the sound of his voice, he drew his cloak over his head, and covered himself close, hardly daring, at the moment, either to see, or hear.

A loud knocking, and then a call roused him, and, at last, he heard his name spoken; when, instantly turning at the sound, he perceived, behind the grate, not the dark countenance of the Prior, nor the stern one of his keeper, but that of his beloved and unhappy wife. Hardly daring to trust his senses, he held the lamp nearer, before he became convinced it was her very self. Without question, or one word of endearment, she called tremulously upon him to save himself by flight; and, repeating his name with hurrying fear, entreated him to unfasten the door on his side, telling him that means were provided for his escape, but that he had not an instant to lose, ere the keeper might return.

Then, almost swooning with apprehension, she undrew the outer bolts, and was so much exhausted by the effort, that she clung to the bars of the grate for support. Woodreeve did not now, as on a former night, hesitate to undraw the inner bolts: no; with the eagerness of hope and joy, on this unlooked for meeting and intelligence, he forced back the bolts, and

pected, such was the enchantment of his elation, that the door would open. He had forgotten, that the keeper's key, or the Prior's, was necessary to unfasten it.

With this recollection despair returned, for, all his strength was not sufficient to force the lock. When he had ceased his efforts, and had somewhat calmed the distress of his wife, he inquired by what means she had heard of his situation; for the messenger he had despatched, he well knew, could not, in so short a time, have reached her. He asked, also, how she had gained admittance to his prison. To these questions, she answered, that she had received a former letter, mentioning the time of his landing at Hull, while, with her sister, living in Gloucestershire; and had written by the carrier, to tell him she would abide there, till he should pass thither on his way home. While there awaiting him, she had heard of what had passed at Kenilworth, from one who being at Warwick, when the King took wassel there, had returned almost in his train to witness the festivals at the castle.

There, hearing the name of the prisoner, whose extraordinary accusation of the Baron de Blondeville had become known over the whole forest and county, he had relinquished the expectation of fine sights, that he might hasten to acquaint her with her husband's danger; and it was by his contrivance, that she had gained admittance, and had hoped to effect an escape; that, for two nights, they had walked about the castle; and, when all was still, she had sung aloud, in the hope, that he might hear her voice, and know that she was near him. He now doubted not, that he had heard this, when he thought he listened to a warning of his death.

She was then proceeding to give him some particulars of the plan for his escape, when they heard footsteps ascending the stair. She made no attempt to conceal herself; for, since all hope for her husband was gone, she had nothing more to dread, and she awaited the expected appearance of the keeper, with indifference.

The keeper – for it was he – came on, with lamp in one hand, and a parchment in the other; and, seeing a stranger at the chamber-door, he surlily demanded who she was, and what she wanted. Her answers told part of the truth; on which he seemed somewhat softened, not refusing her admittance to the prison-chamber of her husband. Then, the poor prisoner saw enter it, at the same time, his beloved wife, and the keeper bearing his death-warrant! Happily for her, she saw not this; she saw only her husband, and ran into his arms, and wept upon his breast. What he then suffered, who saw not only the evil prepared for himself, but for her, none may tell.

When Woodreeve could recollect himself, he made sign to the keeper, to conceal that dreadful instrument from his wife, and to withdraw awhile, that he might prepare her for what was to come. This man so far respected the misery he witnessed, as to yield, and leave the chamber. Then, Woodreeve, calling forth all his fortitude to bear him with composure through the relation of his adventures since he had landed on English shore, led her, step by step, to the knowledge of all that had passed. But, when he came to relate the manner of his trial, and all that had happened during it, all his endeavours to prepare her for the sad result were of no avail to his distressed wife; who, before he could come to his sentence, was gone beyond hearing, having swooned, as if dead, by his side.

The keeper, who was brought up to the chamber by the cries of Woodreeve for help, was moved at what he beheld, and aid was administered, which slowly brought her back to consciousness. Soon as it did, they conveyed her out of that chamber, while the keeper showed to the prisoner his death-warrant, which gave order for his execution early on the morrow. It were vain and cruel to dwell upon the misery of this innocent man, thus brought into jeopardy by the repeated crimes of others. How to break the unhappy message to his poor wife he knew not: yet know it she soon must; and he thought it were better she should know his sentence from his own mouth than from any other. So lately met, after long absence, and now to part for ever! He desired the keeper to bring her to the chamber, soon as he thought she had recovered strength enough to hear, without destructive suffering, the truth he must unfold. And here a dark veil of misery falls upon a scene of pangs, too acute, too searching, to be made known.

And to many others in the castle was this night dreadful! To the young Lady Baroness, and to the King himself! How changed, indeed, was the whole appearance of this castle, from that it wore on yester-eve; where, if the inhabitants were wakeful, it was only from the restlessness of joy, and preparation for the grand festival of the morrow! Where were now the mirth and music, with which these walls had rung? where the feast, the dance, that had made every minute pass so quickly to the

211

poor mortals, whose hours were fleeting away beneath these princely roofs? All was changed to grief and silence. The footsteps only of attendants were heard along the halls and galleries; no voice spoke there; it seemed, indeed, as if every one were fearful of speaking. When, perchance, the door of a chamber was opened, no burst of merriment or song came forth, no harp sounded, no hum of voices. The impression of this whole change may be best signified by conceiving what one might feel on another change, on a smaller scale; that in one hall, for instance, of this same edifice, which should have been lately deserted of its splendid guests, where the few lights still burning might serve but to show its lonely grandeur, while one heavy step proceeds about the tables to extinguish these; and then the long sound of the closed door denotes the vastness and the emptiness of all that space.

Now of the King's condition and the things, that befell, on this night, there go divers tales. The truth were difficult to hit, because of the closeness, that guards a King from eye and ear, within his private chambers. Yet there be occasions, when the strangeness of occurrences, that seem not of this world's ordering, surprize and thus overcome the fidelity of servants, nay even the prudence of others, most concerned in them, and they speak of many things, which, at less pressing times, they would keep safe locked, within their secret thought, to feed alone their own fear and wonder. Thus might it be, on this night. There went forth many strange tales. This, which followeth, was much received at the time. Nay there were strong witnesses of some parts of it in the attending pages, and even in words dropped by the King himself, to warrant the passing of the story. But, be this as it may, I tell but what was told, in the court itself.

It was said then, that King Henry, after signing the death warrant of Woodreeve, dismissed every one from his presence, and retired to his chamber for all night. There, he would hardly endure the necessary presence of his pages, while he underwent the usual ceremonies of his wardrobe. No sooner had they divested him of his mantle and surcoat, and helped him with his night-robe, than he would permit no further intrusion upon his melancholy and vexing thoughts. Full of sadness was he and of self-reproach, it may be believed, for the premature death of one he had loved and esteemed, and for whose fall he blamed himself, since, had he not so long delayed to execute,

212

what he called justice on the merchant, whom he was still willing to think a false accuser, the Baron, he held, would be still alive.

He sat thus ruminating, while all was still around him; and what he heard afar was not likely to change the temper of his mind – sad and solemn music it was, mingled as he thought, with lamentation. He listened, and distinguished a choral chant of voices, faintly rise and fall. It was the dirge, which was performed in the chapel for the departed Baron de Blondeville, in that very chapel, where so few days before, his nuptials had been solemnized, in the King's presence, and where strains of joy, and hope and benediction had lately ascended.

Now, ever and anon, the trumpet groaned, and, in dismal and interrupted strain was sung, 'Darkness is my bed – the worm is my sister. I am covered with the mist of death, nor may the sight of man behold me.'

The King went to an oriel-window, that looked towards the chapel, and heard the chant of the choristers swell with these words, 'Eternal rest give unto him!' And then the faint response concluded with, 'Rest in peace!' Then, the instruments sunk low into a murmur, and the voices were no more heard.

Now, the tale goes, that, when his Highness distinguished these words of the requiem, he was overcome with the sad thoughts they brought forth, and he sat down in his chair, and even wept, leaning his arm upon a table, without noticing what lay there. When the King took his hand from his eyes, he beheld a sword – the very sword worn by the Baron de Blondeville, and which Woodreeve had claimed, as the weapon of his murdered kinsman; the same, of which a resemblance had this day been raised up before the King, by the stranger knight, in the field of tournament, who had there pointed it, with deadly power, against the Baron.

On seeing this, his Highness was greatly amazed, marvelling how, and with what intent it had been conveyed. While yet he gazed, the blade became dull and cloudy, and large spots of rust began to appear, which turned to a bloody hue. Then his Highness, terrified by what he saw, and thinking it the work of sorcery, looked towards the ante-room, where lay the esquires of the body, with intent to call them, and perceived some one, as he thought, passing along his chamber. The silver images, which had held lights, stood not there, and a gloom, nigh to darkness, spread through this spacious chamber, save just

213

where some one seemed to watch. To that side the King directed his voice, and then rose up to learn the truth. Now, the hangings of this chamber were storied with the famous siege of Acon, where the first King Richard performed such valourous deeds, and the light so fell on that King on horseback, that to the King Henry he seemed to be verily riding out of the arras, and the sword he held to be gleaming to and fro.

This was but a passing phantasie of the King's own mind, as was afterwards declared: but that, which followed, was said to be no deceit of his fancy.

He had risen to discover whether any person was in his chamber, where there had been that appearance of some one passing; he saw a gleam of light, like unto the glistening of Richard's sword, yet neither substance, nor shape, there. Again and nearer, that light appeared, and did not vanish immediately as before; and, before it faded, it assumed a form and countenance; and the King again perceived before him the stranger-knight. Having now lost all power to summon to him those who watched without, his Highness only heard these words, 'The worm is my sister!'

The King gasping in breathless terror, said, 'What art thou? Wherefore art thou come?'

The voice answered, 'Give me rest – the worm is my sister. The mist of death is on me!'

The King again said, 'Wherefore dost thou come?' to which the phantom answered, 'Give me rest!'

'How may that be?'

'Release an innocent man.'

'How may I know him to be such?' said the King.

'By the sword of justice, that lies before thee. A knight-hospitaller was slain by that sword; it has, this day, slain his slayer, Gaston de Blondeville. The Prior of St Mary's was his accomplice. Punish the guilty. Release the innocent. Give me rest!'

The King, as was said, had now sufficiently recovered from his surprize, to demand proof of the Prior's guilt, on which the vision answered, 'I will call up one, who may no more deceive.'

It is said, that the King's courage here failed, and he called out, 'Forbear!'

'Recall your warrant, then,' demanded the spectre solemnly, 'ere it be too late to save an innocent man.'

At that moment the matin bell sounded.

214

'My time is short,' said the vision; 'if he perish for my sake, he shall not fall alone. Be warned!'

While these words still vibrated on his ear, the King again heard the chant from the chapel, and knew that they were performing the second requiem.

'I am summoned,' said the vision; 'My bed is in darkness; the worm is my sister. Yet my hope——'

The King, on looking up, saw only the dim countenance of the knight; his form had disappeared; in the next moment, the face too had passed away. But who may speak the horror of the King, when, in its place he beheld that of the Baron, but as in death; an expression of solemnity and suffering overspread his visage; and the King heard the words 'My guilt was my doom; I shall behold you no more. The prisoner is innocent. The Prior of St Mary's is gone to his account. Be warned!'

At these words cold drops stood on the King's forehead, and his eyes remained, fixed on the vacant air, where the countenance of the Baron had just appeared. At the same instant, these words of the distant requiem rose on his ear, 'I go unto the dark lane; that is covered with the mist of death, – a land of misery and darkness, where is the shadow of death and no order. The eye of man may no more behold me.'

The the King lost all recollection; his ear was closed against every sound. How long he remained thus none knew; only it was yet early morning, when the esquires, sleeping in the ante-room, were roused by his summons. Then, his Highness despatched one to the constable of the castle, with command to attend him in his chamber, another to St Mary's, to know how it fared with the Prior, and yet another to bring the Earl of Cornwall to him. For my Lord Archbishop, the King as he believed of himself, wished not to disturb the repose due to his age; but in truth he liked not to see him; for he had spoken truths, which his Highness now too heavily feared it had been his duty to listen to.

The messenger, despatched to the priory, had no sooner passed the castle-ditch, and gotten on the outside of the great portal, than he espied carts, drawn up under the walls, in waiting, to carry away the poor merchant, ere those in the castle could behold the sad sight of his removal for the dreadful purpose, that had been determined upon. He spied, too, under the gloomy dawn, the whole of that dismal assemblage silently watching to take away their prey. The page rued the jury's

215

sentence on the prisoner, and he went on his way, with heavy heart; for the merchant was pitied of many.

When he reached the priory, the brethren were at matins; and he was told the Prior was in his chamber. Marvelling, as they did, at the King's early message, one delayed, as little as might be, before he went to acquaint the Prior with it. He struck upon his chamber-door; and, receiving no answer, he went within, and the Prior was found, as had been foresaid; he was lifeless in his bed, stretched grim in death.

He, who beheld him thus, descended the stair, with all speed, to acquaint the brethren then assembled, with what had happened, and found them in consternation great as his own, though from a different cause.

The tapers were dying away, and the only light, that glimmered strongly on the walls, came from a spot, where stood the armed figure of a knight hospitaller. His shield threw a deeper gloom around it on the tombs and even on the tapers of the monks. He pointed with his sword to the ground he stood on, and exclaimed mournfully, 'A murdered knight hospitaller lies below; search for his bones and save an innocent man from death!'

The figure stood for a moment; and, as it raised its shield, the flame thereon flashed, within the hollow helmet, and showed the stern, yet mournful countenance of the knight, such as it had appeared before the King.

Then sunk the figure with the flame, into the earth.

For a while, the brethren stood in utter silence and amazement; then they began to look upon one another, and to ask what this meant; and, even while they did so, a thrilling voice groaned from beneath. Then, without further hesitation, they sent for him whose office it was to dig graves, that search might straight be made, where that sound had seemed to be heard. Such of the monks as, in this tumult of fear and wonder, had time to understand, that their Prior was said to be dead, now hastened to his chamber to learn the truth – others remained in the church.

Some of these dared to approach the spot, where the spectre had appeared; and found it to be over that nameless grave, near to which the poor merchant had found refuge; and where their deceased brother, Anselm, had borne witness to a supernatural appearance. When the lay-brother, the digger of the graves, came, who had not long been in office, he pored over the stone, marvelling that one so little ancient should have neither name, nor date, nor inscription of any kind, on his tomb. There were some standing by and observing, who, if they had been so minded, could have told, that it had not been always thus: but they held their peace.

On raising that stone and turning up the earth beneath, a coffin appeared, bearing this inscription:——

'Reginald de Folville, Knight Hospitaller of St John, slain in a wood of Ardenn, rests here!'

There was neither taper, nor visible flame of any kind, over the grave, yet was this distinctly shown, by a strong light. The coffin-lid, which was of stone, like the receptacle, and was cut in shape of the head and helmet, being removed, there lay exposed to view the figure of the dead knight, in the armour in which he was slain, and such as had but now appeared on the grave; the shield was on his breast; but no sword was at his side. At this spectacle, some of the brethren shrunk, overcome with so sad a sight; others pressed forward, and bent over the grave with intense curiosity.

The features of the knight were entire, though shrunk and changed in death. They were of a noble cast, and bore the very countenance of the apparition. On the forehead appeared the death-wound. While yet they looked, the appearance of the knight began to change, and the countenance to shrink and fade away. Some said this was only an effect of the living air upon mortal features so long shut up in death; others said not so, but that it was, like all the rest, to bring truth to light and administer justice to an innocent man. Then the coffin lid was replaced, and that awful spectacle of mortality was hidden from view, for all time. During this, still music was heard in the air, like unto a requiem, hymning some blessed spirit.

The brethren, while they listened, were hushed in holy peace; some knelt over the grave; others stood, with hands and eyes lifted up, as if following the sound with their attention; and others, drawing the cowl over their eyes, bent their heads and wept in silence. Without the church, the old oaks, swaying in the wind, mingled in high and solemn harmony with the lessening chorus, till their murmur alone remained. Those, who had heard that soothing strain, long stood, as listening, still rapt in the quietude it had breathed forth, till, at length, their peace was enlivened into cheering hope.

The grave-digger, who had withdrawn to some distance,

217

was the first to recover himself, and the sound of his footsteps drew back to present life the thoughts of the holy men around him.

Then, they recollected the death of their Prior, and that the King's messenger was yet waiting for the tidings, which his Highness, by his extraordinary anxiety, appeared to have foreknown. One of them returned to the castle with the esquire, who, when he came near the gates, looking anxiously to see, whether the poor merchant was yet gone to his doom, perceived, that the carts, with the whole mournful apparatus of death, were already departed. On perceiving this, he struck his hands together, in sorrow and despair, with a force of action, which drew the observation of his companion, who soon learned the occasion of his honest emotion, and suffered with him.

How much more would each have suffered, could he have witnessed all, that had passed within the prison-chamber, while those marvels were passing in court, and priory, as already told! How much more could they have seen all the struggles of Woodreeve, for composure and resignation, and, yet harder task! his endeavours to prepare and reconcile his wife to calmer sorrow. Of late, she had refused to allow it possible, that her husband could thus unjustly and ignominiously perish in the cause of humanity; and she would have forced her way to the King's presence, there to have pleaded the truth, nothing doubting she could have convinced him of his mistake, had not bars and bolts withheld her. For the arguments of her husband, on this subject, they were as nothing with her, in this state of desperation. And thus passed the heavy hours of this night to those poor sufferers, till the keeper came to bid Woodreeve prepare for death, the guard being then in waiting to carry him away. Then, the poor prisoner perceived, what until this moment, he had been unconscious of, that hope, in spite of reason, had lingered at his heart; for, now only was it, that he felt the full pang of despair.

And, when he heard the summons afar off, that deep and dismal bell, he stood trembling with horror, unconscious where he was – unconscious even that his wife lay senseless on his pallet! Again it called, that hollow murmuring death-sound! He heard not the footsteps ascending the stair, nor the bars of his prison withdrawn; that shuddering sound alone crept on his ear.

He perceived, however, the keeper standing now not in the

room, but near the door; and he began to recover his recollection, like one, who has been stunned by a blow; yet was there a gloomy and dreadful stillness at his heart and over all around him. He turned to his wife, and leaned over her, without shedding a tear, or uttering a groan. She was pallid, as a corpse; his own cheek was of the same hue; yet he called not for help.

The keeper advanced into the room; others, as if from respect for misery, waited without, at the door. Perceiving the condition of the poor woman, he sent off some one for assistance; and, taking Woodreeve by the arm, he looked upon him, as if he wished, yet feared, to speak. But the prisoner saw not this; for, he raised not up his eyes. Then, the keeper shook him by the arm and spoke; but he heard not the words; he only answered, that he was ready; and then, turning to give one long, last look to his poor wife, he found his eyes could not well distinguish her.

He groaned heavily, and was departing; but still the keeper told him, and, in a voice less rugged than usual said, 'Read this paper.'

'I cannot see the letters,' answered the prisoner; 'my sight is gone; and it is also useless to read my death-warrant.'

'Can you endure to hear it read?' said the keeper.

'Why not?' replied the merchant; 'What have I to fear, in this world?'

'Have you nothing to hope?'

On this the prisoner lifted up his countenance; his sight began to return, and he looked at the keeper; his soul was trembling in his eyes.

Then the keeper ventured to call out 'Respite!' – and instantly the whole aspect of Woodreeve was lighted up, like one called back from death.

But this spirit was short lived; in the next instant he called out, 'My wife! my wife!' and bent over her in an agony of woe. 'Is no help to be had?' cried he. 'She is gone! your respite comes too late.' But, while he so spoke, one, who had been sent for a restorative, returned, and, after long application, she revived.

Then Woodreeve, when his first joy had subsided, began to consider this was a respite, not a release, and that his sufferings, perhaps, were not ended, but postponed. This respite, which now began to be viewed by him with doubt, had well nigh destroyed his wife with sudden joy; to her mind it brought, not merely hope, but certainty of life for her husband. A convulsion followed, and she was, for a short time, in as much danger as before. Hardly had she recovered from this, when an order came from the constable to give Woodreeve his liberty and a chamber in the castle better suited for him. Assured of this, he drew his cloak over his eyes, and stood, for some time, weeping in silence, save that his sobs were audible; then he raised his hands and eyes to Heaven, and bowed his head. His wife remained weeping on his garment, till he took her to his heart, and then they left that prison-chamber, hand in hand together.

When the King had heard of the Prior's death, he was struck with marvellous dread, and with conviction of his falsehood and of the merchant's innocence. He bitterly repented of the favourable opinion he had so long adhered to, respecting the Baron de Blondeville, and of the weak credulity, with which he had listened to the artful suggestions of that false Prior, rather than to the arguments and to the strong conviction of the Archbishop of York. But the former went with his passions, the latter against them; and he helped to deceive himself. Yet, when he did find out his error, he was warm and generous in counteracting it; and, now that he was assured how unjustly the poor merchant had been made to suffer, he loaded him with present kindness, and prepared to repay him hereafter by certain grants and privileges, that made Woodreeve the most wealthy merchant of his guild.

Nor did his Highness forget the forlorn widow and children of the deceased knight, whom he fostered and nobly supported. The miniature of that knight and the golden chain he had worn he returned to his family; and the Jew, who had forsworn himself, at the instigation of the Baron, was punished with heavy fine and imprisonment, the fine being amongst the King's gifts to Woodreeve. But, though his Highness found it now his chief delight to do kindness to the merchant and to the family of his unfortunate kinsman, yet could he not endure to behold him, nathless the expectations of most in the court.

And now that the Prior was dead, many things came out, concerning him, which had not been suspected. He was of birth so low, that no one could learn whence he had sprung; but it appeared, that, not many years before, he had been in arms, and in the class of a follower of Sir Gaston de Blondeville, one of the retainers, whom the latter was obliged to produce, on receiving his gilt spurs.

He was conjectured to have come with him from Gascony; for, he spoke that tongue, and had all the craft and soaring vanity of that people; but he was not born there; he had no foreign sound in his discourse. How he came by his wealth in those lawless times, and the use he made of it to procure him power, may be easily guessed. And it appeared this was well suspected by my Lord of York, who had never looked upon him with a favourable eye, and had constantly endeavoured to counteract his pernicious influence.

When, hereafter, his messenger returned from Exeter, it appeared, that none in that neighbourhood had ever known the Prior of Saint Mary's, such as he had described himself to be. The arts too, practised by this Prior with certain of the brethren, who remembered the interment of Reginald de Folville – and with certain people of Kenilworth, who recollected his story, were now all exposed. Those, who, from education and station, might not have been suspected of such baseness, were now brought to truth, and were fain to hide their heads for shame. The Prior's memory was thus condemned to detestation. Be it remembered, he was no true son of the church.

THE EIGHTH DAY

Here was a drawing, divided into two compartments. In one, was presented an Archbishop, kissing the hand of a crowned king; in another, was the sole portraiture of a prince; who, from his mantle, and the feathers embroidered on it, appeared to be a Prince of Wales.

N THIS day, the merchant and his wife departed from Kenilworth, where they had suffered such extremes of good and evil. They departed, carrying with them joy and blessings. But it was not till they had gone a good distance through the forest, that they felt themselves fully at liberty. Then, as they looked back, and saw afar off the grey towers of the castle, above the tawny woods, nay, that very prison-turret, perched over all, which Woodreeve had never expected to leave, but for death, their hearts overflowed with thankfulness, and tears of joy fell fast. Yet, turned they suddenly from view of it, and then went forward, even faster than before. After leaving these woods of Ardenn, they journeyed homewards in peace.

And many others departed from the King's court homeward, on this day; especially, my lord Archbishop took solemn leave of his Highness, who gave him all due honours, for his wise counsel, regretting also, that he had not sooner followed it. The Archbishop, pleased with the release of Woodreeve and with the bounties since bestowed upon him, bowed himself, with willing homage, to his lord the King, and bade farewell to the young Prince Edward, with affectionate respect and with lofty hopes of what he might hereafter prove himself.

And, this day, left Kenilworth, the unhappy lady, Baroness de Blondeville, conveyed away by her noble parents to their own castle, there to pass in quiet shade this season of affliction. And those, who have mourned with her in this chronicle of her sad story, may haply like to look into the glass of her futurity. There, may they see many dark years of grief and sadness, passed within her father's towers; but onward they will see the gleam of hope and joy striking athwart her path, and further still, the calm sunshine of happiness settling on her home, where she is married to a nobleman right worthy of her. And here we veil this mirror of futurity, and come back to the passing time.

And, on this very day, the King his-self, who now loathed Kenilworth, broke up the court, and departed in all state with the Queen, for his palace, at Woodstock. The eventful days and hours of a very short period had wrought great change in the King's mind, and in the views and hopes of many in his train. Some had profited in wisdom by what they had experienced, or witnessed; others had suffered truth to glide before their eyes, without attention enough to derive one lesson from it.

And now, the King and all his court passing away under the battlements of this stately castle, in the pomp and order, with which, eight days before, they had approached it, his trumpets sounded their last to these towers, which echoed back the farewell; and then they were left to solitude and silence. This was the last gleam of courtly splendour, that lighted up the walls of Kenilworth, in this King's reign. And now the fading woods strewed yellow leaves on the long cavalcade, that wound below, whispering a moral to departing greatness; and their high tops, rustling in the blast, seemed to sigh over those, who were leaving them for ever to their own quietness.

The King's banner still waved on the keep, till his Highness had reached the end of the furthest avenue, the last spot, from which he could look back on the castle, standing, with all its solid masses of tower and bastion, amidst the rich and varied hues of autumn. While he gazed, a cloud overcast it, and then a gliding light showed every battlement and turret, wall and bastion, window and loop distinctly in succession, nay, the very grate and spikes of the portcullis, hanging in the arch of the great portal, under which his train had passed.

Just as his Highness turned into the close woods, his banner on the Keep bowed homage, and then was lowered to be no more raised till long in after years, when the King's camp lay in Ardenn, and Prince Edward planted the royal ensign over the sons of the rebel Montfort, and restored Kenilworth to his sovereign lord and father.

This vision of the living world, which had so suddenly appeared in these wild solitudes, which had, in so short period, carried the joy and mourning of human passions, beneath these

223

shades of Ardenn; which had banqueted and striven, had hoped and feared, had plotted and punished, had fretted and triumphed, had shown the extremes of princely grandeur, and of domestic misery, of deep villany and generous humanity, of supernatural power and mortal weakness, of human craft and of controlling, over-powering justice – this vision was now all vanished as in air, to be no more seen, or traced here, peace and silence closing over the towers where it had been.

The halls, where late the banquet revelled, or the sceptre of justice threatened, now echoed only to the straying steps of ancient menials. In the courts so lately filled with princely pomp and tumult, where the hurrying foot passed incessantly to and fro; where the many sounding hoof trampled, and the hum of voices rose, all was now so still, that, when the solitary sentinel ceased his measured pace, you might hear only the shivering of the ivy, or the distant echo to the closing door of some deserted chamber, murmuring through empty galleries, which, of late, to have looked upon would have filled you with marvel of the high dames and gaudy gentils passing through them. These courts now spoke only at certain hours, when the watch-word went its round, or a single trumpet of the garrison called together the few armed tenants, stationed at gate, or rampart, and the guard was changed.

Thus quickly passed away this courtly vision from these woods of Ardenn. And so from before every eye departs the vision of this life, whether it appear in lonesome forest, in busy city, in camp, or court, – where may be pressed within the compass of a few short days, the agitating passions, with all their varying shades and combinations, the numerous events and wise experience, that make up years of ordinary life and the seeming ages of a cloistered one; for there, pale moment, lingering after moment, like rain-drop following drop, keeps melancholy chime with chants too formally repeated to leave, except on very few, the due impression of their meaning, and with slow returning vigils. Yet even here life is still a FLEETING VISION! As such it fades, whether in court or convent, nor leaves a gleam behind – save of the light of good works!

And thus endeth this Trew Chronique

CONCLUSION

ILLOUGHTON, long before he had finished this *Trew Chronique*, had some doubts, as to its origin. With the enthusiasm of an anti- quary, he was willing to suppose it a real manuscript of the monks, in spite of some contradictory circumstances. The illumina- tions it exhibited, with the many abbreviations and quaintnesses in the writing, only a few of which, however, he has preserved in this, his translation, and those few but here and there, where they seem to have gained admission, by their accordance with the matter then in narration, these traits justified, in some degree, his willing opinion.

Perhaps, one better versed in antiquities would have found out, that several of the ceremonies of the court here exhibited, were more certainly those of the fourth Edward, than of the third Henry, or the second Richard, and would have assigned the manuscript to a later period than that of the title, or than that afterwards alluded to in the book, whether written by monk or layman. And though that same title said this chronicle was translated from the Norman tongue, by Grymbald, a monk of Saint Mary's Priory, it said nothing of its having been composed by one; and the manuscript itself seemed to bear evidence against such a supposition, by the way in which some of the reigning superstitions of Henry the Third's time and of the monastic life in general were spoken of. He must have been a very bold man, at that period, who had dared to utter even from under a cowl, a doubt, concerning the practice of magic, or witchcraft. It is, however, to be acknowledged, that, on some other points, his notions were not unworthy of a monk of the thirteenth century, that is, if he really credited all the supposed incidents of the hall, and of several other parts of the castle. The way, in which he speaks of the melancholy monotony and other privations of a cloister, seem to come from heart-felt experience; yet, if it had been so, he might not have ventured thus to have expressed his feelings.

225

But at whatsoever period this *Trew Chronique* had been written, or by whomsoever, Willoughton was so willing to think he had met with a specimen of elder times, that he refused to dwell on the evidence, which went against its stated origin, or to doubt the old man's story of the way in which it had been found; and he was about to enter upon another of these marvellous histories, entitled 'A *trew historie of two Mynstrells, that came by night to the commandary of Saint John Hospitalier, at Dalby sur les Wouldes, and what they there discovered.*'

But, behold! the beams of another day springing on the darkness! On drawing aside a window-curtain, he perceived the dawn upon the horizon; and, who ever yet beheld those first pure tints of light upon the darkness, more touching, more eloquent to the soul, than even the glorious sunrise, and turned abruptly from them? The towers of Warwick castle soon began to show themselves on the east, their mighty shadows raised up against the increasing light in peace and stillness. The morning-star alone rode bright above them, trembling on the edge of a soft purple cloud, that streaked the dawn.

The heart of Willoughton was deeply affected by the almost holy serenity, the silent course of order and benevolence, that he witnessed in these first minutes of another day; he looked up to Heaven, and breathed a prayer of blissful gratitude and adoration; and then departed to his rest.

To-morrow to fresh fields and pastures new.

NOTES

1. 'Corn and flour'. Leland mentions, from a Manuscript in the Cottonian Library, describing the entrance of Henry the Seventh into York, during a progress, that, 'in divers places of the citie was hanging out of tapestry and other clothes, and making of galaries from on side of the strete over athwart to that other: some casting out of obles and wafers, and some casting out of comfetts in great quantitie, as it had been haylestones, for joye and rejoicing of the King's comyng.'

When the same King visited Bristol, and was publicly received there, the same account says, after the description of a very ample procession; 'And then the King proceded towarde th' Abbey of Seint Austeyns, and by the way ther was a baker's wiff cast oute of a wyndow a great quantitie of whete, crying, 'Welcome, and good luck!''

2. *Ibid*. 'Before the castle-gates.' Of these gates, or of the ramparts, or of the moat, that once surrounded them, there are now no traces left. All that remains of Kenilworth, is already noticed in the introduction to the Manuscript. Such, at least, it appeared in the autumn of 1802, when the writer viewed it, with a mixture of admiration and disappointment.

3. 'Voide.' The following curious particulars relative to this distinguished part of ancient entertainments, are from the articles ordained by King Henry the Seventh, for the regulation of his household: 'Thirty-first of December, 1494; printed by the Society of Antiquaries, from a copy in the Harleian Library.'

'AS FOR THE EVEN OF THE DAY WHEN A VOIDE SHALL BE HAD.' – 'In the even of the day of estate, it is the usher's parte, and it please the

229

King, to have a voide; then the usher must warne the servant of the spicerie to make readie for the spice-plates for the King and the Bishoppe, and for the lordes and estates, after as they bee; and after as yee see necessarie; and also to warne the King's servers and esquires, which must wayte that tyme, and the server of the chamber, for the Bishopp's spice-plate; then yee must goe to the servant of the seller, and warne him to make readie the King's cuppe and the Bishopp's; and as many festeres of wine as yee thinke will serve the people. Also yee must receave the pile of cuppes, and bring them upp, and sett the Bishopp's covered cupp above them, if yee seem it before to doe. Alsoe, yee must warne an esquire for the bodie, to bring the King's cupp to the cup-board, and an esquire of the howsehould to bring the Bishopp's, if the usher will. Alsoe, you must warne the server to fetch the spice-plates for the Kinge, and a server of the chamber for the Bishoppe, and bring it to the cup-board. Alsoe, you must appointe for everie plate, an esquire of the housholde to serve the estates and lordes, as yee thinke best. There what time yee thinke the King is readie to take his voide, then yee must assemble them together, and bring them to the cup-board; the usher goeinge before, making roome to the cup-board; then the chamberlaine goeing to the cup-board, taking with him three of the greatest estates, delivering to the greatest the towell; the second estate the spice-plates; the third estate the cuppe; and when they come to the Kinge with it, the chamberlaine taketh the covering of the spice-plates, giving assay to the bearer; and when the Kinge and Bishopp have taken spice and wine, then the lordes deliver it to the officers againe; then the usher to appoint esquires to serve the lordes and the people largely. And lett the Bishoppe's spice-plates bee served forth amongst others, without it bee an Archbishoppe; then this done, the usher to call in cuppes againe, and sett them in order as they came; and so bring them forth out of the chamber, like as they came; and if it bee in the night tyme, that you must have light at the voide, bee right well advised how many lights you must have, and how many shall goe with the King's spice-plates and cupp, when hee shall drinke; BUT EVER LOOK THERE BEE ODD IN NUMBER AT THE VOIDE.' – *Royal Household Ordinances*.

Mr Pegge, in his 'Dissertation on the obsolete office of Esquire of the King's Body', says, 'A voide was a small collection of spices (a term at that time including all sorts of sweets of the confectionary kind) and rich wines frequently taken by the King and Queen after even-song, which on great festivals was attended with much state. I have no better guess at the meaning of the word, than that it is a transfer of the term from the utensil to the ceremony, a voyder being a kind of tray still in use, under that denomination, for the purpose of moving glasses, &c. from one room to another. Time seems to have contracted the word a little, though its meaning has been enlarged so far as to imply the whole ceremony. "After which there was a voyde," occurs frequently

230

in accounts of ancient high festivals. But what most favours this derivation, is a passage in Sir George Buck's "Account of the Coronation of King Richard the Third". – "Lastly," says he, "after dinner came the Lord Mayor of London and the Sheriffs with a voyder." The Lord Mayor of London is chief butler on a coronation, and serves the King with a cup of wine, and this formerly might be a branch of that office.' – *Curialia*.

4. *Ibid*. 'These were in that great oriel.' The great oriel here mentioned, was probably that made by order of Henry the Third, the expense of which is recorded to have been six pounds sixteen shillings and fourpence.

5. 'Maister Henry.' Of this personage, there are several memorials in the records of the reign of Henry the Third and elsewhere. The treasurer and chamberlains of this sovereign were commanded by writ to pay to Master Henry, the King's poet, a hundred shillings, due to him for arrears of his stipend, and that without any delay, or difficulty, although the Exchequer should be then shut. At another time, 'By virtue of a Writ of *Allocate*, directed to the Treasurer and Barons, allowance was made to Peter Chacepark, keeper of the wardrobe, of several payments by him made, to wit of x*l*. to Master Henry the Poet, of cix*l*. to Alexander, King of Scots, for his corrody upon his coming to the King of England's court, and returning back again.' – See Madox's *History of the Exchequer*. A corrody, it seems, was nearly synonymous with a pension, though it sometimes meant a separate gift. Warton, who notices some of these donations to the poet, calls him Henry of Avranches.

6. 'The four esquires of the body.' This attendance was due to the Sovereign as a knight. Other knights had two; a knight Sovereign had four esquires. The Household Book of Edward the Fourth, before referred to, says, 'Esquiers for the body iiii, noble of conditions, whereof alwey ii attendaunt upon the King's person, to array and unarray hym; to watche day and nyght; to dresse hym in his clothes, and they be callers to the chaumberlayn, if anything lak for his person or plesaunce; theyre business is in many secrets, some sitting in the King's chaumbre, some in the hall, with persones of like service, which is called knyghte's service, taking every of theym for his lyverey at nyght di' a chete loffe, one quart wyne, a gallon ale; and for wynter lyvery, from All Hallowentyde tyll Estyr one percher wax, one candell wax, ii candells peris', one tallwood and dim', and wages in the countyng house; yf he be present in courte, dayly vii d. ob' and clothinge with the houshold wynter and somer, or xl. s. besides his other fee of jewel-house, or of the thesaurere of Englonde; and besides his wachyng, clothing of chaumbre of the King's warderobe. He hath

231

abyding in this courte, but vii servauntes, lyverey sufficiaunt for his horses in the countrey by the King's herberger; and if any squier for the body be lette blode, or elles for watched, he shall have lyke lyverey with knyghtes, litter and rushes all the yere of the sergeaunt ussher of the hall and chaumbre; oftyn tymes these stond in stede of kervers and cupberers.'

Of carvers a former section of the same book had spoken thus:—'A kerver at the boarde, after the King is passed it, may chese for hymself one dyshe or two, that plentie is among. The King will assigne a dishe to some lorde or straunger in chaumbre or hall, elles the almoner woll see to straungers in sache rewardes, if it seme hyme worshipfull, elles all at the Kinge's boarde goethe to almesse. In the Noble Edwarde's dayes' (in household books this always means the days of Edward the Third) 'worshipfulles quires did this servyce; but now thus for the more worthy. Theis kervers and cupberers pay for the carriages of their harneys and other in courte. *Them needeth to be well spede in taking of degree in the schole of urbanytie.*'

But this office of esquire of the body has given occasion to a work, than which scarcely any is more copious of particulars, relative to the domestic habits of our ancient sovereigns. It need hardly be added, that this is the Dissertation of the late Mr Pegge. The following large extract will be pardoned by those, who have the book, and doubtless well received by those, who have it not. After mentioning the duties of this officer in the day time, the author says, 'Thus much for the office of Esquire of the Body *by day*; but the principal, most essential, and most honourable part of his duty, was *at* night; for when the King retired to bed, the esquire had the concentrated power of the *Gentlemen Ushers*, the *Vice-Chamberlain*, and *Lord Chamberlain*, in himself, having the absolute command of the house both above and below stairs. At this period (the reign of King Henry VIII) and till the close of the last century, the royal apartments, from the *bed-chamber* to the *guard-chamber* inclusively, were occupied in the night by one or more of the servants belonging to each chamber respectively. The principal officer, then called the GENTLEMAN (now the LORD) of the *bed-chamber*, slept on a pallet-bed in the same room with the KING; and in the *ante-room*, between the *privy-chamber* and the *bed-chamber* (in the reign of King Charles II at least) slept the GROOM of the *Bed-chamber*. In the *privy-chamber* next adjoining slept TWO of the *six* GENTLEMEN *of the* PRIVY-CHAMBER in waiting; and in the *presence-chamber* the ESQUIRE *of the Body*, on a pallet-bed, upon the haut pas, under the *cloth* of *estate*, while one of the PAGES of the *Presence-chamber* slept in the same room, without the verge of the canopy, not far from the door. All these temporary beds were put up at night, and displaced in the morning, by the officers of a particular branch of the wardrobe, called the *wardrobe of beds*. Beyond all these in the *guard-room* was the *watch*, consisting of a certain number of the *Yeomen of the Guard*. After supper,

232

previous to the King's retiring to his bed-chamber, the proper officers were to see all things furnished for the night, some for the King's *bed-chamber*, and others for the King's *cupboard*, which was sometimes in the privy-chamber, and sometimes in the presence-chamber, at the royal pleasure, and furnished with refections for the King's refreshment, if called for. After this, the officers of the day retired, and committed all to the charge of the ESQUIRE of the BODY. This DOMESTIC CEREMONY was called THE ORDER of ALL-NIGHT; the nature of which I shall now give at large, from an account preserved in the LORD CHAMBERLAIN'S OFFICE. The writer, who was himself an ESQUIRE of the BODY to two successive KINGS, goes circumstantially through the whole of the *Esquire's* business *of the Night*; from whence it will appear, that, even so lately as the middle of last century, the office was of so confidential a nature, that no dispatch, letter, or message, could be communicated to the King *in the Night*, but what was brought to the ESQUIRE on duty, and by him carried in *propriâ personâ* to the King.

The ORDER *of* ALL-NIGHT,
As described by Ferdinando Marsham,
ESQUIRE of the BODY,
To King Charles I and King Charles II

'The ORDER of ALL-NIGHT for the KING was antiently as followeth:–

'The *Gentleman Usher, Daily Waiter*, having the charge of constant attendance upon his Majesty until nine o'clock at night, called to the *Yeoman Usher* attending at the *guard-chamber door*, for *ten* Yeomen to attend him to go for ALL-NIGHT for the King. The *Gentleman Usher* went *bare-headed*, and the *Yeoman (Usher)* to the *pantry* for *bread*–to the *buttery* (i.e. butlery) for two flagons of *beer*–to the *spicery*, for *sugar*, nutmegs, &c. –to the *wine-cellar*, for two great flagons of *wine*, and drank the King's health in both cellars, causing all to be uncovered going and back, having a *Groom of the Chamber*, carrying a lighted torch before the *Gentleman Usher*, until he returned into the *presence-chamber*, and lay all the *services* upon the cupboard there; and so delivers all to the ESQUIRE of the BODY and takes his leave. The ESQUIRE then takes the *inner keys* and charge of ALL-NIGHT calls to the *Yeoman Usher*, or *Clerk* of the *Cheque*, for the roll of the *watch*, and *page* of the presence, with a *silver bason*, with a *wax morter*, and *sizes*, attends the ESQUIRE into the *privy gallery*. Then he (the ESQUIRE) takes the *bason*, &c. and carries it to the King's *bed-chamber*, and stays until his Majesty goes into his bed, and then goes himself to bed, under the *state* in the *presence-chamber*, in a *pallet bed*, sent up from the *wardrobe*. At eight o'clock in the morning there was the ESQUIRE'S breakfast usually brought up to the *waiter's chamber*, where the *Gentleman Usher* attended with the *quarterly waiter* to relieve and discharge him, and to take care of the *daily waiting*, and to see the

233

presence and other *rooms* made sweet and clean. The breakfast was a good piece of boiled beef, of fourteen pounds weight, with bread, beer, and wine; and sometimes a boiled capon, and a piece of veal or mutton.

'There was a silk *traverse* hung up, and drawn by the *Page* (of the Presence,) and the chain turned, and the *page* lay on a pallet-bed without *traverse*.

'After the ESQUIRE of the BODY had carried the *morter* into the *bed-chamber*, and received the *word* of the KING, with his *treble* (triple) *key*, which the ESQUIRE in waiting always had, he locked the *outward door*, leading into the *privy-lodgings*, and then went into the *guard-chamber*, and set the *watch*, and then returned into the *presence-chamber*, where he lodged under the canopy, being the CHIEF OFFICER OF THAT NIGHT.

'In all the time of my duty and service upon my Royal Master, his late *Majesty* of blessed memory, I, being ESQUIRE of the BODY, did always come into the KING'S bed-chamber, without asking leave of any; and I did every night, having my sword and cloak on, bring in the *morter* into his Majesty's *bed-chamber*, and stayed there as long as I pleased, which was commonly till his *Majesty* went into bed; and, having received the *word* from his Majesty, I set the *guard*, and after ALL-NIGHT was served up, *I had the sole and absolute command of the house, above and below stairs*, as his Majesty did declare upon several occasions to be the right of my place. And in the time of war, upon all occasions that required, I went into the *bed-chamber*, and awaked his *Majesty*, and delivered all letters and messages to his *Majesty*, and many times, by his Majesty's command, I returned answers to the letters, and delivered orders. And I remember that, coming to the KING'S *bed-chamber* door, which was bolted on the inside, the late *Earl* of BRISTOL, then being in waiting, and lying there, he unbolted the door upon my knocking, and asked me what news? I told him I had a letter for the KING; the Earl then demanded the letter of me, which I told him I could deliver to none but the KING himself; upon which the KING said, *"The Esquire is in the right; for he ought not to deliver any letter or message to any but myself; he being at this time the* CHIEF OFFICER OF MY HOUSE; *and, if he had delivered the letter to any other, I should not have thought him fit for his place."*

'And, before this time, I never heard that any offered to hinder the ESQUIRE from coming to the KING, and I have frequently brought letters and messages to the *bed side* when the *Duke* of RICHMOND was in waiting. By me,

'FERDINANDO MARSHAM'

It may be pardonable to extend the encroachment upon this interesting part of Mr Pegge's book, so far as to say, that, from the Notes annexed to it, Mr Marsham appears to have been a collateral

234

ancestor of the Earl of Romney, that 'sizes' are still the denomination of certain allowances of bread, beer, cheese, &c. in the University of Cambridge; that a silk 'traverse' is a silk curtain; that the earl of Bristol was of the name of Digby, which family became extinct, as earls, in 1698, and that the Duke of Richmond was Lodowic Stuart, which title ceased in that family in 1672; and that Chaucer was probably an Esquire of the Body to Edward the Third.

7. 'Knights of the houshold.' The Household Book of Edward IV says, 'Knights of houshold xii, bachelers sufficient, and most valient men of that ordre of every countrey, and more in number yf it please the King; whereof iiii to be continually abyding and attending uppon the King's person in courte, besides the kervers, as above sayd, for to serve the King of his bason, or such other servyse, as they may do the King, in absence of the kervers, sitting in the King's chaumbre and hall, with persones of lyke servyse, everyche of them have etyng in the hall, and taking for his chaumbre at none and nyght, one lofe, one quart wyne, one gallon ale, one percher, one candell wax, ii candelles peris', one tallwood et dim', for wynter lyvery, from Allhalowentyde tyll Estyr, rushes and litter all the yere of the sergeaunt ussher, and for keping of theyr stuff and chambre, and to purvey for theyr stuffe; also at theyre lyverey in the countrey, amonges them all iiii yomen; after tyme vii of these knyghts be departed from court, and the three yomen to ete dayly in the hall with the chamberlaynes, tyll theyre sayd maistyrs come agayne; so that the number of knyght's servants be not increased when theyre maistyrs be present. Every knyght shall have resorting into this court iii persones wayters; the remenant of theyre servants to be at theyre lyverey in the countrey, within vii myles to the King, by the herbergers sufficiently lodged; and it may be ii knyghts togeder; also they pay in this courte for the carryage of theyre own stuffe, and if a knyght take cloathing, it is by warrant made to the King's warderober, and not of the thesaurer of houshold. Sometymes knyghts take a fee heer yerely of x marcs, and cloathing, but because ray clothinge is not according for the King's knyghts, therefore it was left.'

This exactness, in specifying the quantities and sorts of the food and other matters, to be received by the knights of the household, could not be thought degrading to them, since it prevailed in the cases of their superiors; the King and the royal family not excepted. Many of our sovereigns, from Edward the Third, to William and Mary, had their own 'diett' described, with nearly as much particularity in their own household books. That, for Edward the Fourth was, 'The Kyng for his brekefast, two looves made into four maunchetts, and two payne demayne, one messe of kychyn grosse, dim gallon of ale. Item at none for his bourde sitting allone viii loves with the trenchers; his servyce of kychyn cannot be expressed at certeyn, but the noble Edward the Third in comune dayes feriall, being no prees of lordes or straungers at

235

his bourde, was served with viii diverse dishes, and his lordes in hall and chamber with v, his other gentylmen in court with iii disshes, besides potage; and groomes and others with ii disshes diverse. Then the King's meate, two pichers and dim wyne, ii gallons ale. Item for his souper by himself, viii loves, with the trenchers in all the kychyn, after the day, or after the stuff that is had within forth, ii pychers wyne, ii gallons ale, besides the fruter and waferer. Item, bred and drinkinges for the King's person, betwixt meeles, cannot be ascerteyned but by recorde of the usshers of the chamber. Item, nyghtly for the bed making, one pitcher half a gallon measure.' With the same accuracy other matters were distributed. 'Item for the King and his chamber also, when the day shortenyth, and no prees of grete straungers, iii torches, one tortays and iii pricketts for the table and cup-boarde, if it be not fasting day; vi perchers, x candells wax, for the sizes of the chamber, ii mortars wax every nyght; and at the festes, or cumming of lordes or other straungers worshipfull, it must be more large by the discression and recorde of the usshers, by oversight of the chamber-layn and others. Item for his own person, one chymney brennyng day and night, xviii shides, viii faggotts for wynter season; and if there be more nedeful chymneys to brenne for the King's honor in the grete chamber, then as the chamberlayn and ussher think reasonable; and dayly all things to be recorded by the ussher into the countyng-house. Item for the beddes and payletts in the King's chamber, all litter and rushes of the serjeaunt of the hall by ovyrsight, for all thinges that growith of the thesaurere of household his charge, must be overseen the expences thereof by the styward and countroller.' Among the curious circumstances of these extracts is the orthography, the same word being differently spelt even in the same line; and this in a book, which must have been frequently referred to by persons of rank, and doubtless had been seen by the King himself—in fact, a state-record.

8. 'The sayers' art. The narratives chiefly fictitious, but partly true, related by the sayers, or Tale-tellers,' who frequented the banquet halls of old times, were often the subjects of poems sung by the minstrels.

It was probably because the custom of listening to these narrators came to us from France, that our ancestors denominated them by so literal a translation of their French title. In the extract, published by Mr Ellis, from R. de Brunn's translation of Wace's Brut, containing an account of Arthur's coronation, we find

'Disours enow telled fables.'

In the list of those, who afforded entertainment at the feast, these *disours* are mentioned last, as are also their rewards from the King.

'Unto disours, *that telled them gestes,*
He gave clothes of wild bestes.'

236

9. 'Until the wayte piped his second watch in all the courts.' A wayte was an established officer in royal palaces, and probably in other mansions. His duties and privileges in the palaces of Edward the Fourth, are thus described in the Household Book, which has been already referred to.

'A Wayte, that nyghtly, from Miqhelmasse till Shere Thursday, pipeth the watche within this courte fower tymes, and in somer nyghtes three tymes; and he to make bon gayte and everey chambre door and office, as well for fyre as for other pikers or perilles. He eateth in the hall with the minstrelles, and taketh liyverey at nyght dimid' payne, dimid' gallon ale; and for somer nyghtes two candelles peris', dim' bushell cooles; and for wynter nyghtes halfe a lofe, dim' gallon ale, fower candelles peris', dim' bushell coles; and dayly, if he be present in the courte by the chakker rolle iiii£, ob. or iii et. by the discression of the Steward and Thesaurer, and aftyr the cunnyng that he can, and good deservyng; also cloathing with the houshold yomen or minstrelles, according to the wages that he taketh; and if he be syke or lette bloode, he taketh ii loves, one messe of greate mete, one gallon ale; also he parteth with the generall giftes of houshold, and hath his bedding carryed, and his groomes togeder, by the countroller's assignement. And under this yoman a groom wayte; if he can excuse the yoman in his absence, then he taketh clothing, mete, rewardes, and other thinges, like to the other groomes of houshold. Also this yoman wayteth at the making of Knyghtes of the Bathe, watching by nyght-tyme upon theym in the chappell; wherefore, he hath of fee, all the watchinge – clothinge that the Knyghtes should weare uppon.'

10. 'A special Suttletie.' At banquets given upon great occassions, it was usual to have several 'suttleties', in every one of which was a representation, or mimickry, of some part of the even then celebrated.

11. 'The whole court.' For a court-festival in a later reign, and for the practical jokes, which were rewarded by general laughter, see the account in Leland's *Collectanea* of the banquetings and other rejoicings, on the arrival in England of Catharine of Spain, ultimately the wife of Henry the Eighth. Then, Henry, his father, had caused the walls of Westminster Hall, 'the which is of great length, breadth, largeness and right craftye building, to be richly hanged with pleasant clothes of arras, and in its upper part a royall and great cupboard, to be made and erected, the which was in length all the breadth of the chauncery, and in it were sett seven shelves of haunshes of a goodly height, furnished and filled with as goodly and rich treasure of plate as could be scene, great part whereof was gould and all the remanant of silver gilt... When the King and the Queene had taken their noble

seats under their clothes of Estate in the said hall, and every one of the nobles were ordered in their places convenient, then began, and entered the following goodly and pleasant disguising, which was convayed and shewed in proper and subtile pageants; the first was a castle right cunningly devised, sett upon wheeles, and drawn into the said hall by fower great beasts, with chaines of gold. The two first beasts were lyons, one of them of gold and the other of silver: the other two were, one of them an hart with gilt hornes, and the fourth was an Elke. In each of these foure beasts were two men, one in the fore part, and another in the hinder part, secretly hid and apparelled: nothing of them was seen but their leggs, which were secretly hid and disguised after the proportion and kinde of those of the beasts that they were in. Thus this castle was by these foure beasts properly conveyed from the nether part of the hall to before the King and the Queene, who were in the upper part of the same hall. There were within the same castle, disguised, viii goodly and fresh ladyes looking out of the windowes of the same. In the foure corners of this castle were iiij children, that is to say, in every square of the castell one, sett and appearing above the height of it. In every of these turretts was a little childe apparelled like a maiden; and all the four children sang most sweetly and harmonious-ly in all the cumming of the castle, the length of the hall, till it was brought before the King's majestie; where when it had been conveyed it was sett somewhat out of the way towards the one side of the hall.

'The second pageant was a shippe, likewise sett uppon wheels, without any leaders in sight: the same was in right goodly apparel, having her masts, toppes sayles, tackling, and all other appeertye-nances necessary unto a seemely vessell, as though it had been sayling in the sea; and so passed through the hall by the whole length, till they came before the King, somewhat besides the said castle. The masters of the shippe and their company, in the counteynances, speaches and demeanor, used and behaved themselves after the manner and guyse of mariners, and there cast theire anchers somewhat besides the said castle. In this shippe there was a goodly and a fayre ladye, in her apparell like unto the Princess of Spain. Out and from the said shippe descended by a ladder two well bescene and goodly persons calling themselves *hope* and *desire*, passing towards the rehearsed castle with their banners in manner and forme as ambassadors from the knights of the mount of love unto the ladies within the castle, making great instance in the behalfe of the said knights, for the intent to attaine the favour of the said ladyes present; making their means an intreaties as woers and breakers of the matters of love between the knights and the ladies. The said ladyes gave their finall answere of utterly refuse and knowledge of any such company, or that they were ever minded to the accomplishment of any such request; and plainely denyed their purpose and desire. The two said Ambassadors therewith taking great displeasure, shewed the said ladyes, that the knights would for this unkind refusall make battayle and assault, and so and in such wise to them and their castle, that it should be grievous to abide their power and malice.

'Incontinent came in the third pageant, in likeness of a great hill, or mountain, in the which were inclosed viii goodly knights with their banners spredd and displayed, naming themselves the Knights of the Mount of Love, and passed through the said hall towards the King's grace, and there tooke theire staunding uppon the other side of the shippe. Then these two Ambassadors departed to their masters, the knights, who were within the mount, and shewed the disdaine and refusall, with the whole circumstance of the same. The knights, not being therewith content, with much malice and courageous minde, issued from the said mount with their banners displayed, and hastily spedd them to the rehearsed castle which they forthwith assaulted, soe and in such wise, that the ladyes yealding themselves descended from the castle, and submitted themselves to the power, grace, and will of these noble knights.' This affaire ended, as might be expected in a dance, during which, 'the three pageants, the castle, the shippe, and the mountain, removed and departed. In the same wise the said disguisers, as well the knights as the ladyes, after certaine leasure of their solace and disport, avoyded and evanished out of light and presence.'

Then, occur two bass dances, which appear to have been minuets— one between Prince Arthur and the Lady Cecill, the other between the Princess Catharine and one of her Spanish ladies, in Spanish dresses.

'In the third and last place, the Duke of Yorke, having with him the Ladye Margaret his sister in his hand, came down and daunced two bass daunces. Afterwards he perceiving himself to be accombred with his clothes, sodainly cast off his gown, and daunced in his jackett with the said ladye Margarett in so goodly and pleasant a maner, that it was to the King and Queene great and singular pleasure. Then they departed againe, the duke to the King and the ladye to the Queene. This disguising royall thus ended, the voydee began to enter in the maner of a bankett, exceeding the price of any other used in great season. Before the voidee, came in five score couple, Earles, Barons, and Knights, over and besides Squiers, having collers and chaines of gould, every each of them throughout, bearing the one of them a spice-plate, the other a cuppe, beside yeomen of the guard that followed them with potts of wine to fill the cuppes. The spice-plates were furnished in the most goodly manner with spices, after the manner of a voidee; and the cuppes were replenished with wine, and universally throughout the said hall distributed. The number of the said spice-plates and cuppes were goodly and marveylous, and yet the more to be wondred, for that the cupboard was nothing touched, but stood compleat, garnished and filled, seemingly not one diminished.'

239

12. 'Arabian jongleur.' The Arabian jongleurs were said to practise a kind of natural magic, and by some means of chemistry to raise up false appearances.

13. 'His Highness himself had once proof.' Matthew Paris records this strange charge made by Henry the Third, in full council, against Hubert de Burgh, his justiciary, Earl of Kent, that Hubert had taken by stealth, from the royal treasury, a stone of the highest value, which had the effect of rendering him (Henry) invincible in battle, and had traitorously sent it to Leoline, King of Wales, his enemy.

14. 'Silver warriors.' Statues holding torches were usual in palaces on the Continent. Cellini, the celebrated Italian artist of the sixteenth century, tell us, in his Life, of twelve silver statues, several feet high, which he wrought for Francis the First, for the purpose of holding lights round his table, at grand entertainments. Such images represented various characters, sometimes satyrs, sometimes warriors, and sometimes fools, or court jesters.

15. 'As he had sitten, at Winchester.' This was in the year 1249; and in the hall of the royal palace, when he commanded, with such impetuosity, that the doors should be shut, for the purpose of detaining the accomplices of robbers, who refused to point them out, and when he loudly expressed his indignation against the whole neighbourhood, as abettors of them.

16. 'The Lord of Warwick.' John de Placitis, or de Plesset, who received the title from Henry the Third, as the husband of Margery, sister and sole heiress of a former Earl.

17. 'Cedars.' Many noble cedars are now growing in the grounds of Warwick Castle, whose silvered branches show beautifully among the dark flakes of their foliage; but we must not venture to fancy, that any of these ever shaded John de Placitis.

18. 'Maria, the French poetess.' Mr Warton, in noticing Hawes's *Temple of Glasse*, (first printed by Wynkin de Worde, in 1500,) which he considers as a 'Copy of the House of Fame of Chaucer,' says, 'In the mean time, there is reason to believe, that Chaucer himself copied these imageries from the *Romance of Guigemar*, one of the Metrical Tales, or *Lais of Bretagne*, translated from the Armorican original, into French, by Marie, a French poetess, about the thirteenth century.'

Of this lady and of her works we have a better record in the ample and curious Dissertation on her life and writings, written by the Abbé de la Rue, and translated by F. Douce, Esquire. From this it appears, that she was probably born in Britany. 'The Duke of that province was the Earl of Richmond in England: many of his subjects were in possession of knight-fees in that honour; and Mary might have belonged to one of these families. She was, besides, extremely well versed in the literature of this province; and we shall have occasion to remark, that she borrowed much from the works of the writers of that country, in the composition of her own.'

Notwithstanding her foreign origin, the subjects of the greater part of Mary's poems were chosen by her from 'the Romances of Chivalry', amongst the 'the Old Welsh and Armoric Britons', – a selection, the policy of which is obvious, since it appears that she was patronized by Henry the Third and his court. Some of these stories she had learned only from having heard them recited.

> 'Plusiers en ai oi conter
> Nas voil laisser ne oublier.'

'Her lays,' says the Dissertation, 'were extremely well received by the people. Denis Pyramus, an Anglo-Norman poet, and the contemporary of Mary, informs us, that they were heard with pleasure in all the castles of the English Barons, but that they were particularly relished by the women of her time. He even praises them himself.'

19. 'Robin Hood.' Although ballads upon the subject of this person are said by Dr Percy to have been popular in the reign of Edward the Third, such were known before that era. One, which he considers as 'of much earlier date', is in print; and it appears, that there was *a* Robinhood in the reign of Richard the First.

20. 'Robert of Gloucester.' A monk of the Abbey there, in the time of Henry the Third and Edward the First.